The

Stillwater

Conspiracy

Georges Carrack

Neville Burton '*Worlds Apart*' Series

Volume 4

Story   by   Georges Carrack

Cover design   by   Joshua Courtright

Print ISBN: 978-0-9906492-5-0

E-Book ISBN: 978-0-9906492-4-3

Carrack, Georges, 1947-

The Stillwater Conspiracy: fiction/historical

Visit our website at www.CarrackBooks.com

This is a work of fiction. It is historical fiction, however, so most ship names, captains, places and time references that appear in this work may be found in historical documents, or are set closely within the time of their occurrence. The protagonist and his family, friends and most close associates are fictitious. The names of all characters, historical or otherwise, are surrounded by a purely fictitious story. Any resemblance to businesses or companies is also fictional and entirely coincidental.

v1.0

A story for

Tasia

The author wishes to recognize the efforts of and thank people who were extremely helpful in accomplishing the publication of this book:

My wife, Carolyn, for her continuous patience and ideas,

Joshua Courtright for cover design

The group of willing "Beta Readers" who provided guidance on the story line,

All those authors of this genre who have gone before, providing the inspiration and a basic understanding of life on a British warship in the Napoleonic era, and

The internet and its contributors, without which/whom the original research necessary to complete such a tale would have been enough to stall my effort.

The Neville Burton 'Worlds Apart' Series

Volume 1: The Glorious First of June
Volume 2: The Experiment at Jamaica
Volume 3: (title to be determined)
Volume 4: The Stillwater Conspiracy

Table of Contents

Notice to Readers:

As indicated above, there are reference materials at the end of this book which may be of help to your understanding of the story.

The Stillwater Conspiracy

Volume 4 of the Neville Burton 'Worlds Apart' Series

1 - "Blockade"

[Early December, 1803] "The Peace of Amien may have ended when France tore up their treaty with us back in May, but the French see no Peace here in Haiti," announced British Commodore Bayntun. "We hear they are engaged in a very brutal war against the blacks and mulattos whom Napoleon wishes to return to slavery. Thousands on both sides have died of atrocity and disease.

"I am not so patient as some others," he continued, "who would wait out here on blockade of Cap Francoise Harbor for month upon month for those ships to come out. Hear my plan…"

"**A**re we hove short, Mr. Johnson?" Commander Neville Burton asked his young boatswain just moments after the sun dropped below the horizon.

"Quite soon, Sir." Those three short words somehow carried an edge of excitement.

"Set storm sails in place of the mizzen- and fore-courses, if you please, gentlemen. Low and small; I wish to be the least visible we can be.

"Anchor up when Mr. Catchpole gives you the word, then, Mr. Johnson, quiet as you can."

"We'll go in on the east, Mr. Catchpole, circle westward 'round-about like, and come back out up the western shoreline."

"Chart says there are rocks to the east, Sir."

"There are, and I remember exactly where. If I can see anything at all in the dark we'll be all right."

"You remember … ?"

"Why is it so hard to believe that I've been into the Cap Francois harbor before?

"It's just that Haiti's French, Sir, and …"

"Shut it, Mr. Catchpole. I've studied the chart again, anyway. Just do as I direct."

The men tramping 'round in a circle at the anchor cable capstan a few minutes later had bare feet, so there was no noise from them, but the clunking of the machine's muffled mauls irked Neville. It was more because he could feel them in his feet rather than hear them. The sound should not be of concern, though, he told himself, because the ships of their French enemy were quite a long way off. The night was near perfect for the escapade. The moon was not up yet. A light breeze was blowing straight out of the east.

Small sails and a light breeze, together, propel a sailing ship very slowly; possibly slowly enough to be caught by rowing boats, which is why Neville made sure that Johnson had their sixteen sweeps at the ready. *Superieure* slid backwards for a minute when her anchor tore loose of the bottom and the breeze pushed her bow off. As soon as the flutter of the jib forward was silenced by tightening its sheet, *Superieure* began to move. Small wavelets began to gossip along her sides.

"Three knots, S-sir," reported Midshipman Foyle, a gangly, stuttering lad of about thirteen years.

"We must be quiet, Mr. Foyle," said Neville, "but it is not necessary to whisper…

"Mr. Johnson and Mr. Catchpole, get your best ten lookouts at the foc's'l rails with Sergeant Denby's marines and keep sharp watch for anything in our path and any likely little ships we might cut out – now or later. Pass word to everyone aboard to keep still as mice or the whole ship will be without grog for a week. If anybody sees something, pass word back quiet-like, so's we don't wake up all the Frogs and we don't hit anything. You can also pass word that if this goes well we'll splice the main brace at dinner tomorrow. Sergeant Denby – no cocked muskets. Get on now."

"Here, Mr. Catchpole, cut in here. Two more points to starboard."

"Did you feel that, Sir?"

"I did. Wind just dropped a knot or two, just like that."

Superieure's momentum allowed her to continue ghosting forward fast enough that they could hear the gurgle of water behind her rudder.

"Dropped again, Commander."

"I felt it. Did we not see stars just there to the east when we turned in?"

Catchpole said nothing for a few minutes, and then agreed, "Yes, I think we did. It's clouds, Sir, I'm sure; they're coming on.. And the wind is now gone to naught."

What's my move now, Neville wondered. *Lurking about the harbor in a light breeze is one thing, but if we're stuck in here with no wind… install the sweeps?*

"The stars are all covered up to the vertical now, Sir. We'll not be able to see a damned thing in another fifteen minutes, and I think I feel a breeze out of the south. What're your orders?"

Great drops of rain began to fall. Not many – just a drop here and there – but very large and wet.

"Starboard some, Mr. Catchpole, while we still have steerage. Let's get what little puffs there are on the beam, cross the harbor, see what we can see, and get out."

There was a quick fluttering of sails. "What's this, then?" queried Foyle. The ship heeled slightly but suddenly in response to a strong puff.

"South wind for sure, Commander, rising fast. 180-degree swing and a bit of rain. Squall coming in, or I'm not English. What now?" asked Catchpole.

"This night's gone wrong for us," Neville said. "No white horses yet, but they'll be along soon. Keep on for the French fleet. We might learn something yet."

Five minutes in a small harbor beam-on to a rising wind in the dark, even under little storm sails, makes for a heart-racing experience. Someone up front yelled, despite all the warnings, and it was a good thing he did: "Ahoy, aft! 74, Sir, dead ahead and coming fast!"

"Starboard, Mr. Catchpole. Put the helm over hard." *Superieure* turned sharply and the booms crashed across the ship to larboard. The sails snapped taught to the now-following wind and she accelerated quickly. Neville heard no sounds of men being injured or knocked overboard. *I'll hope for the best and we'll count heads later.*

The raindrop frequency increased. *Superieure* now had a fresh breeze dead astern and was gaining speed as the sails were eased farther out.

"Six knots," reported Foyle.

Superieure missed an anchored French 74 by a scant ten feet. Someone else forward yelled, "She's raising anchor and her tops'l's are dropping." At this distance they heard the rumble of running feet and the piping, drumming and yelling of setting sail and clearing for action.

"By God, Mr. Catchpole, they're coming out in the squall. Course three points east of north. Get us out of here ...

"Mr. Johnson," he yelled. "Clear for action! All hands! Let those sails out." *So much for quiet.*

A gun fired behind them… a swivel gun, perhaps.

"I heard the gun, but no sound of shot passing us. Anything, Mr. Catchpole?"

"Nossir. Maybe just their signal gun. I can't believe they could see to shoot at us."

"Pass word for Sergeant Denby and his best gun crew to come back here and man the chaser. I doubt they can catch us, but if they even get close I'd like to give 'em a potshot or two. It's a good job we have our storm sails on. We'll stand up nicely in this wind and be out to warn the squadron in no time."

Boatswain's Mate Gerald Johnson appeared a few minutes later when the clearing was done and the gun crews were standing ready. He was a great mountain of a man, quite the opposite of Catchpole. The first thing one noticed were his bulging forearms – possibly as large as Catchpole's thighs. His head carried a boyish face of clear complexion and blonde hair, but apparently going prematurely gray. It was kept neat with a string of small stuff to hold a pony-tail in back. He had bright, clear gray eyes and a quick-witted look about him. Possibly of Swedish descent, he was young; twenty or so. He stood with a straight posture to six foot and two inches. Neville remembered him from *HMS Vanguard*, of course, but there he had always been a minor player. He would have to thank Dagleishe for this 'volunteer'. Under this boatswain the ship had immediately gained the organization it was previously been lacking.

"Johnson, get enough of a gun crew up for'rd there to fire the signal gun. Take a half dozen men with two good eyes apiece with you. We don't want to hit our own. Wadding and no ball, to be sure."

The rain was falling in earnest now. "Aye, Sir," Johnson yelled from ten feet away.

"What do you think, Mr. Catchpole – about half an hour out to our blockade?"

"About, Sir. Wind is a near gale now, I'd judge, but I'd wager it won't blow for long. It's just a squall."

"All right, then, turn the timer glass."

The wind did not abate in that next half hour, and the waves grew to a long swell from the northeast across a three-foot chop from behind them.

"Ship!" Some marine of the foredeck yelled. "Over there."

"Come on, man, what does 'over there' mean?"

"To the right! The right."

"Bloody marines! I'm surprised they can learn to buckle their belts. There she be! Three points on Starboard bow! Four now."

"Loose sheets, Mr. Catchpole; get us under her lee."

"Mr. Johnson, fire a signal gun.

Neville heard a diminutive 'bang' forward and hoped that the noise of it was loud enough to be heard by the blockade ship. "Ahoy, there!" he shouted as loudly as he could manage through his trumpet at the ship towering over them. Through the now-driving rain he thought he saw a man at the rail. "What ship?" he yelled.

"*Theseus*. Who goes?"

"His Britannic Majesty's schooner *Superieure*, Jamaica station. Commander Burton."

"Heave to under our lee."

"'Vast that. They're coming out! They're right behind us! At least one 74. Signal the squadron, man! Signal 'Enemy'."

Neville hung the trumpet back on its mainmast becket and turned to Catchpole. "Steer to starboard as soon as we pass behind

Theseus," he said. "She is number three in line behind the *Billy* and *Vanguard.* They must be ahead of her there. We'll be sure they get the message."

Once out from under the lee of the large frigate *Theseus, Superieure* surged forward, off in search of the two British 74's.

"T-two red lanterns rising on *Theseus,* Commander," Foyle reported.

"She must think the others can see her, at least," said Catchpole.

Neville looked back. The ship and the two lanterns disappeared momentarily in the rain, reappearing much more clearly as the rain decreased. Looking forward, he could see *Bellerophon* [well-known amongst the British Navy as the '*Billy Ruffian*'] ahead, now silhouetted by the stars behind her.

"Mr. Catchpole, the squall is passing, as you suggested. The French won't get far...

"Mr. Johnson, fire the signal gun for the *Billy.*"

Superieure's signal gun fired at the same instant the *Bellerophon's* topsails dropped.

"They've seen *Theseus'* signal, Commander." *Bellerophon's* big signal gun fired and she began turning back toward *Theseus. Superieure* slipped quickly along her windward side with Neville shouting as he went, "They're coming out!"

"**T**hey needed the south wind to come out," said Neville to Mr. Framingham, his second midshipman. "The only south wind would come in a squall, so they were obviously ready and waiting for the opportunity."

"Aye, Sir, and now we but have to catch them," said Framingham.

Superieure began another loop back into the mouth of the harbor to see how many ships had taken the chance to leave. "I'm sorry I didn't confide, Mr. Catchpole," Neville volunteered in a very un-captain-like moment. "I see I could have saved you considerable concern. I had no intention of engaging them – only to see how many there were."

An unrated ship the size of *Superieure* was not allotted a fully-warranted Sailing Master, so Second Sailing Master Martin Catchpole was Neville's assigned man. He was slender as a rail, with a rough complexion left over from smallpox or a bad case of acne as a youth. He might have stood close to Neville's height but for his stooping posture. He never seemed to pay much attention to his hair from what Neville could see, and his upper teeth stuck out at an unusual angle. Neville barely managed to stifle a laugh when he first saw the man, because with his oversized round ears, the appearance of a rodent was overpowering. He had so far proven to be proficient with his navigation and ship-handling, however. Catchpole was obviously agitated by the thought of running back in amongst the enemy. He was gulping and twitching strangely.

"We saw only the three – that frigate *Guerrière* and the two 74's, one of whom took a shot at us. All three slipped out pretty clean in the dark and rain."

"Shot was close," said Catchpole, after another round of gulping.

"Have you seen anything, Mr. Framingham?"

"No Sir, and I took a walk forward a few minutes ago to tell the marine watch there to pass word back on anything at all they might see other than sea serpents or mermaids."

"In the absence of any orders from the Commodore, we shall choose a likely direction for the enemy to sail and give chase. I say north from here for half an hour, then west into the Windward Passage."

Catchpole began gulping again, but after a moment said, "Chase? Chase a 74 and a frigate with a schooner?"

"Yes, chase, gentlemen. I am not saying we shall engage, but we may be the only ship that can see them by morning. We can signal if that's the case."

"Aye, Sir, north for now; night's not so bad, is it?"

"Prepare to come about," Neville said.

"Sand's run out, Sir."

"Helm over, Mr. Catchpole. Let's go find the Frogs."

The Windward Passage's usual north-east wind prevailed through the night. When morning dawned purple Neville sent a lookout up the mast and waited impatiently for a call from above. He'd gotten a few hours' sleep. Catchpole was still below and Foyle was on duty.

"Sail, Ho!"

"Where away, lookout?" yelled Neville. "Can you tell who it is?"

"A point off starboard bow. Looks like English tops'ls."

Brilliant. We've followed our own out here. In hopes of finding the enemy, I fell off more than most would, because I can come upwind faster than the others, but it's for naught?

"Call me after I have some breakfast, Mr. Foyle. I'm going below."

Neville was eating his collops when he heard the lookout's call through his open hatch, "Deck, there, another sail! French 74 tops'ls, I think; four points off Starboard bow. The English has a signal up now. 'Enemy', sure."

Neville ate his last bites of egg and toast and took his coffee on deck.

"We have English t-topsails there," Foyle pointed to starboard. "You can see them from the d-deck here now. I'd guess she's the *Tartar*. She signals 'enemy'.

"Let us go see, Mr. Foyle. We'll head up between *Tartar* and the French. Three points to starboard…

"Ahh, Mr. Johnson. Perfect timing. Let's haul our wind, shall we? Helm down a bit."

The wind continued to hold steady. Neville's clear, bright-blue eyes swept the expanse of open water before them and the details aboard his ship. "North by west, Mr. Catchpole," he said.

Superieure leaned to the different angle of wind. Under the morning's partly cloudy skies, she began shouldering waves aside on Neville's estimated intercept course for French sails. He had every intention of getting in harm's way.

"Why do you suppose *Tartar* signals thus? Would you suppose she can see something from her tops that we can't see from our stubby little mast, or do you think she merely signals in hopefulness?"

"Sail, Ho! English. Starboard, just for'ard o' the beam."

"That answers th-that," said Foyle.

After their turn, *Superieure* now had *Tartar* a few points off her larboard bow, the French sails a few points to starboard, and the other English ship, whoever she was, almost on her starboard beam.

"Our ships are on the chase, but it's unlikely they will be able to catch the Frogs unless we slow them somehow. We have ourselves and *Tartar* to do that, since I believe we are both ahead of the French."

"Ahh, Mr. Catchpole, there you are. Good morning to you," said Neville. The quartermaster rang the bell, turned the glass, and yelled forward to a seaman at the chains, "Heave!"

"Whatever are we about?" Catchpole asked, "I felt the change."

"We are about the chase again," said Neville. "You see *Tartar's* topsails there, the Frenchman there, and another of ours there," he continued, pointing to each. "We and *Tartar* must cut the Frogs off somehow, enough to slow them so our ships can catch them and do some damage. I expect we should reach them by about noon." He could feel his cheerfulness at the thought of some action, but his amusement was obviously not shared by Catchpole, who began gulping again.

"Mr. Foyle, Mr. Catchpole relieves you. Gather Mr. Framingham and join me on the foredeck for a minute before you breakfast, if you please."

Despite the excitement of the previous night, the time was now moving slowly. The night had spread the fleet over miles of ocean. It would be five or six hours before they arrived at that spot on the water where they would all meet. Neville walked to the bow of *Superieure* and watched while the more experienced Framingham gave Foyle a short refresher on calculating an intercept course. The northwestern-most point of Hispaniola was still visible behind them, but it was sinking into the sea as each minute passed. Neville remembered encountering two pirate luggers here. He might have been done for if one of the armed ships of his convoy had not come back to help. It should be different this time.

By 11:00 a.m. *Tartar* and the French ship were fully visible from the deck, and the English 74, whom Neville now recognized as *Vanguard*, was almost hull up. *Bellerophon* was also clearly visible behind *Vanguard*.

"*Tartar* looks to be thinking same as us, Sir," said Johnson.

"Yes, she does," answered Neville. "What are the Frog's options, Mr. Framingham?"

"Well first, Sir, I think she can't haul her wind and cut to starboard with *Vanguard* over there."

"I agree with that," said Foyle.

Neville and Framingham turned to look at him.

"W-w-what?" asked Foyle when he realized he was being watched.

"You didn't stutter that last time," said Neville.

"Excited, I suppose," he said, and continued, "So Frenchie could continue on straight, but both we and the *Tartar* are catching him up. He might pay us no mind, but he must at least recognize the presence of *Tartar*."

"Then last," chimed in Framingham, "he could come down on us, either on *Tartar* to see if he could smash the frigate and then ignore us, or on us to create some sort of diversion. If we are all swimming, *Tartar* might stop for us… or not, if I know Captain Perkins."

But he might, and the French captain could think he would. I didn't think of that last option myself.

"But remember that whatever he does," said Neville, "we will have done our job if we cause him to slow enough for *Vanguard* and *Billy* to arrive. So, Mr. Framingham: you are the senior midshipman. You have made a good synopsis of the situation. What would you have done aboard the *Tartar*?"

"Verily, Sir, I would have left it to the lieutenants and the captain, and do as I was told."

"Then I shouldn't have asked thus, should I? We are not aboard *Tartar*, so if you have no plan the French will cook your goose."

"Aye," said Framingham, quieting to think for a moment.

"We will be close enough to t-t-trade shots with him soon," said Foyle.

"So?"

"So we should annoy him; remind him we are here and draw him to Mr. Framingham's scenario."

Mr. Catchpole made a noise like he had a potato stuck in this throat.

"Why would we want that?" asked Neville.

"Once he goes for us, we make a turn for *Tartar*. We give him our broadside if he's close enough and then we duck behind the frigate. He might turn far enough that he cannot broadside *Tartar* while the frigate gets their first shots in. At any rate, he would be slowed."

"Yes, duck behind *Tartar*," Catchpole croaked.

"It's our best play," said Neville. "Good thinking, gentlemen, although it's flawed. Mr. Johnson, get the foredeck gun crews to work on the long twelve-pounders. Tell them to fire at will."

"What's wrong, Commander?" asked Framingham.

"You've been on that frigate too long. Look out there on the deck. Other than the bow chasers we've got ten ugly smashers, not long guns like *Tartar*. The French ship has long guns as well. Our little swivel guns will do us no good for this work, either."

"*Duquesne*, Sir. We c-can read her name now," announced Foyle.

"Before we could get close enough to the *Duquesne* to give her our broadside, those who are left of us would be swimming amongst our own splinters, for sure," concluded Neville.

The crack of a foredeck long twelve interrupted their conversation, and the smoke of it blew off quickly to larboard. *Well, there will certainly be no hiding in the smoke.* Foyle was still watching *Duquesne* with his glass. "Oho!" he yelled. "The ball skipped. Must have been a nice wave. The ball jumped high enough to smash some windows of her starboard gallery." Men on the foredeck were cheering and slapping each other on the back.

"We have her attention, then. Now we must hope she has no lucky gunners."

A ball whistled across the deck just before they saw the puff of smoke and heard the 'pop' of *Duquesne's* stern chaser. It was low enough to cause two men to flop to the deck. One dropped straight down and the other twirled like a ballerina, blood spurting from his arm.

Superieure's chaser answered; again with a hit, although this one useless. "Our little ball bounced off her hull like spit off a hot skillet, Sir."

"Get me a report on those injuries, Mr. Foyle."

Their first foredeck chaser fired again. A hole appeared in *Duquesne's* mizzen course.

"Here she comes!" shrieked Catchpole.

"Fall off, Mr. Catchpole. Catchpole! Fall off, man!

"Up, helmsman! Tiller up!

"Mr. Johnson, sheets out!"

Superieure had exchanged her storm sails for her standard canvas during the night, and with the much larger sail area she lurched to larboard, leaning heavily to the force of the wind before her sheets were loosened, and then accelerating quickly to run before the breeze.

"She's turning directly for us," yelled Framingham. There was then the bang of at least two long guns each from *Tartar* and *Duquesne*, and explosions of white before them and behind. *Superieure* slammed into a large wave that sent spray half a cable forward. At the stern, Catchpole was suddenly covered with red spots and...

Feathers? wondered Neville. Catchpole's eyes rolled up into his head. He slumped to the deck just when the caged hog began an unspeakably loud squealing. Neville motioned two men back to carry Catchpole below.

"Mr. Framingham, take over there."

A broadside boomed out from *Duquesne*, but it was not immediately clear to Neville where it had been aimed. That may also have been the case aboard *Duquesne*, with possibly some guns aimed at *Superieure* and some at *Tartar*.

"Chain shot, Commander," said Foyle, just now returning aft. The ship shuddered with the motion of the foretopsail going to ribbons and its mast falling, but there seemed to be no other damage. "I can't say if *Tartar* is hit, Sir. She g-goes behind *Duquesne* from us."

The sound of a broadside ripped through the air on the far side of *Duquesne*.

"*Tartar* or *Duquesne*, Mr. Framingham?"

"Can't tell sir, but all masts on both ships still stand. *Duquesne* is turning back to her original course; maybe a bit more south, Sir – running, but more slowly without a foretopsail."

"*Vanguard* has come cracking on under stuns'ls. She's almost in range now, and the *Billy* is not far behind. It looks as if *Tartar* will go around for another go at *Duquesne*, too. Perkins would."

"Now we stand back," said Neville. "That's our fun for today, but we will follow along even if it's only to fish men out of the water."

"One man dead, Sir. Ball must've passed his head by a fraction of an inch. There's not a mark on him."

"And t'other?"

"Lost a hand. Same ball took it right off. I think you saw him spin."

"And what of Mr. Catchpole."

"He's awake in sickbay. White as a sheet though, and that's without the feathers. He just fainted. Surgeon's quite angry about all the feathers."

"Wonderful." He looked back to the stern. "So much for eggs and a chicken dinner, gentlemen, but it looks as if we will have ham tonight." The pig was lying still in his broken cage, with a large splinter from the taffrail sticking out of its side.

"Better him than me, I'll say," said Framingham of the pig. "But there are still two hens in that cage over there."

"Get Chips and Mr. Johnson on those repairs forward," snapped Neville. "Without a foremast we'll be hard pressed to keep up with *Vanguard* and *Bellerophon* on the way back to Cap Francois. I reckon *Duquesne* will strike her colours soon. Then we'll have only a couple hours until they have the prize crew aboard ... and someone throw a tarpaulin over the chicken coop or the stupid animals will soon blunder out and fall overboard."

The island of Tortuga rose from the sea to larboard by late morning of the next day; the town of Port-au-Paix was visible on Hispaniola to starboard.

"It's back to blockade duty for us, I wager," said Neville to Catchpole. "How are you today?"

Catchpole had been very quiet. *I suspect he is feeling the shame of having his debility discovered,* thought Neville, *and unlike Foyle's stuttering or Johnson's lack of self-esteem, I doubt I can help him much. My bigger problem is to decide whether I can afford to keep him on such a small ship.*

"That… yesterday, Sir. Never happened before. All that blood. I thought it was mine."

"I see," said Neville. "What's this, then?"

All five ships were returning to join the blockade of Cap Francois, but ahead of them their squadron was backing sails and surrounding some smaller ship.

"Heave to, Mr. Catchpole.

"Lookout, there. What is it?"

"Dunno, Sir."

"Mr. Foyle. Take your young eyes up and confer with the man and have your own look at it."

Foyle was back on the deck in a matter of minutes. "It ap-ap-… seems a French schooner much like us has sailed into the squadron on the op-opposite course."

The lookout yelled just then, "Commander, Signal from *Billy Ruffian*. Our number. Repair to flag."

"Something different, after all," said Neville. "Launch the boat."

2 - "The Investigation"

Four days later, *Superieure, Tartar* and *Vanguard*, escorting their prizes *Duquesne* and the schooner *Oiseaux*, arrived in Port Royal harbor. *Superieure* had been sent back to 'have proper repairs made to her broken foremast'. Commander Neville Burton stood on the unmoving deck the next fine morning in Port Royal Bay, Jamaica in December of the year 1803. He moved with his pot of coffee to the larboard poopdeck rail to study the details of Kingston and to watch *HMS Vanguard* swing slowly on her single cable as the tide changed. *Not a bad-looking ship for a 74*, he thought, *but although my cabin here is smaller than Vanguard's breadroom and I have to duck every beam as I walk 'round in it, I am glad not to be aboard her any longer.* A flight of pelicans swooped low over the turquoise water in rigid formation, looking for breakfast. Their wide motionless wings skimmed inches above the water for yard upon yard before the lead bird began his upward climb for another pass.

Neville had come across from Gibraltar aboard *Vanguard* as 3rd Lieutenant. He advanced to second when his senior, Lt. Otto Stolz, died of something akin to the ague here in Port Royal. He reflected on that for a moment: *I always feel a sadness for this method of rising to the top, despite that it is in my own better interest, and is the way of things.*

"Ah, Mr. Johnson; here you are. Two weeks we are allowed here," Neville said to his young boatswain. "Put your list together. Chips should have his ready; he's the reason we're in port. Get

Cookie's as well, if you please. Tell him to be sure there's chickens and a pig on it."

Port Royal Harbor was always a more emotional location than he expected. It was here that he had loved Maria Fuller and lost her. That was over two years ago now, but the loss had not yet been completely accepted into his heart. He knew where her house was – on a former sugar plantation now surrounded by the sprawling city of Kingston, but he did not know its occupants. Her father Thomas, a man he'd come to love as a father, was also gone. He finished his pot of coffee. *Maybe writing a letter home will take my mind off these memories.*

HMS Superieure
Jamaica Station   *December 28, 1802*

Dearest Mother and Elizabeth,
The dreadful weather of summer in the Caribees has gone by the board, I am pleased to write. The heat and incessant rain that seems to conjure up all the disease are behind us.

We've not had muche in the way of action – juste several cruises Northe into the Windward Passage and to the Southe of Spanish Cuba. There were two great Stormes that blew several days each, but the locals did not regard them as Huricans. We were thankfully in Porte for each. One man was injured when the Winde tore loose a Boat from the very deck, but we lost no one. Three small Vessels in Harbor were sunk by it.

It has been almost three years since I have been here in Port Royal Bay. I know I haven't told you of it because I am not permitted to tell muche. It's where I was when I "went missing". I can tell you some personal things that have been too painful to mention, though. I think Elizabeth smoked it that I had a girl here. I was to be wed, but she was killed in an accident. Enough said of that for now.

First Lieutenant Joseph Dagleishe of Vanguard continues to be a particular friend. That's a pleasing change from the old Elephant a couple years ago, where I ran up against Lt. Aderaly.

We have another New Year's Gala coming up. You may remember that I wrote you of it last year. The owner of the Stillwater Rum Trading Company puts it on as promotion. It should be a great good time. I hope you have an affair there in town to ring in the new year as well!

Pass my regards and thanks to Mr. Blake for treating you so well. I'm happy of it!

We should be here quite some time, so if you can send me word on of Daniel and his Dad – and big and little Gage, of course - I would appreciate it. I would love to hear how they're getting on. I should also like to hear that Mary and John are well. I think you might understand that I haven't written them.

I shall continue to take the utmost care, and pray you do the same,

All my love,
Neville

His thoughts continued as he dripped the sealing wax on the envelope: *That did take my mind off Maria for a few minutes, but she's back. I'd give God my soul to see Maria being rowed out to greet me. Enough on that. It can't happen and I don't need to be seen crying in the dark.*

Neville sat the very next day with Lt. Dagleishe in the Morgan Arms in Kingston overlooking the harbor. Each had a half pot of ale in front of them, and the crumbs of their meat pies. The afternoon December sun glinted off the water into their eyes.

"I say we move table, Joseph," said Neville. "This spot will be very hot in a few minutes."

"I'll just finish my cup here and move on, Neville, I have a couple errands to run. You need a tailor? Hey, look there, the packet arrives. I'll have a letter from home, for sure."

Neville looked out to where the sails of a small ship were rounding the point at Fort Charles. "It's amazing. They come like clockwork these days. I remember when..."

"When what?" asked Dagleishe. "Why wouldn't they come regularly? Never mind. I'm off to the tailor."

"Fine, then." *I suppose it's time I begin my duty to accomplish Sir William Mulholland's assignment. I shall go off to 'investigate' the mysterious Mr. Stillwater - however one does that -* thought Neville. *Why do I go see that Mulholland? Every time I go he has another impossible thing for me to do. How am I supposed to investigate Stillwater? We commanders aren't just allowed to disappear whenever we like.*

Before Neville was assigned to be Commander of *Superieure*, he did some preliminary work for his investigation of Mr. Chester Stillwater for Sir William Mulholland of The Admiralty at Whitehall. Thus far, most of his efforts were lonely and thankless work, consisting almost entirely of asking questions around the waterfront. He couldn't talk to any navy man about it, and it interfered with occasions when his peers would get together for a pint or a dinner ashore. He did learn that some sort of costume would be needed to do much more; his enquiries, as an officer in uniform, were often met with unusual facial expressions, blank stares, or outright scoffs. In that mode, much more poking about would certainly come to the attention of Mr. Stillwater himself.

He'd also learned enough to raise his suspicions that there might indeed be something to Sir William's curiosity. It seemed to Neville that Stillwater – or some minion – was always about when a prize came in. They would buy any unopened rum – presumable for resale – that wasn't appropriated by the prize captain. That was no particular surprise, except that 'excess rum' was a rarity. But then they would ask questions-, more questions than seemed appropriate. *Were they just gossipy fellows, or was there more? Was hanging around the docks just part of their sales approach, or did asking a lot of questions mean they expected to learn something?*

Once he determined the dangers and procedures necessary for the work ahead, he found a room that he could use for a short-term headquarters ashore. A nondescript canvas bag would suffice to carry civilian clothes. Choosing the clothes was not an easy task for Neville. He'd worn nothing but his navy uniform for many years and paid little attention to civilian custom. His costume needed to be something between that of a common sailor and that of a common working landsman, so at least nothing fancy was needed.

His objective at this point continued to be waterfront gossip, expecting to find it in noisy little bars like the *Boar's Head* on Harbor Street. *I don't want to appear too nosy,* Neville thought, *but I can't take a table in the corner and write letters if I want to find out anything. Just knowing that I know how to write might scare off some of my best possible contacts.*

He entered the *Boar's Head* and walked to the bar.

"Barmaid," he called, "I'll have a pint of your house ale and a meat pie."

Here's a group I might sit near and just listen awhile. "I'll take it over there," he told her.

"When do we go, Captain?" he heard one of the four men at the other end of the long trestle table ask another. The man addressed as 'Captain' did not look to Neville as he would have expected any captain to look. He was dressed about the same as the others except that his clothes were slightly less ratty, he had actual shoes rather than the things the others wore, and his belt held a long dagger..

"When we can find a cargo, Jason, and not before. I'll not…"

The barmaid rattled her tray in Neville's ear and set his pint down with a thump.

"…rum companies here that…" the captain continued.

"That'll be a tanner," said the barmaid. Neville raised his eyebrows. He remembered Port Royal being outrageously expensive, but he hadn't thought that Kingston might carry on the tradition.

"… one our countryman owns. He might be more willing to deal with us." The captain looked around the room. Neville was closest. "You, there. Been here long?"

Neville looked behind himself, assuming he was not the one being addressed. Nobody there. "Me, Sir?" he asked. "I just sat down."

"Aye, you. Nobody else there. And I don't mean at the bar. I means in Kingston."

"Middlin. Why?"

"We know there's rum companies here. It's what this place is famous for." His speech was
'less English' than most. "What we'd like is to carry a cargo of it home to Norfolk with us."

"So?" Neville asked, "You need crew?"

"No, we've got crew. We need paying cargo. Do you know if there are any American rum companies?"

"Well…" Neville paused. He knew the answer, but decided to look like he was trying to remember. "Stemwater, Stemwinder, Stillwinder, Stillwater," he said. "Yeah, that's it, Stillwater."

"Heard o' them, Captain. They deal with the French," said Jason.

"Any others you know of, matey?" 'Captain' asked Neville.

Neville finished his mouthful of meat pie and washed it down with a swig of ale while he gave his impression of being deep in thought. "Nope," he said.

"Thankee," said Captain, and turned back to his associates.

Just like that? thought Neville. *I could probably sit here the rest of the day and not contrive that again.*

"So what difference… letter we've got… half in South Carolina-" was all Neville could hear from Captain, who sat with his back toward Neville.

"We'd better be sure it don't have no French writing on it or the limeys will take it for sure when they stop us. And you know they will somewhere," another of the four said. He was facing Neville's way.

"Best idea… go see 'em… eat here," said captain. He drank the last of his pint, rose and walked out. The others lingered fifteen minutes or so talking about other mundane chores they needed to finish before sailing, and following their captain out the door.

Neville decided to finish his lunch and try some other ale house down the street.

The *Anchor Bar* and the *Three Pieces of Eight* proved useless. Traffic was light. The talk he could overhear was either about farming or old pirate nonsense. He decided to make one last stop before giving up for the day.

Well, I'll be dipped in tallow and lit for a candle, thought Neville as he walked back into the *Boar's Head*. There sat Captain and his three men. *He didn't say 'eat here'. He said 'meet here'.* He decided to take the bold approach. He stopped by the table and asked, "Any luck, Captain?"

"None o' yours," said Captain.

"Sorry. S'awright I sit there?" he asked, adding a slight slur to his speech and indicating the seat he had used earlier. He realized that the three pints he already drank this afternoon improved his unsteady appearance. The breeze outside had mussed his hair and, with the sweat of the hot day, had plastered it to his head. He probably looked more the part of an out-of-work jack than he did before. He could still feel the sweat trickle down his chest from the walk back here.

"Ain't ours to say," grumbled Captain at him, and turned back to the others.

They had apparently just arrived. Their ales thumped on the table and they paid. Neville raised his hand to the barmaid for another ale that he knew he really didn't need.

"He'll do it, but there's a catch," he could hear Captain begin.

"What'll it be, blue eyes?" asked the barmaid.

"Pint o' your house ale, please."

"…wants us to take…" Captain continued.

Now the barmaid was beginning to annoy him. He couldn't hear Captain. "Which one, luv?" she asked. "We've got two this afternoon."

"That's a risk," said Jason.

"The dark ale and the beer. Both same price."

"- like dealing with the French, either -"

"The dark one," said Neville. "The ale."

"- only way he'd -" said Captain.

"You'll quite like it," the maid said to Neville before she walked off.

Now what have I missed? fumed Neville.

"A big fellow," said Captain. Neville could hear the man better now as he began turning his body. "He's the contact man, I'm sure. I heard him talking French to someone in the back room there, and then he come out with the number of barrels we'll carry for him.

"You there," he said to Neville again. His tone turned friendly, "Sorry to be gruff earlier."

"S'awright, Cap'n."

"Do you know where the Isle of Ashes is?"

Neville stifled a smirk. "Yea. Isle of Ash. South of Hispaniola at the west end. Know it well, I do. I was caught there in a hurricane back in…"

"Still need a crew job?" Captain interrupted Neville's made-up yarning.

"Nossir, Thankee." He puffed his chest out and said, "Signed on one of Fuller's barkies just s'afternoon, I did."

"Fine; never heard of him. Best o' luck," said Captain, and turned away.

"What do you think, men? I'm giving you your say," he heard Captain finish his explanation. He was apparently using a bit louder speech to display enthusiasm.

Jason said, "I'm in."

The third man wagged his head strangely, and then finally nodded 'yes'"

The fourth man stared at the table for a minute, after which Neville heard him say, "I don't like it, but if you lot are all for it, I'll go along."

As before, Captain downed the last of his pint, stood suddenly, and walked out after throwing a few more coins at the table.

The other three stared at each other for a moment, and then continued talking in voices so quiet that Neville couldn't hear a bit of it. He decided it would be better to depart than appear to be listening, and if it was anything akin to a mutiny, he didn't want to hear it. He carried his dirty plate to the bar. "Barkeep, can I ask you about someone 'round here?'"

HMS Superieure
Port Royal Harbor   *29 December, 1803*

Sir W'm Mulholland,

Three times I have gone in the Guise of a Civilian into Kingston Towne this last fortnight in search of Information regarding my Assignment. I have a strong opinion that our man's Company has dealings with the Enemy, although it may be his Associate rather than the Man himself. I believe a small Cargo will be carried to a Rendezvous with a French ship at the Isle of Ashe by an American ship this next week. What type of French ship I know not. I believe that another part of the Cargo was paid for by this dangerous service. I have also determined that our man's Company owns a small sloop that is used for Deliveries - which may of course also be made Wherever this ship desires to sail.

I am sorry it is not more. What I have heard was obtained through ale-house gossip, which I must say has not been very effective. I may need to find a new Tactic after I return from another Several Months on the Blockade at Saint-Domingue.

In service of the King, I am

Neville Burton, Commander

3 - *"1792 – 1796"*

United States Navy Midshipman Candidate Michael Stearns sat at the rear of his Norfolk, Virginia classroom doodling in his navigation ledger while his classmates reported their findings to the instructor. Most were giving the same answer. He could simply have written down what they said and replied in kind – perhaps adding some small error to make it look as if he'd done the problem himself. There were a few other students who reported something completely different, and were chided by the instructor for trying to sail their ships in western Virginia or southern Africa.

Michael saw no point in cheating. It wasn't that he wouldn't have cheated. That wouldn't bother him. What bothered him was knowing that to be a naval officer this material was important. Without understanding it, he would never be a very effective officer. Yes, he might last quite a few years as a lieutenant by cheating the system somehow, but he would never make it to captain.

Michael was a good sailor. He did well in a boat, and he enjoyed a day on the water as well as the next, but navigation was an abomination to him.

"Mr. Stearns. Mr. Stearns, you are here, aren't you."

"Ahh, yes. I am sorry, Sir. Yes?"

"Your answer to the problem, please. You're not just auditing my class, are you?"

"No, Sir. I'm sorry. I don't have it." But he knew how important it was. He was out in the Atlantic one day when the fog rolled in, and suddenly he knew what 'navigation' meant. He had a compass, sure, but where was he along the coast? It was only a day-sail in a small boat, and he could go slowly west until he saw land. You wouldn't start taking celestial sights for that situation anyway, but what if he were a hundred miles out and had to find Jamaica or Martinique? He understood his problem.

"Report to my office after class, if you would, please, Mr. Stearns.

"The rest of you go on to problem number two."

In the instructor's office later that day they had the conversation Michael had been expecting for some months.

"Mr. Stearns, is something bothering you? Is there some reason you aren't doing the work?"

"Only that I don't understand it."

"You have done well at sea. You are one of our better sailors, and your small-boat handling is excellent. You seem to be a good supervisor of the training ship's company. Surely, if you put it in your head that you will learn navigation you will learn it in time."

"It's the mathematics. It makes no sense to me at all... might as well be hieroglyphics. I have tried. I've had friends try to explain it. It won't sink in. And I understand the importance of it."

"Well I certainly am sorry to be the one to suggest this, but maybe you should find another career, then..."

The expected letter came to his quarters the very next day. He was dropped from the program. Michael Stearns left his midshipman's uniform in the closet at the boarding house when he stepped out into the street. He had no use for it. He would have to make arrangements to send his sea chest home; he had no idea where else he might send it.

He pulled his collar up behind his ears to fend off the chilly autumn wind coming directly off the Atlantic. He was determined to find a good tavern, far enough away that he wouldn't see any midshipmen candidates. He was realistic enough to know that here in Norfolk there was probably no place he could go where there wasn't a navy officer. That was fine, as long as his classmates weren't there.

"Where to now?" he asked himself out loud, realizing that he felt a bit lighter in his step just for having finally reached the end. It had been worst in the beginning, when he began to realize his problem.

"Hello, there, Mr. Stearns?" called a voice from a bench at the edge of the park he was passing.

"Yes, I am." He stopped to face the man. The officer. The man wore a navy uniform. "How do you know me?"

"I had a chat with your instructor. He speaks highly of you, by the way."

"Sure he does. That's why I'm here instead of in class, isn't it?"

"You don't look to be taking it so hard. Where are you off to?"

"What's it to you?"

"What say we go find a fire somewhere, sit by it, drink a pint, and get out of this wind?"

"That's what I was thinking, but somewhere my classmates won't be. Are you buying?"

"Sure. I'll throw in lunch."

"What branch are you in? I don't recognize the insignia."

"There's a nice little hotel I know a few blocks down with a very cheery dining parlor. Seafood sound good?

"We're in Norfolk, aren't we?"

"Tell me about yourself," was the officer's first question after they found a table and ordered.

"Let's start with your name and why you've asked me in out of the cold."

"I'm Leonard Robinson. Lieutenant, obviously. We'll get to the 'why' of it soon enough – or not at all, depending."

The two stared at each other for a few moments. Leonard, well-versed at this sort of thing, could tell Michael was making his decision.

"All right. I guess it's worth telling a story for a good lunch."

He began with his childhood, which Leonard was not particularly interested in. At age twelve he started to get into some details that Leonard wanted to hear; not that Leonard did not already know Stearns' history.

"Why did you want to join the navy? Just because your father was in it?"

"So you already know the details. Why'd you bother to ask?"

"Just wanted to hear how you told the story…"

"Well, as you know, then, he died when his ship was sunk in the Gulf of Mexico in 1781.

"It was a damned French ship that sunk Father's and it was the damned British who are responsible for that war. I was just twelve then."

"Why join the navy?"

"To get back at the buggers. I'll do my part to sink 'em all. We'll be at war with England again in not too long, mark my words," he said. "I would've got my payback!" His embarrassment after slamming his fist loudly on the table was enough to cause him to turn and apologize to the patrons at the next table. "But now?" he said quietly to Leonard, "How do I go about it now?"

"I said I'd answer your question, 'depending', so I will, but we shouldn't do it here. I think you'll find my proposal interesting…"

"Waiter, the reckoning, please."

They moved to a noisy pub that had a set of booths at the back and ordered another pint.

"Here it is, Mr. Stearns: this insignia, you asked about? I've been allowed to make my own, since no such branch of the Navy actually exists. I'm considering not wearing it after all for that reason. I probably should not announce the concept. Thank you for letting me say that. I've just decided to take it off. But here's the thing, in simple words. We're spies."

"Spies? You're asking me to be a spy?"

"It's still the navy – with navy pay, but you probably won't be wearing a uniform. And you can get back at both the Frogs and the Limeys. You could be very useful to your country. You already know how our navy works. The others aren't that much different."

Michael thought for a minute. He took another swig of his ale. "How do I go on from here?"

"Classes, still, but not years of it, and then field work. You have to know ciphers, of course, but not navigation… nothing that requires cosines and tangents."

"Thank God for that. Where?"

"Some here. We'll start here, but after that it will be wherever we have an instructor for a specific subject. You might have to move around a little."

"When do I start?"

"**Y**ou've graduated, it appears," said Stearns' sleuthing partner of four years. "Boss says you're going to France; a real assignment."

"That's good news. No offense, James, but this standing in the shadows to watch these Brits come and go, waiting to see if they are doing something we don't like, has gotten pretty tiring."

"That's most of the job here in country. It gets much more interesting overseas, and you'd better be real careful in France. Old Boney runs a tight ship. Here's your letter."

"Hey, look. I'll be masquerading as a tobacco salesman from North Carolina. I'd better practice my southern drawl."

"And your French. And your ciphers."

"How am I supposed to find out what Boney's plans are for his navy?"

"You won't be alone. We have people in place over there already."

"So I'm just a messenger, and they do all the real work? Who are they, anyway? It doesn't mention them in this… no details at all."

"Sometimes I have to wonder if you're ready to go. Of course there are no details – we're spies. I know *I* don't want anything written down."

"So, Michael, here's what's not written down. You are to take any ship you find to Marseille. Be sure to go in the status of a salesman. When you arrive…"

Stearns was pleased with the dinner arrangements. This was how it was supposed to be. A group of eight well-off men gathered in a fine hotel dining room in Marseille for a sumptuous meal, conducting espionage like true gentlemen – not slinking around the alleys drinking lukewarm coffee and waiting for something to happen. He had been told who they were and introduced properly. Now he just needed to keep the names straight in his head.

"I will sit you next to Georges Cadoudal," said his contact, a Monsieur Giroux. He is my advisor, and it is probably from him that you will get the papers that must go back to Norfolk – or I guess it will be Washington now. The others may have something, as well, so keep your ears open, but not your mouth, yes? I will be at the other end of the table."

"Where is M. Leclerc? I understand he is the shipyard buyer of tobacco. To keep up appearances, I really must make an attempt to speak with him."

"There is no question of that, but he is at my end of the table. You will have your chance when we move to the other room for cognac and a cigar."

Michael followed the instruction to keep his ears open as dinner progressed, but not so well the instruction to keep his mouth shut. The thing he did well was to act the part of the salesman.

"We have the finest tobacco in North Carolina," he announced between the second and third removes, "Your sailors will appreciate that. I certainly know that. I came into this business after leaving the school for navy officers in Norfolk. Jack Tar loves his smoke and chew."

"The navy, Mr. Stearns? You have left it, yes? Why?"

"Yes. The mathematics of navigation, Sir. It is beyond my ken. My father took me back and put me in sales, and here I am." He turned to M. Cadoudal and said quietly, "You can count on me to do something more than this mundane assignment. I'll make a name for myself in this game."

Cadoudal glanced down the table and gave M. Giroux a slight wag of his head.

"Excuse me, Mr. Stearns. The next course will be a few minutes in coming. Will you join me for a smoke out of doors?" asked Mr. Giroux.

The street lamps were being lit, and the still-dusky sky cast eerie shadows around the detritus of Marseille's commerce. It was a nice hotel, but not in the most fashionable part of town. The business of selling to the navy was conducted, understandably, at least on the fringes of the waterfront.

"I am embarrassed, Sir, not only that I must speak to you but for what you have said. You cannot be talking about any time you have spent in the American Navy in public..."

"What do you mean 'public'. Are these not your friends?"

"There are friends of different sorts, Mr. Stearns. They are not all..."

"Oh, I thought…"

"You cannot assume, Mr. Stearns." He began searching his coat pocket. "Just because I introduce you to one man, it does not mean that everyone at the table is in our camp. Some may be there for their information or for other reasons. Did you not notice M. Foyard's sudden attention to you?"

"I can't say that I did…

"Ah, good evening, M. Cadoudal."

Georges stepped out onto the sidewalk. He passed a knowing look to Giroux and said, "Mr. Stearns, it sounds as though you have ideas about our business with Napoleon… might you share them with us?"

"Yes. In America, we would…" Michael outlined his ideas quickly while the sun sank below the rooftops.

"Thank you for being brief," said Cadoudal. He nodded to Giroux, who now had cigarette in hand, and disappeared back inside. Giroux said, "We'll think about it, but no more at dinner except for your tobacco pitch to M. Leclerc, if you please. We two have to live here, and we like our heads."

M. Giroux knocked on his door at 8:00 a.m. the next morning with a large envelope about an inch thick. "Here is our response to your proposal," he said. "We have made arrangements for you on a ship departing later today. Don't open this. You'd best hurry…"

There were three inches of snow on the ground when Stearns passed through Latrobe Gate into the new Washington Navy Yard. Evidence of construction was still piled in corners beneath the icicles hanging from the cornices. It was all new enough that even those working there were not all able to give him directions to the office he sought, but by 10:30 he had found his way.

"Lieutenant Stone, I'm told you are the one to whom I am to deliver this envelope from France."

"France?" he asked, his head jerking up. He looked Stearns up and down and stuck out his hand.

"Yes, France. Marseille, exactly. Some of us leave the country."

"Thank you, Mr....?"

"Stearns. Michael Stearns."

"Who is your contact here?"

"Fordson. William Fordson."

"Right. I'll see he gets it. That's it for now."

"That's it?"

"Yes. You can't expect him to be in, and to drop everything he has going, even if this did just come from France. Don't leave town until you've been called in, and leave the address of your rooms with the clerk, if you please."

"I guess bureaucracy is the same everywhere, isn't it?" queried Stearns. He turned and left.

It was a week before he heard from the Navy Yard. The day was slightly warmer and the snow had turned to slush. He returned to the same reception area with wet shoes and cold feet. "Michael Stearns to see Mr. William Fordson."

"He's not in. You are to see Mr. Roger Townsend."

"I'm your new contact," Townsend gushed enthusiastically. He popped to his feet and came around the desk to shake Michael's hand. The man seemed to be trying to use up some excess of energy. "You'll like this, I think," he went on.

"They've taken my suggestions?" asked Stearns. "When do I leave?"

"Almost as soon as you wish. I envy you. Warm weather, beaches and palm trees. Bare-breasted women, too, I hear."

"I've been to France, and there's no such thing this time of year, I can assure you."

"Oh, no. Not France. You've been assigned to Jamaica, Mr. Stearns. I know nothing of France, myself. That's Fordson's area."

"That's who I came to see. Why have I been directed to you?"

Townsend slowed for a minute, returned to his side of the desk and paged through the single file that was there. "Oh, it is you, I see." His enthusiasm returned. "Well, no matter. Fordson tells me that his contacts over there didn't want you back. Didn't say why, but he thanks you for the papers you carried for him. Jamaica's better anyway. No snow."

"Is this because of that little slip in Marseille? Did that Frog sell me out, Roger? And for that you're sending me to Jamaica? What good am I going to be in Jamaica? The island is stinking English, you may remember."

"Yes, exactly. You'll be behind the enemy lines, so to speak. It is dangerous, although not so much as France. Is that not what you want – the adventure of it? In a foreign country they will still hang you as a spy if they catch you."

"I'd rather not be among the English. My father was killed by a Frog because he took English advice. Why do you think I got into this, anyway?"

"It's not my business to get into all that, but we need this done, Mr. Stearns," Townsend continued in a more businesslike tone. "This intelligence-gathering business isn't all dash and dagger. Most of it is digging up information about the enemy. HQ has a place in Jamaica where we think you'll fit right in. There's a rum trading business there – the Stillwater Rum Company – that must know every ship that moves about the Caribbean, whether it's legal or not. They all take rum. The owner used to be in tobacco like your father. His son was killed last year and he needs a man to help manage it."

For all practical purposes, Stearns was in mourning for his first years in Jamaica. He denied that he had been sidelined from an active spying career. He became angry about it and wrote letters to the main office. He made excuses for his situation. Finally he accepted it. He improved considerably when he determined without a doubt that it was indeed Georges Cadoudal the Frenchman who had rejected him. But by then he had begun to like the situation with Stillwater, the warm weather and the ability to live so well. He also began to notice Marion Stillwater as she matured from a little girl to the beautiful woman she was now at the age of twenty-two.

4 - "New Year's, 1803-04"

"It'll be 1804 tomorrow, Commander Burton. When you were my age d-did you ever think you'd live to see it, p-particularly in a setting like Port Royal 'arbor?"

"I'm not that old, Mr. Foyle. There have been a few times when I wondered if I would see the next day, but just living this long is no surprise to me. Have you always had this stutter, Mr. Foyle?"

"No, Sir."

"Were you also the youngest on your ship? What ship?"

"Aye, S-sir, I w-was. *Elephant*, Sir."

"*Elephant!*" Neville exclaimed. "I didn't see you there. Ahh, wait. You probably weren't there when I left her. No matter."

The sun was climbing fast. Neville could feel the breeze flagging and the heat rising. The colours above his head, that had been so gaily flying, began to droop.

"Well, what started the stutter, then?"

"First Lieutenant Aderlay started it, Sir."

Aderlay. My God, I hoped I'd never hear that name again. "How could he start your stutter?"

"He s-scared me to d-death, Sir... had me in the t-tops more'n once. I got 'fraid to s-say anything, I did. He thought it f-funny. And then when the s-s-stutter s-s-started, the other m-mids made s-s-s... fun of me." A tear squeezed out from his right eye and rolled down his cheek. Neville wouldn't have seen it at all but for the strong sunlight. To the boy's credit, he made no attempt to wipe it off. "B-b-bright sun ain't it, S-sir."

"You've heard of Demosthenes, then?"

"Who, S-sir?"

"No matter. We'll have you cured of it in no time. Nobody on this ship will make sport of you, either, I'll promise you that." He couldn't tell if there was any reaction at all on Foyle's face.

"It's been a good year in my b-book after I left Elephant. For that I thank you."

"Your thanks should be directed more at Captain Walker. *Superieure* was his capture and he put me in her. We'll have a little prize money out of his work, as well."

"I could use the p-prize money. How many was it?"

"Three, I think. That 74 *Duquesne* will pay the most, just because she's such a big ship. The prize money will be split between us, *Bellerophon*, *Vanguard*, and *Tartar*, though. What're you smilin' about?"

"Just remembering Mr. Catchpole covered wi' f-feathers, Sir."

"Ho, ho! That was funny, yes… Then there was the little brig *Papillon*. We helped with her when *Vanguard* brought out the last of those starving Frogs at Saint-Marc. And we were part of *Tartar's* capture of the frigate *Clorinde*. I think that's all we'll get credit for…

"Who's on duty next?"

"Mr. Catchpole I be-be-… think, Sir."

"All right. I think I need to get on, Mr. Foyle. We've been invited to that party the Stillwater Rum Company throws every year. I need to see to my uniform. And you might, too. Your arms and legs are sticking out an inch more than they were when you came aboard.. Mister Chester Stillwater, the owner of the Stillwater Rum Trading Company, declares it is merely in appreciation of the considerable amount of rum the navy purchases from him. It is not a navy affair, though, so your participation is not mandatory."

Neville went below to tidy his uniform and to think. *Here we are again. Another New Year without Maria. I'm here in Port Royal - or Kingston - but she's not. If I had only taken another street, I might be with her today. It is getting harder to recall the feel of her face against mine or the twinkle in her eyes or the – oh yes, the little scar on her knee. That's enough of that.*

He stepped through the door into the Stillwater's banquet hall. The party was already well under way. *I must keep my eyes and ears open. There may be something I can learn about Mr. Stillwater. I would expect his business associates would be here – although not the French ones.*

An older man in servant's garb was working his way through the crowd with a silver tray of hors d'ouvre. The little bits of food on the tray were becoming fewer and fewer as he approached Neville. Another person caught his eye on the far side of the room. It was the big fellow he had met last year; the one who came and collected... *ahh, yes, that beautiful creature that reminded me so much of Maria. I should look 'round for her.*

"Roasted Shrimp, Sir?" asked the man with the tray, "It's the last one."

"Yes, I'll try it. But excuse me. Do you work for the Rum Company?"

"I do, yes."

"Can you tell me about that big fellow there? I was introduced last year, but I don't remember his name."

"That would be our Mr. Stearns. He's been with the firm maybe seven years."

"From where, if I might ask?"

"Somewhere north in the Americas. Carolinas, I believe. He seems to like it here now. I don't think he did when he first arrived – found fault with everything. Then one day he just stopped complaining. Sorry to ramble on, Sir."

"Is there any connection..."

The waiter lifted his tray back up into position for walking through the crowd. As he turned away, he said, "Sorry, Sir. I don't know much more, anyway, and I must get back to it."

-between Mr. Stearns and Miss Stillwater, I wonder? No matter, I'll ask her myself. He chatted with the guests. He asked what he could about his host.

"He's American," said one. "He's from Virginia, if I have it right. His father was in tobacco and he came here to Jamaica to check out the possibilities for expanding the business. He discovered rum and started the business. The 'rest is history', as they say. He's done well, and I'm bloody glad of it today," he added, raising his glass.

"First Lieutenant Joseph Dagleishe, as I live and breathe. It had fallen from my mind that you might be here." The two hugged and thumped each other's backs.

"Most of the officers in the fleet are in here, Neville," Joseph commented, "Even the Americans."

"And most of the councilmen of Jamaica, too, I'd wager," said Neville; "and Kingston's prominent businessmen. Did you try that French wine from that drinks table in the corner? It's wonderful. I would have thought it would be all rum."

"They enjoy their rum here, there's no question of that. How is the old *Vanguard*, Joseph?"

"She's just fine, Neville, and all the wardroom well. How's that little jolly boat you're sailing? I see you now and then, dashing about hither and thither."

"It's a bit lonely, I'm afraid. There's not another officer aboard to confide in."

"That's the lot of the captain, anyway, Neville. You might as well get used to it. I have moved well up the Navy List, by the way. By this time next year you may have to salute me."

"I shall hope for it, of all things, Joseph, for you more than any other. We must get together for catching up before we go back to sea, but right now I see that girl I met last year; Miss Stillwater. She deserves another 'hello', don't you think?"

"Good luck getting through that cordon of officers. Half of them are probably your senior, I might add. At least a couple are captains. 'Excuse me, Sirs' will not cut it."

"I managed a word last year. I'll do it again. I'll begin with the wine you suggested," Neville said, "and I'll find you later, my friend." *I feel like some voyeur, but I simply must meet her. If naught else, I must see her more clearly. I have been rather thick. While it might be a great pleasure to meet her, it is also my duty to get to know her. It is her father I must investigate. She must know him better than any other.*

He decided on the most forward approach he could imagine: taking her a glass of wine and boldly walking straight into the fray.

He took a second glass and turned her way. She was but twenty feet distant.

Neville circled slowly, like a lion circling its prey. He enjoyed what he saw. Marion stood about five feet and two inches, with a very straight posture. Hair of a color between brown and blond hung to just above her shoulders. Her empire-waisted dress, currently the style in England, showed her well-formed young figure extremely well. After a hunt of close to a quarter hour, Neville saw his chance. Miss Stillwater had finished her glass of wine and began to fidget awkwardly - but rather daintily, he noticed – with her glass. None of her admirers were offering to take it from her. A quick glance around found him the drinks waiter, and before the others could react, he slipped in through the circle.

Somewhere faintly in the background, at the very edge of his concentration – the tinkling sound of silver on glass. Someone was calling the room for its attention. The group of officers around her turned toward the speaker, and Marion said to them as they did, "Excuse me, gentlemen, My duties as hostess summon me." She turned away from their attention with a hint of a courtesy – or maybe just a nod – directly into Neville's advance.

Only three feet away now, he forced the arm that held the glass up to her. It had been Neville's intention to address the lady again in French, but suddenly thought better of it. Last year they were not at war, but this year the Peace of Amiens was history, and the French were their enemy. He didn't want the officers around them to treat him with suspicion, and she might not want it known that she spoke French, either. "A glass again this year, Miss?"

Marion's face was alive with the amusement of the party. She was a petit girl. The slight tan on her clear complexion was evidence of tropical life. Small facial features included a short nose and thin lips. Her smile and twinkling eyes showed that she was enjoying the attention of several uniformed men. The smell of plumeria from the flower in her hair – just as Maria had worn – threatened to turn him feeble.

"Oh," she said, "it's you again. I hoped you would come." She looked back at him with the same confidence that Maria had worn so well. *I had forgotten the similarities to Maria. How could I do that? Is it good that this woman brings back my memories of her? Is it bad that this one stirs feelings I thought were dead?*

He handed her the glass and took her empty. He said very softly close to her ear, "Could we meet again later? After dinner, perhaps, on the veranda?"

"I look forward to it," she said. Over her shoulder she added, "Thank you very much for noticing my glass, lieutenant."

Neville found Lt. Dagleishe again and made his request to sit with the officers of *Vanguard* for dinner. The dinner guests were not all seated so carefully here as they had been in Neville's experience at Newfoundland, except for the captains of ships, the local politicians, noteworthy businessmen, and personal friends who were organized at the host's tables furthest from the doors. Marion lit up the room beside her father. Neville knew the silver-haired man beside her was Mr. Stillwater because he had greeted the man in line. He distinctly remembered his awkward feeling - ashamed or duplicitous or something - for accepting of the hospitality of a man who might be his enemy. *But this is war, isn't it? What now? And what could my feelings for his daughter be?*

Although he would have preferred to sit with Marion, he knew that was not possible, so he sat with the officers of *Vanguard.* He was glad of it, too, for if he had been alone, his thoughts would have returned to Maria, or to Miss Stillwater or, worse yet, the time might have dragged at a snail's pace. At this table the camaraderie was a rare joy for him. They faced a group of officers from *HMS Bellerophon.* Conversation was lively, and the dinner passed quickly. The men were offered rum and the women sherry, and the room returned to general milling and mixing. "I must step outside for a bit of fresh air, Joseph," Neville said, "and to meet Miss Stillwater."

He waited by the veranda railing for a few minutes, hoping that it would be possible for Marion to find her way outside. The view of the harbor grew dim with the falling of dusk. He continued to watch the glow of sunset fading to oranges and grays amongst the patches of azure blue. He was relieved that the view was not the same as from the veranda of Thomas and Maria Fuller's plantation house, or his emotions would certainly have overpowered him. When the unmistakable smell of plumeria reached his nostrils, he whirled about to see if the source of it was what he hoped for. It was. Marion approached.

She smiled widely, "It is very nice to see you again. I have remembered you a few times during the year."

"Pray tell, why is that? Have you nothing better to do?"

"That's a rather impertinent question, so I'll just say that it isn't you I remember, just those blue eyes... and that's a change, isn't it?" she asked, pointing to his shoulder.

"And I thought you didn't know navy ranks. Yes, I am still a lieutenant, but my position is 'Master and Commander' of the *HMS Superieure*. She's a..."

"So you're a captain now?"

"By duty I am, yes, but my rank remains lieutenant, although I move my epaulette to the left shoulder."

"Most confusing. You're a captain who is a lieutenant."

"Or I'm a lieutenant who is a captain. They call me Commander."

"Miss Stillwater, I would very..."

"I know this is rudely forward, but I will not call you 'Commander' in private. If I may call you Neville, will you please call me Marion?"

"Marion is a beautiful name. Thank you." *She didn't just remember my eyes, but my name, as well!*

"How do you manage to escape all the admirers for a moment with me? And don't I remember a large gentleman who came and removed you from my sight last year?"

"I know my way around the house, is how I escape the wolves for a moment. And yes, that fellow, Mr. Stearns, can at times act like he owns me, but I assure you there is nothing to it." She said this with a slight edge, somewhere between annoyance and exasperation.

"I know this is also very forward, then," said Neville. "May I see you again?"

This time Marion blushed. "I would love it, I think, but I seriously doubt father would allow me to be visited by – no offense – a mere lieutenant, even one called a 'Commander'."

"Then I might ask your father's permission to call on you on another day?"

"You may ask his permission, and he would appreciate it greatly, although it is not his to give." Her eyes twinkled the way Maria's did when she was announcing to the world that she would run her life her own way.

"Yours, then?"

"Oui, je voudrais en profiter, (Yes, I would enjoy it,)" she said, and held her hand out for his kiss.

He gave it, and she added, "…although you may be just as aggressive as the other wolves."

"Who do we have here, Marion? I don't believe we've met," the stranger said.

Neville turned to see the same robust man he had seen the previous year. Mr. Stearns, as Neville now knew his name to be, was thirty-five or so, square-jawed as a marine sergeant and a good fathom of height, dressed in a fine suit of civilian clothes. Together with the question he just asked, the smooth good-looker's confident approach indicated his familiarity with Marion. He had obviously noticed that Marion had been standing with only one officer, not six or seven.

The new arrival spoke with a flat American accent that contained a hint of – what did they call it – southern drawl? It was akin to what Neville had heard in Norfolk in the American colonies. This man looked as if he would be stiff competition for Marion's hand, assuming there could ever be such a contest. *I could understand what Marion might certainly see in him, although I think I just got the impression she is rankled by his possessiveness.*

"Commander Neville Burton of *HMS Superieure,*" he said. "We met briefly last year." *The best defense is a good offence*, he told himself. "I must thank you for a second lovely evening, sir." He extended his hand.

Stearns shook it. "Michael Stearns of the Stillwater Rum Trading Company. I'm sorry, Sir. There are so many of you, and I often deal only with your pussers. But you are quite welcome. We are pleased to show our appreciation to the navy's defense of the country. We couldn't operate here without it, could we?" *THE country, I heard* *him say — not **our** country. But he is smooth, I'll give him that. He must be their salesman.*

"Excuse me, but can you two please come with me?" Mr. Stillwater himself stepped out on the patio to make his request of Marion and Mr. Stearns. "It is nice out tonight, isn't it?" he said with apparent surprise. He looked Neville up and down, gave him a polite nod, and turned to go back inside.

"Please excuse us, Commander Burton," Stearns said, and took Marion by the elbow to guide her away.

"Very nice to see you again, Commander," said Marion, "But now I must return to my duties as hostess. Don't give up." She turned and floated away, a swishing pale yellow blur.

"What was that about?" Neville could hear Stearns ask Marion as they returned to the party.

"Just something he was telling me…"

5 - "Chester's Permission"

"**T**he squadron will not sail for at least another eight days, gentlemen," Neville announced to his immediate reports. "I have some unfinished business ashore, so expect I will be out and about often. If you have something that needs my attention, do not be bashful about stopping me to ask it when you see me." *With such success at the party, I do not wish to lose my momentum.*

Neville's first thought was a ship-visit to Dagleishe at *Vanguard*, but he changed his mind due to the formality of it, and invited his friend aboard.

"It is as small as I remember it, Neville," said Dagleishe, "I don't know how you can stand it." When he saw Neville's face fall, he added, "I'm sorry, Neville, I mean no offense. I'm sure it is different when she's yours."

"It is, Joseph. All the difference in the world. Can we step astern for a minute's conversation? I would have come to *Vanguard*, but they would pipe me on and pipe me off. It gives me a great pleasure, for sure, but it's embarrassing knowing that I would be there just to ask for advice in a personal matter."

"What is it then, Neville?"

"I wish to call on Marion Stillwater, and I feel I should ask her father's permission."

"Yes, so?"

"Do I go to the rum company as if his daughter was business or do I presume to call on him personally at his home; his mansion? Either sounds preposterous for me."

"I am flattered that you would ask me, but I have no experience in such things. The closest I ever got to calling on a girl was back home, and her father lived in a mean little rabbit-hutch at the end of the lane in the woods. I see you are disappointed with my answer. I'll give my opinion, then. I would go to the business. I think it presumes nothing except that you knew where to find him."

Neville had seen the impressive business façade before. This one was impressive, although rather in an industrial sense. It was not a retail operation, after all. He had gone in once, using the perfectly legitimate excuse that he was looking to supply his ship with rum. *Superieure* was too small to carry a purser, so that left the purchasing duty to Neville – at least for parts of the supply that weren't provided directly by rear-admiral Duckworth's shore command. The place was impressive inside as well as out. *More like a courtroom than a business*, he thought. He'd once seen a courtroom. He could think of no other similar interiors outside of Whitehall. Three booths with small conference tables in each were along the left wall as he entered a double door to the large waiting room. He recognized the purser of *Vanguard* speaking with a man in civilian attire in the second booth. He could imagine that when the harbor was filled with shipping there might be several pursers waiting here for their chance in a salesman's booth. No other buyers were there this warm day. An information desk to the right held an elderly gentleman working on some papers. In the center was a door to the rooms behind, three of which had windows to the waiting area. A man Neville believed to be Mr. Stillwater was sitting in the center one, his head bowed as if he were reading.

"Excuse me, sir," Neville said to the information clerk, "Is Mr. Stillwater in?"

"Your business, lieutenant?" he asked.

Neville felt himself blush. "It's a personal matter."

"I must tell him something. Your name or ship, at least."

Neville suspected that most 'personal matters' meant some inability to pay, and he also suspected that Mr. Stillwater knew neither his name nor that of *Superieure*. "Hmm. If you could tell him that it's his daughter's request, if you please."

At the mention of Marion, the man gave him a hard stare indeed. However, since it was his duty to announce visitors, he motioned to the row of wooden chairs and went off without anything further being said.

As Neville waited, he tried to avoid staring at the office window, where he did notice Stillwater turn his head away from the window as the clerk went in, then turn again and look out at Neville, and then back to speak with the clerk. He also had a thought that worried him: *Other than the chance meeting last year, he has known nothing of me. Now he will know who I am, and I'm out asking questions about him. Any indiscretion on my part could get back to him very quickly.*

The clerk took several minutes before returning. *Took the time to go out for a smoke, I'd wager. Stillwater probably told him not to hurry.*

Some sort of small timing bell rang. The clerk stood and walked over to Neville. "You may enter, Lieutenant. Mr. Stillwater has time now."

Chester Stillwater, owner of Stillwater Rum Trading Company, was dressed in his favorite red and black checkered waistcoat with twelve brass buttons and matching knickers. His ruffled white shirt and neck-cloth, white stockings, and freshly-blacked shoes – with real silver buckles – completed his costume, except for the long jacket that hung on the hook by the door. It was Jamaica, after all, and some consideration to the climate could be taken in the private of his office.

Neville was mildly surprised that Stillwater stood to greet him. *Always the salesman, I presume.*

"Good morning, Mr. Stillwater," said Neville. "I am Commander Neville Burton of *HMS Superieure*. I appreciate your taking the time to see me. I apologize that I didn't give my ship or name, but I expected you wouldn't recognize them."

They shook hands and Stillwater returned to his seat behind the desk. He motioned for Neville to take the visitor's chair. Stillwater leaned back in his chair and spent a moment taking out a cigar. He did not offer one to Neville. "I must admit that I didn't know your name, but now that I see you I believe I recognize you from our party a few days ago."

"Thank you for that, Sir. You had quite a few people there. You must have quite the memory for faces."

"I'd like to think so." He returned to his business. "I am aware that *Superieure* is in the harbor. We keep very close track of our potential customers."

I see, thought Neville. *That explains why he's being so polite. I'm a potential customer. I still feel awkward, but I must persist...*

"The reason for my visit is your daughter."

"Yes, so you said. Her request, you say? She receives a great number of uninvited admirers."

"She is a beautiful young lady; no question. But yes, Sir. Our conversation at the party was very short. She suggested I come by to request your permission to continue it."

"She said that, did she?" he said with a smile. *I suspect he misinterprets the importance of his permission. She may have even more visitors than he knows of.*

"And your intentions, Commander?"

"She reminds me very much of another I was very close to, God Rest Her Soul. To spend a little time in her company would be a great pleasure to me."

Mr. Stillwater stopped fidgeting with his cigar and finally lit the thing. He thoughtfully puffed a perfect smoke ring and stared out into the lobby. "You might suspect that I don't approve of navy callers... certainly not those under the rank of captain. Until an officer has... 'made post' I think you say, there is no assurance that he will ever be a man of any means."

"Is it not the lady's choice, Sir, in this advanced age?"

"A lady may join the hunt, as does a man. It's wonderful to see her enjoying the company of all the young men at the New Year's parties, but they cannot be considered her suitors. The final decision will always require the father's permission. He must be sure she marries well, don't you think?"

"I am not asking to be considered a suitor, Sir. Simply spending some time would be a great joy – with your permission, of course."

"Your case is unusual, I must admit. We don't see many commanders here – and certainly not polite ones. Your position places you on my list of potential customers, which I can't ignore. It also puts you a step above the average lieutenant, I must say...

"She is not without a suitor, though, you realize?" It appeared to Neville that he had added this last sentence as an afterthought... *didn't think it was serious?*

Stillwater seemed to be in a chatty mood, so Neville continued, "Oh, I hadn't realized. Might I ask who it is?" At this question Stillwater gave him a curious look. *Getting too inquisitive?*

"Mr. Michael Stearns, my right-hand man."

"A big fellow? He was at the party, for sure. What does he do for the Stillwater Company?"

"He's my Sales Manager. It's him we'll send to Washington or Norfolk and the like to work up United States Navy contracts. And to cities like New York to visit restaurant supply firms."

"I hadn't realized the complexity of it. There are two other offices here. One is his, I assume. Whose is the other?"

Now Neville realized he was beyond the bounds of his curiosity. Stillwater answered more curtly, "Yes, one is his. The other is my daughter's"

"She works here?" Neville asked in an incredulous tone that brought a laugh to Stillwater.

"Ha, ha! That's the reaction of everyone. Not that I think it a joke, by any means. If she had her way she would be the Sales Manager rather than Mr. Stearns. She is not the demure thing she appears, I warn you. Although I have no doubt she would do as well as Mr. Stearns, it's just not a lady's place to have a profession, is it?"

I should quit while I am ahead. "I suppose not, Sir. I have your permission then?"

Stillwater blew another perfect smoke ring and then stubbed out the cigar. "Yes, why not? You may visit with her. I suspect you won't be around long, anyway. She'll see to that, even if the navy doesn't." He looked down to the papers on his desk, as he had been when Neville entered the lobby.

"Thank you, Sir. Good day."

"Mmm."

6 - "A New Year"

On the Monday one week after the new year began, Marion Stillwater bustled into the offices of the Stillwater Rum Company. She caught her father's eye through the glass as she walked toward her office. He looked up with a smile.

"Good Morning, Father," she said. "I thought I might find you here. How are you this fine day?"

Chester had been up for several hours. He was casually dressed for a day when he expected no visitors.

Chester's wooden chair creaked as he swiveled to face his lovely daughter. He glanced down to be sure his hand placed the burning cigar safely in the little pewter tray on his desk. It certainly wouldn't do to begin the new year with a fire. The fragrant smoke of it filled the large room. Marion enjoyed it. Her father never smoked one long enough to overpower a room.

"Is your office our New Year's Morning tradition?"

"It may be. I find it to be a peaceful place when there's nobody else about. Did you have an enjoyable stay in Spanish Town? You look to be in a sparkling mood."

"I did. The hotel has a new chef, and his lamb is better than ever. I have a feeling 1804 may just be a wonderful year. I wish mother and Freddie were here to see it."

"So do I. It's been a long three and a half years since your mother passed, hasn't it?"

They sat quietly for a minute. Marion broke the silence. "You've been writing. What are you up to already this year?"

"Not much. A few letters. I'm not trying to sort accounts or anything like that."

"Marion, do you remember a lieutenant… No, I'm sorry, a commander… to whom you gave the suggestion to ask me for permission to visit you?"

"Your permission…?"

"Now don't start with that, young lady. Did you suggest it to him?" She watched with interest as her father's countenance changed. The reaction was immediate, but she thought it unsure. Did he know what his own reaction was? Was he angry? Defensive?

"I certainly would not… blue eyes? Six feet tall? One ear a little droopy?"

"Yes, that would be him. You did, then?"

"Yes, I did, now that you mention it. I feel like I know him from somewhere. He came by?"

"He did."

"And you said?"

"I said he might, but that you would probably send him away faster than the navy will."

She gave him a perky, "Oh," and then added, "Thank you." She walked off across the hall to drop the packages she was carrying in her office.

Her father stood up and followed. He stopped at her door and leaned on the frame. "I also told him you had a suitor," he said.

"Why would you do that?"

"Because you do: Michael."

"That's not how the game is played, father. Really. We're not engaged." She was quiet for a moment, and then added, "I hear you and Michael are making plans for him to take on the Washington sales trip."

"Where did you hear that?"

"Come on now, father. They say that on a ship every man knows what every other one knows. Do you really think the Stillwater Rum Company isn't just another ship tied to shore?"

Since neither had sat, Chester turned around and returned to his desk; she followed He sat and fumbled in the top drawer of his desk for another cigar. "Yes, I am sending him to work the Washington accounts."

"And neither of you were man enough to tell me?"

Chester's mouth moved a bit, but no words came out. He resorted to blowing a smoke ring.

"Why are you not sending me?" she asked

What's wrong with Michael? He's been our sales manager for four years and has a fine potential with us."

"HE has a fine potential with 'US'?"

"Again…?"

"You say 'US', implying that this company is ours, not his, and in the same sentence you say *he's* the one with the 'fine potential'. I have been working in sales and management for two years now. You trusted me with that trip to Washington last year, unless you've forgotten, and you know I was a hit on the party circuit. That's not just to claim my feminine rights to men's' attention, but I was an absolute success for this company's sales, and you can't deny it."

"Mr. Stearns was with you. You weren't alone."

"Oh, Father, really. I am a good – no, a better – sales representative than he is, and you know it He was hardly writing down the orders as I went about our business. He really wasn't much help, if I must say it, but I can say he was not the most attentive escort a woman would want." *Except for the pass he took at me, which was really awkward. I don't think he's done trying yet, either.*

"Why can't you trust me for this? So now you propose to send him alone? As if he will be even half as successful. You wouldn't have been sending Mr. Stearns instead of Freddie."

"I wish you hadn't brought that up. It was just a simple disagreement. I miss them."

"I do too. I'm sorry."

Marion sat opposite her father and swung her legs up onto the other side of his desk. It wasn't the least indecent. She was wearing her long travelling skirt and tall boots. It was just a bit belligerent.

"Cigar, please," she said.

"I don't like it when you get like this," he said, but it didn't stop him from leaning down to fish one out for her.

She took it. He lit it for her. *Maybe I shouldn't complain,* she thought. *Except for the fact that I would do a better job for the company, Mr. Stearns will be gone for a while and I could work on my 'Paris plan'.*

They puffed for a minute, each in their own thoughts.

Chester broke the ice, "So, it's 'professional jealousy' is it? If this will be your company someday, do you not want an experienced salesman on board?" His chair creaked loudly as he leaned back.

That simpleton Stearns didn't even meet the British attaché in Washington. It's a good job the attaché found me. I have no idea how I would have found his equivalent – either American or British.

"You simply must oil that, father. Mine is quiet as a mouse."

I must admit that I enjoy the idea of finding myself in a dangerous situation. If that's what it takes to avenge Freddie's death for father, that's what I'll do, she mused.

"On the other hand," she said, "if I stay here while he goes, I could spend more time with Neville."

"Him again? And on a first-name basis already, is it?" said Chester. "You were not interested in anyone you met in Washington, and those are surely some of our country's finest gentlemen. If you're not interested in Michael, then you don't need some unreliable navy boy. This Burton is only a commander. Do you not remember that I said that if you are interested in the navy, the man must be at least a captain? In Washington, it should be a senator or a congressman."

"There were certainly some interesting men in Washington, father, but none had the right combination of youth and – what do you call it? – basic manners, maybe. But I don't need Michael. I don't need a man to manage me. And, he's certainly not the salesman that I am. In truth, father, I suggest that you stop pushing Mr. Stearns at me. He's just not going to be my final choice."

Chester sat up, stubbed out his cigar and looked directly at her. "Now it's 1804, and you still aren't getting any younger. Maybe I should insist you go and just hope you will run into the right man."

"Maybe you should."

"No, no, no. no. I can tell when you're manipulating me. I say again, a navy man will do you no good. They're all the same. A girl in every port. Again I say, I forbid it."

I knew he'd say it.

Mr. Stillwater wagged his cigar in the air, implying some form of emphasis.

Marion didn't take it that way. She knew her father. She thought it comical.

"Hmmmpf," she said. She changed her voice to the sing-song that she had always used to manipulate her father since she was old enough to talk. "That's not what you said before."

"Oh, as you had it, then. Just don't bring any indecent dalliance to my house."

Ha!" she laughed. "Always the last word. Never mind. I'm in a good mood and intend to stay that way. I wish you a wonderful new year, and I'll see you right here next year to hear your new story." She leaned back again and took another puff Then she followed her father's example and snuffed out the cigar.

"I have something better than this conversation," she said. "Are you interested?"

He glowered at her, and probably would have left the office if they weren't in his, but after a moment or two he said, "All right. I'll bite. What is it?"

I don't have it all together yet, but I can give him the idea. "My 'Paris Plan'," she said.

"Sell to the French navy?"

"You are quick, father."

"I've had the notion before, but I haven't figured out how to sell to the French when we live on an English Island."

"That's because you haven't had me on it. I'll need you to write a few letters."

"I've written before."

"Maybe, but now it's my turn." She walked out the door.

7 - "Independence Hall"

"**A**nnoy French trade, Commander Burton. Those are your orders. Rather straightforward, I would say. Most of the vessels we have captured have been of similar size to yours... little barks and ketches, a few sloops. So you would have the advantage of speed over most of them. I'd like you to concentrate on the trade routes at the north end of the Windward Passage and up toward Florida...

"That's all Commodore Loring said, gentlemen, almost verbatim. Straightforward orders, but also quite open."

"Our objective then, if it were up to me- May I, Sir?"

"Yes, Mr. Johnson, go ahead."

"- is to gather ourselves as much prize money as we are able to spend."

"I think that is indeed a good way to look at it, Mr. Johnson.

"Mr. Catchpole, you look worried. I will assure you that this doesn't mean we will be sticking our noses into the business of any French 74's — or frigates either, unless they chase us. French trade, Mr. Catchpole. Merchants; lightly armed ships, we would hope."

Neville suddenly yelled forward, "Mr. Foyle! Mr. Foyle, there! Get that jib in or we'll be all week here in the Passage."

The group heard Foyle's muted yell from forward, "Aye, Sir."

"Mr. Catchpole, does it not seem rather brisk out here today?"

"Aye, Sir. Christmas Trades are acting up."

Superieure leaned heavily to larboard and shouldered an unusually large wave aside. Even though Neville was near the stern he turned his back for a moment to shield himself from the spray from its crash on the bow. This second day out of Port Royal they were on the return tack from Spanish Cuba back toward the cul-de-sac of Haiti.

On the third day, well inside the cul-de-sac, the wind died away with the rising sun, the seas went flat, and they began to bake in the stillness.

"It's hot for January. Unusual weather for this time of year, ain't it, Commander?"

"Yes, do you think it portends anything, Mr. Catchpole?"

"I'd say it portends only…"

"Sail, ho!"

"Where away, Mr. Mulgrove?" yelled Neville to the lookout. *I'm pleased that I am finally learning more of their names. I feel I've been rather slow at it on this ship.*

"Due north, Sir. Point off starboard bow. There. One square topsail."

"Does she look to have wind?"

After a moment's pause, Mulgrove called down, "No, Sir. Looks dead like us."

Johnson and Framingham sauntered back the deck to where Neville stood. "Not a very big ship, then, Commander," said Framingham. "What shall we do?"

"Sweeps?" asked Johnson.

The entire group turned to stare at him for a second. "You must be very hungry for a little sack of coin, Mr. Johnson," said Framingham. "If Mulgrove up there sees only one topsail, and if she is about the size of us, then she must be three leagues or more distant. Would you propose we row over there?"

"No, I suppose not."

"We wait, gentlemen. There's the only way," said Neville. "But hey, look there. Turtles, Mr. Johnson. There's a prize worth going after." The sea was littered with the backs of sun-bathing turtles, many with small white birds standing on them. "Soup for all, by the look of it. Sway out the boats. And while you're out there catching dinner, see to towing the bow around to the nor-east. Mr. Foyle and Mr. Catchpole, reset the sails for a breeze coming up from there." He held his arm out straight to the east. "We can be set to run after that topsail as soon as the wind comes up."

The breeze returned after *Superieure* had been towed around and a pile of turtles sat dripping on the foredeck. "I just hope Cookie learned what to do with 'em," said Foyle. "I didn't care so much for his last attempt."

"Amen to that," said Catchpole. "Is it gone, then?"

"Is what gone?"

"Your stutter, Mr. Foyle - I didn't hear it at all."

"When I d-d-don't think on it, or if I'm n-n-not thinking about the Elephant."

"Jolly good for you, then. As to the soup, I think our good commander got Cookie a new recipe from *Vanguard*. The soup should be much better."

The jibs fluttered. The two booms wagged their sheets like dog's leashes, and then slowly swung alee. "Avast your gossip, gentlemen," said Neville, "Let's catch a merchant. I hope she's French."

In half an hour the wind had removed wrinkles from the sails. *Superieure* was cutting a neat furrow northward across the cul-de-sac of Haiti – the great bay within the western arms of Hispaniola. The square sail ahead was easily visible in the morning sun.

"Three knots and a half, Commander," announced Framingham.

"Deck, ahoy!" called Mulgrove's replacement from the masthead. "She's not flying her colors, but she looks French."

"And we look American, if anything," said Neville to those on deck. "Hoist American colors and continue the chase. Call me if things change or in an hour, whichever is sooner." He went below.

He took the time to write a letter home to his mother and sister, expecting that he would be back in Port Royal within a few weeks. *Maybe much sooner if we make a prize of our chase and take her in.* No sooner had he affixed his blue sealing wax than there came a rap at his door frame.

"Master's compliments, Sir. Would you step up, please?"

Given the number of times he had been in such situations, Neville was surprised at the reaction in his body. He could feel his heartbeat speed up and a tingle of some sort race through. He was alert for whatever might happen, but he forced himself to sit still for a minute. "Tell Mr. Catchpole that I shall be right along." *We mustn't have the men think I come running to every little change, must we?* he thought.

He was surprised at the nearness of their chase when his head reached a point above the bulwarks that he could see her. She was hull up. No glass was needed to see the entire ship.

"She's a ketch, Mr. Catchpole." Her mainmast was stepped amidships and her shorter mast was aft, opposite the *Superieure*. Although her larger foremast was entirely square-rigged, she carried large jibs and a lateen mizzen course. "She should be relatively fast when close upon the wind, as she is now. I'm surprised we have caught up so quickly."

"She's indeed a Ketch, Sir, and we caught her quickly because she wasn't all that far off. See how small that tops'l is? Catching her may not signify at all. I expect she will be very nimble when we come in close."

"How many guns? Can you tell?"

"Mr. Foyle has gone up with a glass. We should have the benefit of his eyes soon."

"Why does she stay this course do you suppose, and not fall off to run?" Neville began looking to windward toward Haiti, and found his answer before Catchpole spoke. "The island. Ile de la Gonave. It is mostly an inhospitable thing, with rocks about it, but she might have a rendezvous waiting there. She thinks to go somewhere we cannot. I'd wager she is of less draft than we are, and if you say more nimble, we don't want her playing games in there, do we?"

Foyle's feet thumped on the deck behind him. "Six guns and small chasers is all, I believe," he said.

"There you are, then, Mr. Catchpole. He certainly does not think to blast us to pieces."

"Mr. Foyle, what else did you see?"

"She is carrying at least some lumber on deck, Sir, but still no colours. What might that mean?"

"Methinks the most part of it is that her captain is a very cautious fellow. He is thinking hard now. If we are American, and he is as well, then he would be safe. He should also be safe if we were French, but why would the French put up the 'stars and stripes' and give chase, unless that ship was actually British? If we are French under false colors, we wouldn't chase either an American or a Frenchman. For that matter, why would an American chase except possible to speak. If we are pirates, he is not safe no matter what his nationality. So that means he is a scared Spaniard or Britain with a French ship?"

"A Britain should not fear an American," said Foyle. "We might stop them for some strange reason, but there should be no harm done. Americans, even looking for some contraband, should allow almost any ship to go on her way after a search."

"Then I am afraid she runs simply because she is being chased. Haul down the 'stars and stripes', Mr. Framingham, and hoist our proper colours. We shall see what she does then. Perhaps we have caused ourselves undue annoyance."

The Flag of Britain soon reached the top of her hoist.

"She's raising American colors, but she does not throw her sheets to the wind or slow in any other way I can see," said Catchpole. "Do you think her still just cautious?"

"Now I say she is either a very cautions American or she is, indeed, French. We shall keep on. These are our waters, and her captain knows it. We may not have a perfect right to stop an American and search, but she knows we assume the right. There is no reason not to stop unless she has a very strong belief that she can get free of us or carries some contraband. Do you suppose we are close enough to try a shot at her? Pass word for Gunner Jimson."

"We are closer on the wind than she is, but now I wonder if we might not weather the island, Mr. Catchpole. I think she will, though, so if we don't catch her before the rocks we will have to tack-and-tack and lose hours of time."

"Do you think we will catch her first, then, Commander?"

"Possibly not, but if we can do her some damage she might not be able to weather the island either."

"But what right have we to fire on an American vessel?"

"Suspicion of contraband, I'll say, if she proves not to be French. Go aloft again, Mr. Foyle, and see if there is any other thing to be seen. If she's a merchant, there should be no uniforms aboard."

"Mr. Jimson, ready a foredeck long twelve for a shot across the chase's bow. Fire when you think she'll bear."

"Aye, Sir," Jimson said with a big grin, and went off quickly.

"Deck, ahoy!" called Foyle. "No uniforms, and I see only eight men. Ship's not real tidy, Sir."

"Merchant, then," said Neville, "French or contra…"

Jimson's cannon fired. The smoke drifted quickly off to the west.

"Where, Mr. Foyle?" Framingham yelled up.

"Din't see it. Sorry."

"Pass word for Mr. Jimson to fire again and ready the other forward twelve as well, Mr. Framingham," Neville said. "Our chase has not changed a thing." *Superieure* was now within a cable.

"A reasonable gunner should be able to make it clear that the chase should heave to," said Neville.

His sentence was followed by the 'bang' of Jimson's second shot.

"Off her windward bow, Sir!" yelled Foyle.

"Oi, Commander, there she goes!" yelled Catchpole. "She's like a rabbit!"

The ketch wheeled suddenly to larboard as if she were a ballerina on stage. The moment she was before the wind, she fired a gun at *Superieure*. A short length of chain whistled across the water between them, and a big hole appeared in the forestaysail.

"Nimble, the bugger, I'll say!" said Catchpole.

"American colors coming down, Sir."

"Fall off to larboard, Mr. Catchpole. Now!

"Call all hands Mr. Johnson.

"French colors going up, Sir," said Foyle

"Fire the larboard gun, Mr. Jimson!" Neville howled. "Fire!"

Forever it takes him. What on earth could take so long to… he heard the bang of Jimson's gun.

"I saw splinters fly from the taffrail, Sir," announced Foyle with his eye still at the long glass.

"Her name is *Le Serpent,* Sir."

"Of course it is. What an appropriate name for a merchantman." *I never thought this ship would feel so cumbersome.* "Helm up!" he yelled. "Loose sheets there! Mr. Johnson, get those men to haul there larboard! Haul, I say!"

Superieure slowly began to respond. Not slowly, possibly, but in Neville's mind the comparison between the performance of his prey and his own beloved ship was embarrassing.

"Mr. Foyle. Run forward there and tell Mr. Jimson not to stop firing until I give him leave."

"Again to the other tack, Commander!" shouted Catchpole. "He tricks us! How can an undermanned ship haul her wind so quickly?"

Le Serpent this time fired all three of her starboard guns as she sprang off at right angles to *Superieure*. *Superieure's* spritsail yard exploded into splinters. The sail dropped into the water and dragged under the hull.

"Haul our wind, Mr. Johnson! Helm down, Mr. Catchpole! Damn his eyes; he'll not get away from me! Mr. Johnson, send men up there to cut that rubbish away."

Foyle arrived by the binnacle, and Neville sent him back forward, "Chain, Mr. Foyle. Tell Mr. Jimson to use chain. Let's tear out his rigging.

"She's bought herself a bit of time, Mr. Catchpole, but now I'd say we can weather the point as well as he can."

Superieure climbed up the wind to find *Le Serpent* had gained fifty yards in the process. As directed, Jimson fired again. Only a small hole appeared in *Le Serpent's* mizzen.

"Pass word to run out larboard, Mr. Johnson. If she does that again she'll get more than a ball from our chaser."

Jimson fired again.

"I thought I saw the mizzen jerk, Sir, but it's still up."

Neville heard another small 'bang' from *Le Serpent*, and a man forward shrieked. Wood flew from one of the boats stacked amidships. "They've hauled a gun aft."

The shot was returned by Jimson. "I don't see any…" began Foyle. He stopped mid-sentence as they all watched the mizzen lateen boom drop straight down across the deck. It broke in half; one half off drooped off each side of the ship. *Le Serpent's* speed began dropping as quickly as her colors were coming down.

"That's the end of that," said Neville. "Thank you, gentlemen. Pass word to Mr. Jimson that he may cease fire now.

"Ready the swivel guns at both ends and prepare to grapple alongside."

"Her master's waiting for you, Sir. We are grappled."

Neville crossed from *Superieure* to *Le Serpent*, where her master was standing by his binnacle. He was looking quite annoyed and defiant by the time Neville arrived there.

"Pourquoi est-ce que vous a fait voler le drapeau américain? (Why did you fly the American flag?)" he demanded.

"Pourquoi avez-vous exécuter? (Why did you run?)" asked Neville.

As he had seen in previous incidents, the man seemed to deflate when confronted with a French-speaking opponent. The conversation continued in French.

"You have cargo?"

"Yes."

"Does it need any special care? It is not animals, is it?"

"No. Only products of the land from Cartagena."

"Understood. We will take your ship to Port Royal, then. You and your mate and half your men will come aboard *Superieure*. We will place several of our men aboard your ship. Mr. Foyle will command. He is young, but he will do your ship no harm. Our bo'sun, Mr. Johnson, will assist him."

Given the small numbers of men to be exchanged and the similarity of the ships in size – meaning an ease of stepping from one to the other – the transfer took very little time. The two ships freed themselves from each other and turned for Jamaica before sunset.

Mr. Framingham sidled up to Neville after the two ships parted. "Thank you for not sending me as prize commander, Commander," he said in a quiet voice.

"Never mind, Mr. Framingham, I try to make my decisions about the good of the ship. I can't have my senior midshipman away when I've sent off my boatswain, can I? I have need of you here."

"Aye, Sir, of course."

"She sailed well until that hard blow just north of Jamaica, Sir. Then she went right crank," Foyle began telling Neville after they had completed the transfer of *Le Serpent* and her company to the Jamaica Station shore forces. "By God's grace we had their most excellent petit officer aboard, who was himself not interested in drowning, or we might all have done. I feared for my life on one big wave that we were about to broach..."

"I thought we were done," interrupted Johnson.

"...but he swung her nose down and we slid down that wave like a sled in winter. She's a very different ship, that ketch."

"They are, Mr. Foyle. I should have given you some warning, though I've not sailed one myself. Not to make light of your adventure, but what was her cargo?"

Foyle's eyes lit up with the news he was to deliver: "Logwood, Sir. Logwood and mahogany from Spanish Cartagena. I think it's quite valuable."

"That cargo doesn't come from the Spanish Main. It comes from our own colonies in Honduras. Whether our Master is a good trader or he's into mischief, *Le Serpent* is a legitimate prize. We'll have a nice share from her since we captured her with no help from others.

"I expect *Le Serpent* will sit here for some time while they deal with her, but that's naught to do with us. We could be ordered to sail at any time. I will allow some shore leave when you, Mr. Catchpole, Mr. Framingham, and Mr. Johnson can make me a proposal for keeping it organized. I'll expect that by morning, because I have some plans ashore myself."

Neville had taken his time in the evening to create a simple note to leave for Marion Stillwater at her office. He did not want to spend any time loitering about the premises. The thought of meeting either Mr. Stillwater or Mr. Stearns was not at all to his liking.

Port Royal harbor　　　　　　　　　*12th January, 1804*

Dear Miss Stillwater,

I admit I'm at a loss as to how to approach. I do not wish to interrupt your Worke, and I am not familiar with Kingston to the extent I can propose an appropriate Meeting Place.

I pray you will be able to offer the suggestion of a location where we might continue our conversation tomorrow. I humbly request the Favour of your Reply this afternoon.

Sincerely yours,

Neville Burton,   Commander, HMS Superieure

Neville's 'gig' – that is, *Superieure's* little jolly boat – deposited him on the strand opposite the end of King Street shortly before noon. He ordered his coxswain to collect him at dusk. He began his walk up to Water Lane, where he turned right. A half block down on the right were the two big entrance doors. He swung the right one open and strode boldly into the lobby, scarcely daring to look into the office windows. The clerk sat at his reception desk, head down. Neville walked forward the few steps to his desk and stopped there. He stole a glance at the windows as the clerk's head was rising. There was a silver-haired head in the center office, and the back of another brown-haired man's head with him. Marion was not in her office, at least from what Neville could see.

"Yes? May I help you?" said the clerk. He gave no sign of recognition.

Neville's hand trembled ever so slightly as he placed the note on the clerk's desk and said, "If you would be so good as to deliver this to Miss Stillwater, please. I shall return later for her reply. Thank you for your assistance." *What a farce I am. I can sail my ship into the mouth of a cannon and stand defiantly while the bullets fly past my head, but I cannot deliver a note to a woman and face her father without trembling? He stole another glance at the window as his head rose from speaking to the clerk.* Mr. Stillwater was looking at him, and the other was turning to do the same. *It would be wrong not to recognize him,* thought Neville, and nodded politely in his direction. The other face came around. It was Mr. Stearns. Neville nodded again, turned, and departed at the most leisurely pace he could manage.

That was quick. Would they read my note, or divert it from Marion? he wondered. *Now I have time to kill before I go back in hopes of receiving an answer.*

Expecting just this situation, Neville had brought his portable writing case. He headed for the Morgan Arms. His mother and sister would appreciate news of his situation — not that they would read about Marion...

There was a note waiting for him when he returned to the Stillwater Rum Company. The clerk passed it to him when he arrived as if he were passing a lump of tallow.

Neville carried it to the street before breaking the seal and slipping the neatly folded paper out of the envelope.

Stillwater Rum Trading Company

Commander Burton,

Luncheon tomorrow at Stillwater House?

(Father at work, staff present)

M. Stillwater

Neville noted the flowing hand — *quite sensual by itself,* he thought.

"**W**hat's this, then, Mr. Catchpole? Looks like a Station boat, if ever I seen one."

"It does, doesn't it?," queried Catchpole. "We'd better call down for Commander Burton."

"Packet for your captain," said the shore boat's coxswain when it bumped alongside fifteen minutes later. Neville was on deck by then, waiting for whatever they were bringing. "No need of response."

Neville took the packet below to open it.

"One never knows what we'll get," pontificated Framingham to no one in particular. "Could be orders to keep secret 'till we're at sea."

"Well, it's not," said Neville, already climbing back up the companion ladder, "but it is orders to shove off with reasonable haste – to go back out and catch another, one would presume."

"May I speak, Sir?" asked Foyle.

"Come ahead."

"Just passing this along, Sir. It's not my question, but some of the men are asking when they might see a bit of coin from the last."

"My God, Foyle. The body's still warm. It's that grasping Kilburney, isn't it?"

"Aye, Sir, 'tis."

"You may tell him, and let the word go 'round with it, that they should be lucky the wee boatie's not navy or we wouldn't be seeing a thing for a year. Admiral Duckworth will probably settle the bill right here in Kingston, and right quick-like, but none of us will see a groat 'till we're back in next, and maybe another cruise as well."

"Aye, Sir. When do we sail, then?"

"Sooner gone, sooner back, eh? Well it won't be today, and not tomorrow, either. We've still to complete our water, and... what else, Mr. Johnson?"

"Bloody wood, Sir. Always the wood. Hills full of trees here, and the wood takes an age. It should be here tomorrow, though, if them ashore can keep a promise."

"Right, then, it's day after tomorrow on the morning tide. We've had wind every day, so then shouldn't be different. Pass me letters, if you've got 'em. I'll be off again about six bells in the forenoon. And, Mr. Foyle, raise the Blue Peter in way of acknowledgement to Station."

Independence Hall, as Chester Stillwater had dubbed the place, was more imposing than Neville had remembered it from the New Year's parties. The house was a mansion, sure, but it was not out of keeping with the style and size of several others in St. Andrew or Kingston Parishes. It was the great hall to the side, where the parties had been held, and the gardens roundabout that bestowed it the air of wealth. Neville had at least thought to hire a carriage in which to arrive rather than trudging in by foot, and the first thing he saw when arriving from the front was the centerpiece of the garden – a huge old plumeria tree. Sea-faring party-goers who did not hire their own transportation had been shuttled up from the harbor for the parties via the lane to the side of the 'functions hall'. Neville had therefore never noticed the tree and had assumed the entire smell of it emanated from Marion's hair decoration.

The jingling of harness and light thumping of hooves on the fine gravel of the entrance road was enough to alert the staff to organize for Neville's arrival. The ostlers of *Independence Hall* whisked both horse and driver around back, and a butler in tails and white shirt gave him a shallow bow while gesturing with an outstretched arm for him to enter the house.

Marion's "I'm so glad you could come," was the first music his ears heard as he entered the doors, which he estimated to be ten feet tall.

"I would have been sad indeed to have missed the opportunity. You look positively lovely, Miss Stillwater."

"Thank you, Commander Burton, but it's Marion, remember, Neville?"

"We in the navy continue to be quite formal aboard ship for reasons of discipline, I'm afraid, but I would love it of all things to think us that intimate. Your house, by the way, is even more remarkable than I realized."

"Father has done a superb job – with mother's help on almost all of it. Money changes everything, as you know. Well, I'm glad you've arrived a bit early. I can give you a tour of the first floor while the staff is setting out our lunch in the garden. Take my arm, please."

From then forward the conversation flowed freely and easily, beginning with the walk through the parquet-floored halls to see views from the windows, paintings by American artists of such subjects as the Hudson River and mountains of Vermont, porcelain from China, and a glance into Mr. Stillwater's study.

"You must tire of giving the tour," Neville said when it ended at the door to the back garden.

"Oh, I rarely give it. We don't oftern have guests in since mother died three years ago."

"I am sorry to hear of…"

She cut him off. "Your mum still with us?"

The question gave him pause. He rarely talked about his family. "Yes, she is. And I've a sister and nephew back home in Suffolk."

She's trying to change the subject.

"It's a beautiful day for lunch out here, don't you think?" A simple metal table and two chairs stood on a flagstone patio between flowering bird-of-paradise plants. The table was covered with a blue and green checked cloth, and silverware was already set.

But I'm not quite done with it. She expects me to believe she doesn't have suitors around often? "With the crowd around you at the party, I would have thought your tours to be a regular thing."

"You must think me quite the trollop," she said. Her eyes twinkled mischievously. He held her chair to sit.

"Why me, then?"

"I don't know what it is. I feel like I've known you all my life; like my brother or something, God Rest his Soul."

"Where's he, then?"

"My older brother Freddie was killed by French privateers just last year. It has been a hard time." A tear dripped from her left eye. Neville fought the urge to grab her and hold her in his arms. It would have been most inappropriate.

"I'm very sorry."

Their conversation stopped while a waiter arrived and arranged two small plates of cold shrimps and a red sauce in front of them.

"I thought I felt it at the very first when you addressed me in Spanish; then a bit more this year. Now I am sure of it. Somehow we know each other."

"I feel the same. You could almost be my sister, though she may be a bit more spiteful."

"That isn't very flattering, you know."

"The whole thing doesn't seem so romantic as I'd hoped."

She put her hand on his arm and looked him in the eye. "As I said before, though, Neville, don't give up. Don't let father cow you.

He will if he can. It's just his way." Her touch was startling, even through the cloth of his jacket.

The touch of St. Elmo's fire, I hope, he thought.

"I'm being terribly brazen," she continued. "Don't think me a tart for it, but I hope it can be."

"Can be what?"

"Commander Burton, don't be thick." She blushed, and then continued in a hushed tone. "Romantic, Neville. I've never met a man before that had any such effect on me, and I have dealt with some of America's smoothest."

Marion gave the slightest signal to the waiter who had been standing far enough away to allow a private conversation. While he was removing the little dishes she returned to a less intimate subject, "What did your father do?"

Neville gave her his whole story of youth and family. It was something he had not done with anyone that he could remember, but it was so comfortable and easy with Marion. He blabbered on and they both allowed the previous conversation to sit lurking in the background.

Lunch finished, they tossed their napkins on the table. "I'd like to show you something," Marion said. They stood and walked together into the house as they had on the tour. "This is something I discovered about the house when I was a young girl – maybe thirteen," she said. They turned a corner into a small windowless foyer that held a small side table with a tiny oil painting above it. "What do you think?"

Neville leaned close to take a look at the painting. *What could the subject of such interest be?*

He felt her body press his from behind. "It's not the painting, silly. It's the room." He straightened up and turned around – into her arms. "It can't be seen from any angle, save the entrance," she whispered. He needed no more invitation to bend down and push his lips against hers. They held each other and kissed again, softly but urgently, and tears rolled from her eyes.

"What could make you this way, Maria?" he asked.

The reaction was instant ice. "What could indeed? Who is Maria? Father said you sailors have a girl in every port. Why did I think you different?"

"Wait, wait, I'm sorry. Maria was..." *she doesn't want to know it all...* "Maria is..." he hung his head. "...with your mother." And now the tears fell from his eyes. *I have not often wept of this,* he thought.

"Oh. Oh, I am sorry," she said, now soft again. "Married? You didn't say..."

"No, but engaged. Three years ago now. Can we sit somewhere a minute?"

"Yes, certainly. Over there."

They sat close, but formally; not touching, which was just as well because their lunch waiter came by just then.

"Is everything all right, Miss?" he asked while giving Neville a stern look.

"Yes, Carlos. Of course. I was just telling my caller about Mummie. He's lost... a girl as well."

"Ah, I see. I'm sorry, both of you. May I bring you something?"

"A tea would be nice. Yes, please."

"I would have told you soon enough, but it is still painful," Neville said when Carlos had gone. "You are very much like her; beautiful and strong. Very strong. I would offer you promises and assurances of all sorts if we could but have more time. Could we? Can we see each other more?" A humorous thought suddenly hit him, and he asked, "May I have *your* permission to see more of you?"

"Yes, you have *my* permission," she said with a crooked little smile. "Much more, I hope."

"How do we send each other messages? I feel very awkward walking in to your office in front of your father – and that Mr. Stearns. It makes me feel that I must skulk around the back stair. And just walking up to this house is rather presumptuous for a simple navy man, is it not?"

"I solved that problem as a young girl, as well," she said. "It's quite easy, really. Pass a note to Miss Fletcher at our butcher's in Kingston on Harbour Street. The shop has a silly name – the 'Pig's

Tale'. If there's no order from us that day she will see it here one way or another, and I will be sure she has an answer for you the next morning. You may also address a letter there, if your heart dictates that you should write me."

"Wonderful. How positively devious."

"I agree that we don't want father or my charming Mr. Stearns to see you often. They would certainly get the wrong idea," she confirmed with another sly grin.

"Speaking of the wrong idea, I think I should have another look at the tiny painting before I go, don't you?"

8 - "Desiree"

HMS Superieure
Port Royal Harbour   *January 19, 1804*

My Dear Miss Stillwater,

I am writing to express my utmost appreciation for your hospitality during the luncheon at your home Wednesday last.

I believe I forgot to tell you of our Orders to Sail 'post haste' the following day, but this is the way of things for a navy man, I am afraid. By the time you read this I expect I shall be an hundred miles Easte of Jamaica keeping a keen eye out for our French friends. As always, I shall endeavor to keep You and Yours safe from their encroaches.

I also wish to express my sincere Desire to meet with you again. I will Notify you at the Earliest upon my Return (whether or not the Stillwater Rum Company has already reported Superieure's arrival to you).

Sincerely yours,
Cmdr. Nev. Burton

Neville arranged to have this letter carried to the 'Pig's Tale' butcher shop on Harbour Street by the first boy he saw loose on the waterfront before *Superieure* set sail the next day. *We'll see if her message system is working,* Neville thought. *And what a dunce I've been. It's time to write another, but that can wait a few days.*

HMS Superieure
At Sea, Easte of Jamaica   *January 22, 1804*

Sir W'm Mulholland,

I am writing to report a finding of the simplest order, but I will leave it to you to determine its importance – if there be any at all.

The spy-craft, if such you call it, is right in front of us. The Stillwater Rum Company don't hide it. They boast of it. They don't lose a customer because of it. They track every ship in and out. Merchants, single and convoys, naval and privateer, We are all customers. They know where we all are, and when. They probably know when we're going to sail and even when we're expected back. They can walk into Admiral Duckworth's offices and ask, for all love, all in the name of trade – and for the gift of a bottle of rum or two to the clerk, no doubt.

To top that, I am quite sure they trade with the enemy – merchants and privateers and pirates, at least – and might in similar fashion know the movements of them as well.

On the personal side, I have good news and bad, and they are one and the same. While my soul still aches for the loss of Maria, there is a girl here so similar that I am compelled to seek her company. If that is not Enough bad and good news together, there is more. She is the daughter of Mr. Chester Stillwater, and she works for the Company, so if he is guilty as you suspect – although I see no proof of it yet – she might herself be implicated. In the meanwhile I am condemned to skulk around her snooping out her father. I must admit that my emotions push me close to confounded.

I expect to post this with the first Advice Boat that comes my way in the hope of having some Answer from you not long after my return to Kingston in a few Monthes.

Sincerely yours,
Cmdr. Nev. Burton

P.S. There is another man here - Mr. M. Stearns - whom Mr. Stillwater refers to as his "right-hand man". There's not much I can add to that, except that he is also an American.

This letter he sealed in a proper navy canvas dispatch envelope with three red seals, and addressed it simply to "Sir William Mulholland, Navy Office, Whitehall". *I may very well be questioned by the Commodore over this,* he thought, *but I will pray he forgets it before we have the chance to meet. If it is in the official dispatch pouch even a Commodore would not dare delay it, and it will be gone from his sight.*

By the time Neville was finished writing his second letter the north shore of Jamaica had sunk to the west of them, leaving only a thin ribbon of low white cloud beneath a clear blue sky.

"What is our position, Mr. Catchpole?"

"Here, Sir," reported the Second Sailing Master while he pricked the chart with the fine point of a divider, "Wind's about a fresh breeze, and not fair for our destination, but we are full and bye, moving well this morning on a course four points south of east. The log just came in at five. Seas are maybe four feet, as you can feel."

"Any sail?"

"Not of any country at all, Sir. We seem quite alone out here. Church is rigged, Sir."

"Tell the lookout to stay sharp. We will be nearer the remaining capital of the French on this island every day."

"Aye, Sir."

But they saw nothing that morning or the next day or the one after that, and Neville decided to tack north into a familiar bay – that of Bahia de Neiba on the south coast of Hispaniola and only eighty miles west of Santo Domingo.

"We might find French shipping at anchor here, gentlemen, but we'll have to be careful not to find an abundance of outsized protection by their navy. Coming up from the south and having the land to our larboard, we will have no way to enter with the sun behind us.

"Mr. Catchpole, propose a course to take us in to the head of the bay with the setting sun to larboard as best we can, if you please. It must be as difficult as possible for any ships in there to identify us easily. I want to be able to turn and run quickly if need be, and before any one of them might raise an anchor to chase us. It will be best at dusk, as well. We might need the dark to evade them.

"Mr. Framingham, hoist the French colors, please. We have a proper name for this deception.'

"I count six ships anchored in the bay, Commander," reported Foyle after spending some time at the masthead with his glass. "There's two big 'uns. First is a medium-sized East Indiaman, I must guess and second looks like she might be a frigate, but I can't be sure from this distance. Three are merchants for sure: brigs. The last is a small lugger. Can't tell much more about her, either, the way she's swung dead-on to us."

"So out of the six there are three to look out for, eh?" mused Neville. "And we sure enough cannot sneak in from around a corner to cut one out. The bay's too big for that. Ideas, Mr. Framingham?"

"Not right off, Commander. I've never been asked such a question."

"Hmmm."

Neville continued to stand at the leeward gunwale staring at the anchorage as they approached, pondering any action he might take.

"Mr. Framingham, Mr. Foyle, or Sergeant Denby, might any of you fancy leading a cutting-out party? I'd prefer a volunteer, because it's going to be risky, I think; but it could work and I shall myself go in one boat. I'll not think worse of you if you don't want to go on this one.

Foyle, Johnson and Denby all stepped right forward, parroting, "I'll go, Sir."

Framingham hesitated, as Neville expected, but he gave the man a minute to think on it. Finally he said, "I might, but I'd like to hear your plan first."

"Fair enough, gentlemen, I'll have to choose, then, because we cannot all go. Someone has to sail this ship smartly away from here if my plan goes wrong. My plan is thus:

"We are arriving pretty well at dusk, and should have the anchor down just as the sun goes. That's important, because we don't want them to see us very well. We can't look like British navy, but we can look sort of privateer-ish – a few more men than a merchant for example. Firstly, Sergeant Denby, I need you to go right now and hustle all the red coats below. And you others, get at least half the men below. You mids ditch your hats and turn your coats inside out, if you haven't something else. We'll certainly use your marines in this business, Sgt. Denby, so have 'em find something to wear that's not red. Tarpaulin jackets would be better, so you can use the shock of seeing them to our advantage later. Not a one on deck now, though, if you please, including you. Get a cold meal in everyone right now, as well. When that's all done come back for the rest of it. No more squeaky whistling than you'd hear on a merchant, Mr. Johnson."

Superieure slid slowly toward the anchorage as the sun drooped lower over the land to the west of them, finally leaving them in the shadow of the low hills ashore. Neville's officers returned.

"The ships at anchor are pretty well lined up there, with the Indiaman and the frigate at center. That schooner at the seaward end of the line is our target. We'll slide 'round behind her and come up along the same anchoring line and drop there – not too close. I can yell some greeting in French as we go past. The Indiaman won't be able to see much of us at all, and the frigate behind her even less, I should think.

"Then we will wait 'till it's just a bit darker. The moon is three quarters tonight, but it won't be up until maybe four bells of the evening watch. That should give us at least two hours for this, and it shouldn't take more than a half of one, if we do it smartly.

"Then we're going to load all the men we can fit in our three little boats over on the side away from our friends – so they can't see what we're up to, of course – and set off for that schooner when it's dark as pitch. Our men in the boats clamber aboard quickly, take her by surprise, cut her cable, and we're both away.

"What's our course out of here?" asked Catchpole. "east or south?

"Good question. I say south down the peninsula, around Islas Beata and Alto Velo…"

"In the dark?"

"Moon will be well up before we get there, if not the sun, Mr. Catchpole, right? We'll give it a good offing, anyway."

"Right, Commander."

"Then west along the southern shore of Hispaniola. We can do it, and so can the schooner, I'll wager, but the frigate, if he chases, cannot fly so tight to this wind, and he must fall further and further offshore of us. We'll run with no lights. The moon will do. Rendezvous at the Isle a Vache or go on to Port Royal, depending on what the wind allows us. Shall we do it?"

"I'm in," said Sgt. Denby.

"Me, too," said Foyle.

Before Framingham could answer, Neville said, "That's it then. Mr. Foyle will command the prize. We've only three boats, and you others are the ones I'd've chosen to sail *Superieure* home if we don't come back. Look sharp and be ready to crack on hard if that happens."

Superieure followed a lazy path around the seaward end of the line of anchored ships, dropped enough sail to ghost slowly past the schooner. At close range she looked to be a well-armed merchant; possibly a pirate or privateer and carrying, it appeared, ten guns. She flew no colors and showed few men aboard.

As they passed, Neville used his speaking trumpet to yell a greeting across in French. "*Superieure*. Good evening. All quiet here?"

The answer was only two words, without a trumpet, "*Unique*, Aye."

"Fair enough. Mr. Johnson, ready at the anchor."

"Just here, Mr. Catchpole. Turn in."

"There's only about fifteen minutes of light left, Mr. Johnson. It's dark enough now to get the boats over the side. Sgt. Denby, fill them with the men. Remind them – no cocked muskets."

"What's this, then, Commander?" asked Framingham. "See that boat there?"

"Clever frigate captain; he's made his own harbor patrol, I think. Get the marines up here with their muskets. Have them stay below the gunwales and be ready to pop up. We'll invite the harbor patrol into the spider's web."

Twenty French sailors rowed the frigate's launch straight toward *Superieure*. Neville stood at the main chains, high and visible, as they approached. He waved.

"Good evening," he yelled again as they neared. "Are you the harbor patrol? Ha, ha!"

A lieutenant – or maybe only a midshipman by the sound of his young voice - called across, "We are, Sir, from the French People's Frigate *Desiree*. Why are you here?"

"Monsieur Downey," Neville said to Johnson's mate in French. "Take that painter there." He expected that Downey had no idea what had been said, but it was obvious what the command would be.

"Up!" Neville commanded at the moment Downey grabbed hold of the rope that was tossed over.

The top rail of the gunwale was suddenly lined with twenty muskets. The sound of them all being cocked above their heads was enough emphasis to staunch any illusions of resistance on the part of the French.

"Nobody move or make a signal or you will all suffer for it. Pass up your weapons; then all of you get out and come aboard!"

"See them below, gentlemen. Then we need the marines back up here. Borrow a few hats. We have another boat now, but less time. The frigate *Desiree* will wonder where her patrol boat is very soon."

"They're all stowed," reported Sgt. Denby ten minutes later.

"Excellent. Let's get under way. Mr. Downey will take the jolly boat now. You take the frigate's with all your marines in one boat."

There was a little shuffling and confusion due to the changes, but most of the seamen, prepared for the attack, had been sitting ready in the launch and jolly boat during the harbor patrol visit.

"Shove off," commanded Neville. All four boats began the row toward the dim lights which showed where the schooner floated.

The surprise attack was far less dramatic than even Neville had expected. The schooner *Unique* had no guard posted – or at least no guard awake. *Superieure's* men swarmed aboard from the four quarters of the quiescent vessel in under two minutes. Neville was amazed to find the Master already in his bed. The Mate and two others, who appeared to have some status above seaman, were caught playing at cards. Five seamen lying about the deck were trundled down into the frigate's barge without struggle, and the remainder of the *Unique's* thirty-man crew were trapped in their mess below.

"Sergeant Denby. I think we'll exchange twenty. Eight of yours will stay here with your corporal. March them up now. We need to get along."

On deck, the captured French were being urged into the boats at cutlass-point. *Superieure's* barge was the first away, pulling hard for their ship. Then the jolly boat with only two prisoners in it.

"Cut the cable as soon as you have a sail abroad, Mr. Foyle. I'm going down now."

Four marines guarded the largest number of prisoners in the frigate's barge. *Unique's* fore topsail was dropping even as it shoved off. The whole operation had taken only twenty minutes including the row across from *Superieure*.

"Put your backs in it, men," urged Neville. "We've no time to lose."

A musket fired ahead in the dark – somewhere near *Superieure*, and some sort of candle was lit. It glowed bright red.

"The frigate has sent out another boat to look for the first one, I'll wager," said some seaman forward.

"Aye," said Neville, "and they're making a signal to their ship. You two marines in the bow keep a close watch for that other boat; and you two aft, watch these Frogs carefully. When we get to *Superieure*, we'll leave the Frogs in here and shove 'em off." He told the French the same in their language.

"*Desiree's* coming alive, Commander," said one of the rear-facing rowers. "You can hear her calling all hands. She'll come chase us for sure."

"Marine – forward there. One of you shoot at that red light.

The marine's musket barked in the dark, shooting a long yellow flame toward the red light.

"Someone screamed, Mr. Grimby," his mate said. "A lucky shot, indeed."

"Here we are. Get aboard. Shove them off, Mr. Grimby. Have your mates shoot a couple holes in the bottom of that boat to keep them busy. We won't have to deal with them, at least."

"Mr. Johnson, are we all back?"

"Aye, Sir, all that's coming."

"Get the anchor up, then, and fast! We'll have *Desiree* after us. There goes Foyle ahead of us already."

"Two more men with muskets… take a couple more shots at that red light. Maybe we can delay *Desiree*'s search for her patrols. They won't be happy to find a batch of slovenly pirates in their broken launch, either, ha, ha!"

Two musket shots.

"Anchor's hove short, Sir."

"Ready Mr. Catchpole? Mr. Framingham?

"Aye, Sir."

"Raise it."

Superieure heeled slightly to the breeze, now shifting toward her beam. The gurgling of water astern informed them that they were under way, and the little wavelets of the harbor began gossiping down *Superieure's* hull.

"One point west of south, If I remember right, Mr. Catchpole."

"I agree, Commander.

"Helm up a bit, quartermaster."

The starlight was not yet enough for them to see what *Desiree* was doing nor enough to see *Unique* ahead.

"Mr. Johnson, get four men with two good eyes apiece onto the bow. I would prefer no collision tonight. And then two gun crews at the stern chasers, if you please. Get these silly French colors down."

Six bells chimed.

"Moon, Sir. There she peeks, at the horizon."

"Four knots," called the log-thrower from the main chains.

"I see *Unique* just there, Commander. She's clear now in the moonlight. She's got half a league on us. A cleaner bottom, maybe?"

"Or Mr. Foyle's cracking on to save his soul, more like. She's getting clearer as the moon rises. I knew we'd be able to see, but we'll not be able to hide at all, will we?"

"No, Sir, and *Desiree's* easy to see behind us as well, but I can't tell if she's even under way yet."

"Let's pray she takes her time."

"Don't spare a trick to keep her moving, Mr. Catchpole. I'm going below for a few hours' sleep. I'll be up with Mr. Framingham."

When Neville returned to the deck at two in the morning, *Unique* was slightly further ahead, and *Desiree* was undoubtedly under way, but at least three leagues distant. She was hull down, as best they could tell in the night.

"Six knots, Sir. Breeze has freshened. Everything we have is up, but that frigate can hold as close to the wind as we can along this coast."

"How long to the islands, Mr. Catchpole? I'm beginning to think this was ill-planned."

"Six to seven hours, if the wind holds. It will be daylight when we get there."

"Well, that's good. We can go between the islands to save some time. Unless he's very experienced in these waters, I doubt he would try it. Now we just need to get Foyle to slow down so we can lead him through."

"Between the islands, Sir. Do you really think to…"

"Yes, Mr. Catchpole. I have done it before. Here's Mr. Framingham. You should get some sleep."

The moon, still hanging in the western sky, turned a dim white as the sun rose to larboard.

"All night she's come on, with us plain to see as the fingers on the end of your hand."

"And she's catching us up, I think," said Catchpole.

"Fire a gun and signal *Unique*. Try, 'speak' I suppose."

"She's got it, Sir," Mr. Johnson said ten minutes later after a forward chaser was fired and the signal flag flew. *Unique's* sails were fluttering as she spilled wind to slow for *Superieure*. Two hours later she was alongside. Both ships were back at speed, and Foyle had found a speaking trumpet.

"…going between the islands… follow us through…"

"There's the point there, Commander," said Catchpole.

"We cannot turn at the point and go inside Isla Beata. We must go 'round it, and then within Isla Alto Velo. From here that looks to be three leagues. I'll have my breakfast, then," said Neville. He went below.

HMS Superieure, at Sea
Southe of Hispaniola   *January 27, 1804*

My Dear Marion,

I hope to send this the moment I am returned to Jamaica, and I now see a chance of it being soon. We have had some luck in finding a few French ships at anchor on the Southe Shore of Hispaniola and last night we 'cut one out', as they say. We are at sea now bringing her home to Port Royal.

I must report being pleased with the performance of my little ship, and with that of young Mr. Foyle, whom I have set aboard the prize as commander for her return. I'll have to introduce the boy to you. I am sure you will enjoy his enthusiasm.

I also wish to repeat my sincere Desire to meet with you again. I will ask at the Pig's Tale for a note from you as soon as I am in.

Affectionately,
Cmdr. Nev. Burton

"Come ahead," Neville called to his sentry when he heard the rapping at his door.

"Mr. Catchpole's compliments, Sir, and can you please step up to the helm?" asked the messenger.

Neville squinted north as he made his way to the binnacle, trying to better gauge the distance to Desiree.

"Somewhere between two and three leagues, still, is my guess, Commander," said Mr. Framingham, "and that's closer than she was."

"Look forward there, though. Here's your Beata Island. And I think I see that other 'un low on the horizon a couple points to starboard."

"You're right on both. It's almost time to turn. Signal *Unique* and have the men stand by on the sheets."

Five minutes later Neville stood by the helm to give his own personal directions to the quartermaster. "Now, Quartermaster. Helm down. Come up two point to starboard…

"Another two now.

"Is *Unique* following closely, Mr. Framingham?"

"Aye, Sir, she is."

"Stay this course, Quartermaster. Oh!" Neville's stomach knotted, but he decided to say nothing more. He watched a huge rock slide by beneath the ship. *This water is so clear that I can't tell if that rock is down one fathom or five,* he thought.

"What is it, Sir?"

"I was… I just thought… We'll pray that frigate doesn't dare cut through here just because he sees us do it. As I see it, one of three things may happen. He may follow us through with no trouble at all, he may try to follow and find some rocks, or he may decide on the safe course around Isla Alto Velo. We must pray for one of the latter two."

"Rocks, Sir!" exclaimed Sgt. Denby, who was leaning at the rail.

"Hush, Mr. Denby!" cried Neville, "And the rest of you as well. Keep it calm. I tell you I have been through here before. Our draught is less than ten feet. That frigate will draw over twelve and will strike much harder than we ever might… if it happens."

As if to underline Neville's point, the ship shuddered ever so gently. His men looked to Neville, and he returned a strange thin grin, "Let that frigate try than one," he said, knowing they had just scraped the top of a rock. "We are committed. Keep on.

"Mr. Johnson, get a man in the chains with a lead. I think we've come through it now. Does *Unique* still follow?"

"She does."

"Seven fathoms, Sir."

"Keep him calling out."

"Aye, Sir. He says three now."

"I heard."

"Four and a half."

"Three." They watched another rock pass beneath, wondering how they had missed it.

"Six."

"Seven and a half."

"Five."

"Eight." There was more sand than rocks visible below now.

"Seven."

"Ten and a half... twelve."

"Unless we have really bad luck, that's it. We are through. Put us on our new course, Mr. Catchpole: two points north of west.

"Haul our wind, Mr. Johnson, Mr. Framingham. Let's see if old *Desiree* can come anywhere near so close on the wind as what we're about to do."

Superieure leaned well over to larboard and began shouldering small waves aside.

"Full and bye, Sir," reported Framingham.

Neville looked behind to where *Unique* was doing the same. *Desiree* would not be visible again until she came into the opening between the point and Isla Beata, and then later again the opening between the two little islands. An hour passed, and then two.

"Sail, Ho!" cried the lookout at three hours. "Frigate at the islands."

They could all see from the deck as the frigate passed across the gap between the point and Beata. Her topsails could be seen as she sailed behind the low island, and then she appeared at the next opening. They watched.

"She's turning in, Sir," said Framingham, "to follow our wake."

Desiree did not turn to point directly at them. She could not go that close to the wind, and so presented an oblique picture of her rig. After fifteen minutes on that tack her sails began to change color in the late morning sun.

"Lookout, what do you see of the frigate?" Neville hollered up.

"Sails a-flutter sir. No. They're aback. She's turned chicken, Sir; turning back!"

A hesitant cheer rippled through the ship's company. The men had been aware of their peril, and they heard the lookout as well as Neville did.

"She'll go around Alto Velo," Neville said. "We've bought ourselves some time. Now we crack on for the Ile a Vache or Port Royal."

All day they pounded west northwest. *Unique* slowly came up again and took the lead. *Desiree* was now barely visible to the southeast, but she hadn't given up. When night fell, *Unique* burned a light. There was no chance *Desiree* could see it at that distance.

"Wind's veering, Commander. Come up some?"

"No change. Hispaniola is still to our north. It's good for *Desiree*, though. She'll come up towards us. Nothing more to do this night but keep on, I suppose."

"Good morning, Commander," said Catchpole. Neville knew it was Catchpole by his voice – not because he could see the man in the dark. "Sun will be up soon. You can see the glow to the east. It's coming purple already."

"Get the lookout up, if you please." He slurped at his coffee cup.

"Deck, there! Sails!" the lookout yelled down a half hour later. The sun wasn't up, but the light was enough to identify *Unique* half a league ahead and *Desiree* four to the southeast.

"A new plan, gentlemen," said Neville after gathering his officers. "We fall off some to gain a little speed and head due west to clear the southwest point of Hispaniola. Because *Desiree* is south of us we can't fall off for Port Royal without crossing her path. As long as we stay ahead and gain sea room, we will be able to sail closer to the wind into the Windward Passage for our escape. If something goes wrong with that, we'll have to try doubling back behind the frigate and count on our nimbleness to evade them."

All day they charged ahead. By six bells of the afternoon watch it was apparent the new plan wasn't working.

"The wind has veered too far for us, Sir. And we must have less wind in here than *Desiree* out there, as well. She catches us steadily."

"Aye. Time to change to our plan of sailing behind the frigate in the dark. Signal *Unique* to come close by."

Neville passed word of his new plan to Foyle. Using the same night conditions that permitted their cutting-out of *Unique*, the two ships turned about at dusk and sailed southwest into the night.

"This captain is getting on my nerves, Commander Burton," said Framingham several hours later when the moon rose. "He has seen us, I'm sure. You see her rig straight on, not from the side. She may have us by morning."

"Same all night, Mr. Catchpole?"

"Aye, Sir. She's quite close now, as you see. But we have sea room aplenty now. We can haul up close on the wind whenever you order."

"Thank you, Mr. Catchpole. We'll have breakfast first, I think."

"Sail, ho! Deck, there; three sail to the west... no, Sir; four."

"Whose, can you tell?" Catchpole yelled.

A minute passed. Two.

"Ours, Sir. Now five. 74, two frigates and two smaller."

Desiree fired. Neville saw the ball skip and then hit a wave just half a cable away. Then they saw the smoke blow off *Desiree's* bow and heard the bang of the gun.

"My word!" Exclaimed Neville. "That's a long gun indeed, and a good gunner."

Just before they saw another puff of smoke and heard the bang of a second gun, a length of chain whistled across the deck. The mainsail flung wide on the wind, causing *Superieure* to lurch drastically to larboard and expose her side to *Desiree* as she shot off at right angles to the oncoming frigate. The distance between the two closed rapidly before Mr. Johnson's men had a new sheet on the main.

"Hard to larboard!" yelled Neville, counting on *Superieure's* nimbleness for her safety.

The big frigate charged past. She was well within range of her guns, but having expected no such opportunity in that time, her ports had just been flung open and her guns only half run out. Two fired in haste. A hole appeared in the mainsail and a great shuddering was felt throughout the ship as a ball stuck hard somewhere.

"Now we're in for it, Commander," said Framingham.

"I don't think so," replied Neville. "There she goes. I'll wager she'll not even slow down. Our frigates will chase." He breathed an obvious sigh of release. "Splice the main brace, Mr. Johnson. That's an order."

"A floating bomb, she was. That's what you had me bring back. Forty barrels of powder, Commander Burton!" blurted Midshipman Foyle when he reached the deck of *Superieure* at Port Royal Harbor. "Forty! And the rest of the hold full of lignum vitae. So if we didn't all blow up when that frigate shot us, we'd have surely burned away to charcoal."

"Oh, Mr. Foyle," cooed Catchpole, "Don't be so dramatic. Look at you standing there richer than you was before we left and complaining about it. Anyways, you think that frigate didn't know what you were carrying?"

"He's right on that, Mr. Foyle. That might be why they chased us so far. The powder might have been for them, and their carpenter would certainly have been pleased with some of that wood. At any rate, Mr. Foley," said Neville, thumping him on the back, "I'll overlook your disrespectful outburst and praise your damned fine sailing. Jolly good show!"

"Sorry, Sir, and thank you. And I have something for you. Some sod from the Rum Company ashore what can't tell one schooner from another left this off with me." He held out an envelope. "Can't read *Unique* from *Superieure* either, I suppose."

"Thank you, Mr. Post-boy," Neville joked. *I'll look into this below.* "But now we must discuss the disposition of your ship and crew. Come below…"

After their discussion and the departure of Foyle, Neville pulled the envelope from his pocket. He had been hard pressed to think of anything else during his meeting with Foyle.

To: Commander Burton   *Feb. 1, 1804*
HMS Superieure

Dear Sir,

*We at the Stillwater Rum Trading Company take seriously the
State of Affairs of our Clients. When last your ship was in
Harbour you purchased no rum. Now you have been away at
least two weeks longer, so we must assume you are close to the end
of your Allowance.*

*Please drop by at your earliest convenience to discuss how we
might help assure your ship of an uninterrupted supply of rum.*

Your most humble servant,

Mic. Stearns,
Manager, Stillwater Rum

*Just a letter of trade! I had so hoped for a response from Marion. But I
suppose it wouldn't be delivered that way, would it.*

In the morning Neville had himself conveyed to shore, giving
the need for a simple walk for exercise as his reason. It wasn't
entirely a lie; he took a walk to the *Pig's Tale* and inquired for Miss
Fletcher. A medium-height dowdy young woman with wild dark hair
appeared from a back room wearing a gray dress and blood-stained
white apron. "Yes, Cap'n?" she asked.

"I, uuhhmm… Is there a note here for a Commander Burton?"

She looked at him through suddenly brighter eyes. "There might
be," she said. "You 'im?"

"Yes, I am he."

"Well then," she said, and went back through the door. She
reappeared in a minute with an envelope and a meat cleaver. "Here
'tis," she said, holding it out for him. "You won't cause her no
trouble, will you?"

"Certainly not, Miss Fletcher. I would never."

"No, you won't," she reaffirmed in a calm, quiet voice while staring him in the eyes and wiggling the cleaver, "because if you do, this'll be for you, too!"

The envelope was addressed to: 'Cmdr. Burton, *HMS Superieure*'. He took it outside after mumbling, "Thank you."

Inside, it read:

Neville,
You see? Easy!

I too look forward to seeing you again. You could begin with an official visit to the office as soon as you're in. I'm sure you're well, but 'Seeing is believing', they say.

Marion S.

9 - "The Meeting"

One of Marion's weekly responsibilities at work was the very mundane task of reconciling the lists of rum shipments with the receipt notes. It usually took her all morning, and often required several short walks back to the warehouse to ask some question of the shipping supervisor.

The smell of oaken casks and aging rum filled the spaces in the air that were not already filled with the sounds of wooden hammers pounding bungs and staves.

"What's this, then, Mr. Powers – a two?" Marion asked in a raised voice. His was not the best penmanship in town

"Why, it's a seven, Miss. You see? This is a two, like this. And all our little rundlet casks are seventeen and some gallon anyway, so it must be; you know that."

"Mr. Powers, I am beginning to think you make these mistakes just so I have to come ask you questions. You're just a flirt."

"Not me, Miss, I would never!" he insisted – with a wink.

She departed the warehouse through the large doors to the front of the building and returned to her office. Through her window she could see a man in uniform standing at the receptionist's desk in the lobby. His head was down because he was speaking to the clerk, but he looked familiar, nonetheless. She knew Neville's ship was in, and this man was the right size. Because he had told her, she knew that he wore the epaulette of a commander – not the average lieutenant. She kept her eyes on him while she moved behind her desk to sit.

His head came up, presumably at the end of his conversation, and he looked her way. Yes, it was Neville. And he had apparently noticed her motion, because he looked directly at her and smiled wide. He gave her a polite nod – almost approaching a bow. She returned his smile before he turned to find a seat in the lobby where he was directed by the clerk.

Marion watched him walk to a chair. She noticed, as he did so, the slightest of limps. She sat when he did, doing her best not to be noticed staring at him. She placed her shipping documents in the center of the desk in front of her, and began to sort through them. There was no reason to sort except to kill a few minutes while she tried to decide whether she should go out to the lobby and greet him. The clerk was up and walking into the office hallway. Was he coming to collect her?

No. He turned the other way. She glanced over to see him enter the office of Mr. Stearns.

He wouldn't really come in here and ask for Mr. Stearns and not me, would he? She wondered.

After a minute in Stearns' office, the clerk emerged with Stearns a few steps behind. *Maybe he didn't ask for any specific person?*

The two men from the office walked out to the lobby. The clerk returned to his desk and Stearns went to greet Neville, who stood when Stearns arrived at his chair.

Marion watched the two men move to one of the sales booths along the side wall. They spoke for a few minutes, and then they both turned and looked across at her. She looked away; down at her desk, knowing she had gone red with the presumed embarrassment of it – or maybe anger?.

By the time she stood they were no longer looking her way. She marched out from her office, out the office door and across the lobby to the booth where they sat talking.

"I'll not have it, you two," she announced in a hushed but very stern tone. "You will not sit here making me the butt of your jokes."

Both stumbled to stand the instant she entered. Stearns' chair upturned and clattered to the floor as he rose, and what few people were in the lobby turned to see what it was about.

"If you have something to say, either of you," Marion said, "This is the time to do it!" Her eyes paused on one and then the other.

"We weren't talking -" began Neville.

"About me, Commander Burton? Why look my way, then. I have eyes."

"It wasn't -" started Stearns.

"- any of my business, perhaps, Mr. Stearns?"

"Why are you here Commander?" she asked

"I was invited by Mr. Stearns..."

"He's a customer, Marion..."

"Don't you 'Marion' me, Mr. Stearns." She stared at them both for another moment. *Perhaps it is indeed the case, and I am making a fool of myself.* "If that's so, Mr. Stearns, we shall expect an order." With that last remark, she turned her stare back to Neville. "If you please, kind sir."

She turned to leave in a proper huff, then hesitated, and turned back to them. "I thank you for the compliment of your admiration, but I shall not be made fun of." She stomped out.

She could not see what happened behind her, of course, but the men in the lobby soon went back to their business – very quietly - as if signaled. She returned to her office and sat as she normally would, determined that they would not cause her to change her routine to suit their comfort. She used the repetition of her task to take her mind away from the incident as best she could and to cool down. Then she took out a writing paper and wrote a note:

Stillwater Rum Co.

Feb.3, 1804

Cmdr. Nev. Burton,

I am embarrassed by my outburst in the office today and certainly apologize for my behaviour. It is of course natural that you would have been invited by our Mr. Stearns and I must repeat his entreaty that you might become one of our valued customers.

I should never have taken your approving looks in my direction as anything other than a compliment, and I am in hopes that I might have the pleasure of your company to express just that.

*If I might be so bold as to invite you to join me for a luncheon at
the Golden Strand Hotel on Church Street on Monday next.
The hotel maintains a fashionable dining room and a novel
menu. If you could make it,*

I would be Gratefully Yours,

Marion Stillwater

She reviewed her wording and decided it was reasonably proper, though certainly forward. When she was finished she looked up to see that the sales booth was empty; Neville was gone and Stearns had apparently crept back to his office on the other side of her father.

"You are quiet today, Miss Stillwater," said Stearns. He had walked past the door to her office several times in the course of the morning. It was now after lunch, and he had not had time – or dared – to speak with her. He had apparently decided that he should not allow the day to go by without contact.

Marion turned slowly to look at him. He lounged against the doorsill like he owned the place. Her father was not in, she could see that. "Would you mind coming in for a minute and closing the door," she said as sweetly as she could muster.

"Would you mind telling me what was said yesterday between you and Commander Burton?"

"It was innocent, Miss Stillwater." She noticed that he continued to refrain from using her name. He was normally not the formal type, and he did usually call her by her first name without repercussion. "I had sent him the customary invitation to discuss his ship's rum requirements. When he appeared I made all haste to address his questions. No derogatory comment regarding you was made."

"I hope you don't think me overly self-conscious, but I have never seen the like before – two men having a conversation about rum suddenly turn and look at me. There must have been something."

Stearns wasn't normally the nervous or bashful type, either. He was more the type to become angry or self-righteous. So seeing him quietly fiddling with his pencil did not lead Marion to believe he was as innocent as he professed. *Choosing his words.*

"I believe he could see you from where he sat, and he made the comment that I must be a lucky chap to work with such a beauty."

"Just out of the blue?"

"Yes, if I remember right."

"And how did you address that?"

"I don't remember my exact words, but something to the effect that he should stick to the business at hand and that my companion is none of his business... or associate. Associate, I said, I think."

"Mr. Stearns," Marion said, leaning closer to him and direct on, "I don't think that's how it went, because he was not facing my way when you began. He had to turn 'round to look, remember?" To her own surprise, she managed to remain very calm, "But whatever you said, exactly, if you were at all close to it just now, is enough to repeat what I have said to you before, and I tell you now that it is also what I have said to my father; that I shall not be referred to as 'your companion', that we are not betrothed, that it is unlikely that we will be, and that I will run my own life as I see fit. Do we understand each other?"

He might possibly have taken her speech it as a challenge rather than the threat it was intended to be, because his reaction was not what she expected. "For now," he said with a growing smile. As he stood, he added, "I will endeavor to behave as you wish, Marion..."

He opened the door. "But things change," he said, and walked out. She thought she heard him softly whistle a little tune as he walked down the short hallway to his own office. "Yankee Doodle", perhaps?

Marion Stillwater arrived home at the end of the day in a less-than-pleasant mood. She brightened the moment she entered her room and found a note in Neville's hand on her dresser.

Miss Marion Stillwater,

I apologize for what must have seemed an affront.

Please believe me when I say that none was intended.

Simple admiration by both of us prompted the incident.

If you will but offer me the opportunity to do so, I will humbly explain.

In anticipation,

Cmdr. Nev. Burton,

He hadn't got it before he wrote this, then, had he? Rot!
The next day was Sunday, with church on and the butcher shop closed. She considered writing another note to pass over on Monday early, but then she realized that if he had delivered this note of his to the Pig's Tale after the incident at work, then he must have picked up her note at the same time. Although the situation left Marion with time to brood, that thought helped.

"You're looking more yourself today, Marion," her father said when she arrived at work early Monday. "You seemed rather distant yesterday, also."

"Just keeping my thoughts," she said, and added a bit of a lie, "I found the sermon particularly interesting."

"Really? I was thinking the man needs a new writer. Anyhow, I'm sorry you didn't make the morning carriage in."

"I'm sorry, too, father. Miss Aughton had a problem with this dress, and I had an errand anyway."

"Are you happy with her?"

"Who, Miss Fletcher?"

Chester paused. "No, Miss Aughton. What's the butcher have to do with this?"

"Oh, nothing. Yes. Yes Miss Aughton is just fine."

Chester gave his daughter a questioning look, and then a kiss on the forehead, and he went off to his office.

Marion had gone to the butcher's in hope of a reply to her note, but had found nothing there. She asked Miss Fletcher to have a boy run up to the rum company with any message that came in and went on to work.

It was almost eleven when a small brown boy of about eight years peeked his head in the door. Seeing that it was indeed the lobby of a large business, he appeared to gather his courage and strode boldly across the wood-planked floor to the information clerk's desk. He placed an envelope in the center of it under the old man's watchful eye and held out his hand.

"Off wi' you, you gutter snipe!" hissed the receptionist, "You've been paid to bring it already, and you know it."

The boy left. The clerk took the note in to Miss Stillwater's office. The note was scrawled with some sort of rough pencil. *Maybe he just got it this morning.*

> *Miss Marion Stillwater,*
>
> *I accept.*
>
> *In anticipation of Monday lunch,*
>
> *Cmdr. Nev. Burton,*

Marion left immediately. She had already made certain that there was nothing on her calendar.

Neville was standing in the hotel foyer when Marion arrived. She didn't apologize for being late. "I arranged for a table on Friday last. It should be ready."

"Neville, this is Miss Ellen Aughton, my personal assistant." Marion had taken a carriage from work out to *Independence Hall* to collect her handmaiden before meeting with Neville. The girl had been instructed to be prepared for a sudden departure.

"My pleasure, Miss," said Neville. Marion saw his eye wander quickly across the girl, who was about the same age as Neville and of similar height.

"This way, Miss Stillwater," said a waiter who appeared suddenly from behind a curtain to their right.

"Is Miss Aughton not coming?" asked Neville, as they began threading their way through tables to the far corner of the dining room. It was indeed a nice room in the modern English style – high ceilings, but with plaster frescoes painted more in Jamaican than English colors.

"She has agreed to sit opposite, Commander, to allow us a bit of private conversation; it's one of the advantages of being allowed a young chaperone rather than some old battle axe. She will do her duty, but she can also act more… quickly. And you'll get no ideas on her, either. I saw that look."

"My eyes are for you only. I think you know that already."

"Very charming response, Commander, but I look forward to seeing you prove it."

"At the earliest, Miss Stillwater."

They were seated now. Due to the early hour, there was nobody seated within three tables in any direction.

"All right, Neville," she said, "You may call me Marion. It's just that Mr. Stearns' attitude quite galls me at times. Before we turn to a nicer conversation, I would like your version of the incident at work on Friday."

Neville began the right way, she thought. He was straightforward. "It wasn't coarse at all, Marion, the way some men talk with their mates. I don't think I'd count Mr. Stearns as one of my mates, anyway. He indicated that he was surprised I'd come see him rather than wait for your to invitation. Well, I told him this bit was business, and he was the one sent me this invite. I thought it might be rude to put him aside for a gentlemen's mutual interest in a woman."

He looked down at the table for a moment and added, "And, I thought you might also feel me a bit out of station for doing such a thing, as well."

"That wouldn't have been the case, Neville. When I'm there I try to act the salesman just like Mr. Stearns."

"Anyway, then he said, 'This is not a rivalry, Commander Burton. That woman will be mine in time, and I don't need you playing the spoiler. Just look up there. Turn round and see what you're going to lose'. That's when we turned, and I was trying to decide what to say. I'm sorry for the rest of it."

"So the conversation was about me, then? I thought so."

"Yes, Marion, but I made no claims on you... And you were beautiful even in anger."

"Well, you do a much better job of digging yourself out of a hole than Mr. Stearns."

"Does that mean we might meet again?"

"It certainly does, but I cannot think of any place at all where it might be private."

"Ahh, Here are our glasses of wine. Where does Miss Aughton fit it?"

"She's a wonderful girl. And she's my protection. Just for your information, Commander Burton, you must be nice to me. She carries a dagger."

"I think you're safe with me. Surely you noticed the sword at my side?"

"It's you she protects me against, you silly thing – and all the other wolves at my door. I would like some time alone with you as badly as you wish it, but I think here at home it cannot be. We must be happy with times like this. It is my understanding that I would never be allowed even this lunch, with Miss Aughton sitting over there, if we were in London. It might be 'poor form' in Boston, even, but thankfully we are not in those places. The rules of society are far less in 'the colonies' here. I do not often see someone 'of society' to worry about, either, although I might notice one of my acquaintances running about with a man alone, and wonder about her... But I have no one with whom I might gossip about her. I'm also a professional woman who deals with men; many questionable men, I might add, and on a regular basis. I have proven to my father that I am responsible and that I will insist that all these men will treat me with respect. I have 'earned my gold buttons', as they say. Having said that, I am still too well known here even to go off riding without an escort... Miss Aughton is an excellent rider, though. We could go..."

"How is it your Miss Aughton is an excellent rider, carries a dagger, darns your stockings, I assume..."

"I'd rather you focus on me than Miss Aughton, although I admit she is an attractive girl."

"She is that. Where does she come from? Here in Kingston? Did your father choose her?"

"Since you are so interested in her, I will tell you just a little..."

"Compared to you, I have no interest in her whatsoever, so if you prefer not to tell..."

"No. You shall know. My father did not choose her. Have you not yet learned that I make my own decisions?"

"I suppose I am still learning. Fascinating."

"We met in Washington, in the United States."

"You went there? When?"

"Will you let me tell the story?"

"Yes, Miss Stillwater," said Neville, now wearing a silly grin.

"Mr. Stearns and I went on a sales trip there two years ago. He thinks he's the world's best sales person, but I assure you he is not. Modesty aside, I did far better with the Washington set than he ever could."

"I can believe that," interjected Neville.

"So I really needed an assistant, because Mr. Stearns couldn't be counted on for much."

"What was he..."

"We're not talking about him at the moment."

"No."

"Miss Aughton was recommended to me, and we got on well right from the beginning. Her domestic skills are wonderful, and she has had some defensive training, if you can believe that."

"That does make me feel better about your safety. I wonder where a girl would get defensive training."

"She assures me she has had, and I know she carries that dagger. At any rate, she was willing to come to Jamaica, so I brought her home and father seemed quite noncommittal, so here we are. Do you want to know more about her?"

"No, thank you."

"When do you sail next…?"

"Another week, at least."

"…Oh, that reminds me. Have you heard of the ague aboard *Bellerophon*?"

"I had, yes. A bad case. I've heard over an 'undred ill with it, with one dead already. I pray it does not spread."

"And here's lunch. I chose the sand dabs."

"Did I tell you that was my most favorite things?"

"You didn't, but I know now."

10 - "The Understanding"

By mid-March Neville had been to another lunch meeting with Marion at the *Golden Strand* Hotel, and then at sea for a month. Neville was now back in Kingston again. He found himself in a carriage with Marion and Miss Aughton, with Marion's regular driver at the reins.

"I didn't think you'd mind a trip out here to the cemetery," said Marion. "I try to visit my mother and brother fairly often."

"It's a beautiful day for an outing, no question. What are those, there?"

"What sort of thing are you pointing at?"

"The trees, there, with the big round fruits; and that tree, there, with different fruit."

"That one's a breadfruit tree. They've been planted all over of late. That large one is a mango. I thought you'd been to Jamaica before."

"I have but it's been quite some time." The question brought up the remembrance of Maria and a time early in his recovery when she had brought him local fruit. He could remember no 'breadfruit' or 'mango'. The carriage came to a halt beneath one of the trees. Neville asked, "I find these interesting. Can you eat them?"

"Yes, of course you can, but the importance of the breadfruit is food for slaves on the great plantations. We'll arrange to try some later. Captain Bligh brought them from Tahiti, you know, and started their cultivation at Bath some ten years ago now. Maybe someday we could take a ship out to Port Morant and, from there, horses up to the Botanical Garden. I'm told it's a beautiful garden, but father would never allow that ... yet."

"Captain Bligh? The Captain Bligh of HMS Bounty?"

"Yes, the same…"

The day passed happily, until the carriage rounded a curve on the road home to reveal a view of the harbor.

"Oh, that's the *Bellerophon*, isn't, it?" Marion asked.

"Yes, verily, and flying the yellow flag of quarantine. Why do you ask?"

"It's worse, Neville. We are told there are over a hundred and fifty ill with the ague now, and fully fifteen have died. As much as I hate to say it, I'm glad you've been away. Our men refuse to take the rum out and breathe the same air. They'll only deliver it to the shore and leave it…"

There was one advantage to Neville's second month of patrol. Marion had the idea during the previous cruise to simply walk in to the Jamaica Station Headquarters and ask if she could post a letter to the *Superieure*.

"No problem at all, Miss," she was told. "Place it there. We'll put it in the packet for the advice boat. She finds most of our patrolling ships two or three times a month."

She wrote; he responded:

HMS Superieure   *12ᵗʰ April, 1804*
At Sea West of Hispaniola

Marion,

Don't be alarmed as you read this. Everything is quiet now, and no lives were lost aboard Superieure, though it did become rather Exciting for a while on Tuesday last.

We came upon a large brig hiding in the little bay behind the Ile a Vache and quickly determined her to be a pirate, plain and simple. She was not well armed, but she did manage to get off a lucky shot that took down our foremast topsail yard before we came alongside and boarded her. The falling top hamper broke Seaman Moore's right arm. It did not take us long to overpower the brig's company, however, they being drunkards all.

I have sent her in to Port Royal under the command of our Midshipman Foyle, who has proved himself quite capable of suche duty. I am muche amiss at having not introduced him yet, and shall do so when I am returned.

The brig is renamed 'Revelry' by a very sloppy hand, so I do not know her real name. Perhaps when your men see her they can identify her... a Jamaican merchant, perhaps?

I know that it will be just another week before you read this, since I am sending it in with Mr. Foyle to the Pig's Tale. (I suspect it best to reveal as little of our communication as we can.)

When I arrive, might I make the request that we meet... Etc., etc.

In admiration,

Cmdr. Nev. Burton

HMS Superieure arrived at Port Royal a week later as promised, but her arrival was one of Neville's more frustrating experiences. For a day they sat becalmed outside the harbor after having had a luxurious easy sail southwards down the coast of Haiti. Then the wind came up from shore in the morning, just enough to disallow warping the ship in with her boats or using her own sweeps. Another day passed as she drifted farther from the harbor. On the third day a breeze arose from the east. This was enough to make rowing unnecessary, and with the aid of a slow flood tide *Superieure* ghosted into the harbor at the speed of growing grass until her anchor finally splashed in late afternoon.

"Mr. Foyle is almost here, Commander."

"That didn't take him long."

"He's had almost three days to watch us crab in, Sir. I'm sure he swayed out his boat as soon as he saw we would finally come in."

Midshipman Foyle hauled himself up the side at the main chains in another five minutes. Neville leaned down himself and clapped ahold of his hand to help him up the last few feet.

"Welcome aboard, Mr. Foyle," Neville said after Foyle saluted the colours. Come down for a bit of supper, if you please."

"I would Sir."

Below, Hajee set out a pair of claret glasses and left them to drink some wine while he roused up their dinner.

"We're all done in '*Revelry*', Sir. Prisoners have been taken, shore marines are aboard for a guard, and the cargo has been counted. There was a small chest of coins of all the realms here: French, English, Spanish, and even some Dutch, and a larger chest of plunder. They had some captain's silver tea service and the like. In the hold were fourteen barrels of flour, two of saltpeter, and four of molasses. Not much, but it should pay the men a few pounds each. Have you heard anything about prize money from *Le Serpent* or *Desiree*?

"I've just got in, haven't I, Mr. Foyle? I'd say not."

"S-sorry, Sir."

"I see the '*Billy Ruffian*' still has her yellow up. How does she fare?"

"Over t-two hundred sick, but the worst may be over. Seventeen dead, Sir, and they have moved an 'undred to the hospital ashore. There might be more who die there. I know two have."

"Thank you for that, and I wish to congratulate you on another fine job of acting as prize commander. You'll be all set to play captain soon."

"Aye, Sir, I hope to!"

"Let us turn to more pleasant things. I think you know I have seen a most charming lady ashore – Miss Marion Stillwater."

"Aye, Sir. No disrespect meant, but I think all the men know. We hear she is uncommon pretty."

"That's true enough. Well, it's time you've met. I've writ of you, and it seems rude not to introduce you. I'm sure I'll have an answer in a few days as to when and where. So you and the prize crew can come back aboard tonight?"

"They look forward to being back with their mates, aye."

"Excellent. I'd like to ask a favor. I'm going to dash off a quick note. On your rowing about the harbor, will you please find a boy to take it to a butcher shop ashore before you bring our men back?"

"Butcher shop?"

"Aye, the 'Pig's Tale' on Harbour Street. Have him take it, and bring back an envelope for me, if there is one. Here's sixpence to take it. Tell him there's this other sixpence for him when he's back. Oh, and Mr. Foyle, you needn't tell your men what it's about."

"I can't tell anyone, Sir. I don't know what it's about myself." Foyle departed with the note.

Marion,

I am sure Superieure has been the butt of the port's jokes for the last three days now, but we have arrived.

I admit to being most anxious to see you again. Is it possible we might meet tomorrow - lunch?

Nev. Burton

When he returned with the prize crew in an hour he had the response Neville expected:

Cmdr. Nev. Burton,

I am annoyed, as I am sure you are, about your unfortunate experience outside our harbor. When you are anchored, I would enjoy your company, but it cannot be Wednesday. I am promised to attend an important company function with Mr. Stearns that afternoon.

I expect a note at your earliest to confirm.

M. Stillwater

He read the note below decks, and then searched for his calendar. *Tuesday, it is. Rubbish! And she's out with that annoying Stearns fellow. That infuriating wind! Now I must wait.*

"You seem cheerful today, Commander," said Framingham on Thursday morning.

"Yes, I feel better. Sorry about yesterday."

"Not a problem, Sir. After that awful arrival, having to tend to a thousand little annoyances here in port would drive any man to drink, sure."

"Aye, but your captain should never let it show, should he? Never mind, I'll be off before noon - at about five bells, if you'd be so kind as to have my gig ready."

He met with Marion and Miss Aughton at the Golden Strand again. Her shining smile pushed away the cobwebs of monotony that had gathered in his mind after a month at sea. She gave every indication that she was equally pleased to see him. Once again Miss Aughton respected their desire to have a private conversation; they spoke easily of events at the Rum Company and Neville's experiences with *Revelry*.

"I do envy you at times," said Marion. "Such adventure! Do you enjoy the danger?"

"I don't think I've ever thought of it that way, Marion. That certainly seems an unusual thing for a woman to say. Wait; look there. It's Lt. Dagleishe of the *Vanguard*, and Lt. Miller, as well. Could they sit with us?"

"Miss Stillwater, may I present my friend and *Vanguard's* First Lieutenant Joseph Dagleishe? You've met before, at your New Years' parties. And, this is Lt. Miller, *Vanguard's* fourth."

"Third, now," Miller corrected him in a somber tone. "I did see you Miss, and I thank you for the parties, although we did not meet. Rather a busy time for you, I'd say."

"Thurin took ill of the ague. He was taken ashore, and we've just been told he'll be sent home," Dagleishe informed Neville. "That's why we've come to the best dining room in town – to celebrate Lt.

Miller's advancement – and just to get away from the ship for awhile. We'll only sit with the lady's permission, though." he added, "This looks serious."

"On one condition," she replied, "That my assistant might join in. I think it's time Commander Burton discovers that she's a little more than just a maidservant. You are not interrupting anything serious. We have simply found that we enjoy each other's company."

"Certainly," Neville said, suddenly feeling a touch of embarrassment for making exactly that assumption about Miss Aughton. He also noted his pang of concern about Marion's last remark.

Neville had stood. They shook hands all 'round and sat, after the staff had pushed another small square table against theirs and added three chairs. Neville personally crossed the room to fetch Miss Aughton. He then returned to the head of the combined table, with Marion at his left corner. When he seated Miss Aughton diagonally from Marion, Miller sat to Neville's right, leaving Dagleishe opposite Aughton.

"Tell us what you've been up to, Commander Burton," said Dagleishe.

After a long pause when he didn't get a response, Joseph looked to Neville, only to discover everyone else present looking his way.

"Wha…?" he began. He looked down as if to see if his uniform was ripped or he had made some other mistake.

"I'd be happy to answer you, Lt. Dagleishe, but it's considered polite to look at your host, which in this case I believe to be me, yet you haven't taken your eyes off Miss Aughton since you sat down… Not that the rest of us noticed."

A long and lively luncheon ensued, with accounts of the exploits of *Vanguard* and *Superieure* and of the ladies' adventures in Washington. Ellen Aughton did seem to be more than a maidservant. She didn't speak like one. She was bold like Marion and stood her ground well with the officers around her. She was clear of eye, notably observant and, Neville now knew, would not fade into the background unless she chose to do so.

Three hours passed before Lt. Dagleishe announced, "I am afraid we must make our excuses to leave. Captain Walker will be wondering if we have deserted."

"Us as well," said Neville, so they all stood. "Joseph, will you stop by *Superieure* for supper?"

"After this?" he asked, patting his belly.

"A brandy, then."

"No, you'll come to *Vanguard* and have a look round the old ship. The rest of 'em will be pleased to see you. I thank you ladies for the best afternoon we've had in ages." Dagleishe and Miller gallantly kissed the back of the ladies' hands and took their leave.

"I'll signal for the carriage, Miss," said Ellen, bustling off for the maître d'hotel's station.

Neville leaned close to Marion's ear. "A scrap of paper passed from Miss Aughton to Lt. Dagleishe. That was as fast a connection as I've ever witnessed, I think. Should I tell him of the *Pig's Tale*?"

"I think she just did," she said with a wink. "Who do you think carries half the messages?

"Carriage, Miss," announced Ellen.

They strolled to the hotel foyer as Ellen went out.

"While I'm in the mood, I must confess to telling a little white lie earlier," Marion said in a hushed tone. "I would prefer you didn't carry it home."

"What would that be?"

"I told your friends that we just enjoy each other's company. That's true enough, but my heart says it's more serious. I'd give you a big kiss if we weren't in the middle of this busy foyer. I'm going to ask father to at least relax enough to have you over for supper one day. It will be supper. He doesn't usually go home at noon..."

"I will look forward to it. Here you go," he said, pushing the door open for her.

"Might you accept a ride?"

"I'll walk. My heart is too joyful for riding." He led her down the three steps to the carriage holding her hand. "Good day, Miss Aughton. It was wonderful to meet you."

"And you.

"Off you go, driver."

Aboard *Vanguard*, Neville and Joseph took a leisurely walk around the upper deck.

"Once we go below we'll not have a chance to talk, you know," said Joseph.

Even now they were interrupted by men from Neville's' previous divisions giving their greetings and asking about those few who had joined *Superieure* – like Mr. Johnson.

"What do you know of that amazing creature?" Joseph asked.

"Which one?"

"Don't joke, Neville. I mean Miss Aughton, and you know it."

"Little more than I learned today. Her name is Ellen, though."

"Ellen, is it?"

"Yes, but be careful. I'm told she has had defensive training, and that she carries a dagger."

"I can believe it, verily."

"What was the note?"

"You saw it?"

"We commanders see everything."

"Right. I don't know what it means, though. It said '*Pig's Tale*'."

"It means everything to you, then. I'll explain. Let's go below for a brandy, shall we? How's Miller…"

Neville returned to *Superieure* in the evening a much less burdened man. *I think I was close on giving up,* he thought. *Here in Jamaica I am constantly reminded of Maria. I can feel my melancholy over her even worse when I'm at sea spending much more time with my thoughts. I meet with Marion, but we can't be even close to intimate. I yearn to hold her in my arms and kiss her, yet we can scarcely speak freely. It was so much easier with Maria. The plantation was so much more* **rural**, *and she was far less encumbered by society. Marion's father is not my friend, as Thomas [Maria's father] was. I also fear that she is playing me off against this Stearns fellow. Until today, when she saved me from drowning in these thoughts, I wondered if I was just wooing her to stave off the depression that remains of Maria. Thank the Lord for today. I am over the moon.*

No invitation for supper with Marion's father came from *Independence Hall* before *Superieure* set her sails again for the south coast of Hispaniola. Neville and Marion met several times. They took a carriage to the cemetery again, had lunch at *Independence Hall* and arranged another encounter with Joseph and Ellen at the *Golden Strand*. The association of Joseph and Ellen was obviously progressing well, judging by their smiles, cheery conversation, and a few hushed words. All-in-all they passed an enjoyable two weeks.

Before leaving, Neville walked up to the rum company, enjoying the thought of dealing with Marion rather than Stearns. He pushed the large door aside and stepped in to see the usual scene. The old clerk was at his desk. Today the offices of Marion and Stearns had people in them. Chester sat by himself, and he glanced up when he noticed the motion at his front door. He stared at Neville for a moment, and then nodded an acknowledgement of Neville's presence. *Well, that's something. I wonder if he and Marion have had a chat. As much as I'd like him to call me in and offer an invitation, I'd rather deal with Marion today. I hope he doesn't decide to play salesman.*

Three men were waiting to be served. Two in civilian clothes had been talking since he walked in, though not loudly enough for the information clerk to understand them. The third, also in civilian clothes, but with the appearance of a navy purser, sat a few chairs down the row. Neville took a seat two chairs away from the talkative pair, annoyed to find that he could still overhear the chatty fellows quite clearly. One of the best things about being off his ship was that he could enjoy some time when he could not hear the incessant babble of human speech. Their gossip caught his ear, though...

"... father and that other fella spend a lot of time with the Frogs. That's her, there - that wench. I'd wager she's a terror, eh? Har, har! She's gonna marry a Frog, they say... maybe already has. She even speaks Frog, she does." Neville could feel his temperature rising and was considering confronting the man about his insults, but then they changed the subject: "I saw their barky, y'know the *Rum Royale*, out at the Isle of Ash t'other week..." He shifted his position and continued, so Neville couldn't hear quite so clearly now. "...into a Frog launch..."

By now Neville was fairly convinced that the Stillwater Rum Trading Company was dealing with the French as well as pirates, privateers, the Spanish, Dutch and any other ship that came near. He knew the time was coming when he might have to talk with Marion about it. *That would ruin our relationship for sure. Should I speak to Chester directly? It's not my job to enforce the laws in this area unless ordered to do so. I would seize the contraband if I caught them at it, of course, but it's not even my job to investigate – just an errand for Sir William. And what of the Rum Royale? I hadn't even been thinking about that ship. I should learn more – a lot more.*

Chester finally decided to act the salesman. He came out from his office, nodded politely to Neville and the purser, and led the two annoying gossipers to a sales booth. A few minutes later, Marion's guest left. She had the reception clerk see Neville in. He caught a glare from Stearns as he walked back into the office area.

"This is it, then?" asked Marion, "Off again?"

"After we put some rum aboard, yes. I've come to see my favorite salesman about that."

"Not a very good salesman, I'm afraid. I haven't sold the captain of the rum company on a single supper yet."

"I have every faith in you. I shall look forward to your letters and your words of success upon my return. But now I must bargain for enough rum to keep my men pleased for another month."

The April-to-May patrol cruise was uneventful, and another month at sea passed slowly. The monotony was broken occasionally by letters that arrived by packet, an unsuccessful chase that took *Superieure* half way to the Caymanos before they abandoned it, three days of storms and two of calms, and one day of collecting an abundance of turtles. It was mid-May when *Superieure's* best bower dropped into the azure waters of Port Royal harbor. This arrival was normal; they simply sailed in like a proper British warship.

"The harbor's full of shipping, Commander. There's a convoy collecting, I'd say," said Framingham.

"Aye. No question," added Catchpole.

"We'll find out soon enough. Oh, look there at the *Billy Ruffian*. Her yellow flag is down."

"That's a bloody good thing," said Dr. Trimbley on one of his rare appearances among them. "I was getting worried we'd have the ague here one day."

Neville wasted no time making his excuses to go ashore for a walk - to exchange notes from the Pig's Tale. He walked in to find Miss Fletcher at work behind the counter. She passed him an annoyed glance when the little bell jangled at the door, followed by a double-take and a big smile.

"'Ello, Cap'n. Nice to see you're in. Certain somebody'll be 'appy. Just a minute," she said, and retreated into the back room.

"T'other miss brought it just this morning," she said when she came back with a small envelope, "with another for *Vanguard*. You lot must think I'm the bloody Royal Post," she finished with a wink.

"Is she in? I hadn't noticed."

"Who, Miss Ellen? You don't see her do you?"

"Not Miss Ellen, *Vanguard*."

"Oh, no. Out a week Tuesday, I think it was."

"Thank you very much, Miss Fletcher."

The little bell jangled him out into the street. His patience was not enough to see him back to the ship before he opened the note.

> *Dear Commander Burton,*
>
> *I am pleased to extend our invitation to Late Tea on Thursday next. 4:00 p.m. would do nicely.*
>
> *In Anticipation,*   *Marion*

An interesting combination of formal and friendly, he noticed. I shall take it that I have improved in her favor.

Neville busied himself with ship-duties for the next three days, including exasperating Hajee by fussing over his uniform. Thursday finally arrived; Neville disembarked from his hired carriage in front of *Independence Hall*, precisely at 4:00.

The Hall's ostlers whisked the horse and carriage away. The same butler in tails and white shirt gave him the customary shallow bow and gestured him in. Chester was not waiting there inside, giving him some idea of his importance, but Miss Aughton stood just to the right as he entered.

"Miss Stillwater sends her regards and wishes me to inform you that she will be a few minutes late," she said. She gave him a warm smile with a nod, and left. The butler led him to Mr. Stillwater's study, rapped on the doorframe, and announced: "Your guest, Sir."

"Oh, hello there, Commander. Good of you to be prompt. I find myself a mote peckish today. We'll have to wait for my daughter, but such is always the way with women, isn't it?" Chester didn't rise from his overstuffed leather chair. He also did not motion Neville to sit.

"I've not had much experience, Sir."

"No, not with fine ladies, I should think. Sherry?"

Is he trying to get my goat, I wonder? He's not offered me a seat. "I would enjoy that, Sir."

"What do you think of the convoy, Commander?"

"I see it is gathering, but I know naught of it."

"I would think you kept yourself more informed. It is all the talk about the waterfront."

He is trying to annoy me. I won't rise to it. "I have seen the ships of course – one couldn't miss them - and we have speculated that it is a convoy, but other than assuming it will proceed to the United States or on to England or to both destinations, I have learned nothing. I have no orders related to it."

"Hmmm."

"Here we are." The butler carried in a silver tray with two glasses of amber fluid. They each took one. "Thank you, Gregory."

"I'm sorry, Commander. Where are my manners? Please be seated."

"While we have a minute, Commander, I'm going to say something to you that I don't want my daughter to hear me say," Chester began in a lowered voice. "You are here at her invitation, not mine. I am doing my best to please her in this. Since the loss of my wife and son, she is the most important thing I have left in life, and I assure you it would go very poorly for any man who causes her pain. Have you had serious intentions with other women?"

"I have, Sir, but it is of no consequence."

"I think you are wrong. I suspect it would be of great consequence. Where is this woman?"

"She's dead these four years past, Sir. A great accident; hurricane. She was much like your daughter. Headstrong, if you take my meaning."

Chester almost coughed out his wine. "Do I not?" he said. "I am sorry, then. Where did she live?"

Neville considered his answer carefully, taking a sip of sherry. "Here in Jamaica."

"Here, four years ago? There was a hurricane, I know for a fact. It took out half my warehouse. What was her name?"

"There are some things in my past which I am forbidden by the Navy Office from discussing. Any more comes too close to one of those things, but I assure you it is true, and it could be proven at some point in the future if such were necessary."

Chester stared at him strangely, and then changed the subject. "I have told Marion that I do not approve of her taking up with any navy man of lower rank than captain, and I think you know why. You lieutenants have no assurance of reaching the rank of captain or of ever having any money to speak of. How would you ever provide for her? You see how she lives."

Neville paused a minute for effect, taking another sip of sherry. "I have said nothing of this to your daughter, Sir, and she seems to like me none the less for it; perhaps she assumes the same as you – that I am typically penniless. I admit I am not royal. I have no title, but I have a pound or two at Hoare's in London. I can provide."

Chester repeated Neville's pause and sip. He was a skilled negotiator. He took the direct approach. "What is 'a pound or two', Commander? I have met a good many people who think a hundred pounds is a small fortune. It's not that I need to know your business, but we are talking about my daughter, and I am not going to gamble with her future, you understand?"

"I do, indeed, Sir, but I would ask your confidence in this. I would rather she did not know of it. I would much prefer to be convinced that she would continue to enjoy my company even if I bame a pauper. Do you get my drift, Sir?"

"You are an unusual fellow, after all, aren't you? How much at Hoare's then?"

"Your word, then?"

"You have it," he replied with something of a smirk.

"Close on two hundred thousand pounds, Sir. I am also due more in prize money."

The number obviously took Chester aback. "I've never-" he said, "I've rarely met a navy man – even a captain - who could claim any such thing. From whence came such a sum? An inheritance?"

It was Neville's turn to cough into his sherry. "Excuse me, Sir. Would that my family had any such! But no, that is part of my history of which I am forbidden to speak. I will offer that it was pirate money."

"Here she is," Chester blurted.

They both jumped to their feet, and Neville turned to see Marion standing in the doorway. "We are visited by the queen," he said. "Charming."

"I've never seen this dress, have I?" asked Chester.

"I've been saving it for a special occasion, and I think this is it. It was the wrong size, but Miss Aughton has done a marvelous job, don't you think? Now if I could get you two out of this dark office, we could enjoy a conversation in our seldom-used drawing room before the sun goes down. It has a beautiful view of the garden.

As they made motion to leave, the light glinted off a small glass ornament on a shelf near the door. When Chester followed Marion out, Neville had a chance to walk close enough to it to see that it was an award of some sort: an engraved glass plaque. He could read 'Chester Stillwater' and 'Harpers Ferry Armory', but none of the fine print. And now was not the time to indulge his curiosity.

Supper conversation continued smoothly into the second and third courses. "I thought you would relate best to an invitation to 'Late Tea', you being English and all," Marion said. "We Americans don't stand on so much ceremony, but it is an English island."

"Yes, I took your meaning. I'm afraid I bothered my coxswain something terrible about my uniform."

"This dish is one of our cook's best, Commander. Lamb."

"I am surprised that father hasn't been bothering you with a dozen questions by now. Is there not something you would ask the Commander, father – about how he might be an acceptable suitor, for example?"

Chester and Neville immediately looked each other in the eyes. They could not contain it, and they both laughed.

"You mock me?" queried Marion. "How could you, Neville…father."

The men gathered themselves quickly. Neville gave a slight nod to indicate that Chester should lead their defense. He did a superb job. "We have both noted that one of your finest – and most endearing qualities – is your straightforwardness. You have just proved it again."

"We would not change it," added Neville. "It is only the mutual observation that amused us, I assure you."

"Hrrrmmpf," she said. "You two had better behave after that."

"As to your question, dear," Chester said, "I believe we have an understanding."

Marion looked questioningly to her father and then to Neville. She apparently came to the realization that she would not get a better answer at supper. The subject was quickly changed. Conversation went to lighter things: the weather, number of ships for the convoy, and then the prospects for incumbent United States President Thomas Jefferson against Federalist Charles Pinckney. Of the latter, Neville had absolutely no opinion or knowledge.

In a larger gathering, Marion would have been relegated to entertaining the ladies, but since they were only the three, they all retreated to Chester's study for a glass of Madeira. The moment Marion had finished it, she excused herself, but stopped at the door to ask Chester to come out for a minute.

She's going to ask about our 'understanding', Neville thought. *She is probably beside herself about it. I'll have a minute to look around.*

His first action was to find the glass plaque and read the fine print, which indicated the armory's appreciation for Chester's sales efforts. *He probably expects nobody to ever see this. His desk is not clear. What are those papers?*

Neville walked to Chester's desk and found, lying atop a short stack of correspondence, a letter from the same company in the United States. He began to realize his disappointment in not learning more about that new country. The letter he found from the Harpers Ferry Armory was regarding sales of the Model 1803 Flintlock Rifle. He turned to the second page.

He started when Ellen Aughton's voice asked, "Would you like something else, Commander?" She crossed the room to him quickly and pushed his hand down to replace the letter to its original position. "He's on the way back, Neville," she whispered. "Best leave this, and think nothing of it."

Confused, but understanding, he said, perhaps a bit louder than necessary, "Thank you, Miss Aughton. Another Madeira would be nice. The last went down too quickly." *She used my given name? I must think on the meaning of this… maybe confer with Joseph.*

As Chester entered, she was giving him a short bow and backing away. "And you, Sir?" she asked. "Gregory will be right back."

Neville and Chester sat for their last Madeira of the evening. *In England we would be by a nice fire*, he thought. *It's too warm for that here, though.*

"She is near incensed, young man, so this is your warning. I have respected your wishes as we discussed earlier, so it will be your business to explain my comment about 'reaching an understanding' – or not, as you see fit."

That was the end of it for the evening. Nothing more was said other than the 'good evenings' and other pleasantries on closing a dinner party.

What have we here, Mr. Catchpole?" Neville asked in the late morning as the two stood with their pots of coffee by the binnacle.

"I've no idea, Sir, but I believe it's the shore patrol. They bring messages at times."

The eight-man launch rowed to their position and thumped alongside in the blinding sunlight.

"Clap hold of that painter, there Mr. Foyle," ordered Catchpole. "A prize captain can still handle that job, can't he?"

"Dispatch pouch," the coxswain said, and slung it up on deck.

"Let go, Midshipman.

"Shove off, lads. Make way."

With that they were gone, and Johnson picked up the packet. He handed it off to Neville, who took it below to his cabin. There was only one envelope within. It bore the Jamaica Station's heavy seal. He returned topside after taking a few seconds to read the short note within.

"What's the news, Commander? You look as if you've seen a ghost," said Catchpole.

"Good news and bad, Mr. Catchpole. Good news and bad. It's orders, We're to join the convoy with *Bellerophon*."

Oh, My Good Lord. How could this happen? I have finally made progress at Independence Hall. Stillwater! Could he have seen to my departure so quickly? I thought we had decreased our differences. Maybe he set this in motion before last night. Maybe he thought my excuses too unbelievable. Maybe it has to do with my comment about the Navy Office – that might scare him if he is a spy, as Sir William suspects. Maybe this has nothing to do with him at all, and my orders are simply to serve the navy's needs. Whatever the cause, I doubt it can be undone now. I must make arrangements to communicate with Marion, of all things.

"Sway out my gig. I must send a note to Captain Cook requesting instructions."

"June 8, Gentlemen. That's the date for the convoy's departure. We are taking the merchants north; some are bound for ports in the United States and some will proceed to Britain. *Superieure* be a forward scout. I believe we will go no farther than Philadelphia before returning. Mr. Johnson and Mr. Framingham, our preparations fall largely on you two; estimate a month each way. Water, wood, and so on. You know what we need. I'll bargain the rum. We have almost three weeks, so it should not be a problem. Carry on."

Three weeks was longer than Neville normally had in port, so he was determined to make the most of it. He spent as much time as he could with Marion. He did his best to explain his 'understanding' with her father without mentioning his money, although he suspected she distrusted his explanation. He felt less unwelcome at Independence Hall, and the two took advantage of the situation to enjoy lunch together there – and all that went with it - several times.

The day before they were to leave, a shore boat appeared alongside with a passenger. Neville was summoned.

"A passenger? Where are we expected to quarter a passenger? Who is it that can command a berth on my ship?"

"It's a Mr.... let's see... Mr. Stearns."

"What? Let's go up and see. I can't believe what I'm hearing."

It was Stearns; one and the same. He had climbed up the side and was on deck by the time Neville arrived. "Explain yourself, Sir!" he demanded.

Stearns passed him a letter in a hand that Neville by now recognized as that of Captain Cook of *Bellerophon*. It ordered *Superieure* to carry Stearns to Philadelphia.

"It's your cabin, Mr. Foyle. I'm sorry, but we have nothing else."

"I don't mind, Sir," said Foyle.

Neville turned to retreat without saying anything to Stearns.

"It wasn't my idea, either, Commander Burton," said Stearns. "Let's try to make the best of it, shall we?"

"No choice, I suppose," answered Neville. He stomped away.

11 - "Up the Coast"

"Signal to sail, Sir," reported Midshipman Foyle shortly after the break of day on June 8, 1804. *"Billy Ruffian's* cable is straight up and down."

"Heave short, Mr. Johnson," commanded Neville.

"Haul away," Johnson yelled forward, and the stamping of feet began, quietly at first. Turning the capstan only pulled the slack out of *Superieure's* cable to drag her forward a few yards. With more noise, the strain increased.

"Keep going, Mr. Johnson. Raise anchor. We'll take advantage of our forward momentum to tip the anchor out. She should go easily enough in this quiet water. Prepare to raise the mains'l. We'll be out before they're done tramping in circles over there."

"Anchor's up, Commander," called Mr. Foyle from forward. *Superieure* continued to drift lazily forward without a sail up. The goings-on aboard *Bellerophon* could now be plainly heard: a hundred men and more were tramping around her capstan, carrying her stinking wet cable to the hatch and sending it below. She had topsails set and they were beginning to draw.

"Raise the main. Let's go see if the water is still blue out there, shall we?"

"She's a pretty sight, Jamaica, isn't she?" Stearns asked the air around him as Neville passed. "I'm glad I'll be back soon." He turned and gave Neville a leering grin.

The dung heap, thought Neville. *He thinks I'll never be back, so he can have Marion when next he steps ashore.*

Superieure moved purposefully out past Fort Charles on a light northeast breeze. The undulation of a long swell beneath her keel increased with distance from shore. The little ship seemed to be raising her spirits at the prospect of a long free run. Beyond the point, she began to lean to the pressure of a wind which blew undisturbed by the land.

"Six knots," cried the seaman who tripped the log.

"A nice beginning," said Neville to Catchpole. "I think that breeze will serve *Billy Ruffian* to come out well."

"It should."

With the ship on a steady course, her officers gathered at the binnacle for new orders. "Must we keep station, Sir?" Catchpole asked.

"No, thank the Lord," answered Neville. "We are a scout, as I had hoped. We stay out front and keep *Billy's* signals in sight. We should pull in closer at night. Next stop: Philadelphia. Carry on, gentlemen. I am going below for breakfast." *And to write a letter.*

HMS Superieure   *June 8, 1804*

The Caribbean Sea Easte of Jamaica

Dear Marion,

I pray you take no offense that I address you in the familiar, for it is how I feel.

We are under way now, with a good breeze and comfortable seas. I must assume you know that we have your Mr. Stearns aboard. I am most displeased with it, and I am sorry to put any word of complaint into my letter to you, but there is no one aboard to whom I can rant. He irks me terrible and makes implications that he will be happy to have me away from Jamaica.

I am afraid I must wonder if his presence is something of your father's doing. How else could he be got aboard a navy vessel – particularly mine – when there are so many merchants in the convoy? But why does he go, I wonder? If you can tell me this, please do so.

Again I am sorry to complain. I shall address mine to you at the Rum Company, as you suggested, to avoid any chance that any letter from me might "go astray" at Independence Hall. I plan to write at least once per week, and beseech you to do the same. Send your letters with any British sail going forth, to the British Navy Admiralty in London with "HMS Superieure" at the bottom and a note that our destination is Philadelphia, and then the Downs— or wherever you have last heard we might sail. If you are lucky to find a fast ship it might catch this dawdling convoy before we reach our first destination.

I pray this finds you well and cheerful,

Affectionately,

Neville Burton

The Windward Passage held to its reputation this time out. Wind from the northeast, where they had to go, blew a fresh breeze day after day, forcing the convoy to slow to the speed of the worst sailers among them. To and fro they tacked, and on the fifth day made almost no progress in their intended direction. Captain Cook of *Bellerophon* was apparently taking no chance on getting his convoy too close into the cul-de-sac of Haiti —which meant that they all stayed out in the most adverse winds available, but out of sight of land.

"We've spent at least a full day's time hove to, just waiting for them to catch us up, Commander," complained Catchpole. "This bloody Wind'rd Passage will never end."

"Aye, but look to the good. Every indication is we'll round Point Maisi and be over Spanish Cuba on the morrow, even if it be late."

The wind shifted, as is normal, when the convoy sailed past the northeastern rocks of Spanish Cuba at Point Maisi.

"You can feel the stronger influence of the trades here, can't you Mr. Framingham?"

"Aye. With the wind behind us, even our sluggards are waking up and beginning to sail like proper ships. Pray this holds, and we'll be seeing Florida in five days' time.

Their prayers were not answered, and two days more brought a total calm. They became surrounded by bobbing ships.

"Rig awnings before we all die of sunstroke, Mr. Johnson, if you please. Throw some splinter nettings in the water, as well, for any who might like to splash about."

"Aye, Sir. And I have a request from Mr. Dunne to take out a boat with some fishing gear. He says this is the place for 'dolphin-fish'. He can't help lickin' his lips when he says it, either."

"Wish him luck, and remind any of them as doesn't want any of this that it would be a good time for 'make and mend'. We'll all be wanting our tarpaulin hats in the Florida Current, if I remember the passage in June."

The wind was back the next day, and it held most of the way to the Carolinas.

"Gunroom's compliments, Sir. Will you join us for a dinner of magnificent fish? Mr. Dunne brought in four and has given us one. Cookie is making a fine stew for the hands with the rest. You can smell it from here."

"I am honored, gentlemen. I shall bring a few bottles of a fine Madeira I found in Kingston."

"My humblest thanks. I'll not forget this. Dolphin-fish right on the Tropic of Cancer over Cuba," Neville announced as they were patting their bellies after dinner. "Fetch me Cookie's cup for a splash of this wine with our thanks. We must review our chart, Mr. Catchpole, to prepare our course in the Florida Straits the day after next."

Orion and Ursa Major began to rise higher in the night sky as they sailed north, but the humidity of the Caribbean continued to hang about them. In the morning they woke to huge towering piles of white cloud stretching up and up over the Great Current in front of them to the west.

On June 18, Catchpole pricked the chart halfway between Andros Island of the Bahamas and Florida. The convoy altered course more to the north. A few wonderful days of sail followed as the wind shifted to southerly with the great stream. It remained surprisingly warm. On the 24th of June, however, the weather deteriorated. They had hauled their wind forward two days prior as they began the drive nor-nor-east for the cape at Hatteras, but now they relaxed the sheets and ran before a wind that was rising on the starboard quarter.

Dark slabs of gray clouds replaced the puffy white cotton of morning. Flat, menacing things threatened rain – or worse - as the season approached the time of hurricanes.   Thunder rolled ominously across the barren ocean, loudly enough to be heard above the wind that drove the ship into the pounding of waves on her bluff bows. Levin leapt between the ponderous clouds. The fresh breeze that had been with them for the last two days was even fresher now, puckering the heaving sea, strumming the rigging, and threatening a gale. In three days the gale, for gale it was, did come. The water gained a dark, leaden cast as it was denied sun. Foam crested the undulating wave tops. *Superieure* now slammed her way north under close-reefed topsails, sheets hard-stretched as she leaned away from the wind in her right ear. The great southern current, flowing at full strength out of the Florida Strait, carried the discomfort of humidity with it as *Superieure* sailed north watch after watch. Lookouts, admonished to keep a sharp watch for shipping, would see no land and few ships of the convoy, if this weather continued.

The gale blew itself out in another three days, however, and as they climbed up the eastern seaboard of the United States, the wind remained well abaft the beam most days. The great clouds provided considerable shade from the baking sun in addition to occasional drenching rains.

"Commander Burton, would you suffer a conversation with me today?" queried Stearns after a particularly long shower. The sun came out from behind the clouds, and was busy lifting a mist from the wet decks..

"Why would that be, Mr. Stearns?"

"Only because it is a long passage without much conversation. I notice you remain rather aloof from your people."

"And I am to feel sorry for you?" The two stared at each other for a moment.

"No, certainly not," replied Stearns, "and I will admit I haven't tried very hard to be friendly. Whether we talk or not, I assure you that I have every intention of winning Miss Stillwater's hand."

"As do I," stated Neville, glaring back at him.

"It's fair enough that we understand each other. We can speak of other things. This is at least the sound of another intelligent voice."

"True enough. So how did you end up in Jamaica? You're not from there, I understand. You have an accent that I am told is from the Carolinas of the United States."

Stearns leaned on the starboard rail and peered at a flock of small white birds floating on the sea. "I was in tobacco sales for my father to begin with," he said. "We were trying to get the French market, and finally I got a chance to go over and give it a try. I was a pretty good salesman, I think, but I ran into a man there who ruined it for us. I'll never forget him; Georges, his name was."

It couldn't possibly be, could it? Neville wondered. He kept his gaze distant. "What was his last name? I know it never happens, but I have a French friend named Georges."

"Cadoudal. A scurrilous fellow if ever there was one; but in good with those who buy things for the navy. If he turns you out, you're done. And he did – for no good reason. It took me some time to figure that out, but I couldn't get anywhere with the Frogs after that."

Georges Cadoudal! Why would this dullard meet with Georges? This is not what he makes it out to be, I am certain. "So then what?" *Maybe I was not interested before, but I am now. Don't let him know it.*

Stearns continued his usual story about some connection between a crony of Chester's in the US suggesting he might give the rum business a try. "I didn't like the place at first. Just a lot of stuffy Brits, heat, bugs and muggy air. But then I started to realize it was not unlike North Carolina in the summer, and I got on well with Mr. Stillwater. A couple years ago now the Stillwater boy – Freddie – was killed by French privateers, so then Mr. Stillwater really needed me. And then I began - take no offense, this is just a statement of fact - began to take notice of what a beauty Miss Stillwater is, not to mention how smart she is. So, all things together, I think I'm in a place I don't want to leave."

I notice there is no first name basis here… for my benefit, or they've just kept him at arm's length?

"What about you? Ever been to Jamaica before this?"

Neville blew a long breath out through pursed lips. *I don't feel that I need to tell him anything. For all I know he'll use it against me. Marion already knows about Maria. She'd better get the same story from him. I know he'll tell her what I say for her to compare for any lies.* "I would have married a girl there, but for a hurricane almost four years ago. I thought I would live here forever." He saw Stearns perk up. "Don't get ideas. Marion already knows, and so does Chester." He couldn't say 'earthquake'. He had no idea if there had been one four years ago, but anyone would believe 'hurricane'. Chester had confirmed that, as well.

"You work fast. First names, then? What was the girl's name?"

"You'll never get that. But it wasn't a three-week romance. I was here – in Jamaica - two years. I was… connected to important people. This girl was not of low station. She was the equivalent of Marion - so much like Marion it would make your head spin. I am not…"

Stop. Control yourself. Already too much emotion.

"Despite my age," he continued in a calmer voice, "I know Jamaica better than most. I know this Caribbean. I know her waters, her hurricanes and her history, and-" he turned to look into Stearns' eyes, "I will not disappear. I have the means to return whenever I wish." *Let him stew on that!* "Another day, Sir."

Neville returned to his favorite spot by the binnacle and turned to watch forward. *Superieure* was a fine ship. Seas approaching nine feet rolled up from behind, but they slid comfortably beneath her stern. The bow rose and fell with a smooth motion; the seas hissed along her sides. He noticed that Stearns stood at the rail for some time. *Brooding?*

The lookout was not to call out whenever he saw a sail, or he would have gone hoarse. He was only to call out if one approached steadily or if he saw a signal from *Bellerophon*. Neville was finding it increasingly difficult to stay within signaling distance. Small white flecks of sail were seen following – on and off throughout the day, but no ship caught them. In the huge bight off South Carolina

Neville decided he must spill wind and wait. *Superieure* would do the convoy no good if they couldn't be seen, even though Neville considered the chance of encountering a French ship to be small.

They were close enough to shore to observe small coastal traders and fishing boats, but at about two hundred miles offshore, no land was visible to the west, even on a clear day. Large numbers of sails were seen crossing their course, both before them and aft. In the vicinity of Charleston, and then Norfolk, the shipping was considerable. But they saw no French – at least none flying French colors. To the exasperation of the ship's company, sail changes were continual from the Carolinas north.

Burton stepped onto the deck in the morning off Nag's Head to a sight that gave him pause. The doctor, Mr. Catchpole, Mr. Johnson and a small group of seamen were standing on the foredeck looking ahead as the ship ghosted forward before a light southwesterly breeze. He turned slowly to follow their gaze. Land was visible as a low purple line to larboard, lit by the midmorning sun. He judged it some two leagues distant. There was sunlight – the weaker sunlight of the northern latitudes; but while it buttered the freshly-stoned decks, it fluttered and darted and seemed not fully sunlight, but some enigma of shadow and light flying between the lines above. Looking forward, he viewed a vertical wall. The ship was moving toward it; or maybe it was moving toward them. *Simoom*, he thought in a sudden panic. *But no, not here. That could not be.* The wall appeared to be of similar consistency to a simoom, but neither angry nor brown; it was gray-white, as a thick cloud. Fog it was. A great towering monster of fog that now, as he took his first step aft, swallowed the ship whole. It was thicker than any he had seen, and now that it had swallowed the ship, it began sending tentacles into it. It gathered the men at the rail into a ball that obliterated them. It sent cold fingers into his jacket. Sails could not be seen above, although the breeze did not die. Mr. Catchpole's disembodied voice called out calmly, "Shall we alter course two points starboard, Commander?"

"I think we should, aye.

"Mr. Johnson, call all hands."

The usual whistling of pipes and slapping of calloused feet on wooden decks began as it should, but it was followed by much confusion and surprised calls when the men ran up the companion were stopped by the sight. It was perhaps more likely the lack of sight, however, that made them trip and fall. Those who did were trampled by more who followed them up. By now these men could do their duty on the darkest of nights, but this was somehow worse. Not even a lantern could tell them fore from aft, and they had to resort to the blind man's game of feeling their way. Now the men were visible to Neville again, but ethereal; a group appeared with no legs – only their upper bodies. *Like the 'Last Supper',* he thought – *with no table. What has happened to us?* He moved farther aft.

"Commander, is that you there?" called out Foyle. It brought him back to reality.

"Aye. Have Mr. Johnson call the off watch down."

"Mr. Catchpole says these fogs can last for days," mumbled Framingham from behind, causing him to start. Men appeared and disappeared now, with or without actually moving, for the next hour. They all became more familiar with their ghostly surroundings, and the day resumed a relatively normal pace. No navigation sights were taken, of course, because nothing could ever be seen above the crosstrees. The sun was never its familiar round self – only a whiter blotch above them gave away its existence. That endless day morphed into an endless night as the ship's wake indicated forward motion, and on the second day of this they were all becoming more anxious about their location. A light rain – more like a heavy falling mist – began to dampen what cheerful spirits remained, and they heard thunder roll across the water with no hint of the direction of its source.

By three bells in the afternoon watch patches of flickering fog could be seen to precede the thunder.

"By God, what now?" murmured Foyle aloud. "Do we sail with Odysseus?" Which remark was answered by a bolt of lightning that split the fog from on high to the water on their larboard side. The water would have been heard to sizzle had the immediately-following clap of thunder not been so intense as to cause one man to fall to his knees holding his ears. Another clap of thunder to starboard and another forward filled the air. No man spoke, and for several minutes few could hear anything beyond the roar in their ears.

Superieure moved steadily north by northeast through the lightning, or the lightening moved steadily on to the south. Whichever was the case, it took the rain with it as well as the light, and another miserable night followed. Morning did finally come, for this time fingers of light filtered and flickered through the haze. Barely enough to be called sunlight, it was welcome, for it seemed to all that it kept the foggy fingers out of their jackets. The men gathered in little groups about the deck following breakfast and spoke quietly.

Seeing the man at the rail, Neville asked, "Mr. Stearns, how are you at navigation?"

"It's my disgrace," he replied without so much as turning to face Neville. "I'm no help to you."

"Come with me below," Neville then requested of Catchpole and Foyle. "We must see to the charts again.

"Mr. Framingham, get the men aloft and be prepared for any sudden change. If this cursed fog remains we risk the shoals that we all know are ahead."

With somber looks and pursed lips, Foyle and Catchpole followed their captain down the companion, leaving Framingham the watch as Johnson's pipes and the tramp of feet began again.

Neville heard a sound as he descended the steps, setting him on edge: a rolling whoosh ending in a thump. Burton recognized this sound but could not place it. There! Again the sound, exactly the same. And a smudge in the fog, darker gray than the rest, appeared slightly astern and to the east.

"There are almost an 'undred ships out here with us, though I thought us well away from them when last we could see," he said when below. "If the convoy have taken a smarter course farther offshore they may not be in the danger we face here."

A voice shrieked from somewhere above; possibly the fore crosstrees, that could be plainly heard below. "Surf to larboard!" came the voice at its loudest, in unison with the mainmast lookout. "Hard to Starboard!"

Neville, Catchpole and Foyle ran up the stairs. The sound again. *How could I be so stupid?* Neville asked himself. *Surf! I haven't heard it in months!*

Neville noticed a lighter patch where the dark smudge had been - a fleecy enigma — to the southeast. But he looked to larboard where the surf had been reported. From deck he could see nothing. In the next second, so fast as to cut short even his thoughts, the entire forward half of the ship was instantly swaddled in sunlight, and the low sand dunes of Carolina's barrier islands showed their long low mustache of white water, not three cables off the larboard bow. The lookout was still pointing and waving and yelling. Then Framingham and the after deck emerged from the wall of fog as if a theater curtain had been pulled open.

Neville joined Mr. Johnson in his chorus, "All hands! Hard to Starboard!

"Get a man on the lead line." *Why haven't we been sounding all along? Why wasn't I thinking?*

The creaking and groaning of cordage, yards, and booms came even before the tramping boots of marines heading aft had subsided, and the ship leaned slightly to larboard as her turn began.

"Ship! Starboard beam!" Again the united shrieks of the lookouts.

My smudge! thought Neville.

Every eye flicked forward to see the bulk of a bulbous dark ship that had also just appeared from the fog and was now attempting the same maneuver *Superieure* had just made. But the undermanned ship was slower to turn, first presenting her full larboard side to *Superieure's* bow, not half a cable distant. The instant stillness aboard *Superieure* permitted them a moment to hear the pandemonium aboard their ghostly visitor.

"By the mark, five!" yelled the man in the chains.

My God! We're almost inside the surf line.

"Beat to quarters, Mr. Johnson. Run out!" The order and following drums and whistling shocked Mr. Catchpole out of his sudden stupor.

"Captain, she's an American Merchant. No doubt of it. Small two-masted brig."

"Belay that order," yelled Neville. "'Vast running out."

Moments later the other ship's larboard quarter loomed only yards ahead. They would see her stern momentarily. The collision was going to happen. The only question was how bad it would be. He could see the lookouts above clinging hard to the masts.

"*Lady of Marion* - Connecticut," observed Catchpole. "Marion is a city there," he announced to no one. They all looked forward. Each followed the same mental exercise in sailing. They could not fall off far to larboard or the shoals would have them. Neither could *Lady of Marion*. A collision was favorable to the surf, although the surf might have them both anyway if the shoals extended very far to sea. If they hauled their wind in an attempt to miss the *Lady's* starboard, they might hit her stern even harder.

"Let all fly! Mr. Catchpole," commanded Neville, "Keep the helm up. Maybe our way will come off fast enough to lessen the damage."

Time moved very slowly as they approached the *Lady's* stern. Every man watched as sails filled sporadically on *Lady of Marion* ahead, doing what she could to escape. They might miss her starboard aft quarter, yes? No!

A day later the two ships floated quietly beside each other on the low undulating sea. With the wind now gone entirely, the ships themselves were quiet, with no rush of water along their painted hulls. Any sail still abroad hung damply in the hot sun, emitting wispy vapors that appeared anxious to join their kin in the fogbank still looming to the southeast. The two rode the low southern swell, still within earshot of the visible breakers on the beaches, but there was no quiet for the crews aboard. Sweating in the muggy air while repairing the damage of the collision, their efforts broke the silence. *Lady of Marion's* mizzen no longer tilted to starboard and her stern rail had at least some lumber tied across the hole made by *Superieure's* bowsprit. *Superieure's* bowsprit was straight again, but Chips had not given his permission yet to bend any jibs or fore-staysails.

Since American ships were neutral in the conflict between England and France and neither of these vessels posed any threat to each other save the sort of incident just behind them, an air of camaraderie seemed to have descended upon both. Catcalls across the water between the companies sparked a sort of contest to see who would be repaired first, and Midshipman Foyle had been dispatched with an invitation for the merchant's master to visit for dinner; special watches were assigned to be sure fog did not overtake them while he was away.

A short and pudgy red-faced man greeted Foyle as *Superieure's* jolly-boat arrived at *Lady's* sally-port, "Have ye been sent to apologize?" he huffed sternly down at Foyle before the jolly boat was tied alongside.

"Nossir. To invite. Permission to come aboard, Sir?"

"Aye," from another swarthy man to his right. All eyes were on them.

Stepping over the brow, Foyle reached into his jacket and retrieved Burton's letter. Handing it to the Master, he said, "I am ordered to wait for the favor of a reply, Sir."

"Wait there, then, Midshipman," said the man, and walked aft.

Two hours later, Master James Beeton of *Lady of Marion*, with his First Mate Jonas Bryars, were at dinner in the *Superieure's* gunroom. Neville's cabin could not accommodate.

"Just an accident, Commander Burton; I'd agree. Things happen at sea."

"Aye, Master Beeton. We were fortunate the fog cleared when it did, or our bones would be on the beach now."

"True enough. And the damage isn't so bad. Shall we toast your King, Commander?" Beeton's face was now pink from wine rather than red from anger.

"Where bound?" Neville asked, to which Beeton replied in a tone somewhere between guardedly and proudly, "To England, by way of Newfoundland, with a cargo of America's finest tobacco."

"We've just got you early, then, I assume. If you're to join a British convoy, then we're part of your escort. We'll do our best not to hit you again. What can you tell us of the rest of our run up to Philadelphia?"

"**M**r. Stearns, we meet again," said Neville when he found the man hanging on the larboard rail watching the shore as *Superieure* followed the *Lady of Marion* into Delaware Bay. At least seventeen ships of the convoy were directly behind, with *Bellerophon* within signal distance.

"So we do. Why do you lower yourself to speak with me today?"

"We're almost there. You'll be shot of me soon. Have we missed anything?"

"Anything we really care to discuss? I doubt it. Whence do you sail from here?"

"On to England. Don't know when yet. A week? A month? There are no hurricanes to worry about in the North Atlantic."

"You enjoy that cold, damp place, then. After I finish my business here, I'll be returning to the warmth of Jamaica."

"Not much warmer than here this time of year."

"That's not the warmth I was referring to."

"I think you overestimate the warmth of your reception, Sir."

Stearns' response was not hot and passionate. It was cold – calculating? "That's it," he snarled, turning only partly toward Neville, but his face went red and his voice colder, "You've made implications all this way north that she'll not have me. You say she is low enough to take up with a navy man – a *British* navy man, at that. You insult me, and you insult her. I insist on satisfaction for these offenses to the lady's honor, Sir." Stearns drew himself up to his full height and faced Neville. "I demand you face me in a duel."

"A duel?" Neville almost stammered. "A duel? We aren't permitted to duel. It is a comedy of the past."

"It is a custom not yet dead," said Stearns. "Cowards may not duel, either. If you were a man you would stand for your honor – if you have any."

Neville went from astounded to angry in seconds. He felt his color rise. "It cannot be aboard ship, or I would find myself in irons."

"So much the better."

"It will be ashore. If you pursue this aboard, you will find yourself in irons. It's still my ship."

"So be it. Weapons? I have a fine set of dueling pistols with me."

"You carried dueling pistols? You expect me to believe now that this wasn't contrived? You are a miscreant, Sir. Swords. I'll enjoy seeing you bleed."

"As I will you. I was actually hoping you would be old-fashioned. I am an excellent swordsman, as you will see."

"Don't count your chickens," said Neville. He walked off.

HMS *Superieure* swung at her anchor where she had been directed by the Philadelphia harbor patrol. It was four days after the challenge by Stearns. Neville had been summoned to *Bellerophon* with the rest of the navy captains and informed that they would sail in a week – excepting some unforeseen problem with the assembling of the convoy to England.

"There is time, gentlemen, to conclude this sad affair. We four will go to the beach this afternoon and take horse to some nearby copse where we will not be disturbed. Mr. Foyle here will stand by me, and, Doctor, I understand that you will second Mr. Stearns. Neither of the two of you are to join in this, so your only crime, if anything comes of it, will be simple association. Your job is simply to witness that we have concluded our disagreement to a final satisfaction.

"Doctor, I want you to know that I will hold nothing against you for this, as I assume you do not wish me particular ill, but have merely been asked by Mr. Stearns because he has few friends aboard. Frankly, it might be a stroke of luck that we will have a doctor with us. Please bring your kit.

"As to the reason for this foray ashore, we will say that our intention is to purchase certain personal supplies and to put Mr. Stearns ashore. We will put the coxswain and his men to the task of moving his dunnage to the indicated hotel while we are away. They may smell a skunk in the woodpile, but we will keep our business to ourselves, agreed?"

The other three nodded to him.

"Mr. Foyle, have the launch ready at the conclusion of dinner and Mr. Stearns' dunnage at the sally port."

Horses for hire were easily found in the city, and by three bells of the afternoon watch the four were walking their mounts south out of town. In another half hour they had found a small clearing off the lightly-traveled road to Wilmington.

"This will do," said Stearns.

"Yes, I think so," agreed Neville, "if our seconds will be good enough to clear some of this brush and move that log out of our way."

The four dismounted, tied their horses and removed their jackets.

"We will not be terribly formal, gentlemen," Doctor Trimbley announced when he and Foyle were done. "We have all read the 'twenty-six commandments of dueling' as Mr. Stearns has kindly provided from his pistol case. I proclaim this clearing to be your 'Field of Honor'. Honor will be served when the first blood is drawn, no matter how slight or serious, and the winner is the one who drew it. Are you ready, Mr. Stearns?"

"Yes," said Stearns. "I look forward to your humiliation, Commander."

"Are you ready, Commander Burton?"

"Aye."

"No words?"

"None."

"Draw your swords and begin."

The two swords slid quietly out of their leather guides.

"You jest, Commander. You cannot hope to beat me left-handed."

Neville pointed his sword at Stearns' nose. "It's the hand I was dealt, as they say. En garde!"

Stearns assumed a strange stance, with his left hand behind his back. And in the same moment took a swing at Neville's outstretched sword.

Neville moved his sword aside and let the other blade slice the air. "I hadn't assumed we were at a stage play, Sir," he said.

"Even now, you mock me," retorted Stearns, taking a slash and lunge at Neville.

Neville had never fought with swords as an art form. It had always been survival, and he assumed the same held true now. He slapped Stearns' blade aside with the flat of his and lunged forward, stabbing Stearns through the soft part of the right shoulder. Stearns yelled "aaaay!" dropped his sword, and clapped his left hand onto his injured shoulder. Red oozed between his fingers. Just that quickly it was done.

"I do not mock. I have fought hand to hand in many battles. Every time has been for my life.

"See to him, Doctor."

"Sit there on that log, Mr. Stearns," said Dr. Trimbley. "I have brought the right kit for the work at hand: bandages, needle and thread, and a bottle of Stillwater rum. Take a drink and then I'll pour some over the needle." Trimbley began his work.

"It wasn't entirely my idea, "said Stearns. "Mr. Stillwater put me up to it."

"He got you onto my ship?"

"Yes, but he didn't have to force me. I will do what I can to push you away from his daughter. And those are his pistols. I hoped you would choose them. I am a better shot than I am a swordsman."

"I would hope so."

"I've never fought a battle with a sword – only fencing. Your left hand didn't help me."

"That explains it."

"He would prefer me for his daughter, you know. He'd rather not have her 'in the navy'."

"Your business of selling rum to the enemy is less dangerous?"

Stearns looked up at him and held silent for a full minute. "It's not me. I've seen him with the Frogs often enough, though. He's in contact with all of them – knows where every ship is going and who is buying rum for whom..."

"I still don't understand why you came here; just for this?"

Again Stearns kept his tongue for a few moments, then answered, "Rum sales in Washington. This is just a bit of diversion."

"Fair enough. But I will write Marion of this. I will leave out your accusations of her father, though. He won't fire you on my account."

"He'll be all right to ride, Doctor?"

"He will."

"Thank you, doctor. Mr. Foyle, let's be off."

How much of that tripe should I believe, Neville wondered. *Are these all Stearns' own ideas or was he put up to it by Chester? I'll ask Marion to see if Chester has his dueling pistols. Is all the trafficking with the enemy - rum... and guns - all Chester? Maybe Sir William can sort it out. I'll write him, too.*

"Think of it, Mr. Foyle, you have your living space back." He spurred his horse to a trot.

12 - "The Navy List"

Do my chances with Marion sink with that anchor? Commander Burton wondered. The anchor cable attached to *Superieure's* best bower raced out the hawse at England's Downs anchorage on an unusually warm eleventh of August in the year 1804.

"What are we to do now, Commander?" asked his Second Sailing Master two days later when Neville returned from *Bellerophon.*

"I can happily report, Mr. Catchpole, that it involves no convoy. Captain Cook has informed me that he has no orders for us, and does not expect any for a month, at least, so it is my intention to petition for a minor refit and for personal leave to be off to London."

"Might we be paid off?"

"We could be…or sent straight back," said Neville, "I pray for the latter. You've been in the navy long enough to know that you never know until the anchor's up again." *Maybe Sir Mulholland could help me with that.*

Travel to London in June proved to be relatively easy. It was not a particularly wet year, but there was enough rain to keep the fields pleasantly green and the dust down. Upon his arrival he considered avoiding his mentor, Sir William Mulholland, at Whitehall. *I know he is a long-time family friend and would be disappointed, if not insulted, if I do not visit. For that reason alone I should go. He always seems to have another assignment for me, though, and his assignments are usually dangerous. But I am not required to see him and I could refuse his* *missions. Technically, he is not with the navy. So why do I keep going to see him? Do I long for the danger? Do I have some wish for death?*

He procrastinated. He went first to the Navy Office to check on the Navy List.

"Are you on there, Commander?" asked a lieutenant in the small room where the list was publicly posted. "It'll be some time before my name shows up, but I like to see if I know anyone on it."

Neville put his finger at the names on top. "Yes," he said, "it seems the war is taking its toll. That's me there. The fifth name...

"And the second one, Joseph Dagleishe, is a capital fellow. I count him a good friend, and I wish him the best of everything." He ran his finger on down the list, passing several he knew, until he reached one at the bottom. "And here's yet another that is far overdue," he said; "my childhood friend Daniel Watson, just recently added."

The lieutenant peered over his shoulder. "Commander Burton, is it? May I shake the hand of an officer so properly employed?"

"I appreciate your sentiment, and I don't count myself as particularly sentimental, but I shan't shake on that until the day comes."

Neville left Whitehall and took a hack to the offices of the Chancellor of the Cheque.

"Burton, you say?" asked the clerk at the counter within.

"Aye, Neville. Lieutenant."

"Ah, here 'tis. For the ketch *Le Serpent?*"

"Well, yes, but is there nothing of the frigate *Duquesne?*"

The clerk left the counter and spent another few minutes looking in another book at a desk in the rear of the room. When he returned to the counter, he said, "The *Duquesne* is not concluded. Are you interested in *Le Serpent* or no?"

"Yes of course."

The clerk's index finger ran across the line to the right side of the page. His eyebrows raised. He looked back at Neville and said, "Four thousand, two hundred fifty-one pounds, twelve shillings and threppence."

"I am pleasantly surprised at that, I must say." *My Lord! This large amount must be due to my position as captain and having no other ships involved. It's more than three times what I expect from the Duquesne!* "And another one, my good man, the schooner *Unique*."

"You have been busy, haven't you Lieutenant?" mumbled the clerk.

"Aye. That's my job, isn't it," Neville queried, "And it's Commander."

"*Unique*, yes. She's here. One thousand, eight hundred sixty-eight pounds, one shilling and six."

Neville departed a happier and richer man. He did not carry cash but rather a paper that would allow the money to be transferred from the Chancellor of the Cheque to Hoare's bank. Hoare's Bank, at the sign of the Golden Bottle on Fleet Street, was his next stop. There he passed in his paper and asked for an accounting of his balance on deposit.

"Two hundred ten thousand pounds and change, Sir," said the clerk. "Here's the record." He passed Neville the ledger.

"I hadn't noticed this deposit before. Would you have any information on a deposit made in 1715 of eighteen thousand pounds?"

"Only what's there, Sir. There may be some notes in the back, or maybe you could find the family Bible is all I can suggest."

Neville turned to the back of the very old book. There was only a single note. It was in his own hand. 'Dad promises to write Mum'. *I remember that, but she has never said anything. I wonder if he did and it was lost, or if mother just doesn't dare say anything.*

He took a third day just to stroll about town, but finally he decided that he could no longer delay his visit to Whitehall.

He could see no significant change in the lobby of the yellow building beside the Admiralty. The building was quiet compared to the usual stream of officers coming and going through the central portico of the other. He was accosted, as on every occasion before, by a marine sergeant asking his business. This time he had no letter of introduction, but he had knowledge of the place, and he knew where he was going.

"I wish to speak to the secretary to Room Four, if you please."

"I cannot allow you to pass, Sir, I am sorry."

"Send your man, please, with my name. I'll wait."

The sergeant beckoned a sentry, who had been watching from the far corner of the lobby. When the messenger arrived in front of his sergeant, Neville said "Please pass word that Commander Neville Burton requests an audience at his Lordship's convenience. I shall wait on a reply."

The private walked away purposefully, and the sergeant waved his arm at a set of four chairs near the sentry's post. *It's a good job I've had breakfast*, Neville thought. He took a seat, prepared for a long wait.

The response was quick, however, and not altogether unpleasant.

"He's gone home on summer holiday, Sir. Not back for another three weeks, at least."

"Oh, brilliant. I'll see him there, then," said Neville.

"You won't be allowed to see him there, I'm sure, Sir," said the marine, "and I don't know where that is, anyway."

"I do, and my mother thinks I can," said Neville with a crooked grin. He left the bewildered marine and walked outside to find that a short summer shower had passed. Thousands of tiny puddles between the street cobbles twinkled in the afternoon sun that was beginning to peek out between gray clouds. *It's my lucky week, I see. A lovely English summer, prize money and another reason to go home.*

Neville sat in a well-stuffed wingback chair in the back garden of *Stonelake*, his mother's residence since she was married to Mr. Andrew Blake a few years before. His mother, as pretty a lady as any in Bury, looked older than when he had seen her last; but her spirits were good.

"This is a nice house, Mum. I've only stepped inside a couple times to visit. I must admit that even with you living here the place feels more like a stranger's house than my family's. We had less when I was little, although it meant nothing to me then. This is a city gent's house for sure. The country was more fun for us as children, I think."

He had found it easily enough, after the Royal Mail coach from London had clattered to a halt in front of the Angel Hotel in Bury St. Edmunds, Suffolk, four days after his visit to Whitehall. He still remembered the smell of raspberries in the brambles around the Roman ruins across the way that had greeted his nostrils when he stepped down. He had decided that he would see family before Sir William Mulholland, but he sent a boy with a note round to Mulholland's to be sure the man didn't return to London before they had a chance to visit.

"It's a right proper place, yes. Andrew provides well," she said

"And don't you ever forget, Mum, that if you need anything, you can have it off me. I have money in the bank, you know."

"I'm sure you do. But you'll need it yourself one day. Some day when..."

"What is it, Mum?" he asked. Her eyes had teared up.

"I forgot. I've been so happy to see you. Mary's husband, Lieutenant John Towers, was killed eight months ago at the Battle of Assaye in India; and she with the little one. At least they think he's dead. They never found the body. I'm sure I wrote you. With him and Gage gone all the time, Mary has been like another daughter to me. Her mother's not doing so well."

"I don't think I read it. He was with Gage's unit, yes? And how old is the child"

"Did you meet John – or little Martin?"

"Neither, no."

"Martin is three; a little older than you when Dad went missing."

"I'm sorry to hear it. How about Daniel's family – Angelica and Alice. The girl is what – also three?"

"Three, yes. A little older than Martin." She sniffled. "They're both fine, and wonderful little friends. You really must go round and see them all. Maybe Angelica or Elizabeth would go to Mary's with you." She knew Mary and her son had been young sweethearts, and that Mary had waited for him until he went missing for three years. *Was she contriving something? Mothers do that.* She knew something had happened in those three years, but she knew nothing of Maria and he had so far left Marion out of his letters.

"Daniel and his father both are at sea now, Neville. It's a shame you missed Daniel. He was here just a month ago. He stopped round and inquired of you. I read to him some from your letters," said his mother. "Thank you for that, too. You're much better at writing than you used to be."

"I've had a little more time, I suppose. Do I understand that Daniel's got into a new ship?"

"Yes, he's just gone to *Thunderer*. He thought he'd be second, though I don't really understand what that means."

"Still with the big ships, is he? I don't envy him. How about his dad?"

"Edward is first in the frigate *Dryad*. Daniel says he complains that he has seen little action and has therefore moved slowly toward captain. But it seems to me he can't be all that far off."

"He should see action in a frigate. Time will tell. That's where I'd like to be."

"I must say, Neville, you military men may like your action, but I am glad I found Mr. Blake. I feel sorry for Mrs. Watson with rarely a man about the place. My corn merchant's life may be dull, but I see him every day. It's a very good thing your sister has Gage's parents – and me, of course. Well we have your whole visit to catch up. We'll start with Elizabeth tomorrow…"

"You are in hot water, Sir," said Neville when he shook hands with Sir William two days later at the Farmer's Club. They had agreed to meet for lunch by messenger-boy. Neville suspected it would not be a short meeting.

"I think the queen knows little of my activities," he joked.

"The queen of England, maybe, but my mother said, and I quote her now: 'The sneaky old rascal. He comes in town and I don't get so much as how d'ye do?'"

"Oh, I have missed a step, haven't I? Capital to see you, though. I thought you were still in Jamaica. I just received your letter mentioning Mr. Stillwater… A brandy to start? Here's the waiter."

They ate their lunch while catching up on the local gossip, but Mulholland insisted on moving their get-together to his house before they spoke of navy matters. "There seem to be ears everywhere these days, Neville – even here in Bury."

Mulholland rapped on the locked door of his own home. They heard the lock rattle and then Spencer, his butler, opened it for them.

"Come in, Neville. Come in."

"I dropped by to see you at Whitehall, Sir, but they told me you'd gone home."

"How do you come to be here?"

"In *Superieure*, my little schooner. I came in with *Bellerophon's* convoy."

"Ah, that's it, then. We don't so much watch the unrated ships... no offence."

"None taken. But there's a story in that, as well. We were all provisioned and ready to sail when Mr. Stearns came aboard..."

"Stearns? I don't think I know the name."

"Chester's right-hand man..."

"Chester?"

"Yes, Mr. Stillwater. I've made progress."

"So it seems. Go ahead."

"Chester has enough pull there in Kingston to have Captain Cook put a civilian aboard my ship to be delivered to Philadelphia..." Neville continued his account of what small talk there was on board ship from Jamaica to Philadelphia, the provocation of a duel, and Stearns' admissions afterwards. He added his discovery of an unknown connection to the Harper's Ferry Armory and his conversation with Stearns about meeting Georges Cadoudal in France some years before.

Sir William listened carefully. At the conclusion he commented, "I admit that I didn't know you were coming, and it has been some time since I spent much time thinking about this issue, so forgive me if I take a moment. I don't have my notes with me."

"May I refresh?" Neville asked, holding up his glass.

"Yes, yes. Over there. If you get it yourself you'll have it before Spencer would even get here."

He will assign me some mission — or he will try to — unless I say no, thought Neville while crossing to the sideboard holding the brandy bottle. *But it will be something to do other than sit with all the other officers waiting for a ship. I might get back to Jamaica sooner if I argue my case to continue the investigation of Chester.*

He carried their two glasses — now filled — back to Sir William. "Is it possible I could stay with *Superieure* if she will be sent back to Jamaica?" he asked.

"What?... No, no, Neville. You are well up on the Navy List now. You've looked, yes? It will not be long 'till you're made post, and a posted captain needs a post ship; he would rarely be seen commanding an unrated ship the size of *Superieure* Your career requires that you wait for a proper posting," said Mulholland. "Maybe after you are made post we can find something..."

So I would expect...

"I really will have to think about this. Stop by Whitehall on your way... Where is your ship now?"

"At the Downs, but she may go in for a small refit."

"All right, then. Stop by Whitehall on your way there. This Stillwater thing seems increasingly complicated. I'll take another look at that dossier, and we'll see if I have worked something out."

"There you are! Look at you; no worse than last I saw you. No more scars, and you have all your hands and feet," jabbered his sister Elizabeth when she appeared early at *Stonelake* early the next morning. "Hold the door there, please, Gage. See to your manners."

"My Lord!" exclaimed Neville. "Look at you, Gage. You're almost as tall as your mother. I expected to see a small boy. I have forgotten your age, for sure."

"I'm nine now, Sir," said Gage.

"Mum said we should come by for breakfast," Elizabeth continued, "so here we are, and we'll go straight off afterwards to see Angelica and Alice – and maybe Mary," she added, looking into Neville's eyes. She had noticed the pain in them three years ago when he had come home and had suspected then that he had lost someone. But they hadn't spoken of it.

"Why's your epaulette on a different shoulder than Lieutenant Watson's? Does that mean something?" asked Gage.

"My epaulette is on the other side because I am the commander – the captain – of a small ship," Neville finally answered.

"You've made captain?" Elizabeth exclaimed. His mother turned round to look as well, and Gage yelled, "Hooray!"

"Yes. No, not captain the rank. I'm still a lieutenant like Daniel, but I am captain of an unrated ship."

They both stared at him. "You shouldn't joke like that, Neville," said Elizabeth. "It's wicked."

"It's not a joke…"

"The new vicar has come, Mum," said Elizabeth, intentionally cutting Neville off. "He seems nice enough."

"I'll see him later today, dear. Here are your sausages. The toast is there in the rack by the cupboard, Neville, if you would get it, please."

"Where's Mr. Blake, then, Mum? I thought he would join us."

"Gone this week to Ipswich. I thought you knew."

"Forgot, I suppose," Elizabeth answered. "Isn't the weather wonderful today? There's not a cloud."

"I understand, Sir," Gage said to Neville. "The ranks are different in the Army, but I've studied the navy, too, because of you and the Watsons."

"Don't get the idea I'll let you join the navy, either," admonished Elizabeth. "I prefer my men living. Look what's happened to Martin's dad."

"That was brilliant, Mum. I don't often get such a breakfast," Neville said to change the subject again. He had nothing left but his cup of coffee.

"Thank you for the compliment, but it was not special enough for my… captain," she said. "You three go off now. I'll take care of this little mess."

"Thank you, Mum," said Elizabeth, and leaned across to give her a goodbye kiss. Gage dutifully reported to his grandmother for the same. Elizabeth turned to Neville. "Come on – captain.

"You may go off with your friends now, Gage," she said.

The door to Angelica's flat on Hatter Street opened after Elizabeth's knock to reveal his childhood friend Angelica. The sight almost took Neville's breath away. After one child and ten or eleven years, the pretty girl he remembered from his sister's wedding was now a stunning full-figured woman in her prime.

"She knew you were coming, Neville," said Elizabeth, noticing his reaction.

"I did dress, yes," said Angelica. "I expected to go out, and I certainly wanted to look my best if I will accompany a navy officer. You look as dashing as Daniel. He was just home, you know?"

"There is no question why he married you," was the only response that came to Neville's mind.

"Manners, you two," said Elizabeth. "May we come in?"

"Oh, yes, Yes. Sorry," said Angelica. "Mind the dolls and the little pram. It was tidy this morning, but Alice has just been horrid. She's earned herself an extra morning nap, she has. Let's have a tea, and then I'll get her up. She'll be better with Martin around."

"We are going to Mary's, yes?" She asked, looking first at Elizabeth and then at Neville.

Elizabeth took charge. "Yes, I think so.

"You need to do the right thing someday, my brave navy officer brother, so it might as well be today. You are expected."

Neville put on his sociable smile. "It certainly should. Is there a biscuit for the tea? I would love something other than hard ship's biscuit."

"I tell you what," said Elizabeth, "I'll go fetch them. She lives just around the corner on Churchgate. You have your tea and catch up whilst Alice finishes her nap. I've had enough tea for the morning." She backed out the door and left.

Neville and Angelica spent an enjoyable half hour walking memory lane. Elizabeth's rap at the door woke Alice, so Angelica sent Neville to the door and ran for the nursery.

Outside, Elizabeth had taken little Martin's hand and pushed Mary to the door in front of her. When the door opened, Mary and Neville stood face to face. Neither spoke for a moment.

Mary coolly broke the ice, "Good morning, Neville. You look well." She was prettier than Angelica, if that was possible.

"Awiss?" asked Martin.

"All right, you two." A horse and buggy rattled past behind her. "In you go," commanded Elizabeth.

Neville stepped aside, and the three trooped in. Neville still had not figured out how to greet Mary, so he knelt by Martin and put out his hand for the little boy to shake. Martin stepped behind his mother's skirts, so Neville stood again.

"That's what he looked like, my John. Just like Martin." Her chin quivered.

"Mary, I'm so sorry," Neville finally said.

"Not all that sorry!" she exclaimed at him. "Where did you go?" She demanded. She slapped his face. "Why didn't you write?"

"Mary!" cried Angelica.

Alice screamed and both children began to cry.

"It's all right, ladies, I understand. I truly do," said Neville. "May we have a few minutes alone?"

"In the garden then," said Elizabeth, "We'll have the children calm down and play in here."

Mary and Neville stepped outside. It was indeed a beautiful English summer day. A few puffy clouds roamed the blue dome above them. Angelica's garden was well tended, with a small box of sand for Alice to play in on one side and a small patio with a wooden table to the other. The table had a bench on each side and a sand pail in the center. They sat facing.

"You can't possibly understand," Mary spat at him. "First I lost you. No letters. Nothing. We thought you dead. Three years, Neville. Three years! I got past that and found John. He's... was... a wonderful man. We had beautiful little Martin, and now I've lost John. You can't possibly know unless it's happened to you." She was crying now.

Neville reached for her hand. She pulled it back.

"I know how you feel because I also lost someone. It still hurts when I think of her... right here," he said, tapping the center of his chest with his knuckles.

"Yes," she said, "right there. And I'm angry. I'm always angry. Angry at nothing. Angry at everything. I have to be very careful with Martin."

"That's good," said Neville. "After a time I was angry, too, but I had a release. We came into a battle and I'm afraid I was inhuman. It passes with time."

"Time," she said. "Where were you for three years? And whom did you lose? How could you be gone three years and have an entire love affair directly after leaving me?"

"The Caribbean – Jamaica. I was injured early on. If you watch closely you will see a slight limp. My leg was broken badly when a cannon exploded nearby, and they despaired of me losing it for a time. And my memory was gone… had no idea where I came from. My nurse was a beautiful girl. She reminded me so much of you, I think, but I couldn't place you then. You would have loved her, too."

"What happened to this girl, then?"

"Killed – in an earthquake, with me watching. Sucked into the very earth, she was." His tears began to flow. "I almost died myself. They found me on the beach," he said, "with everything gone. Everything. The city had a ship in the middle of it. We were to be wed in another few months."

He pulled himself together. "By then most of my memory had come back…"

"Why didn't you write, then. Surely they have quill and ink in Jamaica." She was angry again.

"They do, but I couldn't. I'm sorry."

"Why not?"

"Navy business. By then I found myself in a situation that required secrecy. I was forbidden to speak of it – still am." He lied, but it was either that or have her think him mad – or completely callous. "And then the earthquake, and they ordered me home."

"Navy business? Did Sir Mulholland know of it then? He said he knew nothing. We all inquired of him. Did he lie to us?" Her complexion had passed a simple pink and was approaching blotchy red.

"They thought me dead, and that was that. He knew nothing then – could find no trace of me. He does now. He couldn't have helped."

"Neville, I can't imagine what you got yourself into, but this had better not be a lie."

"They ordered me to sail a ship home. Aboard as captain I stayed to myself. I skulked around and ignored my command. It's a wonder I'm still an officer. Then I became angry – like you are now; as you say, at nothing and at everything. That will pass for you at some time, whether quickly or slowly. The battle smashed mine, as I said. After that you may tell yourself that John's death was your fault. It wasn't, Mary." He reached out with both his hands, and this time she took them. He looked in her eyes and said, "It wasn't, Mary. None of it is your fault. I beseech you – every time you look at Martin, remind yourself that it was not. He is your reminder that it was not."

A quiet moan began from her lips, and she began to cry again. Neville moved to her side of the table, sat beside her and put his arms around her. She grabbed him and held on fiercely for several minutes until her fit of sobbing passed. Neville's jacket shoulder was soaking wet by the time she looked up into his face.

Neville fished a handkerchief from his jacket and handed it to her.

"I'm so glad you came," she said, while dabbing her eyes. "I thought nobody would ever understand. I've had no one to talk to. Elizabeth and Angelica are friends anybody should be envious of, but they don't understand. Even the vicar doesn't understand, though he pretends better than most."

"Have you spoken with our mother? Elizabeth's and mine. She lost my dad, remember. It has been a long time, and she is a very strong woman, but she would do anything to help you, I'm sure. She told me you were like another daughter to her."

"I hadn't thought of that. She said that?"

"She did. And we could write each other again?"

"I should love it, of all things. There are no more letters from John," she concluded with a quivering chin. "Thank you. You lift my heart, without question."

"Let's tell your friends that you feel a bit better now, and maybe we can have our lunch out here."

"Absolutely not, Sir. We are dressed to go out," she declared.

Upon his return to *Stonelake* after luncheon, he found his mother had gone out. He fumbled about her writing desk for a few minutes looking for a quill and paper. When he had found the necessary implements he took some time to write Marion:

Bury St. Edmunds   *2 Sep., 1804*
Suffolk, England

Dear Marion,

My visit home has been an emotional one. Though not much has changed, the people have grown older. I had not realized how truly long I have been away. Mother and sister are well... &c.. &c...

I wrote you of my duel with Mr. Stearns. He apparently made an assumption that a navy man could not defend himself. I am sure your father will be unhappy with me over that – for wounding his best man, but it was a reasonable outcome from my perspective. Nobody is dead. I assume he could still do his work in Washington, which is where he said he was going.

By this letter it is my intention to ask you if you might wait for me – to implore you not to involve yourself with another until we can at least meet for a proper discussion of our mutual intentions. I know it is muche to ask of one with whom I have no binding arrangement and from whom I expect to be apart for some time.

I shall advise you the moment I know anything of my future.

Your devoted admirer,   Neville

Despite - or possibly because of - Mary he stopped short of professing his love for Marion. What should he think of his situation? Yesterday he could think of no one but Marion, and today he was confused between the two. *Without Marion about, depression creeps quickly back into my soul.*

By the end of September Neville was in London. Before checking in with the Admiralty he stopped in to see Sir William. His mentor was too busy to receive him for two days, during which time Neville began his search for a flat that he could lease for an extended time.

On the third day Mulholland's clerk ushered him in to Room Four.

"A busy week, Sir?" asked Neville. "Oh, yes. Old Boney is giving us a fit with his approaches to Spain. Did your visit home conclude well?"

"Yes. I had not realized how long I'd been away. I saw Mary Mitchell."

"Aah, yes. That is a terrible shame. Will she be all right?"

"I'm sure she will. I recommended she spend some time talking with mother about her situation. I couldn't imagine anyone better. And I offered financial assistance if she needs it."

"That's right. You have a few guineas at the bank, don't you?

"Yes. Have you had time to think about what you might ask me to do?"

"Yes, but I think we should not do anything extreme at the moment. You are waiting for your captaincy. You have a ship that should be out of ordinary in a week or two. I have looked again at the Stillwater file and, while it is not a high priority for the war right now, we should probably not drop it while we are 'in the hunt', as it were. All I have done, then, is pass a suggestion that you might be left in the *Superieure*, as least for another few months, and the Admiralty might have their way with you. Sound good?"

Neville breathed a quiet sign of relief. It seemed a good compromise. "Yes. Thank you, Sir. May I ask yet another favor? This one is pretty passive."

"Passive?"

"Yes. It can probably be handled by your butler, Mr. Spencer. May I use your address to communicate with Miss Stillwater in Jamaica?"

Unexpectedly, Sir William thought for a moment before answering. Neville had not expected any hesitation at all.

Neville added, "I haven't mentioned her to mother or Elizabeth."

"What's to mention?" asked Mulholland warily.

"Nothing I want mother or sister to even suspect. They are very close with Mary, and…"

"And…?"

"And we may be… involved."

"Who is 'we'?" the perceptive man asked, "You and Mary or Marion?"

"Yes, Sir, that's it exactly. I am presently confounded."

Mulholland thought for yet another minute, but then said, "Yes. You have good taste, I'll give you that."

"You've met Miss Stillwater, then?" Neville asked.

"Oh, no. No," Mulholland answered quickly. "But I know Mary. If you have nothing more, though, I must go."

"Nothing. I'm looking for a flat here in town. I'll give you that address when I have it."

"Cheers, then, Neville."

They shook hands and Neville left. *Very strange. Out of character for him. I'd swear he was flustered.*

"**D**o you have any idea why we're sailing for the Med, Commander?"

"Of course, Mr. Foyle. But I was not at liberty to say before we left port. We have a packet aboard for Admiral Nelson at Toulon, and before you ask – No, I don't know what's in it.

"When do we expect to round Ushant, Mr. Catchpole?"

"Another three days if this wind holds, Sir."

The three turned their backs momentarily to shield against a cold spray from a crossing wave. "There must have been quite a blow over towards the Irish Sea a few days ago to cause a northwest swell this large," said Foyle.

"Aye," said Framingham," just then arriving at the helm. "We can thank the Good Lord we didn't have it last month when we sailed with *Dryad* to take Admiral Lord Gardner to the Irish station."

"Amen to that," said Neville. He shivered slightly. He hadn't fully acclimated to the northern climes. None of them had. It had been less than four full months since they left Jamaica. "We must also pray that the swell is less after Ushant. The Bay of Biscay can be bad enough in December without that."

"She seems to sail well after the refit, doesn't she, Mr. Catchpole?" queried Framingham.

"Aye. I think they've raked the mainmast back a few degrees. You notice the boom is lower here aft. You tall fellows had better learn to duck when we come about, I think."

"It's worth it for a little more speed," said Neville, "The Frogs out of Brest up ahead – or his Spanish lackeys out of Coruna or Cadiz - would love to catch a packet for Nelson, wouldn't they? You all know where it is in my cabin, yes?" He looked round to see them all nod. "If we strike, it goes over the side, even if I'm dead. It has its lead weights in it."

"Aye, Sir," said Framingham. Neville saw him shudder. The cold or the cold thoughts? Probably both.

"That's quite the system they have us in back at Spithead, isn't it?" asked Foyle of no one in particular. "They say they can send a telegraph message from the Admiralty to Spithead there in three minutes. And how many of us advice-boats do you suppose were there?"

"I counted twelve that I was sure of," said Framingham. "Another four came and went while we swung at anchor, and there must be three times that many out somewhere. Think of it. We'll be gone a month at least; probably longer, just to go and come 'ome."

"Thank you, gentlemen. That reminds me of two letters I received that I haven't even taken the time to open; we received such urgent orders to leave – tide or no. And will you send Mr. Johnson down. I meant to ask him if we left anyone behind."

"We did, Sir. Three or four."

"Who?"

"Mr. Pulker, Caulker's Mate, for one. Dunno who else. Mr. Johnson will have it."

Independence Hall   *4th November, 1804*
Kingston, Jamaica

My Dear Neville,

I have much news for you. First, I received yours of 2nd and 8th September and certainly give you my permission to address me warmly, as I will you.

I am sorry to include news of Mr. Stearns in my letters to you, but in this case it affects me directly. He returned here a month ago due to illness related to the wound you inflicted on him. It is not mortal – he should recover fully in another month or so. I am glad to have received your letter advising me that he was the instigator, because he implies otherwise. I don't approve of dueling, but I thank you for defending my freedom from him. Father is angry, as you suspected, but with Mr. Stearns defeated he will not pressure me further.

But here it is: Mr. Stearns is ill and the business must go on. So I will go to Washington for sales work within the week. It has been a great rush to prepare! I will have arrived there by the time you read this, as I am sure it will go on the same ship from here to Washington.

I have been before, remember, and I will have Ellen with me. I suspect she would be a more fearsome defender than Mr. Stearns, so don't worry.

Thank you for providing the proper Admiralty address for forwarding letters. You mustn't write me here while I'm gone. For a month or two you can post your letters to me at the Capital City Rooming House on Pennsylvania Avenue. I will leave them a forwarding address when I go. It is a very comfortable place located between the new Navy Yard and the new Capital Building. It will be quite exciting during the winter season, I should think. I wish you could be with me . I will remember our meetings at New Year's.

Affectionately,   *Marion S.*

Neville knew he would worry. He had never been to Washington, but his expectation was that the Navy Yard, even if it was new, must still be in the city's waterfront district; probably a dangerous place for two extremely attractive women. Now he wondered whether injuring Stearns was a triumph. The end result was to place Marion in danger. Even if not in danger, she was back amongst a pack of the strongest rivals for her hand that he would ever have.

The second letter was from Mary:

> *Churchgate Street*   *12th November, 1804*
> *Bury-St. Edmunds, Suffolk*
>
> *My Dear Neville,*
>
> *I apologize for having delayed my writing. It has been difficult to address a letter to you rather than to John, but I have forced myself now.*
>
> *I truly thank you for your compassion on your visit. Your suggestion to discuss my feeling with your mother was tremendous as well. She is the most marvelous person, and said that she was only waiting for me to ask – didn't want to intrude. My heart must be fifty stone lighter.*
>
> *I swear that before your visit Martin was the only reason to drag myself from the bed, but now I am out and about some.*
>
> *I pray this letter finds you well,*
>
> *Affectionately,*   *Mary Towers*

That's right, Neville thought, *It's 'Towers' now, isn't it?*

"As such voyages go, we shouldn't complain, should we, Mr. Johnson?"

"No, Sir, I wouldn't. An ordeal of forty days and forty nights, if you please: it should be tenth February by tomorrow when we're in to Spithead. The wind was mostly fair, we had no serious winter storms, even in the Bay of Biscay. There was your typical foul current at the gut of Gibraltar, a few days' delay by Nelson while he wrote his replies, only a single side errand to Corsica, and one chase."

"That about sums it up, I'll agree," said Neville. "And that chase was the only worrisome thing."

"Aye. When that Corvette came out of Brest I thought he'd have us. I still wonder how he got by the blockade."

"I do as well, Mr. Johnson, but he did it. What I can't figure is where he went that second night. Would he not assume we were heading for Gibraltar? Why would he suddenly turn off? Did he think we were getting clever and did the same, so that by morning we would be his sitting duck?"

"We'll never know. He could have had urgent orders for Cadiz and used the night to breach our blockade there as well. He must be good at it."

"Right. Well, there's the south end of the Isle of Wight, unless I forget the coastline entirely. Send my complements to Mr. Catchpole and ask him if he would step up here and help me decide if we should try to go in yet today or whether we must stand off for the night."

"Aye, Sir."

"I am as anxious to drop our anchor as the next man, Mr. Catchpole," said Neville when he arrived, "but given the late moon, the tidal currents, traffic, wind and shoals, I am afraid we should stand off until morning. What say you?"

"I agree, Commander. We should stand off," was Catchpole's final comment.

Neville had letters he had written to his family and to Marion that he was anxious to post, and he expected a few from them. He had sent one from Toulon on a ship bound directly for the

Americas, but any letter home he had decided to carry himself – as well as a sack of letters and packets from the fleet.

There was the question of orders to Jamaica, as well, but even that was secondary to the Navy List. He should be well up by now, if not made post already.

Neville ordered the launch over the side as soon as the anchor splashed. Since they had been stationed at Spithead as an advice boat, he was required to remain aboard for any abrupt orders to depart with a packet. An advice boat might leave a man or two behind who were in on various duties, but it couldn't sail without the captain.

"Straight back, now, Mr. Framingham. Drop our bags off and bring the same from shore."

He wasn't back for three hours.

"Here he comes now, Commander Burton," said Foyle. "There, see?"

"I don't. Your young eyes are better than mine."

"Just left of that semaphore tower there," Foyle said, pointing to a scrap of white beneath a similarly colored building nestled in the green countryside, "Launch has her sail up."

It thumped alongside in another twenty minutes, and Framingham heaved a post-sack up the side.

"Why so long, Mr. Framingham?"

"They couldn't find our sack, Sir. When they found it they said they hadn't expected us for another fortnight. Sorry."

"Well how did they expect to add any... never mind. Come on up. Send that down to my cabin."

Neville went below to open it and to sort official mail from letters. He looked at the official mail for anything that looked like sailing orders. There was one. He put that aside and then sorted through the mail for any personal letters. There were several.

"Hajee, call for Mr. Johnson to come get the ship's post, if you please."

Mr. Johnson appeared a few minutes later. "Will we be in long, Commander?" he asked as he was picking up the post-sack.

"You can wait, if you'd like the answer to that. I think this one here might be sailing orders."

Neville broke the green wax seal with a knife and took an envelope out of the canvas enclosure.

"It is indeed from the Admiralty, Mr. Johnson. One moment." He broke the red wax seal on the enclosed envelope and retracted the orders.

"It says," said Neville, scanning the words, "that we are – oohoo! Sorry, Mr. Johnson. It says we are off advice-boat duty. We..." he read further, "...we have two weeks to complete for – oh, Lord!... convoy duty, taking... oh, not so bad, then... only a single ship to Jamaica. To Jamaica, Mr. Johnson! Back to someplace warm. You're not excited, I see."

"Not entirely, Sir. Some of the men will be very disappointed, and some even angry. Here they've at least a chance to see home. But that's just my opinion Sir. They're all navy men, Sir; they'll go where you lead them."

"Thank you for that, Mr. Johnson. But it does mean we have some time. Take Cookie and go into town. Fetch back enough good fresh stuff for a salmagundi for supper, if you would, please."

At the thought of fresh food, even though supplies of any such thing might be slim in February, Johnson's eyes brightened and he hurried off with the post.

His next attention, even before that of the letters from Marion, went to another admiralty packet. Why or how he had chosen the first as the ship's orders and why he suspected this to be personal business he was not sure, but the first had indeed been the ship's orders. He opened it.

The letter inside was the culmination of years of day-dreaming.

The Seal of the Admiralty

Sir,

By the hand of Admiral John Jervis, First Lord of the Admiralty, and my Lords Commissioners of the Admiralty, Having been Pleased to Sign a Commission promoting you from the rank of Master and Commander to the rank of Post-Captain in His Majesty's Navy;

I have been given their Lordships command to acquaint you therewith.

I am, Sir,
Your very humble servant,

Tho⁵ Langston,
Secretary to the Admiralty

Attachment

The second page:

*The Seal of the
Admiralty*

***The Honorable
First Lord of the Admiralty,
John Jervis, First Earl of St. Vincent***

Seventh January, 1805

Commander Neville Burton,

*By virtue of the Power and Authority given the Lords of the
Admiralty by His Majesty, We do hereby order you to join with
the company of His Majesty's Frigate La Désirée, now lying
Jamaica Station, and go aboard her before she sails from thence
on or about May of this year and to execute what orders are given
you from your Admiral or any other of your superior officers.
Hereof none of you shall fail as you may answer to your country
at your peril.*

....signatures &c....

HMS *La Désirée... Could she be the same frigate that chased us out of Hispaniola last year?* he wondered. *She was fast.*

He'd read the orders for *Superieure* to depart in two weeks. There was much to do, but his men had been informed and they knew their roles. There was no need for him to jump up and run about at this very minute; he would look to his other letters.

The letter from Sir William Mulholland, written the second of January, congratulated him on his being made post and sought to advise him that he should soon receive orders to sail to Jamaica. *Wonderful sentiment, indeed, and proof that he was somehow involved, but old news now. I must thank him for it.*

The five letters from his mother, sister, and Mary were, as always, a great comfort to receive. The content was almost entirely the news of Bury St. Edmunds, but two of them contained a page each from the letters of his brother-in-law, Major John Gage Hall, who was still in India, and his friend, Lieutenant Daniel Watson, now of *HMS Thunderer.*

I must admit that I am not so interested in the affairs of the army, but I must send some comment of consolation to Elizabeth- But look at this from Daniel:

"...We [HMS Thunderer] will be sailing to Plymouth for a refit soon. Rumor has it that we shall be paid off. I am afraid that makes my immediate future quite uncertain. I might be held for the recommission following a few months or I might be assigned to another ship. The best news is that whichever happens, my dear Angelica, I shall be home again soon to spend some time with you and Martin. I look forward..."

Daniel should be almost home now. I've missed him again!

Another thought occurred to him. *I must write Joseph Dagleishe with my most sincere congratulations. His name was above mine on the*

Navy List, so he must be made post. Where would they have sent him, I wonder?

Then there were the six letters from Marion. He removed them from their envelopes, arranged them by date, and began to read. He was extremely pleased to know that she thought of him often. The letters were weekly:

She wrote the eighth of November as her ship stood from Jamaica.

She wrote on the fifteenth, twenty-second, and thirtieth of November with news of the passage, the weather, and the other passengers.

She wrote on the twelfth of December to advise him that she had arrived safely in Washington to find his letter from Toulon waiting for her; for which she was 'extremely comforted'.

Enough of all this. I must get up and be active. After I set everyone to their duties for completing stores, I shall have just enough time to go into London. I can make arrangements to have the furniture I ordered delivered to my flat, arrange for payments of the rents, and drop by Sir William's to thank him personally. Then it will be off to Jamaica and Marion – and my first proper command of a frigate!

13 - "Acceptance"

"This passage has gone well, Comman... Captain, has it not?" queried Midshipman Foyle a few days before *Superieure* expected to begin seeing the low islands of the Bahamas. "I'm sorry. I suppose I'm just not used to it even yet. "Your epaulette looks better on the right shoulder."

"Thank you for that, and I agree that the voyage has gone well. It is now almost three weeks since the first of March when we weighed anchor in Spithead. I think the more northerly route of crossing served us well; I should thank Mr. Catchpole for his suggestion. We are lucky, too, that *Blessing* sails well."

"On the subject of promotions, Mr. Foyle, have you thought about sitting for lieutenant?"

"I certainly have, but I don't have the time in yet, even with a year of false muster. I must wait yet another one. I am working with Mr. Framingham, though. His experience is great, and I think he may be planning on sitting again himself, after all this time."

"He would be excellent for you to study with, no doubt of it. He might sit, you say?"

"Aye. Serving on a small ship changes everything, he says. You see the ways of the captain first hand. He says that would never happen on a rated ship."

"He is correct in that. I am pleased to learn he wishes to advance. There's nothing worse than a sour old midshipman."

"Sail, Ho!" the lookout cried from the fore.

"Where away, Mr. Mulgrove?" Foyle yelled back.

"Starboard quarter. One sail."

"Keep an eye, Mr. Mulgrove."

The quartermaster of the watch rang eight bells. "Pipe the hands to supper, Mr. Johnson," yelled Neville forward.

"Pass word of the sail to each watch, Mr. Foyle. There is little likelihood it can catch us in a single night, but everyone should be reminded it's there – if it follows. After supper we'll have gun drill, just to be sure we're ready for her. Beat to quarters after second grog and run out both sides. Put a watch on it."

"Aye, Sir."

"Mr. Johnson," He had walked aft after piping dinner. "Take the names of any who can't stand at gun drill. We'll see if any are saving rations."

"Aye, Sir."

Neville and his officers were feeling prickly on the following morning. It was not the weather, which remained fine, with a fair fresh breeze and a patchy sky. The air temperature was rising as they sailed south as well. There should have been feelings of increasing comfort.

"The islands are up ahead. We'll see them soon," said Mr. Catchpole when the sun had scarcely purpled the eastern sky. "Maybe today."

"Get a man up, Mr. Foyle," said Neville. He was feeling the tension like the others. "Be sure to have him look aft for a sail and forward for land. Have him take a long glass today."

The ship began to wake up. Eight bells of the Morning Watch sounded. Neville could hear Mr. Johnson and his mates rousing the men below. They straggled up and soon the sound of holystones began. There was still scarcely enough light for the lookout to see anything more than two cables away, but that would change quickly.

Neville decided to climb up and take a look himself. A little exercise before breakfast is always a good thing.

"Sail …" began the lookout in a loud voice, and finished with, "oh," quietly as Neville appeared beside him.

"Where's *Blessing*?" asked Neville.

"She's there," he said, pointing about three points off the starboard bow.

"Where's the other, then?"

"There aft." He pointed. "Much closer than it was last evening. Two rectangles one above the other; maybe two pairs of them."

Neville looked through the glass for a minute and then handed it back to the lookout. "Any idea what she is?"

"Too early to say, Sir. Could be any two- or three-masted barky from what we can see now."

"Good work. Keep a close watch on her. Call down if you can identify her."

Back on deck, Neville called Catchpole, Foyle, and Framingham.

"Whatever happens, we must be sure that *Blessing* is not captured. I have told you who is aboard, have I not?"

"No, Sir. You've only mentioned 'an important person'."

"My apologies, then. I had not meant to keep it secret forever. She carries Sir George Nugent, Governor of Jamaica, back to that colony...

"*Blessing* is not defenseless; she has guns - fourteen each eighteen-pounder carronades, but those should only be used in the worst emergency. So, Mr. Catchpole, shape a course very carefully to lie between her and this sail until we know her intentions. That should be easily done.

"Mr. Framingham, signal *Blessing* to increase sail."

After a few minutes Catchpole suggested a two-point course adjustment.

"*Blessing*'s setting stun'sl's at her fore and main. She should begin to pull away from us soon," said Neville. "Let's see to our visitor."

"A French corvette, Sir, is what I think she is," said Framingham. "Three-masted, something like a frigate, but low of freeboard, without the fo'cs'l and quarterdeck. You see, even now we rarely catch sight of her hull, and she's much closer."

The day wore on. *Blessing*'s sails became smaller and smaller and the corvette's larger. Dinner passed.

"Spill some wind, Mr. Catchpole. Let's annoy this Frenchman as soon as we can and as far from *Blessing* as we can manage. For that matter, I think we should go right at her. Whatever the case, we must not let her slide past. If she's as fast as she seems and we let her by, she'll have *Blessing* for sure."

"Seven knots now, Sir," reported the seaman at the log.

"Slow to three or four, then, Mr. Catchpole. Frenchie should be on us in a couple hours."

"Deck, haloo!" yelled Musgrove, now returned to the watch platform at the main.

"Go on, man," hollered Framingham.

"Corvette for sure. French flag. I count her as 24 guns."

"Thankee, Musgrove…

"We'll have our work cut out then. And she is sailing fast. Must be steady on twelve knots or so. Do you judge us still in her path, gentlemen? I'd say we are."

They all agreed.

"My plan is thus," began Neville, "We shall shape a course to steer close across her bow such that she must take action and not simply sail by. She will fire at us as we come, but she will not want us to cross her bows, because we might rake her badly as we cross. What would you expect her to do, Mr. Foyle?"

"She should turn to starboard as we close, Sir, in order to give us a full broadside. If she carries cannon rather than carronades we may be badly damaged before we are close enough to do her much damage."

"So I expect; but she must slow to avoid a collision, and we can return our broadside of carronades when we are in close. Load chain or canister for the first broadside and ball for the second. We probably have as many men as she does. We should seek to grapple alongside and board if we can't disable her. Be sure your marines are ready, Mr. Denby."

"We are, Sir!"

"She's about a league off, now. Let's get our speed back up close to hers. Beat to quarters, Mr. Johnson, and run our starboard."

Neville studied the enemy craft as the noise of clearing and running out rose to its normal crescendo.

Superieure closed precisely as planned over the next half hour, bashing across the low mounding seas to place herself across the Frenchman's bow. With his glass, Neville could see that her guns were out. She was no sham. There was a gun in every port.

"Three cables, Sir."

"I can see, Mr. Foyle…

"Fire a chaser across his bow, Mr. Johnson. We might as well be formally introduced."

"Ball's bounced, Sir, did you see it," Foyle asked.

"No. Did we hit her, then?"

"I think so. Look, she's furling her courses."

"We've angered her captain, then. She begins her turn. Mr. Framingham, fire as she bears."

The corvette fired first.

"A full broadside, gentlemen," said Neville as the whine of it passed by. A hole appeared in the fore topsail and a piece of rail amidships flew to splinters, and a man screamed in pain.

"Chain. And from this distance, if must be from cannon," yelled Neville. "They have made their mistake and fired too early. We will be close enough to give them our first broadside before they reload...

"Hold fire until you're sure we are close enough!" he bellowed forward.

The two ships charged onward.

"She's turning to avoid a collision!" yelled Foyle.

"Fire as she bears!" Neville roared.

Superieure's guns spoke one at a time as they passed by the bow of the corvette. Her forward rigging came to pieces, causing her bowsprit to droop almost to the water. A cheer arose.

Superieure sailed a graceful curve past her bow into the range of the corvette's starboard guns, and there the chase ended. It seemed to Neville that his whole world was full of hissing, whining noise. Then crashing, as *Superieure's* foremast went in half below the yoke of the fore-aft course, and the fore topmast fell down to hang limply.

"Strike, Mr. Catchpole!" Neville yelled to the officer he saw closest to the flag halyard. "Haul our colours down before he bashes us to splinters!"

Ten minutes later *Superieure* had lost her momentum and bobbed lazily in the lumpy water.

"We were lucky, gentlemen. They are French and they fought as they were trained – to fire high into our rigging. The butcher's bill is only three and some injuries."

"Here comes their boat, Captain. They don't look French navy to me."

"So I see. I'll be sorry to part with this sword. I will probably never see it again. We have done our duty, though. They could sail all about us and smash us to pieces, but with the damage we have done to their forward rigging they could not hope to catch *Blessing*.

"Just call me Captain Murdock." The French ship's captain spoke English with a northern accent.

"Captain Murdock, good afternoon. I'm Captain Burton."

"Thank you for the sword, Captain Burton. It's a fine one. So how does a British captain find himself on such a wee boatie?"

Not willing to provide all the details, Neville said only, "Transportation to Jamaica for a new command."

"So I might see you again, eh? I'm not sure I'd like that."

"You're not French navy, are you?"

"Do we look navy to you? Ha, ha, haaa! Privateers, Captain. Privateers. I'll not bother you with where we sail from. But what to do with you, that's the question? Your schooner is a nice one, for sure; American, and new, so we'll keep her. She should bring a pretty penny, but it's a shame you have no cargo. Some of your men might join us, I think, if they can act a bit more French or if we need their specialties. But you? I don't need another captain aboard, so I think I'll have to put you off. And your marine sergeant might be more trouble than I need, so he can join you. But we can keep the boys and the rest for now. We'll not hurt a soul as long as they cooperate."

"Land, ho!" yelled the lookout in French.

"That's it, then. Your new home. We'll set you off there. It should be Samana Cay. Since you've interrupted our chase, we might as well stop there for some water. Enough chit-chat, then." Murdock concluded. He turned and walked away.

"Not a very big island, is it, Mr. Denby?" queried Neville. They had been sitting on the beach under a palm tree waiting for the two ships to leave. It seemed the thing to do. Now they watched the sails grow steadily smaller.

"No, I don't think so," said Denby. "Are we dead men, then, do you think?"

"Not for some time," answered Neville. "There is obviously water, and there are at least coconuts. They were good enough to leave me my dirk, so we can cut things – maybe catch a fish. It's getting close on dark now, so that coconut there will be dinner, I think, and anything more we'll have to find in the morning. Excuse me, but I have a letter I'm going to read over. If you must be active, find a rock to beat that nut open with."

"Aye, Sir."

Neville opened his jacket and extracted the last letter he had received before setting sail from Spithead. It was Marion's letter of ten January. There was not much news in it, but he was greatly cheered to know that she continued to write. She complained of the winter cold and the snow in Washington. It was not something a lady from Jamaica would be familiar with. Then she added that she would be leaving 'soon'. He assumed that meant she would be in Kingston waiting for him when he arrived. That was a thought that could carry him through even this ordeal.

"Let's have a look 'round, shall we, Sgt. Denby?" Neville asked at first light. They had eaten coconut flesh for their supper and drunk of its water, and then slept on beds of sculpted sand. Even in the tropics, however, the cold had sunk into their bones by morning, and they were both anxious to get on.

"Where were they getting the water; up this way?" asked Neville.

"Aye. I was too angry to follow them then, but they've left the trail of a thousand cows."

They found a pond with a stream leading to it from high ground. "Up there on the hill we might see where we are," said Neville. "Let's go." They both drank heartily before beginning the climb.

"I haven't seen anything else human, Sir, except a few really old campsites. If I had to guess, I'd say it's old indian pottery bits and a few mounds of shells. That should mean there are clams or oysters here."

Neville had time to think as they trudged upward for something like an hour. They removed their jackets about half way up and hung them on tall poles so they could be found on the way down – one red and one blue.

I have for so long thought of Maria; that I could not go on or be with another after her passing, but I may finally be able to let her go. She is gone, as are Thomas, Vincent and Anne. They cannot come back to life, and I am 'stuck in it', am I not? There are no women here to confuse me, just sand and a few trees surrounded by the sea, and all of it bombarded by the sun. If I come through this I shall be a better man for Marion. Mary is certainly a great temptation when she is near, but she seems so far away now. I have the feeling that Marion would be by my side even here, as Maria would have, if she could.

"This is it, then," said Denby, suddenly breaking his revelation of thought. "Nothing on the island but us." He stood on a rock that was the absolute highest point on the island.

Neville looked fully around and saw very little that was promising other than a few clumps of trees that might be good shelter. "The sea, then," he said at last. "We must look to the sea for fish and shells. We have water. If Indians could live here, so can we. Today we should gather wood for a fire, find a few more coconuts, and make ourselves some thatch mats to sleep on. Tomorrow we fish. Agreed?"

"Aye, Captain. Let's go down for another drink. I'm going to miss my grog."

Neville took one last look, scanning the horizon for sails.

"I see no sails, Sgt. Denby, but we must be ready to make a large, smoky signal fire if we do."

They spent the afternoon making palm thatch mats and gathering coconuts and dry coconut palm fronds for a fire. They woke in the morning with far less discomfort than the preceding night.

Neville sat up first, thinking he would take a more objective review of his immediate surroundings. They were beneath a grove of coconut trees that was perhaps a quarter mile long on the shore of a truly beautiful little semi-circular bay of turquoise water. The arms of the bay protruded far enough to break the large swell, at least when it came from the northeast, resulting in small wavelets that lapped gently at the sand. *This is not hurricane season,* he reminded himself. *Things might be very different then.*

He squinted out to sea, where some white bird floated low to the water. *A flight of pelicans?* He wondered. When they did not rise again to swoop as they usually do, he paid more close attention. The birds did not rise and swoop. They stood steadily on.

"Denby. Sgt. Denby. Please wake," he said to the lump beside him.

"Wha...?"

"Out and down, Sargent. Out and down. Come see what we have here. I have been watching a flight of white birds that seem to have converged into a sail. I need your eyes. Am I just imagining?"

They both stood and ran to the western end of the beach where it culminated in a rock of about ten feet in height. "Up, there! Go on up. I'm right behind you."

Before Neville had clambered up beside Denby, Denby was already looking to jump down.

"The fire,' he said. "We must make the fire. It is indeed a ship!"

The two ran back to where they had piled dry palm fronds in preparation for building a fire and began pulling the pile out onto the beach.

"How do we light it, Captain?"

"A bow. We must make a bow and find a string. Some of this fine coconut stuff will do as kindling." He looked again to the sea, but stopped his motion. He dropped his arms to his side. "Never mind, Sgt. Denby."

"What is it? Are we too late? Will she sail by?" His voice sounded more desperate with each question.

"None of it, Sergeant. I think we do nothing. I think she is coming here. See, her fore and main remain one ahead of the other, though she is not yet hull up."

"She might change course. Why would she come here?"

"Our privateer friends may not be the only ones who know there is water here."

"You are right, of course, but can we not light the fire anyway? You may teach me how, and I will have something to do other than worry that she will sail by without seeing us."

"You are right, of course. Let us get to it."

Closer the ship came, first the sails rising from the sea and then the hull. A black hull with yellow squares along her side.

"English navy, she is,"

"No question. She should be at anchor in an hour."

"Her boat's in the water now, pulling for here."

They remained in the shade some twenty feet from the water and waited until the ship's launch scrubbed ashore. After two seamen jumped out into the water and steadied the bow, they called out: "Haloo!" and began walking closer.

Immediately they found themselves looking at the small end of a pair of marine muskets.

"Come no closer!" some marine yelled from the boat. They were in truth only thirty feet apart, and it was undoubtedly that surprise that alarmed the boat. After a moment a tall, thin, blond-headed British navy lieutenant stepped to the strand and approached a few feet. He and Neville stood staring at each other, unspeaking for a moment.

The lieutenant motioned for his marines to lower their muskets, and then, seeing a captain standing before him, he said, "Uniform's a bit scruffy, Neville, and you could do with a shave. How's the water here?"

"You're late, Daniel," replied Neville. "Could've been here yesterday. That's not a proper greeting for a captain... and the water's fine."

The two stomped forward through the fluffy sand and embraced, and to the amazement of the boat crew, their officers wept tears of joy and gave each other great thumps on the back.

Neville's duty upon arriving at Kingston was to report to Admiral Duckworth the loss of his ship – for which he could expect nothing less than a court-martial. He also needed to report his arrival for duty aboard *La Désirée*.

"This combination of reports will vex him greatly, I am afraid," said Daniel.

"I am sure it will, but there is nothing I can do to change it." The two old friends had enjoyed more time to catch up on everything from family and home to naval exploits and careers.

"How did you come by this ship, Daniel?"

"*Thundered* paid off in Portsmouth when she came in. When I got back from Bury St Edmunds, the *Blancife* here was in need and about to sail. She snatched me so fast I had no time to disagree. Why would I? She's a frigate, and I'm first lieutenant. I should finally have enough action to move myself up the Navy List, as you have done so well."

"Jolly well said! Here's a toast to your success."

Daniel, who had been home to Bury St. Edmunds more recently than Neville, if only by a month or two, was able to report the health of everyone there and what he called 'the grand improvement of Mary.' "She is a lovely girl and deserves no such trauma as she has been through," he said. "I am pleased to see more spark in her than last visit, and particularly so to know the spark is from you."

Neville decided to hold his tongue on that, though he was glad of it. "I have received her letters," he said, "and she sounds well. Your Angelica has grown to be quite the beauty, Daniel. I hadn't seen her in at least two years; and little Alice is smashing!"

Despite the good cheer aboard *Blancife*, the day came when they arrived at Port Royal Harbor. Fearing the worst, Neville dressed as well as he could in his only uniform and went ashore. The command center was easily found.

Inside he found an unexpected reception from the clerk. "Sit just there," the man said when he heard Neville's name. He stood up immediately and disappeared through a large door to his left. He returned in moments, coming out the door and holding it for a senior officer who followed him; an admiral.

Neville could feel his heart rate jump instantly.

"Captain Burton?" the admiral asked.

"Aye, Sir," he said, aware of his instant nervousness.

"Welcome to Jamaica. Governor Nugent was most impressed with your action to defend the *Blessing* on his way in, and asked that I greet you personally." He extended a hand to be shaken, and Neville took it.

"What of your ship, Captain? Damage?"

"Aye, Sir, both masts damaged. I was forced to strike to insure *Blessing's* escape. She was taken by French privateers. My marine sergeant and I were marooned on a small island."

"Bloody bad news, that is. It means a court-martial for sure, we can't avoid it, but I expect the Governor will put a good word in. Well, carry on, Captain. Good to meet you." The clerk held the door for him to return to his chamber.

I may be in hot water, but nobody here has to know that yet, thought Neville. *Before I take the next step here in Jamaica I am going to see Marion. For all I know they will carry me off in irons before I take command.*

His decision was to visit first at the Stillwater Rum Trading Company. It was as yet only 9:30 in the morning. He enjoyed the walk down Water Lane at this time of day; relatively quiet with the cool air and longish shadows of morning. *Perhaps this is the calm before the storm.* With some trepidation, he entered the Stillwater Rum Company through its large doors and found himself looking at three empty office windows. There was no Marion, no Stearns, and no Chester, but there was the old 'information clerk'.

"Good morning, Sir," he said to Neville. He looked up to see who was there, but then went back to his writing. Probably because he saw so many people come and go, in or out of uniform, and because Neville had been gone for ten months, there seemed to be no spark of recognition at all.

"Is Marion Stillwater in?" he asked. It was also apparent that asking for Miss Stillwater was not unusual.

"No, Sir." Not the most hospitable greeter, this time he spoke to the desk. "Gone abroad."

"Abroad?" asked Neville. He had expected her to be home by now. "Abroad where? Still in Washington?"

That caused the clerk to look up at him. Not many knew where she went. "You'll have to ask her father, Sir."

"Is he in, then?"

"Yes," He turned and looked at Chester's window. Chester, as Neville already knew, wasn't there. "Stepped away for a bit. You may wait." He swept his arm out to indicate the chairs in the lobby.

"Thank you, I will."

Ten minutes passed, then fifteen and twenty. Neville was considering returning later in the day when he saw movement in the window. Chester was returning from wherever he went; the warehouse, most likely. He probably had Marion's duties to perform as well as his own. As is a proprietor's manner, his eyes scanned the waiting room for customers before he sat. They stopped at the only person there: Neville.

Neville saw him staring for a minute. *He's probably trying to decide if he should have me thrown out, or if his curiosity requires a meeting.* He sat with his back to Neville.

A few minutes later the clerk rose and walked over to Neville. "Mr. Stillwater will see you now." He never did determine how the clerk was signaled.

Neville followed the clerk to the office hallway door, and the man held it open for him. He knocked on Chester's door frame, and Chester said, "Come in, Commander."

"It's Captain now," said Neville.

"I see. Have a seat. I didn't hear that *Superieure* had come in."

"She hasn't yet. I came in on the *Blancife.* "

"Your new ship?"

"No, but I have a good friend aboard. I am to take command of the *La Désirée.* "

"I see. How can I help you?"

"I would very much like to find your daughter. We have corresponded, and her last is of tenth January. In it she says she is to leave Washington 'soon'. If she is not here, I am concerned for her. Your clerk has told me she is still abroad."

Chester smiled. "She is, yes. You shouldn't worry."

"May I ask where?"

"You may ask," Said Chester. "Europe," he volunteered. "Why would I help a violent person like you find her. My employee, Mr. Stearns, returned from Washington some months ago, ill with a wound you inflicted on him."

"At his provocation. He apparently thought navy officers can't defend themselves."

"He says you challenged him."

"I am surprised at such a breach of honor. That was his point, after all, wasn't it – honor? It was his challenge. With your pistols, I might add. Why was that? Was this contrived?"

Chester deflected. "You can ask him yourself."

"Where is he, then?"

"Also abroad." Chester smiled again, "He didn't die of his wound."

"Same place as Marion?"

"You would like to know that, wouldn't you?" His smile broadened into a grin. "You needn't write her," he added, "Certainly not here. If you need rum for *La Désirée*, please call on us. Is there anything else I can help you with today?" he asked in his smoothest sales voice.

"No, it appears not. Good day." Neville rose and exited the building.

Deep in thought, he walked more slowly down Water Lane than he had come up. Reviewing what he knew, he came to the conclusion that the tone of Marion's letters was not such that he should expect her to stop writing. There must be another letter 'in the wind' somewhere. But where? He comforted himself with the knowledge that if she addressed it to the Admiralty, as she had done the last letter, it would find him at Jamaica. But how long would that take? Between now and then, he could only write letters and stack them up. Would it be faster to send one to the Washington rooming house and expect them to forward it?

The harbor came into view as he turned the corner onto King Street and proceeded toward the strand. A small ship, not yet anchored, was moving slowly to the left. It was familiar to him, yet not one that he had often viewed from a distance. He questioned whether his mind was playing tricks on him. Did that ship merely look very similar to *Superieure* or was it actually the *Superieure*? From this distance there was no way to read her name. Superieure had recently lost her main topmast. This ship had a topmast. But that could probably have been jury-rigged, if not completely repaired, in a very short time. The foremast, then; it had been shot in half. This ship had... a very short foremast with no sail above her course.

Neville began to run. This ship was *Superieure*. He trotted down King Street to the strand, and then along the waterfront, keeping *Superieure* in view until he found a shore boat to give him a ride out.

The little boat hoisted her single tattered sail and was able to use the same wind that *Superieure* was using to follow her to her mooring location. The first hail was not heard above the noise of dropping anchor, but the second was answered with, "Who goes?"

"*Superieure!*" Neville himself hollered back.

"**W**e looked for three days, Captain," said Catchpole. "We checked every island within a few hours' sail," added Foyle, "but since we were locked below when they put you off we had no idea where to look."

"I can't believe you've beat us in," said Johnson. "How on earth..."

"I'll get to that, all of you. The bigger mystery is how you got away so soon. I thought I would never see any of you again."

The chorus began again: "There was no mystery to it, Captain," said Foyle.

"They just couldn't handle us," spoke up Framingham.

"After they had taken..." began Johnson.

"All right, gentlemen. Enough! One person. Who acted as commander?"

"I did," said Foyle humbly, almost ashamedly.

"It should have been me, I know," said Framingham, "but I'm not quite ready for command. I will be soon, but not yet, and Mr. Foyle has taken two prizes in with great success, so we elected him."

"Elected? This isn't a pirate ship!"

"But I'm no navigator, Captain. It couldn't be me," said Johnson.

"And I'm not a commissioned officer," said Catchpole.

"Neither is Mr. Foyle, and he's but... but...."

"Fifteen now, Sir, I am." Despite the situation, Neville smiled with the realization that the boys arms and legs were sticking at least two inches farther out of his uniform than when they had first met.

"And not commissioned, either, I remind you all. Never mind, never mind. Mr. Foyle, the account if you please, and I expect a report of it writ fair on my desk by the morning."

"Aye, Sir. The gist of it is this: We were locked below when they put you off and they got the water, remember? After that we sailed for some time. We could hear arguing above. Then the way came off her, you know? No more sound of the water along the hull and all, and a couple boats came and went. Then it went quiet-like, and we heard nothing for a while.

"By the time we decided they had just left us and bashed our way out, we could only see their royals at the horizon. They would have liked to have had our ship, I'm sure, but wouldn't trade us for it. Their corvette is bigger than *Superieure*, with more guns, and faster – you saw that. The only way to take *Superieure* would have been to drown us all, and I don't think they had the stomach for that, or to put us all ashore somewhere. I think they were afraid of us, though, and rightly so. We had more men aboard than they had. Putting us ashore would have required letting us all loose, at least for a bit.

"So they held us all on the foredeck with big guns on us and the rubbish of the battle all around so we couldn't move easy, and then they took everything they thought was valuable out of the hold. Rum went first, of course. Then most of the food, our long guns and the swivels, half our cordage and spare sail canvas, most of the gunpowder that Mr. Johnson didn't have hid under the bread-room deck, your silver service…"

"I just bought that…"

"Sorry, Sir. And the spare spars. I heard them laughing about leaving us 'two sticks to get home with'.

"Then we looked for you, like we said, for three days. The only sail we saw was an English frigate, I think – maybe like that one over there," Catchpole said, pointing to the *Blancife*.

"Ho, ho," laughed Neville, "You found me, then. I was aboard that ship. My friend since we were two years of age strolled ashore like we were in Hyde Park and picked us up. They took on a bit of water and we came on ahead of you. I thank you heartily, all of you. I'm starving now. Is there something for dinner?"

"Not much until we get some from shore," grumbled Johnson.

"Whatever it is, I'm sure it's better than two days of coconuts," said Neville.

In the morning, armed with Mr. Foyle and his report, Captain Burton returned to the command center of Jamaica Station. Neville warned Foyle that he could be confronted by an Admiral so that he might not appear the fool when questioned. But he wasn't. They were instructed to wait while his report was taken in. "Get comfortable," said the clerk, "It may be three or four hours, and I've seen worse."

Several captains, one of them marine, came and went. A marine lieutenant was summoned after about two hours of waiting. He was in with the admiral for a few minutes, and then came out and walked over to where they waited.

"Captain Burton?" he inquired.

"Aye," said Neville. He stood up and stretched his back.

"The Admiral has asked me to pass you a message if you were still here."

"Still here? Why would we not be?"

"He said, Sir, and I don't understand the words, but I deliver them exactly as I remember he said them, are: 'I do not know why he should be out there at all, as this report makes the matter of a court-martial moot and naught but a waste of my time. He should be aboard *La Désirée* making preparations to sail on the morning tide'. That was it, Sir."

"Thank you, lieutenant."

Music to my heart, that is, thought Neville when the noise of a proper ship's greeting began to emanate from the frigate *La Désirée*. Drums and boatswain's pipes sounded. Mr. Foyle had asked for the honor of transporting him to his new command, and had yelled back '*La Désirée*' in response to the ship's hail when his 'gig' from

Superieure neared her hull. He could see side-boys and marines assembling to greet him as a captain deserved, and a good number of seamen hanging over the rails or in the rigging to get a look at their new commander.

At 36 guns, she was larger than either his first ship, the 32-gun *Castor,* or his beloved 28-gun *Experiment,* but still she sat low in the water and required only a few steps to reach the sally port. In the modern navy she was a fifth-rate. He stepped across the brow as sedately as he could manage, rather than hopping in like a five-year-old as he felt like doing. He saluted aft.

A lieutenant greeted him by touching his hat, and Neville returned the courtesy. "I'm First Lieutenant Towers, Sir. Welcome aboard."

"Captain Burton," said Neville. "I am pleased to meet you." He leaned forward and shook Towers' hand. "Please assemble the men."

Never much for speeches, Neville strode to the appropriate spot at the forward quarterdeck rail and waited for the usual shuffling, mumbling and coughing to die down before beginning the ritual of reading himself in. His experienced eyes prowled the decks and men while he spoke. When he finished reading he indicated to Towers that he had nothing more to say.

"Dismissed," roared Towers. Compared to his stature, his voice was huge. He was a man of average height, about five feet and eight inches, but without the burly chest that one would normally associate with such a roar. He was rather more on the slender side, with a narrow face, short nose and sad-looking eyes. He stood ramrod straight, though, giving him an authoritative appearance that was enhanced by a swarthy complexion.

"Lead me to my cabin, if you please, Lt. Towers."

Once inside, Neville glanced about the place, and then turned to Towers and asked, "I fear we are in a hurry. Are there orders here?"

"Aye, Sir. Top desk drawer."

"Cap'n's Sea chest, Sir," said a voice at the door.

Neville whirled around to see Hajee Ayoub standing there with it. "Hajee, did you just come with the chest, without orders to do so?"

"Aye, Sir. Well, no. Mr. Framingham sent me along."

"Did the Captain's coxswain remain with the ship, Lt. Towers?"

"No, Sir. He went with Captain Whitby."

"Then get to work, Mr. Ayoub.

"Wait here a minute, Lt. Towers."

Neville fished the customary order packet from the desk, broke the seal, and read the letter within.

"We are indeed in a rush, Lt. Towers. I am sorry not to have been here earlier, but here I am now, and we are to sail on the morning tide with a squadron under *Vanguard*. Are we ready?"

"Can be. Does it say how long we are to be out?"

"Not specifically, but I'd say it implies less than a month."

"Then we can, Sir. At worst we might have short rations for a few days. We must complete the water today, too."

"See to it. Thank you. Who are the other lieutenants?"

"Only one, Sir. Lt. Coughlan. We're short one."

"Midshipmen?"

"Just three."

"But you make do? Sail and fight?"

"We do, Captain."

"Pass word that we sail in the morning, then. I need some time to write a few notes, and then I'd like to meet the gunroom. Have a boat ready to take a message to the frigate *Blanciffe* shortly, if you please."

"Aye, Sir."

By the time *La Désirée* approached her anchoring location in Port Royal Harbor a month later Neville had learned a great deal about his new ship and her company.

"Lt. Towers, as soon as we drop anchor, please have a boat out. Do you remember that I sent a note over to the *Blanciffe* before we left, and that I visited *Vanguard* when we sat becalmed off Santo Domingo?"

"Aye, Captain, I do."

"The note was to my friend Lt. Watson asking him to carry a request up to headquarters. I wrote the request for him as well, so he needed only carry it. A captain being reassigned is normally allowed to take a man with him to his new ship. In this instance I am not counting Mr. Ayoub, as I did not actually request him, and I suspect the navy doesn't care much where he goes. So I requested a particularly capable midshipman – a Mr. Foyle. I will go personally to collect him if the request is approved, or to the *Blanciffe* to inquire upon it if *Superieure* is out."

"Aye, Sir."

"The visit to *Vanguard* was particularly fruitful for us. There is a very sharp junior lieutenant aboard with whom I had occasion to serve as the prize captain of a frigate some year or so ago. He was particularly keen on joining a frigate, as I remembered his interest. I went across to inquire if his interest remained. As it turns out, it does. Having seen so many frigates in the harbor, he thought it possibly his most likely opportunity for a transfer to a frigate to be granted. His request had progressed only so far as his captain, and so when I appeared, 'hat in hand', as it were, the deed was done. Captain Evans would not release him, however, until the end of this cruise and approval of the transaction by Admiral Duckworth."

Towers' countenance seemed to lift. "Captain Burton," he began, "I told you that we are able to sail and fight this ship with the officers we have, but there is no question we would be much better off with a full complement – for watch-standing if naught else. I was going to suggest that we appeal to the Commodore."

"There will be no need of that now, I hope. Ah, look. We are in luck for the first part. *Superieure* is there. I am going off to visit her and pay my respects to her company. I expect to return with Midshipman Foyle…

"Take command, Lt. Towers," he said clearly before stepping down into the boat. *La Désirée* had found her spot and dropped her best bower. She was still swinging slowly, seeking her line with the afternoon's light breeze.

Superieure's company had watched *La Désirée* arrive and were prepared to receive their previous captain in style. He was properly piped up the side, found Mr. Foyle ready to go, walked 'round the ship giving his regards to any man who stepped forward, shook hands with Johnson, Framingham, Catchpole, Trimbley, Denby and the new commander, one Lt. Fromow and retreated to his boat all in a short half hour.

"How do you find Lt. Fromow, Mr. Foyle?" asked Neville on the row back to *La Désirée*.

"He'll do well, Sir, I'm sure. You have set us all to rights. This last cruise went very well, indeed."

"Excellent. You will like this new ship. There's room to stand below decks, for one thing. I'll be leaving you to get acquainted for the next couple days. I expect you and Lt. Towers will get along handsomely."

"And whence do you go, if I might be so bold as to ask, Sir?"

"Errands, I suppose you would say." He left it at that.

Neville's first stop ashore the next morning was at headquarters. *Vanguard* had arrived a few hours before *La Désirée* the previous day, so Neville assumed that Captain Evans had reported immediately to inquire of orders for the squadron. When he did so he would have dropped off his packet – which would include Lt. Miller's request.

Just on a hunch, and to allow time for Admiral Duckworth to review *Vanguard's* packet, Neville's first undertaking ashore was to stroll up Harbour Street to the butcher shop. He received the usual grouchy squint from Miss Fletcher of the *Pig's Tale* when the little bell at the door jangled. She gave him a big grin when she realized who it was calling, but could only offer, "I've nothing from her, Love. Not a thing since the two of them left some five months ago. Your friend Joseph's not pleased, either."

"No, I suppose not. Where is he, do you know?"

"No, cap'n. I ain't seen him in some time … a month, maybe."

"Thank you, Miss Fletcher. Good day." The little bell rang him back out into the hot spring sunshine.

As much as he longed to read a letter from Marion, he decided to wait on the post until the next day in hope there might be an answer to the request for Miller. For the remainder of this day he would attend to something he had been thinking about for most of the month gone by. His mission to investigate Chester Stillwater was no longer just a vague assignment from Sir William. Chester had made it personal by his loan of dueling pistols to Stearns and then his refusal to assist Neville in locating his daughter. Neville understood it, but it was still personal now.

He located the dumpy little room he had used before as a personal headquarters for his sleuthing about town. He had carried the nondescript canvas bag with his waterfront civilian clothes with him, and he now set to changing from a captain to an out-of-work tar. A little dirt from the street would complete his disguise, and he would resume asking questions at the local bars. He had new questions to ask now – about muskets.

He returned first to the *Boar's Head* on Harbor Street where he had had some success before, but it was deserted. He tried the *Fox and Squirrel* and the *Gun Locker*, but found little activity at either one of those. Finally he found a crowd at the *Figurehead*. Possibly he had just begun too early in the day, and now it was the supper hour which created the traffic.

"That little 'un there taken?" he asked the barmaid, indicating a small round table in the center of the room.

"Nope," she said, "Only one chair, ain't there?"

"I'll sit there then, and take a pint."

After only a few minutes it became apparent that he was not going to learn anything from simply listening. The conversation around him was about women in Tahiti, some unpopular petit officer aboard one of the frigates in the harbor, and much more mundane nonsense. It would be necessary for him to ask a few questions.

"You, there," Neville said to one of the seamen. "You been here long?"

The three at the next table looked at him blankly.

"A while. Who are you, and why do you want to know?" asked the closest of them.

Neville ignored the 'who are you' part of the question. "I need to find something."

"Good for you, matey. We all got needs, ain't we?"

"Guns," said Neville in a low voice. "Muskets for twenty men."

"Twenty?" queried the next one over. "Where's this army going?"

"Nowhere without the muskets. You know somebody, then?"

"Not us. Maybe that lot over there," he said, pointing to a group of four very rough-looking men.

"Aw-right. Thankee," said Neville, and went back to his beer to contemplate how he might approach.

He gave the distant men a few glances. He finished his beer. The three beside him had remained quiet after speaking with him, and they soon left. As he was paying the barmaid the four also rose to leave. *Now or never.* Neville stood and headed for the door.

Outside, darkness was falling. He had squandered the day – perhaps.

He hesitated by the door until the four came out. "Excuse me, kind sirs..." he said to the group.

"We don't give handouts," one said.

"Not looking fer no handout, guv," Neville said. "I got business."

The four stared at him. They were imposing; threatening. All stood an inch or two taller than Neville. All had collarless dirty white shirts with a single silver button in the center front. They stood close, and he smelled rum and something like lemons. The tallest one had lost his leg below the knee, and it had been replaced with a stout three inch diameter pole.

"What kinda business?" the speaker asked.

"Muskets. Can you get me twenty?"

They passed glances between themselves and at their surroundings.

"Who wants 'em?"

"Friend 'o mine."

"Where will they go?"

"You care?"

The speaker stared at him again while sucking at his cheeks.

"How'd you find us?"

"Somebody in the bar."

They looked at each other again, and one of the others said, "It's Billy. He's got a big mouth."

"Might could find out," said the speaker.

"Can you do that and meet me somewhere later?"

"I could, yea. Where do you know, since I'd guess you're new here and all?"

"There's an alley behind the *Boar's Head*. That do?" suggested Neville.

"I know it, yea. It'll do. Ten." The four walked off into the gathering darkness.

Neville returned to the *Gun Locker*. He thought he remembered a meat pasty on their board, and it was neither the *Boar's Head* nor the *Figurehead* where he might be recognized as the inquisitive one. He could return to anonymity for a while.

At 9:30 he left the *Gun Locker* and walked to the *Boar's Head* to take a better look at the alley before his rendezvous. It was deserted, with trash barrels in the center by the bar's door. There was a stump by the door as well, likely used as a seat by some cook when he got a few minutes off. He was pleased to see the alley was open at both ends, but there was no light except a slice of moonlight that shone between the bar and the next building.

He sat on the stump and waited, not entirely sure what he expected to happen. After fifteen or twenty minutes he heard the sound of rough boots on the cobbles and the low rumble of men's speech.

He heard, "In here, he said." He sat still on the stump. From there he could see five men. One was shorter, and Neville thought he saw the glint of silver hair as the shorter man passed through the moonlight. He pulled his tarred hat lower over his forehead. *It couldn't be Chester, could it? Even if he was involved in illegal gun sales he would never come out himself, would he? That would be foolhardy, at best.*

"Go look, then," a voice said. Neville thought it sounded like Chester.

The four advanced. "Oi. That you as wanted a musket?"

Neville attempted to disguise his voice by lowering his tone, "Aye. Can you get 'em?"

"Twenty, you say?"

"Aye."

"We can. Not cheap, but the best. Harper Rifles, and new; not old muskets."

"When?"

"Where's the money."

"Ain't got it with me."

"Go get it."

"I'm not stupid. I'll send a boy in later with enough for one. You send one out w' 'im. If it's good we have a deal at three guineas each, yea?"

"Go on, then. We'll wait. Better not be long."

Neville stood from the stump and turned away from the fifth man. "You'll see a boy soon," he said.

The fifth man called down the alley, "How you going to carry twenty, sailor?" Neville's blood ran cold. It sounded very much like Chester. The man added, "Do I know you?"

"Dunno. 'oo are you?" he growled.

A moment passed, and the man made some sort of a signal to the big four. Even in the dark, Neville could see knives coming out. He ran for the other end of the alley.

Five steps to go. Four, Three. A pistol fired behind him. He felt the whiz of the bullet pass close and pluck at his left sleeve. He turned the corner and leaped across the street in front of a late hack on its way home. Startling the horse created enough distraction for him to escape down an alley opposite and roll under the bottom shelf of a discarded heavy wooden work bench. He controlled his breathing. Two men ran by. They soon walked back, grumbling to each other. "Could've had his whole sack of gold if Cap'n hadn't shot off his bloody gun…"

He waited for quite some time… an hour, maybe, before rolling back out from under and cautiously finding his way back to his temporary lair. He stuck to shadows. His shoulder began to ache. When he put his right hand to it, it came back bloody.

In the morning he packed his canvas bag. The left shoulder was just a scratch, though he knew he should ask the ship's surgeon to look to it when he got back. He put his uniform on and walked back to the *Gun Locker* for some breakfast, and then to the clerk of the post at Jamaica Station Headquarters. The clerk quickly found the sack for *La Désirée*. It was not as full as Neville had hoped. He noticed a rough bench along one side of the room, and decided he should look to the official letters before leaving. If his answer on Miller was not there he would want to inquire directly. He sat down and opened the satchel. The clerk gave him a disapproving look, but he persevered.

The top letter of two from the navy was the hoped-for scribbling from Admiral Duckworth approving Miller's transfer. He returned it to the sack. The other was a very unexpected order from the Admiral reassigning *La Désirée* to Admiral Nelson's fleet. Neville had heard a rumor about Nelson being in the Caribbean but had discarded it as nonsense. He had also noticed a larger number of navy vessels in the harbor, but had not yet taken the time to investigate who they were, or why they were there. He had certainly been obsessed with his own missions. He slipped that letter back into its envelope as well.

He took another minute to rummage through the sack looking for any letter in a very pretty flowing hand, but he found nothing from Marion.

14 - *"The Crumpled Letter"*

Since he had been gone from his ship for a day and a half already, Neville thought it prudent to remain aboard long enough to disseminate the new orders and become comfortable with preparations for the long passage back to Gibraltar, which was planned to begin in about three weeks.

"Lt. Towers, Mr. Worth; Please come below."

The three descended to Neville's cabin. He had yet to become comfortable with the splendor of his new accommodations. The cabin was similar to *Experiment's*, but considerably more modern and larger, since this was a 36 rather than a 28-gun vessel. Furthermore, it was French-built, having more elaborate carving of the cabin's wooden appointments than English vessels.

"This was in the satchel when I picked it up ashore, gentlemen." He saw no reason they couldn't read it for themselves. While they were doing so, he asked, "What have you heard of this? Anything at all? Are some of these ships here from Admiral Nelson's fleet?"

Lt. Towers finished reading the short message. He looked up to Neville and passed the page to Worth. "Just rumor, but it's probably true. Some of our men know others on those ships, and they know they sail with Nelson – or at least they did."

"Send this note across to *Blanciffe* and this one to *Vanguard*. Have your coxswain wait on a reply from each. The first requests that *Blanciffe's* first lieutenant, whom I know well, be allowed to visit me for dinner and a conversation on the Nelson situation. The second requests that our new Lieutenant Miller come across. I have invited the captains, as well, if they are interested. *Vanguard*, at least, should have more information than we do."

"Mr. Towers, how do you find my Mr. Foyle?"

"Exceptional from what I've seen so far. He's second to Midshipman Hicks, though, by a year."

"Hicks should be about ready to sit for lieutenant, then?"

"I'm not sure on that," said Towers, "He's not the heaviest maul in the locker, as I thought you noticed on our last cruise. You might want to question him well before you put him forward - just my opinion, Sir."

"I assume we have charts for the route from here to England, Mr. Worth?"

"We do, aye."

"Thank you, then, gentlemen. Now that you know what we have to do, you may get to it. Pass word for Boatswain Wynde and Pusser Clinker. Have them bring me their lists, if you would, please."

"It's a fine bottle of claret, isn't it Lt. Watson?" asked Wilson.

"It is for sure."

"Hajee found three in Whitby's locker," said Neville. "I have no doubt he meant to take them, but they should certainly not go to waste."

Lieutenants Watson, Wilson, Towers and Coughlin were sitting at dinner with Captain Burton. The captains of *Blanciffe* and *Vanguard* were either too busy or had decided they would never see *La Désirée* again and therefore had no need to meet this junior Captain Burton. They had politely begged off.

"Captain Evans has had the news from Admiral Duckworth himself," announced Wilson, "Admiral Villeneuve escaped the blockade at Toulon in April when a storm blew Nelson's fleet off station. Nelson first searched for Villeneuve in the Eastern Mediterranean. When he sailed to the Caribbean through the Strait of Gibraltar, Nelson gave chase, but now he can't find the Frogs at all. We suspect Villeneuve joined with some Spanish ships, and it is possible they have gone to some Spanish port here, rather than a French one. The word is that Nelson will search through this month, but if he doesn't find anything he will return to Gibraltar. He has asked for every ship he can get."

"That explains our orders, then," said Neville, "Admiral Duckworth must consider us his least valuable; maybe it's just me." *It's wonderful as far as I am concerned*, he thought. *I have no chance of finding Marion here.*

"These ships in here are in for supplies, then?"

"We assume so. They don't tell us much," said Wilson.

"**W**e part ways here in the Western Approaches," announced Neville to his officers at dinner in the gunroom. "Nelson is taking the fleet directly back to Gibraltar, but the Admiralty has ordered three of us to Chatham for minor refits. Before you ask questions, let me say that these orders are based on changes that the Admiralty has in mind and reports by Captain Whitby. He had far longer with this ship than I have had, so I will not argue at all."

"How long is this refit expected to take, Captain?" asked Marine Lt. Carlyle.

"Only two weeks, I am told, but that may mean four or five, if we are forced to wait before they begin, and then they take longer than scheduled."

"I would wager both will happen, if I know the navy…And then what?"

"And then we will rejoin Admiral Nelson, wherever he is at the time. You should all expect two weeks ashore, at least."

"**N**eville, what are you doing here at Whitehall? It seems you only just left," exclaimed Sir William Mulholland.

"It may seem that way to you, Sir, but it has been ten months, and I have been twice across the Atlantic."

"Sit, Captain, and tell me of your exploits. Captain! I can scarce believe it. I congratulate you to my utmost."

"Thank you Sir." The heavy wooden chair made a screeching sound as Neville dragged it around to face his mentor. "I have news of Mr. Stillwater. I did not bother to write it because I would have expected to carry the letter all the way myself."

"First things first, Neville. How do you come to have been sent home from Jamaica, where you so badly wanted to go and I assisted you to accomplish?"

"Do not despair, Sir William. All is well with it." Neville told the story of the privateer corvette, the marooning, the appearance of Daniel Watson, the reappearance of *Superieure*, his assignment to command the *La Désirée* as planned and without censure, and finally the appearance of Nelson's fleet.

"That last I have heard... but he returned?"

"Aye, Sir, still in chase of Villeneuve, and I am transferred to his command. All went to Gibraltar except three of us who were sent in to Chatham Dock Works for minor refits. We must rejoin him after repairs, which I estimate to be around the end of August...

"Would you like to hear of the Stillwaters, then?"

"Of course. I thought it was your desire to be within the orbit of young Miss Stillwater."

"It is, certainly, but she is not in Jamaica. Her father would only tell me that she went 'to Europe', and so I did not mind at all to be ordered home. Do you know where she is now?" he asked.

"Now? No," Mulholland could honestly answer such a specific question, "Why do you think I would?"

"I am always surprised at what you know. Why would I not ask?"

"Ha, ha. I see. Tell me what you have found out."

"I do not have much more than I had before, other than stronger suspicions of Chester." He related the stories of their meeting and of his sleuthing episode. "The four men in the alley did speak the words 'Harper Rifles', and the fifth man who fired a pistol at me sounded like Chester. For all I could see it might have been the man himself. He also questioned if he knew me, even though my face was blacked and I had a tarred hat on. Stearns told me that the pair of dueling pistols he carried to Philadelphia were Chester's. If he is partial to his dueling pistols, he might have taken one with him that night. Stearns was home in between."

"But you never saw the pistol in Jamaica?"

"No, Sir, I did not."

"Hmmm."

"Did you find anything on Stearns?"

"No. He has a curiously empty dossier."

"Did you find anything else?" Neville asked.

"Mr. Stillwater gives a most convincing appearance of being simply a rich rum-merchant, with most of his trade being legal, but he certainly engages in questionable activities. There is very little that is new, except a few more letters from him destined for France, and what you have told me. We have many reports of offshore meetings with French privateers, and there is your report of his ship delivering something to an un-named French ship. We now think it more likely that it was Harper's Ferry Rifles, and not rum. Was there any more from your questioning the locals?"

"No. After that last, and my orders to join Admiral Nelson, I decided to discontinue asking. It seems to me that the danger of skulking about town alone asking questions is increased if the questions are about arms rather than rum. I was hoping you might find out something about Mr. Stearns, because I am not sure how much of his tripe to believe."

"We haven't learned anything, even with what you reported," he said. We still believe Mr. Stillwater to be an agent for France, even if Mr. Stearns…"

"We?"

"There are tidbits from other places, but so far they don't amount to much fact."

"And Marion. Do you think she's involved?"

Neville noticed a curious twitch of Mulholland's face. He said "Not of more than carrying her father's messages, or being the sales person. If she goes to France, they are trading with the enemy, but technically she is American and therefore not the enemy of France. The Rum Company would be, however. Furthermore, Miss Stillwater may know nothing of any letter's contents. I should think such a pretty girl would be very successful selling to the men of France."

"I thought you said you'd never seen her," said Neville.

Another twitch. "One hears things, Neville. Apparently her beauty is much the subject of rumor."

Mulholland returned to the discussion of Chester. "I have tried to determine Mr. Stillwater's motive. I really don't know, but I think it could be some American sentiment. The Americans are friendly to France, despite his being an American living in British Jamaica. His company sells rum to everyone, thereby giving them access to a significant amount of information concerning troop and ship movements. Could it be that he is simply helping to 'pay France back" for their help in the American Revolutionary War?"

"Could it be that your motive is correct, but it's not just him alone; that it's some American group that directs what he must do?"

"Any one of these things could be true, Neville, and there just isn't enough information to condemn him. We may have to put this entire investigation on hold anyway. The war is taking all my attention these days, and Stillwater seems to be very much a minor character."

"Yes, Sir. I know I will have little time for such diversion once I join the admiral."

For the first time in his recent memory, Neville had very little to do. He was 'on holiday' from Mulholland's schemes. He had a ship, so it was not required that he spend day upon day soliciting the Admiralty for an assignment. Furthermore, his ship was in ordinary for minor reasons, so he had no need to pay close attention to its repairs. He considered making another visit home to Bury St. Edmunds, but two weeks wasn't long enough; that left him with time to attend the furnishing of his London flat. 42D Bedford Avenue would be the first 'home" that ever belonged to him and wasn't afloat.

The furniture he had ordered before leaving had been delivered and deposited within. It was strewn about the place in no particular order. There was no organized kitchen - not even a stove. Neither was there a cook to use it. It did not take Neville more than a few hours to determine the ground he was on was so unfamiliar that it would be necessary for him to hire some sort of agent to complete the decorating. He sought out the manager of the house. From there he was referred to a Mr. Healy at 196 Tottenham Court Rd. After a short wait and a short conversation, Mr. Healy agreed to accompany him back to the flat for a review of the situation.

"We can certainly furnish this space to your satisfaction, Captain," said Mr. Healy after an hour of measuring. "We'll need to paint first, of course, and clean these wood floors. I can direct you to a shop for some lovely carpets. Do you know where you will find a bed, Sir? I notice there is not one amongst your things."

"Bed. Oh, yes, I think the same shop would have one." *I'm such an idiot! No bed!*

"This would be our charge. This for the paint and this for the cleaning of floors," he was now saying while he poked at a scrap of paper upon which he had been scribbling. "We could begin tomorrow, but we'll need you out for a few days. Well, I guess you're not in, though, are you? No. Couldn't be," he said, more to himself than to Neville, while his eyes drifted around the hollow space.

Neville looked at Mr. Nealy's scribblings with some surprise. The total was well beyond his expectations. It was also well within his means. *What else have I to do with my money, anyway*, he wondered. "Proceed, then, Mr. Nealy. Can you recommend a cheery little pub? One with a room to let, as well?"

"*Sign of the Golden Pheasant*, I would say, also on the Tottenham Court Road. A key, if you please, Sir."

Neville pulled a key ring from his pocket. He did indeed have two. He handed one to Mr. Nealy. *So I have a flat in London, but I'll be living in a pub?*" He also took a glance 'round his empty rooms, locked the door behind, and descended the stairs to walk back to Tottenham.

It was a nice summer's day for a walk, and not too busy along the street. Neville's thoughts wandered between checking at the Admiralty for letters, considering purchasing a few sets of civilian clothes to wear in London and leave in his flat, writing letters home, wishing he had a friend to share London with, wondering where he would find a housekeeper to tend to cooking and cleaning when he was in town...

"Neville? Neville, is it really you?" asked a familiar voice.

He raised his head to see a well-dressed couple in front of him on the sidewalk. He realized he had been more watching his feet than watching the people walking by. They were still fifteen feet away. Should he know this couple? Their attire was not familiar. He was apparently a local civilian gentleman and she a well-dressed lady of town. Neville, of course, was far more recognizable wearing his uniform; thus far he owned naught else.

"Neville," the man said again. "'Vast your wandering and speak, man!" They had now stopped in front of him, blocking his way.

"Joseph? It's you, isn't it?" The only recognizable thing about the man was his face. He wore not a shred of naval attire. "Joseph Dagleishe, you're here in London?" Neville stepped forward and embraced him and thumped his back. "You must tell me everything,"

"You're being rude, Captain Burton," said Joseph. "Do you remember…"

Dagleishe's words whirled off into the ether as Neville's attention turned to the female face at his side. He had not recognized the woman – the woman as a fine lady – Marion's maidservant, Miss Ellen Aughton. That meant Marion was here; she must be here, and she must be close.

"Are you well, Neville?" asked Dagleishe. "I've never seen you so distracted."

"I am. I am. Even better now. Miss Aughton, my apologies. How could I not recognize you. Does your presence mean that Miss Stillwater is here in London?" He was gathering his wits quickly.

"She is indeed," said Miss Aughton. She held her hand for his proper greeting kiss. "She volunteered to stay back and read her book while Captain Dagleishe escorted me on a walk this fine afternoon. Sir, I believe Miss Stillwater would allow me to say that she would be over the moon to see you. She had been close to distraught at her lack of letters. You can imagine where one's thoughts might go. What would you two dashing captains say to walking back to our rooms and fetching her for a nice meal this evening. Restaurants in London are open to all hours."

"Ho, ho. It's an excellent idea, and we'll walk you back, Miss Aughton," said Joseph, "but we'll not wait. I have learned that lesson. We shall return to collect you at half eight. Captain Burton and I will find a pub and spend some time catching up."

The two men had first gone to the *Sign of the Golden Pheasant* on Tottenham Court Road and arranged a room for Neville. There they had a pint and told their tales. They were surprised to find their ladies waiting and ready when they arrived at Stillwater's rooms.

Marion and Ellen both looked as beautiful as Neville could ever remember when they came down the stair to be escorted out. However, despite what Ellen had said about Marion's state of mind, Neville felt a slight awkward chill to her greeting. Small talk on the ride to supper was more formal than he had expected and seemed strained.

"Just there, coachman," said Joseph as the hack opened Kingsway Street from Aldwych. The hack jangled to a halt and the four stepped out into a surging crowd.

"Is it always like this?" Neville queried the group.

"We've not been here for a very long time," answered Joseph, "but this seems unusual, even for London...

"Excuse me, Sir," he said to a man hurrying past, "Hold on a minute. Can you tell me what's the hullabaloo?"

"You ain't heard? Admiral Nelson's here. He saved the Indies from an invasion by the French fleet, and he's chased them back into the Med, he has. He's come back to confer with the big brass, as it were – the King, maybe. They say the man himself is down this way. Come along, Cap'n!" He trotted down the street with the crowd.

"He's come back from the Indies, has he?" quipped Neville.

"Ha, ha! You'll have to tell us how that was done, Captain Burton. I'm particularly interested in the influence rum had on the conflict," laughed Marion.

"I shall tell a grand tale, then, but you ladies must tell me how you come to be here. I had the very distinct impression from Captain Dagleishe here that as long as you are here, he didn't ask and he doesn't care. Not that I blame him for the sentiment. Your father, Miss Stillwater, would only tell me that you'd 'gone to Europe'. And in his version, 'selling rum' was only implied. He also wouldn't say if Mr. Stearns had gone with you. I have been most concerned."

"Oh, really," Marion said, "Yet you couldn't find a way to write me. And I do know what you did to Mr. Stearns?" They were swallowed for a time by the noise and bustle of the restaurant. *So is that it? She's only annoyed about not getting letters? Surely she didn't mind seeing Mr. Stearns get stuck in the arm. But then he told the story differently, didn't he? Or is it that she doesn't want to discuss her business — why she's here, or who she's here to see?*

To Neville's dismay, small talk continued before starters. Between starters and the first course, however, he was more than pleased to see Joseph and Ellen paying less and less attention to anything but themselves. In the middle of a crowd, he then felt much more alone with Marion. He could finally say, "I've missed you. I thank you for writing, but I can't say the letters didn't make me miss you more."

"I've missed you, too, Cap... Neville, but there are some things we must talk about..."

"The duel was not my idea. It was Mr. Stearns who threw down the challenge."

"I suspected that. He had it coming, then."

"Not writing, then? I didn't have a current address..."

"It's not the letters, either. I understand the difficulty of keeping up with addresses when people don't stay put. It's my business. This trip is my idea, not father's."

"But you're willing to talk it out with me?"

"As best I can-" There she paused, and blushed at some thought. "-and share somewhat more than that. Like they do," she said, giving a little nod indicating Ellen and Joseph, obviously lost in their own little world across the table. She leaned close to his ear. "They are smitten, Sir," she managed with a little giggle.

"How do you manage if your handmaiden is off on her own business?" he asked quietly.

"I don't need that much to manage. We're Americans, you remember, and I'm a capable woman, after all. And please don't think of her as my handmaiden. She's much more than that to me. She's quite the lady, don't you think?"

"She is indeed. I might chase after her myself if... ow!"

"Oh, here's the soup..."

A light fish course followed, and then one of duck. Joseph and Ellen retreated for a time to their own planet. "Do you have a room, Neville?" Marion asked.

"I have both a flat and a room," he answered, "but the flat is under the hand of a decorator for a few days. The room is in a little pub on Tottenham Court Road, near where we met."

"A flat here in London. I'll be interested to see that."

"Marion, I could never ask you over there."

"By myself alone, you mean, don't you?"

"I'm sorry. I certainly could have you come with..."

"That's not what I had in mind, either. I know you wouldn't suppose impropriety , which is why I'm making the suggestion. But it can't be for a few days, anyway, if you know what I mean," she concluded with a wink.

"There will be a smell of paint, for sure."

"Oh, Neville, you are simply pitiful."

Four days later, Neville had moved from the pub to his flat. It wasn't exactly as he had pictured it, and a smell of paint and turpentine still permeated the place, even with the windows open, but it was now at least livable. A knock had come at the door at about three in the afternoon, and he opened the door to find Marion and Ellen standing there. Marion was carrying a larger purse than he had seen before, as was Ellen, which struck him as odd.

"Ladies, good afternoon. Please come in; see my new home. I can't offer an afternoon tea, I'm afraid, but I think I have a bottle of sherry. Perhaps you'd rather have some lemonade this warm afternoon? No Captain Dagleishe?"

"He's waiting for me in the hack," Ellen said, "I'm not staying. I am sure you can see Miss Stillwater home."

"Go on and find the sherry, Neville. I'll be right along."

Neville went, suddenly feeling a touch of nervousness, but he could hear most of their conversation around the corner.

"Be careful," Ellen said, and "I envy him,".

"You should. He'll be..."

He thought they kissed, as women do. Marion said, "Tomorrow, then. Lunch?"

The door closed and Marion appeared in the sitting area.

"Glasses, Neville said. I've found the sherry, and now I must find glasses."

"They are just over there," she said, "in plain sight." She walked toward him, crossing the space remaining between them in only four steps. "Let me have that," she said.

He handed her the bottle and she placed it on a handy coffee table. Then she pushed her body against his and moved his arms around her. She looked up into his eyes, and said, "Neville, I must admit that I am not here for the sherry. I am here for you to make love to me. Neville, take my virginity before I'm an old woman."

Marion's dress was floor length and made of a relatively thin light blue fabric. Its neck was a great V shape, displaying the skin of her neck, which was rapidly gaining a pink hue, almost to the shoulders. A bright yellow sash was tied high below her breasts, with a large bow on the left side.

Neville leaned down to kiss her waiting lips; he stroked her back and pulled her tightly to him. She did the same, and their lips and bodies remained glued together for several minutes.

"Marion, how could you claim to be an old woman. Your beauty takes my breath away."

"I'm twenty-three now. I need you to keep me young."

"I think I have wanted you since the first time I saw you at the New Year's party two years ago," Neville finally said.

"I thought you interesting, too, and I mentioned you to Father the next day. He would have none of it. 'A navy man must be at least a captain', he said. I am glad you were there last year. After that I knew I wanted you. Pull the bow, Neville," she said. You may have as much of me as you would like. There is nobody here but us, I assume."

He pulled the bow, as requested. It had been tied simply, like a gift-ribbon, and when it opened the sash fell to the floor.

"May I?" he asked, slipping his fingers beneath the shoulder of her dress.

"Please."

Neville pushed the two sides of the neck outward and, as he suspected, the neck was wide enough when opened to pass over her shoulders. The blue fabric fluttered to the floor, leaving Marion standing with a sheer white petticoat. Her remaining garment did not leave the shape of her breasts or her nipples, hardened by the chill air, to his imagination. He ran his hands down her back again, taking hold of her buttocks and pulling her up to him. He held her hips hard against his and kissed her again. She wriggled her feet out of her simple shoes; he carried her to his bed.

Once there she pulled off her petticoat and displayed her naked body in the most suggestive way she could imagine while he fumbled his way out of his multi-buttoned uniform. "Am I as you expected?" she asked.

"Much more," he answered. "Every part of you is beautiful. Even your feet are pretty." He removed his tunic and shirt. "You wrote me some time ago," he said, "that 'seeing is believing'." He sat and pulled off his shoes, then removed his trousers.

"It is, don't you think?" she queried. "And I like what I see."

"As do I; but I must add, however," Neville continued, "that I further believe that 'feeling is God's honest truth'". He slid down on top of her, his tongue on one nipple and then the next. One hand hand slid up between her thighs. Marion gave little gasp, tipped her head back and arched up to him. She was already wet, and he kissed her neck while he increased her desire to take him in. Finally he could not delay longer. He pushed her wider and they coupled for the first time. Marion's body trembled and they began a rhythmic pulsing, harder and deeper, each giving away everything. They did not stop; could not stop themselves long into the night, finally falling asleep intertwined and thoroughly spent.

At about three in the morning, Neville woke enough to be aware of his situation. He felt the warmth of his lover, running his hands over every part of her. He finally slid his hand up Marion's naked thigh into the warmth in the center of her.

"Oh, you're a wicked brute," she murmured, running her hand down his chest and past his belly to where he was stiffening. He rolled over on top of her and they began again.

"It was your idea, you remember." He entered her slowly.

"I could get used to this," she said quietly, when he rolled off again.

It was light when they woke the next time. The first Neville knew was the weight of her warm body on top of him. The feel of her smooth bare skin roused him again. She encouraged him to find more strength before breakfast.

They met Dagleishe and Aughton for lunch; all were in a warm and glowing mood despite a north-sea blow that had London awash with rain under the cover of dark clouds.

"After this terrible weather I'll be looking forward to a nice warm bed," said Marion, with a wink to Ellen, "but first we must find this captain some proper civilian clothes."

"Do you find Joseph fashionable?" Ellen asked. "We found a shop over on Carnaby…"

When the meal was finished and Captain Dagleishe took Miss Aughton away with some errand as the excuse, Marion asked, "How would you like to see my rooms at the *Saxon Arms*? We can't spend all our time in your flat. You have no food, no cook, and no restaurant on site. We can go to my suite. It is splendid being here in London. Nobody knows me anywhere I go. Nobody knows you are not my proper escort – or even my husband for that matter. Nobody even watches to see who goes upstairs with whom, unless special security arrangements are made. They suppose us all to be adults."

"And in Washington?"

"The same, I assume. Worse, perhaps. It might almost be expected that there is something going on behind every closed door. Why would you ask that? I have told you that I've never met another man that has had any attraction for me."

"What of Miss Aughton? Will she be with us?"

"She, my dear Neville, will be wherever Captain Dagleishe takes her. And I have no doubt that he will take her. 'Take', if you get my meaning. We'll be quite alone. You don't mind, do you?"

"Father would never approve of any of this," she said inside her hotel room after they had taken an afternoon tea. "He allowed me to travel because I behaved so well in Washington. I'm older and more responsible now," she added with her most winsome grin. "I have

Ellen now, too. Despite our liaisons today, I deem her far more trustworthy than Mr. Stearns. I think father was starting to doubt the wisdom of pushing Mr. Stearns and I together and then sending us off as though I was safe with him. I'll have to admit to becoming more concerned, although I said nothing about it to father."

I can't tell her that he tried to shoot me.

"I think a little aperitif would be in order," she said. "There's a bottle in that cupboard, and I have glasses. See them there? I'll be back in just a minute."

Marion's suite at the *Saxon Arms* was opulent, yes, but at the same time somewhat spartan. Nobody really lived there, after all. He found a bottle of some amber fluid that he did not recognize, and two glasses, and carried them to a small table by the windows. Along the wall past the windows was a small writing desk. It looked as if Marion had been writing, and he knew she wasn't writing to him, so he was curious. A crumpled ball of paper lay on the floor beside a tiny wastebasket. That in itself seemed very unlikely for Marion, whom he knew by now to be an extremely tidy person, so he picked it up. He opened it rather absent-mindedly without intention of being nosy, and pressed it flat. What he found was almost enough to make his skin crawl.

It's a letter from Stearns; meeting arrangements in Paris, not Brest. The French Navy yards were in Brest, not Paris. Why were there meeting arrangements in Paris. And what meeting? Marion and Stearns or Marion and some customer? An old memory surfaced: a memory of a letter he had carried from Toulon. The letter was from M. Stillwater to someone in Paris. Was it from 'Monsieur Stillwater' or from 'Marion Stillwater'? *What do I do now? Do I confront her with this? She'll throw me out. Of all things, I don't want that! Do I ignore it? Am I feeling jealousy?*

"What have you there, Neville?" said Marion. He jumped. She was only two feet away, wearing a far more simple gown than she had been before. Very simple. Almost nothing to it.

"Neville, what are you doing? That's mine!"

"Marion. It was on the floor all crumpled up. I just picked it up. Verily, I wasn't snooping on you."

She was angry, he could tell, but she was controlling herself; not something he expected. She stood staring at him, arms akimbo. "Neville, I…" she began. Her face was turning red. She looked to be feeling something other than angry. Neville knew his face was red. It wasn't hot in the room. "I need to discuss something with you."

"Is it Stearns?" he asked, waving the letter at her.

"That idiot?" she spat. She snatched the letter, crumpled it up again and threw it at the wastebin. It missed. "That's why it was there. It belongs there. The fool can't stay out of my business." Tears were forming in her eyes. One dripped down a cheek.

Neville opened his arms to invite her hug.

"No," She said tersely, "Not until we talk. You may not want me after we do."

"I can't imagine that."

"If you weren't in the navy, it might make no difference to you, but I put you in a terrible spot. You know why I'm here?"

"You haven't aid, but it is logical to assume your plan is to sell rum to the French. You are right that it is a problem for me, so I think I decided not to ask. Frankly, I don't think I care if the Frogs have rum aboard their ships, although I hear they prefer wine. Their men are like ours; they have little else for comfort. Forbidding them rum does nothing to help our country win the war. Verily, if you can carry some money out of their country, it might be to our benefit. Our government don't see it that way, though. It's called 'trading with the enemy'. But since you're an American, probably the worst they would do is throw you out of England – and Jamaica, by the way - and forbid you to return. I think you should not tell me. What must I do, if I know?

In truth, she is a lucky girl. What she tells me will go no further than Sir William. With anyone else, it might send her to the gallows until they sent her home. He shuddered to think of that.

An awful thought struck him. "Does Dagleishe know? What does Miss Aughton know?"

"Ellen tells me he knows none of it, and I only tell her the basic travel plans. He has not found a letter, and like you, he would not want to know either. I did not jest when I said they were smitten."

"Who are you meeting in France, and where?"

She was angry again, "That stupid, gormless man!" she exclaimed. "The navy yards are in Brest, yet he writes that he is making arrangements to meet in Paris. And he's going to be there? What is he thinking? Does he think at all? Why does father keep him? I should let him go to Paris and visit Napoleon himself."

"Why wouldn't you go where your business takes you and let him go where he wants? Why should you bother to set him to rights?"

Her performance regarding Stearns was enough to allay some of his jealousy concerns, but what about the danger to her of having him near her in France?

"Father would be angry, I'm sure. And Neville, I am now almost embarrassed to tell you that this whole thing was my idea – my plan to make father stop pushing Mr. Stearns at me, stop him from giving my birthright – the Stillwater Rum Trading Company – to Stearns through marriage to me. I don't need him."

"Why do you say 'almost embarrassed'?"

"Because, while it makes our relationship exceedingly awkward, it is a good plan for the rum company, is it not?" she said with an irrepressible little grin. "Also, as you would clearly understand, French men would find this salesperson irresistible, would they not?" She held her arms out to the side displaying herself. Her mood seemed suddenly lighter, most probably for getting this off her chest to Neville. With a naughty grin, she unbuttoned her top button.

"You little trollop," he said, and grabbed her around the waist. "You wouldn't dare use your wiles… would you?"

"Only on you, Captain," she said, pressing close onto him.

Neville wasn't quite finished with his inquisition, but he didn't let her go. He could feel the warmth of her body through the thin gown – and her shape. "All right, so why are you here in London, then, and not France? An American can travel straight to France with no problems – just not from Jamaica. The US and France are not at war."

"Time, Neville. Just time. I must have a letter of invitation from the government of France for them to let me in. If I wait in the United States it will take months for the letter to go there and find me, for me to make travel arrangements, and then to travel to France. Even worse from Jamaica. It is not my intention for this trip to last a year. Here I am now, a single day's sail from France. As soon as I receive my letter, I am off."

'But you cannot sail from here to France. Again, I remind you that we are at war." He ran his hand down her back. There was nothing beneath her 'gown'.

"I cannot sail from here to France? Again I place you in a pickle, Neville. Smugglers go every day, and you know it, although you in the navy try to stop it. You would think nothing of finding a nice cognac in the bar downstairs. It should be child's play to find a ship - or a small boat, for that matter. My letter will certainly come by smuggler, and…"

"What is it?"

"And it could come any day. I have been here a month already. Then I will need to run, as you must when your ship is ready."

"I am well aware. This has been the most wondrous week of my life. It will end soon. There is not much time before *La Désirée* will be out of ordinary, and there will scarce be time for good-byes. Even now I should be checking in with the Admiralty every day. From what you tell me, though, if you do not have in invitation soon you might as well pack for the return to Jamaica. I would rather see you do that. It would end my conflict between knowing you trade with my enemy and loving every inch of you."

"Oh, Neville, we must make arrangements to meet again. We must. Make love to me again - now." She put her hand behind his neck and pulled his lips down to hers.

Neville awoke in the morning before Marion. He tried not to move, though, happy to watch her face in peaceful slumber. She wore a slight smile – and nothing else, he knew. That made his concentration more difficult. *How much of what she has said should I believe? Is she simply an excellent actress? I understand why she doesn't want me to know much about the business, but what about the Stearns part? Can there be anything there? Would she deceive me?*

He was becoming too excited to let her sleep. He ran his hands over her warm naked body. When she stirred and rolled towards him, he put his face between her breasts. She hugged his head and snaked her legs around his. They made love yet again, slowly and quietly.

Neither Marion's letter of invitation nor Neville's orders to return to Chatham did came. With Neville's new civilian clothes, they entered a new world as unknown young lovers in a large city. They strolled the parks and met Joseph and Ellen for lunches and dinners and they made love at night. And they waited, knowing the end was coming soon.

A knock came at the door of Marion's hotel suite some days later when the four were playing at cards. They shared knowing glances, and the knock came a second time. Neville rose, walked to the door and opened it to find the expected bellboy in a blue and gray uniform. He handed in an envelope addressed to 'M. Stillwater'.

"I think the two of you should take it in your chambers," said Neville to Marion. She and Ellen left the two captains at the table.

"Ours can't be far behind, Joseph. Have you no news of a ship?"

"I have orders, Neville," he patted his jacket pocket, "A frigate, the *Galatea*."

"And you're not already gone?"

"I put it off as long as I could. I can't think about life without Ellen. We have agreed to wed; we just don't know when that could be – or where. I am not late, but I have little time. I shall run now, like the wind. She will leave with Marion soon now."

The two women emerged from Marion's chambers looking solemn. Both appeared to have shed tears.

"We have our invitations. We will leave tomorrow noon," said Marion very resolutely.

"Come Joseph," said Ellen, holding out her hand. He stood, and they left to enjoy what little time remained.

"This sales idea of yours, Marion – what is it, exactly?"

"I can't give you all the details, Neville. You don't want to hear all the details. You haven't taken this much interest in weeks. Why now?"

"Because now I know for sure that you are going."

"Let's not talk of this now. I'd like nothing more than another supper at that little place we found off Aldwych the first night, and to lie with you one more night."

Half an hour after noon Neville closed the carriage door behind Ellen. Marion was already inside, sitting quietly with a resolute face. Both were in traveling clothes, with their daggers conspicuously strapped at their belts. Neville gathered his best spirits and said, "Goodbye ladies. Be careful. You have my love. I'll see you in Jamaica." He slapped the carriage twice, announcing to the coachman that his passengers were loaded. The driver snapped his whip and grunted something like "G'up." The carriage jerked and then lurched forward, and they were gone.

With mixed emotions, Neville stood at the curb watching the coach clatter out of sight down the busy street. While his heart felt the pangs of her departure, several events in the last few days had been enough to make him suspicious of Marion's trip. He also couldn't get the idea of Stearns out of his head. *Why would Stearns go? Maybe Chester doesn't even know Sterns is going — thinks he's in the USA? Is this just a very exotic getaway for the two of them, and she didn't want anyone, especially me, to know?*

He had considered sneaking aboard her ship as a deckhand in order to follow her. His French was probably good enough. He decided against it as being too much risk for a British Navy captain. He would surely be hanged as a spy if discovered. His orders would arrive soon, anyway, and he couldn't miss his own ship.

I have one option left, he thought. *I will contact Sir Mulholland with my latest information and request Georges' help. The two of them will know what to do.*

15 - "New York"

"**G**ood day, Mr. Stillwater," said Stearns. He slid himself into Chester's side chair at the Rum Company office.

"Good day, Michael," said Chester. "I thought you were doing well, but you look rather tired today. Do you still have the fever?"

"No, it has gone. It broke some time ago, and I think that's done, but today I'm just tired, I suppose. You have Marion going to finish the navy contracts?"

"Yes, we cannot skip a year with the navy."

"I could go back. I should be well enough soon."

"The way you look, I think you should wait a bit. She is ready to leave in just a few weeks. She has Miss Aughton for a companion, and she certainly knows our business. Another month or so, when you are better, not just thinking you will be better soon, we can talk of a different sort of sales trip: to the spirits wholesaling companies in New York."

Stearns knew this was a compromise, but it was better than being stuck in Jamaica without Marion about. He would have preferred to leave on the same ship as Marion. But he could go wherever he wanted after he left Chester's watchful eye.

Marion and Ellen went aboard their ship on the seventh of November and sailed for Washington on the morning tide. Mr. Stearns did not follow until the *Star of Brighton* sailed for New York after the New Year. His health had been regained. The only thing left of Neville's insult was a scar on the front and back of his right shoulder. He and Chester had agreed on the accounts he was to visit in New York. Most had been sent letters of introduction, but no replies had been received. None had been expected in a mere two months.

Stearns' passage north was not eventful. The ship was British, so there was little to fear from enemy aggression. The beautiful Caribbean winter weather carried the ship easily north to Florida, except for a rather boisterous bash through the Windward Passage. The 'Christmas Trades' were acting up, he was told by the captain at a dinner function with the officers. Atlantic gales were the concern for sailing north, up the coast in the late American winter.

The *Star of Brighton* docked in February on the East River at the Front Street Pier in a light snowfall, leaving Stearns to wonder why he had thought it a good idea to follow in Marion's wake. He wasn't concerned, however, since his plan all along had been to immediately find a ship back south to Washington. Certainly Marion would be pleased to see him. It was inevitable, after all. He could always return for this business after his personal affairs were conducted.

Stearns located an American coastal lumber freighter the next day and secured a tiny cabin for the passage that should have taken less than a week down the Atlantic seaboard and back up the Chesapeake Bay. Although he was told there was a relatively good road from New York to Washington through Philadelphia and Baltimore, with regular coach service, Stearns was not of a mind to try it in the snows of winter. As fate would have it, the same winter storm that dropped two feet of snow on those roads also was accompanied by gales at sea that delayed the freighter's departure for over a week.

On March second Stearns stepped off the freighter and found a hack for the ride to the Capital City Rooming House on Pennsylvania Avenue.

"Good afternoon, Sir," said the reception clerk when Stearns entered, brushing the drops of a fine rain off his cloak.

"Good afternoon," he said, "Would you kindly inform Miss Stillwater that she has a visitor."

"Oh, no, Sir, I cannot. I'm sorry."

"Why not?" Stearns interrupted, "You do know who I mean, don't you?"

"Oh, certainly, Sir. It is difficult not to notice such a beautiful young lady, but I…"

"Why then, will you not inform her that I am here?"

"Sir, I mean no disrespect. I was simply trying to tell you that she is no longer here... gone almost two months now."

"No longer here? Where did she go? Home to Jamaica?"

"No, I don't think so, Sir. She left a forwarding address. Just a moment." *My God! All this way for nothing? Did I just miss her arrival in Kingston?*

"Here it is, Sir. The *Saxon Arms* in London."

"London?" *Why on earth would Marion go to London?*

"Yes, Sir. Here's a bit of paper and a quill. You may copy it."

"Thank you. And I'll need a room."

Stearns stepped into his room at the Capital City Rooming House on Pennsylvania Avenue and closed the door. The room was spacious and warm, with a reasonable view from the window. The building was not far from either the Navy Yard or the capital. *I can see why she stays here,* he thought. *First I must see to my letters; one to Marion and one to Mr. Stillwater. Mr. Stillwater will tell me why she's gone to London, won't he?*

While unpacking he made the decision not to chase after Marion. If she had been gone from Washington for two months, then where might she be? The whole thing could be an exercise in nonsense – a wild goose chase. He found his travel quill and ink and began a letter to Chester. He had only written two lines before he realized that his letter would announce to Chester that he had gone to Washington rather than New York as they had agreed. Furthermore, Chester may not know why Marion went to London. Could that be? Why wouldn't he know?

He put the letter to Chester aside. It would have to wait until he had done some work on the New York accounts – which, from here, would have to be in the form of letter-writing. Fter waiting a while, he could report that he had received no response from Marion in Washington.

He began a letter to Marion. There would be nothing lost if it never reached her, and everything gained if she responded.

Stearns spent the next week, when the weather permitted, following up on the navy yard accounts in the wake of Marion. It was the logical thing to do, and he had plenty of time. He found everything in order. At the end of the week he found himself in a bar near the navy yard having a pint and grumbling to the man on the next stool. They were just two lonely travelling salesmen.

"A duel, you say," said his neighbor, "I didn't think people did such things anymore."

"It seemed the right thing at the time," said Stearns. "I had hoped it would get that bloody Brit out of my hair for good."

"But you got a hole in your shoulder for your efforts, did you? Where has the lady gone now?"

"She was here. I chased her here, you see, but now she's gone to London, and who knows why?"

"Maybe she's gone after that navy fellow."

My God! Could that be? Stearns rolled that thought over in his head and took another sip of his beer, "I can't believe she would do that," he said. *But she might.* "Her father wouldn't approve at all."

"What fathers don't know won't hurt 'em, they say."

"They say all sorts of things, don't they. If that were true then I'm back to playing second fiddle at every turn."

"Go get her, then. There's nothin' else for it," his neighbor concluded. "That's enough for me tonight," He threw a dollar on the bar, grabbed his coat, and departed.

I have no reason to stay here. I should go work the New York accounts, thought Stearns in the morning. *But I'm in Washington. I might as well take advantage of it; I'm not getting any younger.*

"Michael Stearns to see Mr. William Fordson, if you please," he announced to the clerk inside the Navy Yard.

"You're in luck, Sir. Here he comes down the hall; and I believe his schedule is clear for the next hour or so."

Stearns turned to see the man enter the office where he stood, and put out his hand, "Good morning, Mr. Fordson," he said, "Michael Stearns."

Fordson shook his hand as he would a thousand others that year, and returned a blank stare. "Oh, right," he said after a moment searching his memories, "The one who almost botched the Marseille thing a few years back. Yes, I remember you. I thought we passed you to Roger Townsend. What can I do for you today?" *Always the politician.*

Stearns winced at Fordson's recollection. He had hoped it was forgotten. "Yes, you did pass me to Townsend," he said, "and I have been working with him a few years now. Shipping information from Jamaica, you know. But what I came for... can we talk more privately?"

"Certainly... in here," said Fordson, gesturing to a small conference room.

Inside the little room, with the door shut, Stearns continued: "I don't feel that I am contributing to this country in any significant way, Mr. Fordson. My purpose in Jamaica is less now than it was when I got there. There is less friction between the French and the British simply because the British have all but taken over."

"So?"

"So, the information I provide is worth less than it was, if ever it was worth much to begin with. In short, I'm not as satisfied in Jamaica as I was, and I feel I can make a much bigger contribution. I'd like another chance, whether it's in Britain or in France. Can you find me a more active role? I've been trained for it. I can speak French."

"I get your meaning, Sir, but at the moment our government has no interest in sponsoring any clandestine activities against either of these countries. President Jefferson is not in favor of such activities... His position is that we remain neutral. We have no need for new personnel at this time."

"What if I told you I could sell certain products of this country to, say, France, but that to do so I would need to make connections you already have? Would you be interested in giving a small amount of assistance to a commercial enterprise?"

"If it is truly commercial, it might be possible. Exactly what are we talking about?"

"Rifles. We aren't at war with France, as you have said. It might come back at the British, but not at us, correct?"

"I'll need more specifics."

"Are you sure you want to know? I'll need connections."

"Come back tomorrow. I'll write a few things down for you."

"Write things down? When did you begin doing that?"

"Just checking, Mr. Stearns. Do you have the specifics with you?"

"No. I'll come back."

"I'll have some names."

Michael Stearns had not had any conversation about the Harper's Ferry Armory with Chester Stillwater, but he had also observed the engraved glass award on Chester's shelf. The implication was clear. Chester wasn't selling just rum, but he had not thought to include Stearns in his dealings. It was time to strike out on his own. He couldn't be in a better position. Harper's Ferry was just forty-five miles up the Potomac. Even in bad weather, how long could it possibly take to travel up there and strike a deal as an independent sales agent? It will be late April, with most of the snow of winter behind them. He had the money to sail to France. With Fordson's connections he could find the buyers in France. He was a good salesman.

By the first of May, 1805, Michael Stearns was packing his personal items in his room at the Capital City Rooming House while whistling 'Yankee Doodle Dandy'. It just seemed the right tune to go with an unusual cheerfulness that had welled up within him. He had inked a deal with Harper's to sell their Model 1803 Flintlock Rifle to the French, 'if he thought he could accomplish such a thing'. They had given him a paper to that effect that he was able to show Mr. Fordson in exchange for French contacts. Having ample time before travelling to meet Marion in Paris, he had booked passage on a ship to New York City to conduct his planned business. Everything was going well. On top of all that, he had received a letter from Marion. *The post is amazing,* he thought. *Here to London and back in two months! Incredible!*

The Saxon Arms, London　　　　　　　*April 2, 1805*
Dear. Mr. Stearns,

I was quite surprised to find your letter of March 2 here at the hotel when I returned from touring the Cotswolds. Miss Aughton and I will have a quiet week here in London before we're off again. It is a simply lovely time to be here. I am so impressed with springtime in England – all the little flowers. I'm told it doesn't rain so much in East Anglia, so we shall tour there next. I so look forward to seeing Cambridge.

We will be back to London in time to see the museums and catch a symphony performance by this new composer Beethoven. We'll spend most of the summer here and then pop across the Channel to see some of France. I have always wanted to see Paris, so we should be there in early September if all goes well. Then we'll be heading back to work in Jamaica.

I assume father has you checking my work there in Washington, before you go on to New York, so don't let them wiggle out of any of it. I trust you enjoy the Capital Cities rooms… quite nice, what?

Sorry to be so wordy. Thanks for a note from 'home', and good luck in New York!

Cheers,
M. Stillwater

By the end of April, Stearns had visited all of his intended contacts in New York. He strode into the office of a shipping company that he had heard would take passengers to France.

"Good day, Sir," said the reception clerk, "Freight to ship?"

"Only myself, if you have a berth," said Stearns.

"To where, Sir?"

"Marseille, France. Do you ship there?"

"Hmm. That depends."

"Depends on what?"

"On whether you are willing to take the risk that you cannot land in France. The British navy has had a blockade in place for several years. Their main purpose is to prevent the French navy from escaping their ports, but they will also board and confiscate anything they consider contraband. Do you plan to carry anything?"

"Not this trip."

"We'll not refund your fare if you can't land, but it might be possible to arrange some other method for landing if needed – at your expense."

"I see. You have a berth?"

"*Lady Spencer*... Master is... Reynolds... End of the month."

"Write my name in. I'll come back with the fare."

Van Aken House   *18th May, 1805*
New York, City, New York, U.S.A.

Dear Mr. Stillwater,

I am pleased to report quite good success on my visit to New York. Enclosed is my report detailing the same and copies of the orders I have secured on behalf of the Stillwater Rum Trading Company from various wholesalers here.

I have not received any correspondence from you, and so in the absence of any direction to the contrary, I pray you will not mind my taking a short holiday for a visit to Paris. It is a place I have always wanted to see, and I would not be able to travel from British Jamaica to France.

I am booked on a ship leaving here at the end of May, and it is bad enough that I am told an American vessel may be denied landing.

I also took the opportunity to visit Washington and confirm that the orders that Marion took from there are still in place. I hope you have heard from her and that she is well.

My Best Regards,   **Mic. Stearns**

Van Aken House   *18ᵗʰ May, 1805*
New York, City, New York
United States of America

Dear Miss Stillwater,

I have not received any correspondence from your father, and so in the absence of any directions to the contrary, I pray you will not mind my taking a short holiday to visit you in Paris. It is a place I have also always wanted to see, and I can travel directly from here. I would not be able to sail to France from British Jamaica, so the convenience is significant.

I am booked on a ship leaving here at the end of May, and it is bad enough that I am told an American vessel may be denied landing.

Once I land in Marseille I will make the necessary contacts to meet you and conduct other business I have in mind while I am there.

I so look forward to seeing you.

My Best Regards,   **Mic. Stearns**

P.S. also took the opportunity to visit Washington and confirm that the orders that you took from there are still in place. I hope you have heard from your father and that he is well.

A near gale was blowing off the New Jersey coast when the American schooner *Lady Spencer* emerged from the Hudson's River Bay south of the city and passed through the narrows into the Sandy Hook Channel. The wind was fair for their sail into the North Atlantic, which held the seas to a mere six or seven feet.

"It has been an enjoyable experience, no?" said fellow passenger Charles Mason of Pennsylvania when *Lady Spencer* neared the Balearic Islands.

"Yes, indeed," answered Stearns, "The beginning was not so nice when we left in that gale, and the thunderstorms where we crossed the Florida current were not comfortable, but the approaches to the Azores were as fine as I could imagine a sea voyage to be…

"And the size of the rock at Gibraltar was astounding. I am already glad I came this way."

"Did the master say how much longer we should expect until we reach Marseille?"

"What he said yesterday was that once we leave Mallorca to larboard we should have only another two days. Then he added, 'if the weather holds'. Ha ha. He always adds that."

"Sail, ho!" cried a lookout from above.

"I see him, Mr. Stone," the master yelled back.

Stearns and Mason sauntered back to where the master stood by the wheel. "Why did the lookout cry out, Master Reynolds? We have seen many a sail without he calls down."

"What he's comin' straight for us, ain't he?' answered Reynolds, "And he's British. He'll probably board us and go pokin' round our men to see if there's any he can take, and then snoop in the hold for anything he thinks we shouldn't have aboard. It's a bloody nuisance, at the least."

"**G**ood afternoon, Master," said *Phoebe's* captain. "I am Captain Capel of His Britannic Majesty's Royal Navy. Thank you for heaving to." *Lady Spencer* was tied alongside the British frigate, and Captain Capel stood on her deck with two marines and his first lieutenant behind him. There had not been much choice for Master Reynolds. *Phoebe* had the advantage of speed and firepower. Once she was in range she ran out her guns, and *Lady Spencer* let fly her sheets.

"Didn't have much choice, did I, captain?" said *Lady Spencer's* master, "What with you ready to make splinters of us."

Captain Capel gave him an unfriendly leer. "We're returning to Toulon from Gibraltar. Where are you bound?"

"Marseille."

"We have a blockade on French ports. Were you aware?"

"The United States is a neutral country. We can trade where we please. You have no right to…"

"Some say 'might makes right'. Would you not agree?"

"We didn't agree twenty-five years ago. Why should we now?" responded *Lady Spencer's* master, looking Captain Capel directly in the eye.

"Just so, I suppose. We have no quarrel with your country, sir – just with those who would assist our enemies. What is your cargo?"

"Only staples and passengers."

"We'll take a look for ourselves… and for deserters from our navy. Do you count any of those in your company?" Capel began casting his eye about the ship.

"All American, sir," shouted a crewman.

"Call them up in their divisions, then. We'll have a look…

"Lieutenant, send two marines below to investigate the cargo."

The master paused for several moments, staring at Captain Capel, before he said, "Call them up, Mr. Wilbur. I think we have no choice."

Captain Capel began with a look at Stearns and Mason, and apparently decided they were of no interest as sailors. "What business do you have in France?" he asked them.

"Sales," said Stearns. "Tobacco and rum." He didn't think they would like to hear his idea of selling rifles. "And a visit to the famous Paris."

"Hrrrmmph…

"And you?"

"Food," said Mr. Mason. "If the people wish to eat, we have corn and wheat to sell. We will sell to the British, as well."

That answer ended Capel's interest in the passengers. He turned his attention to the two lines of eight men whom Reynolds had called. He walked down the first line, stopping in front of each man and asking his name.

"Thomas," said the fifth man in response to Capel's question.

Capel's lieutenant looked at the man steadily while Thomas nervously avoided his gaze.

"Yes," said the lieutenant finally. "It is Thomas, isn't it? It's Thomas Morton. You served with me when I was a midshipman on the *Amethyst* some years ago. You're no American. You're one of ours."

"No, I ain't. Not no more," spat Thomas. "I've been in Boston these fourdeen year and I has American citizenship, I has."

"By your law, maybe. Not by ours. If you were born in England, you're English, and that's that. Stand over there." He pointed to the sally port, where two more marines stood with their muskets at port arms.

"Master Reynolds, have you more like this, who claim American citizenship?"

"Not that I will volunteer to the likes of a pirate," Reynolds answered.

"Here's two here!" yelled one of the marines who had gone below to inspect the cargo. "I found these two hiding under the corn." They climbed the ladder to the deck, and the marine shoved the two men roughly toward Captain Capel.

"I won't even bother to ask questions," said Capel to Reynolds. "Innocent men don't hide…

"Stand there with that other deserter."

Capel's review of *Lady Spencer's* men concluded with yet a fourth man that he had sent to the sally port. He then turned to the men now grouped by the sally port, and asked, "You four. Do you volunteer to return to your duties in His Majesty's Navy, or shall I hang you here for desertion?"

"Captain, Capel," began Master Reynolds, "My men are not yours to take. You can…"

"I can what, Master Reynolds? Hang them for desertion? Is that what you prefer I do?"

"No, I was certainly not suggesting…"

"Then I will do as I please with English citizens, and you may stand aside.

"You four. Do you volunteer?"

All four nodded silently, knowing that Captain Capel's alternative was not negotiable. Thomas Morton looked as if he were about to cry and one of the others was visibly trembling.

"That's all, then, Master Reynolds. Good Day," said Capel, and indicated to his lieutenant his intention to depart.

"The Devil take you," said Reynolds. "Get off my ship."

16 - *"Cape Trafalgar"*

The longing in Neville's heart as *La Désirée* rose to the first swell outside the harbor would have been far worse if he didn't know that Marion was no longer in England. She should have been in some comfortable hotel in France for a week now. For all he knew she had conducted her business and was awaiting a ship home – or more likely to the United States.

"What was the news from the Spanish coast, Captain? Did you get anything more than the general rumors?" asked Lt. Towers.

"Not much, but I was officially told that Captain Blackwood of *HMS Euryalis*, who is in command of the frigates that Nelson has watching the coast, brought news to London just yesterday that Admiral Villeneuve has the combined French and Spanish fleets at Cadiz. *HMS Victory* is to be Nelson's flagship, and she isn't ready yet."

"We'll be in the thick of it, then. We sail to join the frigates."

The two stood near the binnacle casting the occasional eye to sea on larboard and to the green of England receding slowly to starboard.

"Every ship feels different, doesn't it, Lt. Towers?" said Neville. *La Désirée* leaned slightly to the pressure of a light northeast breeze. Ever-larger waves rolled beneath the hull once they cleared the shoals at the Nore.

"True, but I have been aboard this one for two years now," said Towers, "I'm not sure I can remember the feeling of another ship."

Neville made no further comment on the subject, but watched the bow rise and fall outside the harbor.

"Set a course to clear the North Foreland, Mr. Worth. Ushant and the Bay of Biscay after that."

"It's third of September, Sir. The weather should be reasonable."

"I don't count myself superstitious, Mr. Worth, but I really wish you hadn't said that...

Neville noticed that the land of France was visible this clear day. "Mr. Worth, how long would you estimate the average sailing time from London to Brest?"

"I'd say four or five days, Sir, all things considered – no storms or calms."

"That's what I would have said, too."

"Why's that then, Captain? Certainly we're not bound for Brest."

"No, no. Not unless you wish to die soon, or spend the rest of the war in one of Boney's prisons."

Marion said, 'It's only a day's sail to France, Neville remembered. *If she had already investigated travel possibilities, she must have known. The harbors for Paris are only a day's sail. Did she lie? Was Stearns' letter correct? Is she going to Paris? To meet him? Joseph had told me that he and Ellen were to wed. Why didn't Marion even speak of it? My Dear God, please let me have some misunderstanding.*

Neville stepped back aboard *La Désirée* after his visit to Vice-Admiral Collingwood's ship, the *Royal Sovereign.* He had not yet gotten completely used to being piped aboard an Admiral's flagship; bad memories lingered.

He saluted the colors aft, and then Lt. Towers, and said, "Call the officers to my cabin, if you would please, Mr. Towers. Senior warrants included, and the doctor."

When they had gathered there, Neville began his summary of the orders he had just received:

"The ships that were here when we arrived five days ago were indeed from the Channel Fleet," he said. "They are under Vice-Admiral Calder, and they were ordered here by Lord Cornwallis a month ago to join with Nelson's fleet – those with whom we sailed up from Jamaica.

"I count twenty-four ships of the line, but I've missed a few. Once Admiral Nelson arrives in *Victory* we are supposed to be at twenty-seven, plus we've five frigates, a schooner and one little cutter.

"How many enemy, Captain?" asked Lt. Coughlan.

"Ho, ho. Keep your eyes peeled, Lieutenant. That's the sort of thing we are supposed to find out. Just as many ships as we have, though, it is believed, maybe more; and some of the Spanish are larger than anything we have. If Villeneuve comes out we'll see a lot of smoke, won't we?"

"Aye, Sir."

"Our orders from Vice-Admiral Collingwood are to form the inshore squadron and patrol the harbor approaches with the other frigates. Once Captain Blackwood arrives in *Euryalis* he will be our Commodore. It is suspected that he will arrive with *Victory*.

"It was stated that Admiral Nelson will keep the fleet over the horizon in the hope that Villeneuve will come out. We are to keep our signaling to a minimum to further hide his presence, and communicate via *Pickle* and *Entreprenante* as best we can. They are the schooner and cutter."

"**W**hat do you think so far, Lt. Miller?"

"Of what, Captain?"

"Frigate duty. I know she's been a month in ordinary, and you've been… where?"

"Home, Sir, in Cornwall. Quite a treat, It was. I'm an uncle now."

"I'm pleased for you. I have my own nephew…

"You've been with us for the sail from Jamaica and a little time now completing for this cruise. Are you glad of the change from *Vanguard*?"

"I'll not go back to a ship of the line, Sir. Maybe when I'm a captain, but otherwise it's all chores and little else. We had a few good goes in the Caribbean, though, I must admit."

"You did for sure. A bit of prize money never hurts. How do you find your cabin, then?"

"Small," said Miller.

"Did you see blockade duty on *Vanguard* before I came aboard?"

"Not before, but at Saint-Domingue, Sir, as you know, and that was rather loose, as I understand it."

"You may yet change your mind about a frigate. We've only been inshore here for a week – and we've had good weather."

"Sail, Ho!" cried the lookout, "Starboard beam."

"Ours, Mr. Clark?" Neville yelled back.

"Looks to be an English frigate, Sir."

"Carry on, Mr. Clark."

"I expect this to be *Euryalis*, then, and we won't see *Victory*. She'll stay fifty miles off or so with the rest of them. Pass word for Mr. Wynde to have his mates to be ready with my gig, if you would please." *My gig. Ha, ha! I have a proper gig instead of a little jolly boat.*

The weather had remained mild, with light winds, so it took a good three hours before *Euryalis* was bobbing, sails aback, with the other frigates.

Where would Marion be now? Halfway across the Atlantic on her way home?

"Signal, Sir. 'Repair to flag'."

"Sway out the gig, if you please. I'll soon know what Captain Blackwood would have us do."

"**P**ass word in the gunroom, if you would, please, Lt. Towers. There was only one small thing in the news," said Neville after he had come aboard, saluted the colors, and touched his hat to the man. "Everything is as expected. The combined fleet of French and Spanish are here in Cadiz, Blackwood is appointed to command, we continue inshore as we have been doing, and our orders are to keep the admiral informed of any and every movement of the enemy."

"What's new, then? Why did he call you over?"

"Ah, yes, that. We are to paint all the insides of our ports a bright yellow. When they are all open our ships will display black-and-yellow checked hulls so we should not be firing upon ourselves. You'd best get to work on that while this fair weather holds."

The weather held fair. The frigates paraded back and forth before the harbor entrance while their companies painted.

"It's a 'moon dog', Captain," said Lt. Miller just before sundown a week later. Neville had been pacing the quarterdeck, watching the moonbeams twinkle across the waves and thinking of Marion. *Where will she be now? Arrived in the United States yet, or still upon the sea, watching this same moon as I see here?*

Neville glanced skyward at the large pale yellow rings encircling the moon. "So I see. And cirrus clouds all day. Have you seen many 'moon dogs'?"

"I haven't, Sir. I was not long at sea before *Vanguard* sailed to the Caribbean. Before *Vanguard* I was in a coastal cutter out of Great Yarmouth. Weather' different up there, Sir, and you don't stay out much."

"Mr. Worth wished us good weather across the Bay of Biscay, but we've had nothing I would call unusual. Three more days, Lieutenant, and we'll be battening the hatches, you'll see. Just the thing for a blockade, ain't it? I'm told we're at full strength now. The last of the frigates was *Phoebe*. We have her, us, *Euryalis*, *Naiad* and *Sirius*, plus the two little ones. If there's a battle, it will be up to us to run all the signals. Pray it's after the blow."

"**S**ail, ho! Quarterdeck, there! Sails in the harbor!" cried Mr. Hande from the main top.

"Signal, Mr. Hicks! Lively, there, man. Lively. Send up 'enemy'."

"Lt. Towers, clear for action. Don't beat to quarters yet. We'll have time."

"I'd say so, Sir. After a week of gales, the blooming Frogs have decided to come out when the wind's gone. Look there. They can't even fill their courses."

"It's a shame for them, then, isn't it."

The signal ball rose to the mast head and opened clean, displaying a signal flag that the light breeze was barely able to lift.

"Signals on *Naiad* and *Phoebe* now, Cap'n," shouted Hande, and I have 'acknowledge' from the fleet offshore.

Almost all the officers lined the bulwarks of *La Désirée* to watch the French and Spanish working to sail out of the harbor.

"Captain Burton," said Dr. Elworth, "this is going to be like watching paint dry. In twenty minutes now only one ship has reached the mouth of the harbor. It will take them all day to come out."

"You are correct, I am afraid, Doctor, but we can't do much about it, and neither can our fleet. We can move no faster. Without some wind, there will not be much of a battle…at least not today."

Neville leaned behind the doctor and said to Towers, "Today will be as normal as we can make it then, but we must be ready for a change of wind at any time. We will follow, whichever direction they go, and will endeavor to move off a league toward our fleet to make signaling easier. If nothing changes by nightfall, have the men sleep by their guns. We can't afford to be caught in our hammocks."

All day the Franco-Spanish fleet straggled from the harbor and turned south.

"They seem to be in no particular order, Captain. What do we report?"

"I should say they have at least three rough columns, but for now just signal 'sailing south'."

"Aye, Sir. We're just reporting the obvious, though, I'm afraid," said Towers. "We can see our fleet's topsails from the deck now, and the Admiral has them pointed the same way."

It was early – three bells of the Morning watch – with the light growing over Spain. The men had slept by their guns for two nights, but the normal holystoning of the decks was now under way. Neville and his lieutenants, midshipmen, and warrant officers had gathered on the quarterdeck to decide whether any change of activity was warranted.

"There's enough light to see that all four of us are still with them, Captain," reported Midshipman Foyle.

"What do you suppose Admiral Villeneuve has been thinking, Captain?" Lt. Coughlan asked. "Yesterday he had them in three columns, but then back to a single line. Do you suppose that's his line of battle?"

The Quartermaster rang four bells. They all heard him say, "Turn the glass and heave the log."

"We might have enough wind to support it," commented Towers. "We had that light northwest breeze all yesterday."

"And it seems to be holding this morning," added Miller.

"Signal!" hollered the lookout, "From Victory." He paused, obviously trying to read it.

"Take your young eyes and go up, Mr. Hicks," said Neville. "We can't afford to get it wrong."

"Prepare for battle!" yelled Hicks from above, after he had been up a few minutes.

"Maybe you're right, then, Lt. Coughlan. Whether he wants it or not, that sprawling line may be his line of battle...

"How close to Gibraltar are we, Mr. Worth?"

"Twenty miles, I would estimate."

"What point of land is that there, then?"

"I believe the name is Cabo Trafalgar, Sir. They should not have a problem to weather it."

"I'm going below for an hour, Mr. Towers," announced Neville. "Call me then unless something noteworthy occurs."

Neville returned to the deck when seven bells rang, "Pipe the men to breakfast, Lt. Towers," he soon ordered. "It's a bit early, but I'd rather they were fed before this begins, and it's looking closer. Our fleet is hull up now. When I went below an hour ago I could only see sails."

"Deck, there! Captain!" yelled the lookout. It was Hande again.

"What is it?" yelled Neville.

"Dunno, Sir. Some of them looks to be turning."

"What's this, now? Mr. Foyle, go up if you would, please. Give the man a hand to understand it. Sorry, no pun intended."

Foyle was quick on the climb, and his return down a backstay was even faster. "Captain, it would appear they are attempting to wear together, but with this variable breeze, it's not going well for them. *Naiad* is signaling 'wear', and their 'enemy' signal is still aloft."

"Good enough. Mr. Hicks, repeat that signal.

"Mr. Worth, sails aback, if you please. We can wait here for them, if they're coming back."

The group watched for most of the morning while the Franco-Spanish fleet struggled in the contrary breezes to reform their line in the opposite direction.

"What could the Admiral have in mind, Sir," queried Lt. Miller. "Our ships are not in any line parallel to the French, but it looks as though he has every intention to engage."

"It does, indeed, Lt. Miller. Pass word for the officers to gather here on the poop. It is time for me to advise you of Admiral Nelson's plans."

"As you know," Neville began when his men were gathered, "I have attended two Captains' dinners aboard *Victory* over the past few weeks. Admiral Nelson gave us the essence of his plans. He has no intention of forming a parallel line of battle against the French. Our fleet will attack in two lines at the perpendicular in order to cut the enemy line into three. If you look out there you will see that it is a perfect day for it. The enemy must be stretched over five miles and they are in disorganized groups. We cannot attack them very quickly, even with the wind fair for it, but they cannot easily move about, either...

"Our duty is to station ourselves between the two British lines and pass signals. *Euryalis* is close behind *Victory* as the first frigate to repeat signals. In order next on the weather side of all are *Sirius* , then *Naiad,* and finally *Phoebe,* The little ships will be wherever they can... which brings me to another important point: Nelson is very extremely experienced, as you know, and he understands that no sea battle is a certain thing. There are always situations of chance. He orders us, therefore, to take our initiative - to attack where we can - to take any advantage. I intend to do just that Questions?"

"Captain, look to our fleet. They are setting all sail. That one forward is the *Royal Sovereign.* She is setting stuns'ls, Sir. Stuns'ls into battle!"

"Verily, I see it, Mr. Wynde. She is Vice-Admiral Collingwood's flagship, and is at the head of one of the two lines. Nelson will take no time to form a line. They will sail in to divide the French line as quickly as they can…

"Mr. Worth, Lt. Towers, let us crack on as best the wind will allow. We're still faster than the flagships. Beat to quarters! Dismissed, everyone."

"Signal from Victory, Captain."

"It's a long one…'England expects'," Neville read.

"Right, Sir. You know your signals, I see," said Caughlin, "that every man…" They waited while the previous hoist on *Victory's* mizzen came down and the next went up.

"… will do his duty'," Neville completed. "I'll say we will. Repeat the signal, Lt. Coughlan."

"Get on it, Mr. Hicks.

"Here's another, Sir. "Close action!"

"After the previous signal is down, repeat that last, and leave it up until we have another."

Moments later they saw the flashes from the enemy's cannon. The flashes were soon followed by the roll of thunder and a rising cloud of white smoke.

"*Royal Sovereign* is out front of all. She will take a terrible beating from French broadsides before her guns will bear at all, Captain."

"Aye. So I see." The smoke blew toward land, leaving the *Royal Sovereign* visible as she broke the French line between an immense Spanish vessel and the next behind. *Royal Sovereign's* foremast went down, and she began to fire. The thunder increased to a continuous roar. *La Désirée* continued to approach the French line at a fretfully slow three knots. A man from the fourth gun leaned over the rail and vomited.

Miller had a glass to his eye, and reported, "*Royal Sovereign's* mizzen course yard is down. So are the Spanish ship's entire mizzen and main top hamper. She looks to list. No other British ship has yet to fire. *Royal Sovereign* is firing far more quickly than the French, Sir."

"Make sure your battery does the same when we engage, Lt. Miller," said Neville. "Load langridge. Our little guns will not damage the hulls of these monsters, but we can cut their men and rigging.

"They converge on her, Sir. *Royal Sovereign* may be doomed, but other British are coming to her aid now."

Neville had been watching the increasing melee with an eye to involving *La Désirée* in the action. *Royal Sovereign* had swung alongside the giant Spanish ship, whose name they could now read, to exchange broadsides.

"She's the *Santa Ana*. Three other French are joining…"

They were much closer now. The thunder of cannon had increased to the point that ears were ringing. "There, Mr. Towers," yelled Neville, "Follow *Belleisle* and *Mars* through the French line."

"They will crush us like eggshells, Captain!"

"It is not yours to decide," Neville screamed back at him, "Helm down!"

A ball from *L'Aigle* howled low across the deck, cutting only a single main shroud. She and *Belleisle* drew up alongside each other and engaged each other with broadsides. *La Désirée* continued to follow *Mars* until she passed *Belleisle* and turned south to assist in the forward part of the French column.

"Lt. Towers! Mr. Wynde!" screamed Neville, "Prepare for a hard Starboard…"

"Lt's. Miller and Caughlin: Fire at will as she bears either side. Fire high. Cut rigging and men."

A moment passed while commands were yelled forward and braces were manned. "Mr. Worth! Now!" yelled Neville, "We must discourage this French two-decker from destroying *Belleisle*."

To the south, the bow of a French seventy-four approached on a converging course as she sought to join *L'Aigle's* battering of *Belleisle*.

"If we turn now we shall stop in front of her!" yelled Worth in a moment of hesitation, "We will be crushed to kindling."

Lt. Caughlin's starboard guns fired a broadside, shivering the decks. The French ship's foredeck rail exploded and her outer bowsprit sagged. Neville turned directly to the quartermasters at the wheel and hollered, "Hard to starboard! Now!" They began spinning the wheel.

"She will turn, Mr. Worth. She must. We may be small, but not so small that she would not be severely damaged. We can fire our broadside at her now, and she cannot yet return anything but a chaser. You will see. And never hesitate on my orders again or you will be relieved."

With the speed of a snail *La Désirée's* bow turned toward the oncoming monster.

Closer she came, continuing on a straight line. Then a slight movement indicated she would not run them down. Her turn was not gentle, as it might have been; not just enough to miss *La Désirée*, but as a knee-jerk lurch to starboard as Neville had hoped.

"Fire as she bears, Lt. Miller!"

A bow-chased fired, followed by the first gun, second, and then the rest as a broadside. Smoke momentarily obscured the Frenchman.

"Hard to port Mr. Worth...

"We must pass her as quickly as possible, even if is it close aboard. She will do us great damage, I fear, but even more so if we strike out diagonally and give her more time. And she will have a difficult time returning to her pursuit of Belleisle

"Fire, Mr. Miller!" Neville screamed again. *La Désirée's* guns roared again, but only a second before the French broadside. Neville saw holes appear in the enemy's sails, and a twitch of her mizzen indicated they had cut enough of its rigging to render it unusable. He saw her name go by. "*Neptune.*" He saw a man on the foredeck cut in half. His two parts fell to the deck in a gush of blood. He heard a great crack above his head at the same time he saw the forward rail of the quarterdeck explode. He felt a tug at his right sleeve, a crushing blow to his chest, and a thump to the back of his head as it hit the deck.

"He's awake, you say?" Neville heard Lt. Miller ask.

"Aye, Sir," responded Dr. Elworth. "Over there."

Neville realized he was lying on a mat beside some trunks in sick bay. His head was thumping. All was not still. He could still hear cannon firing. Lt. Miller's face appeared above him.

"Miller?" he asked.

"Aye. Are you all right, sir? Anything broken, do you think?"

"Miller. Thanks be to God. Not some other."

Neville suddenly sat straight upright. He'd had a thought that woke him thoroughly: *I'll see Marion!*

"Certainly Sir. I thank you for the compliment."

"Is she here? No, of course not."

"Who, Sir."

"Marion. Miss Stillwater."

"Oh, that's who Marion is. You've been a bit delirious. You called out for Maria, I thought…

"Doctor has removed the splinter and dressed your wound."

"Where?" croaked Neville.

"Right arm, Sir. The battle's not over. Now that you're up, can you come on deck, do you think?"

"A rum, please; straight, and I will come up. How long, Lieutenant… Lieutenant…"

"Miller, Sir. Half hour, Sir. You've been cut half an hour."

"I can't believe I am here now."

"I understand, Sir. I think it was a very close call."

"No, not that. A dream? The whole thing, perhaps? Uuugh! My chest feels like an elephant sat on it; and my head – oooh.

La Désirée fired another broadside to larboard.

"aaaahrgh – the sound of those cannon does not help it any, nor does the smoke."

"Doctor says there are no broken ribs, but you'll have big bruises. Mizzen course yard fell across you."

"Why am I alive, then?"

"You were in the middle. The binnacle held one end – the wheel and compass are smashed, Sir – and t'other was on the hog pen. The huge one smoothed the landing of the yard, Sir."

"Fresh pork, then."

"I'd say so, Sir. You seem all right then, shall we go up?"

"I feel very groggy, but help me up on deck and explain what we see."

Leaning on Miller's shoulder, Neville hobbled up the companion to the deck. His old leg wound was acting up in addition to the pain from this latest incident. What he saw around the ship when his eyes came above the gunwales was breathtaking.

"Your strategy to save *Belleisle* didn't work. *Achille* and *Fougueux* came up and battered her bad, and *Neptune* found her way back to help until our fleet fell upon them. *Belleisle* still floats, but she is dismasted. There she is there, about half a league distant. We have not traveled far, between the lack of wind and lack of sails."

Neville looked skyward, where he could see a missing main topgallant mast – and a space where the mizzen course should have been. Fore and main courses were furled. Topsails and jibs still flew – or rather hung limply.

Cannon continued to roar all around them, with smoke so thick that ships downwind could only be seen intermittently. *La Désirée* would do no good as signals relay for *Victory*, as that ship was not visible in a cloud of smoke to the north.

"Who is First Lieutenant? "Powers? Sorry... it's been a year?"

"Towers, Sir. First Lt. Towers; and no year – you've only been out ten minutes or so."

"Aye, That's it, Towers. Pass word for him, if you please."

"Aye, Sir, and we'll bring you a chair."

Lt. Towers arrived carrying a chair.

He placed it by the remains of the binnacle and said, "Please sit, Sir. I understand you are not quite yourself. We've cleared the mizzen course yard, you see?" Towers ran a small rope around the chair and the stump of binnacle to hold it still, but there was not much sea motion to worry about.

"I'll come 'round," Neville said. "What's the situation? I see the dead hog."

"The French van has come up on our fleet, and most of our fleet has run in amongst them."

"What do I see there? That looks to be a French frigate that is taking a run at *Thunderer*. She's more our size. Go at her! Let's take one down, at least... how are we steering?"

"Relieving tackles below deck, Sir; Mr. Worth's plan. It seems to work well, but don't hope for any sudden turns."

"Can we come round to follow *Thunderer*? Pass word for Lt. Carlyle to get his marines ready; sharpshooters as high as they can get. We obviously don't need them at the mizzen course braces, and hand out cutlasses for boarding. I think we'll have a very close action soon."

La Désirée began a slow turn to starboard as Mr. Worth shouted his steering commands down the aft hatch and Lt. Towers roared his sailing commands forward.

"Breeze is coming up, Sir. That frigate's coming on faster."

"Here's our calling. Frenchie there plans to cross *Thunderer's* stern and rake her. *Thunderer* will not change course for a frigate, but even a frigate firing a broadside at a seventy-four from aft can do tremendous damage."

"From here we can put ourselves between, Captain."

"Exactly, Lt. Pow... Towers. We shall follow *Thunderer* so closely that Frenchie cannot get between. That frigate will be forced to run under *Thunderer's* guns in order to place herself where she might broadside *Thunderer's* stern, so we must cut her off from that path; then she must either turn larboard to pass astern of us or starboard to fight *Thunderer*. I would not put my frigate against a seventy-four's broadside without some better purpose. When she passes astern of us we shall turn and close with her."

"We'll try sir; can at least give them a broadside."

"Do you hear me, Mr. Worth? You must be ready to make a hard turn to starboard."

"I hear you, Sir, but..."

"Pass word for Lt. Coughlan to double-shot the starboard guns. We must run up behind *Thunderer.*"

"I see..." began Towers. A huge explosion vibrated the very water they sailed upon, so loud that the roar of cannon seemed to lull for a moment.

"I see your meaning, Sir," yelled Lt. Towers again. "Someone's magazine has gone."

A cloud of acrid smoke wafted across the quarterdeck. Neville's head thumped the harder for it.

"Wind's coming up. We have the weather gage for this," announced Lt. Towers.

La Désirée carved a graceful curve in the ocean, putting herself directly behind *Thunderer*. Neville could see an officer on the poopdeck above them waving.

"May I have a glass, please, Lt. Miller," he asked.

Miller handed him his small pocket glass. It was enough to make out that the officer waving was Daniel Watson. Neville raised his arm to wave, but it only went up about half way before the pain in his chest stopped its motion. "Ohhhh," he moaned. "Lt. Miller, will you return that man's wave for me. I should be most grateful. He is a blessing for mine eyes." Miller waved. Daniel apparently understood, and left the poop.

"Not long now, Captain. Frenchie has not changed course," said Worth.

Thunderer's guns thundered ahead of them. Holes appeared in the French frigate's sails, and her fore topgallant mast flopped off to her larboard, but she came on.

"She's still comin' on, Captain," said Lt. Towers, "Straight on like she is, she doesn't present much of a target for *Thunderer*."

"She's turning to her larboard, Sir!" yelled Worth.

"Turn toward her, Mr. Worth. Make her turn hard. Maybe we can force her into irons unless her captain thinks he can withstand a collision with us."

Thunderer was leaving them behind now, no longer in danger of the frigate's guns.

"She's turning further to avoid us!" yelled Lt. Miller.

"Straight at her, lads! Smash us alongside and grapple…"

"Are you ready to board, Lt. Carlyle?"

"Ready, Sir!"

"Our helm is responding, Captain," said Worth. "We'll strike just right. Her sails are fluttering. They're going aback. She's in irons!"

"Let sheets fly, Mr. Towers," commanded Neville. "Pass word for Lt. Miller to fire the forward carronade at the earliest possible moment."

Time slowed. The ships neared. Half a cable. Bow chasers on each ship fired. Neither was in position to fire a broadside. *La Désirée's* bow rail exploded. A hundred yards. Neville could hear the rattle of muskets begin. Two balls thumped into the deck at his feet. A hundred feet. Miller's forward carronade boomed out. Neville saw a small group of French boarders disappear from their foredeck.

The sickening feeling of his ship tearing its hull against another of equal strength suddenly began. The jarring crash threw Neville from his chair. The stab of pain in his chest kept him there for a moment while the noise of *La Désirée's* first point-blank broadside rattled his ears. The deck shuddered, and with his face pressed against it, he felt it far more than ever before. He raised himself with his left arm to sitting, and then steadied himself on the mainmast bitts as he stood. A musket ball removed his hat.

This was madness! The two ships had collided and been grappled together, and now men from both sides began to throw themselves at each other with cutlasses, pistols, axes and pikes.

"At 'em, men! Go at 'em!" he heard Foyle yelling. He saw Foyle and a group of eight or ten men go over the rail onto the French frigate.

A marine fired the quarterdeck swivel gun at a knot of French sailors preparing to jump from their foredeck onto his quarterdeck. Three fell; one between the ships and two back on their own deck. Six came on ahead.

Neville drew his sword and stood with Mr. Worth and five marines ready to repel them. The instincts of self-preservation consumed Neville. Swords and cutlasses clashed. One Frenchman pulled a pistol from his waistband, but before it discharged it was pointed at the deck and the man was missing three fingers. Mr. Worth was a better swordsman than Neville would ever have expected. His sword was already through the man's neck. The deck was red with blood and slippery now, and the noise slightly less. The ringing in his ears was overpowering his hearing.

A blue French uniform appeared in front of him, worn by a brute of a man who stood six inches taller. He had long stringy black hair; even through the cannon smoke he smelt strongly of onion. Neville slashed at him, but slipped in the blood and went down. He felt a searing pain in his left side, but stabbed upward in defense. The brute groaned and gasped, and grabbed for something to support himself. Not finding it, he landed hard on Neville's chest and lay still.

Neville may have passed out again for a few minutes; he wasn't sure. The pain from having the brute land on his already-damaged chest was excruciating. It was suddenly eased as two men dragged the body off him. Miller and Worth. Marion's face flashed across his mind. *Where could Marion be now? Where was it she was going?*

"Smoke," croaked Neville. "Why so much?"

"Dunno, Sir," answered Miller. "It's coming from below on t'other frigate."

"Cut us loose, then," he croaked. "Throw the lines off! She may blow! I'm all right here for now."

"Aye, Sir. We'll send Elworth. You stay down."

Neville could hear the clashing receding. He rolled on his side to see what remained of the action. Foyle was herding his men back aboard and throwing the French back onto their ship or overboard. Fewer Frenchmen were visible. *Are they going below to fight a fire? Why can't I remember where Marion was going? It's been so long…*

"Cut loose! Cut loose," Miller was screaming forward. Worth was doing the same nearby.

The motion of the ship changed when the last of the grapples were cut. There was no longer the sickening sound of two hulls grinding together. Neville heard one final hard thump before the two ships parted.

Mr. Worth was back in his element: "Lt. Towers, see to the sheets, if you please. We must make some distance… any direction."

Lt. Towers and Bo'sun Wynde began yelling sailing orders. *La Désirée* was gathering speed rapidly in the increasing wind. She bashed into waves that had risen from two feet to four in the last half hour.

"Is all this blood yours, Captain?" asked Mr. Leonard, one of Dr. Elworth's loblollies who had arrived to assist.

"Don't think so," Neville managed, "That big 'un was on top of me." He pointed to the body next to him on the deck.

"Oh, you have a wound, though. I see…"

A rolling roar began from behind them. More holes appeared in their sails, and a crash below led Neville to believe they had been struck below the quarterdeck by at least one ball. The deck shook. A different thundering from the same direction began.

"I see the hole now," Leonard continued, "Here's a hole through your tunic on the right side. I'll wrap you tight and we'll get you below."

"The frigate - *Thémis*, she was - shot at us, Sir," said Midshipman Hicks' voice behind him. " They must have got the fire out and took one last go at us, but they've stopped now. *Dreadnought* is upon them. They'll be out of *Dreadnought's* range, soon, I expect, and follow their fleet off. I doubt *Dreadnought* will chase a frigate. I think we've carried the day."

Again, Neville woke up wondering if he had been out long. He was lying in his cabin below decks without a shirt. His belly was wrapped so tightly with a canvas swatch that breathing was difficult, particularly with his chest still hurting. He felt his right side where there was a definite stinging pain, and found the spot wet. When he pulled his hand back to look, it was red. He was still bleeding. *That big lug must have stabbed me through*, he thought. *I wonder if it is mortal?*

"Oh, I see you are waking," said Hajee. "You stay quiet. I get Doctor."

He decided to wait that long, but not much more. He needed to know what was happening above. There was only the occasional distant blast that sounded like cannon fire. The loudest sounds were of waves and water. The motion of the ship was much rougher now than it had been during the fighting, and the ship was definitely heeling to starboard and moving well.

Midshipman Foyle appeared. "Lt. Towers sends his compliments, Sir, and he will be down direct, now he's heard you're awake. It's not your best day, is it?"

"Certainly not, Mr. Foyle. What are we about?"

"Battle's over Sir, and we've thumped 'em bad, but *Victory* signals that Admiral Nelson has been killed. Collingswood and Blackwood are in command. Weather's come up serious now; blowing a gale of wind. We're ordered to try saving prizes and fishing men from the water. Here's Doctor Elworth now."

"Damned fine of you to sleep a few hours sir," said Elworth. "Gave me time to sew up t'others." He looked to be near exhausted and there was the smell of rum on him. He'd put on a clean shirt, for sure, but his hair was all frizz with streaks of blood in it.

"Butcher's bill, please, Doctor," croaked Neville.

"Only one dead, Sir, however we were so lucky, but twelve injured, counting you."

"Oh," said Neville, with some surprise, "What of me, then?"

"You'll hurt a while, for sure. That French monster poked a hole clean through your right side, but I don't think he hit a single thing of importance inside. We have you wrapped tight to staunch the bleeding. I would recommend you stay below."

"Doctor, I must see to the situation above."

"You can feel from the way the ship moves that it is not pleasant weather."

"Rain?"

"I have not heard it."

"Mr. Foyle, can you help me up, please."

"Aye, Sir."

"Mr. Foyle," said the doctor, "If you take him up, I cannot assure him that he will come back down conscious."

"I understand, Doctor, but while he may not always have the right, he is always the captain...

"This leg first, Captain. Swing it down here."

Neville and Foyle struggled up the main companion. The lively motion of the ship added to Neville's unsteadiness, and when Neville's eyes came above deck, they beheld a scene very unlike the one he had departed after being wounded. In place of ships fighting ships, men and flotsam in the water, clouds of acrid smoke and cheerful little waves flicking sunbeams back into his eyes, there was clear air and eight-foot waves with white spume flying off their tops. When his foot first touched the deck, the foretopsail exploded into ribbons of canvas, no longer able to withstand the stress of a dozen holes.

"Tie me into the mainmast bitts, Mr. Foyle, that I may view long enough to understand."

Lt. Towers walked over to them. "Several prizes appear to have been retaken, Sir, and they are running off," he said. "It would be reasonable that a small prize crew could not hope to sail a strange ship under these conditions. Others without control are certain to find themselves upon the rocks. Vice-Admiral Collingwood has taken his flag over to *Euryalis* because his *Royal Sovereign* is dismasted. He is ordering our fleet to tow any others they can assist."

"Can we help?"

"We cannot tow a seventy-four or anything larger, but there are men in the water ahead. We will try to fish them out. In this gale, even that will be difficult."

"Can we anchor here, lieutenant? We are quite close in."

"We might do. I'll get the lead going. If it is not too deep, we shall anchor by the drowning men and see to the boats, aye?"

"Aye." Neville began panting, and soon he was sprawled unconscious on the deck.

17 - *"Paris"*

"**E**asy, there! Easy!" yelled Master Reynolds as the *Lady Spencer* edged up to the wharf in Marseille's harbor under the guns of Fort Saint-Jean. His ship thumped roughly against the stone and stopped.

He yelled again: "You'll be painting that personally tomorrow, Mr. Poole."

"Not in a good mood, is he, Mr. Mason?" queried Stearns.

"I'd say not, but I can't blame him for it. Four men gone. Three times boarded. Probably no prospect for a cargo home. It makes me wonder how we'll get home from here."

"Mmmm… Where do you go from here?"

"My business is here in the ports of Marseille and Toulon. My contacts will have connections for American farm products throughout the country. And you?"

"I wish you luck. I'll do some touring before September when I must be in Paris. France may be at war with England, but away from the coast I expect life to be simple and the people at peace.

It took Stearns almost two weeks to find Monsieur Giroux, the contact suggested by Mr. Fordson in Washington. "I have come in a very different capacity," Stearns assured Giroux. "I won't be troubling you with the business we had before. I only need a contact for the sale of certain items in Paris, and your personal suggestions for a pleasant holiday in the Loire. Our mutual friend in Washington assured me you would know some people in military purchasing."

"Here are the names you will need, Mr. Stearns," said Giroux. "You will forgive me, please, if I am somewhat suspicious. When we last met I thought you would not be back to France."

Stearns spent the months of July and August in central France, leisurely traveling slowly north and testing the local food and wines. By the end of August he reached Paris and found his contact. "Bonjour, Monsieur D'Aubigne. I have two requests. First, I will need to know how I might sell American rifles to Napoleon. Second, I am looking for a very beautiful American woman here in Paris whom I expect will be trying to sell rum to the French navy."

"No more? I was told to be discreet with your requests, but these two are quite simple. The purchasing organization for Napoleon's army is this," he said, sliding a paper across the table.

"As for the second, you must mean Miss Stillwater. We have few American visitors to Paris these days, and even fewer who are women. Certainly none that both seek to sell rum and are beautiful. I have seen her, and she is as you say. But let me caution you: just because your requests are so simply answered doesn't mean you should not be careful about your business. You will be watched. I do not know your intentions, but she is very much in the public eye."

"Yes, yes, M. D'Aubigne. Miss Stillwater. She is... a close friend of mine, and I look forward to seeing her."

"I would imagine. I envy you, Monsieur. She is staying at the Hotel Le Pont Noir."

"Merci, merci, M. D'Aubigne. One more question, if I may? In order to sell rum to the navy, there are particular people she must meet, *est-ce pas alors*? Might you might know who they are?"

"*Oui, oui, Monsieur.* Of course. It would be M. Vasser. I think she has a meeting tomorrow evening for the dinner. It is there, at the hotel. Oh, you will excuse me, of course. I talk too much, Monsieur. I am not so used to the English."

Stearns did not have much difficulty finding the Hotel Le Pont Noir. It was in the center of the city. Even though Paris was near the size of London, the better hotels were grouped in a relatively small section of town. The carriage driver knew his way through the dirty little streets that led from the seedy area where he'd met M. D'Aubigne to the grandeur of Napoleon's new capital.

He decided to surprise her at dinner rather than interrupt her day. He wanted his first view of her to be when she was dressed at her finest, and that would be for the meeting, naturally. He needed the rest, anyway, after a long two months of travel, and might also need to have his better suit of clothes cleaned or pressed. He checked in and went to his room, which he found quite acceptable.

A thought struck him: Why did M. D'Aubigne seem to know all the details of Marion's visit? Was he not part of the Americans' network here in France? Why would they be interested in the selling of Jamaican rum to the French navy?

Curious, he thought, *but of no consequence. Marion will be surprised at my ability to find her, and I will no doubt impress her with my ability to get things done here in France. Things should go well from there.*

Stearns slept well that night. In the morning, he made his preparations for a grand entrance, which included a substantial tip to the bell boy to determine the time of Marion's evening dinner.

It was the smells he noticed first when he descended the stairs to the lobby floor and turned toward the dining room. Quite unlike the smells of raw sewage and horse dung outside, these smells were of perfectly cooked pheasant and lamb, cheese sauces and roasted garlic. They wafted out into the lobby from the dining area, beckoning hungry guests to come eat in the hotel rather than finding a fashionable restaurant elsewhere. As usual, Marion had made a wise choice – if it had been her choice to make.

Stearns was greeted at the entrance by the maître d' hotel in his black suit. Marion's party was visible at the far side of the room. Despite her hair being up in a rather curious 'horizontal bun' style, there was no question that it was Marion. He saw her in profile. *The Paris fashion of the day, no doubt.* Without claiming to be a member of the party, he indicated that he was there to visit with them, and was allowed to pass.

Marion sat with three men and Miss Aughton at a large round table. They had apparently not gotten far into the meal… only to starters, perhaps. One man had his back to Stearns and was therefore not available for observation. The two others were ordinary-looking for Frenchmen – not particularly handsome.

All the better, thought Stearns. *I will let her know I am here. She can make short work of her business and after dinner we can send these creatures away and enjoy a wonderful evening. But what do I do with Miss Aughton? I had forgotten her. And why does she sit with them as an equal? That's not the place of a lady's maid.*

He advanced nonchalantly, as if he didn't know she was staying in the same hotel. His movement caught her eye, and she looked up as one who might expect a waiter to pass by. He stopped walking when she saw him. She obviously recognized him. She stopped talking and her eyes opened wide. Her lips formed a small 'o'. Ellen and the two men visible to Stearns noticed her distraction and followed her gaze. The third man began to turn toward him as well.

Stearns advanced to within a few feet of the table. "Marion," he said in as surprised a tone as he could manage, "I cannot believe I discover you here at the same hotel! What amazing luck."

Marion had so far said nothing to him. She was obviously trying to collect her thoughts while she continued to stare at the unexpected apparition.

Ellen rose, which required that all the men do the same, her hand apparently feeling for something at her side. The unidentified man stood and turned to face Stearns. He seemed vaguely familiar. "Marion," he said, "this is quite a coincidence, meeting one of your countrymen here in Paris. May we be introduced?"

Stearns thought he noticed the man's brow tighten slightly. He was now face-to-face with the man. A hint of recognition flashed across Stearns' mind. *Surely it could not be, after all these years! Georges Cadoudal, the same man who killed my chances at advancing in the spy game all those year ago? Could it be Georges Cadoudal? If it is, why is Marion meeting with him? These others may be spies, too, or government…*

Marion was saying something. What he heard was "…doudal," and he knew for sure it was the same Georges. Georges held out his hand, and Stearns heard Marion saying, "…Michael Stearns." Stearns stood dumfounded. *I'll scream out who he is!* Stearns thought. *No, I can't rat out Georges. Not here in France. Who are these other fellows? People from the government? They would believe Georges, not me. It would be the death of me, and possibly of Marion, even if I get rid of Georges.*

Stearns was rapidly collecting his thoughts. "I cannot, Marion," he said to her, "This is not the first time I have met this man. He is a scoundrel." His voice was getting louder, and speaking English.

I could demand satisfaction 'for old scores unsettled', or something of the sort. "I cannot shake this man's hand…

"Good evening to all of you…

"Marion, be careful in any dealing you have with this man. I will leave you a message at the desk. I apologize for this… this… inconvenience." He turned clumsily, knocking into the next table, and sending silverware to the floor and a glass of water across the tablecloth. He strode rapidly from the room, his head spinning with questions and confusion. *I must leave*, he thought. *Georges will suspect that I am on the old business, and who knows whose side he is on these days? It is dangerous for me to stay.*

Stearns passed through the blur of the lobby to the stairway, calculating the fastest way to depart Paris as he went.

Let me think. Let me think. Marion doesn't know that I have ever been a spy. I never said anything to her about such a thing, or that nasty creature Georges. Georges cannot possibly know Marion for anything but whatever this business is here. She might even be in danger. I may be a coward to leave her with the man, but Miss Aughton was there. Why was she dressed as Marion's equal?

Nobody knows I am here, other than Marion and that devil Georges now. Chester only knows I have taken a holiday, and surely he doesn't know where his daughter is. Chester was ignorant of Marion's movements before, so I should be able to continue 'business as usual' back in Jamaica and pretend none of this ever happened… but I must leave here now! That damn Georges has undone me again. I can only wonder what Marion thinks. And Miss Aughton… what is that?

By morning he was gone. Marion received no note.

18 - "Double-Cross"

Neville's head had ceased aching about a week after he woke up in Haslar Hospital in Gosport. His chest still felt as if an elephant were sitting on it, the sword-hole in his side pained sharply whenever he moved, and his old broken-leg injury was acting up.

"You're recovering quite well, Captain," reported the doctor.

"I am loathe to complain, doctor, but I don't feel very recovered. I suppose I should be overjoyed that the sword wound was not mortal."

"Verily, Sir, you should. The stab wound may be the least of your worries, though. I am concerned about the crushed chest, although I see no evidence of internal bleeding."

"I shall pray it stays that way. Do you know how I came to be here, doctor?"

"Other than that you were carried in on a litter, I do not. You were one of our lads brought home from the Battle at Trafalgar, I know. That in itself makes you one of our country's heroes."

"Why do you say this, doctor, what news is there of the battle? It was quite fierce."

"We have been instructed not to talk about it with any patient who is not strong enough for some excitement, but it looks as though you may be well enough now. Admiral Nelson's fleet carried the day, but he was killed in the fighting."

Neville immediately knew why the doctor had his orders not to speak of the battle. His heart rate increased, re-starting his headache. The tight bandages around his chest for the stab wound caused his breathing to labor."

"Ah, you see," said the doctor. "Your stab wound bleeds. But you have heard it now, so I will continue...

"Admiral Nelson was shot by a sniper. Admiral Collingwood's ship, the *Royal Sovereign*, was dismasted, so he moved his flag to the frigate *Euryalis*. He and Captain Blackwood did not break off at all, and the French and Spanish were confounded. A great storm came up directly after, causing several of the captured ships to be lost on the rocks. Casualties were great, as you may learn from others in hospital here, but no British ship was lost. It was a great victory, indeed."

"That last is wonderful news. It means that my ship was not lost. The last I remember is that we anchored to save the ship and dozens of drowning men."

"Yes, Sir. Well, you're here now," said the doctor. He patted the bed twice and departed, leaving Neville to lapse back into sleep with mixed emotions.

"**Y**ou needn't treat me like a child, Mother," said Neville, "The King thinks I can command one of his ships, and the doctor at Haslar allowed me to travel."

"Well he shouldn't have, should he?" his mother, now Mrs. Blake, shouted back from the next room. The travel from Portsmouth to her home in Bury St. Edmunds had been more difficult than Neville had expected. Although some autumn rains had softened the ruts somewhat, the jarring ride had loosened his recent scars. "You've bled again, haven't you? Just shush a minute whilst I get you a fresh bandage and after that we'll have some sandwiches."

"Shush," he grumbled. "She tells a captain to 'shush'. It's a good job the men can't hear it."

There was a rattle at the door below. He heard his mother tromp down the stair and a murmur of women's voices. That was followed by footsteps coming back up.

"Who was there, Mum?," Neville asked.

"Just me," came the answer. It was not his mother's voice, but Mary's, and it was she who appeared at the door. "How are you, Neville?"

"Suddenly much better, I think. You look much happier than last I saw you. You look very nice in that dress. No, you look positively beautiful. And I'm fine, thank you."

"That's not what I hear. That's just what we all say to each other, isn't it? Some beast has stuck you through with a sword?"

"Yes, but it's got better."

"That's not what your mum tells me either. She says you need a nurse, and you're far too much trouble for one woman, so I've volunteered."

"A nurse - dressed like that? That's quite a thing, I should say."

"I'll go change before I get all bloody, but I wanted to make a good first impression. I was afraid you might not hire me." She leaned over and gave him a kiss on the cheek. "It's wonderful to see you, Neville. You're a hero come home, too.

"I'll go help your mum with the sandwiches. I am afraid she may already be having too much help from little Martin. I'll start my duties tomorrow."

His mother and Mary returned shortly with the lunch, and they ate together by the bed.

"What's this paper here, Mum?" he asked.

"It's a note for you from one of your men, I'd say. I found it in that dirty thing you call a uniform."

"You're not my laundress, either, Mum, and I'm not penniless. I can have my things cleaned proper by someone else... but thank you for finding the note." He opened it.

"It's from Midshipman Foyle. This is real news, it is," he said after giving the note a quick scan. "He says that *La Désirée* had orders to remain on station with the fleet, with my first lieutenant Towers as acting captain, and that they put me aboard the little schooner *Pickle* to come back to England. She was the ship who first carried news of the victory home; that much I've learnt. He wishes me the best.

"I've sent letters to Sir William and to *La Désirée* asking for the status of things, but I haven't had answers yet."

A week passed pleasantly, with daily visits from Mary to help change the bandage 'round his middle and to steady him when he took short walks. The coach ride from Portsmouth had set him back more than he would ever have expected, but he was finally mending. He could feel his strength returning, but he was not about to forego the opportunity to lean on Mary. She always kissed him on the cheek when she arrived, and again when she left; he could feel his distress rise with each kiss. *Mary is a sweet girl, and I am very much attracted to her, but where is Marion? What had happened in France? Should I write her in Jamaica? Would she write to me on La Desiree? That might be it,* he thought. *Marion couldn't know of my injury. A letter to my ship would probably go there before being back to the hospital and from thence on to Bury. It would take quite some time.*

Neville was sitting with his mother at the little table she had in a little nook by the kitchen when his sister's knock came the next morning.

"There's a letter in the box," she said. She fished it out and read the address, "It's for Neville, Mum."

"I don't recognize the hand," he said. "I hope it's news of my ship."

The envelope contained only a single small piece of paper with a short note. It was not what one would normally call a letter, It was dated October 2, 1805.

> *'M.S. has run off – suspect to Norfolk. No rum sales – double agency. Thought you'd want to know. I've copied Godfather."*
>
> The signature was *'Uncle Georges'*

This message is almost 2 months old. My word! It's direct from Georges – not through Sir William. This would have been a month after Marion left me in London. There must be some mistake. My Marion - a double agent? How could that possibly be? She's just not that devious. She has the feminine wiles without any doubt, but this? Impossible! I would have known something. And why Norfolk? Because she's American, and Norfolk was the first ship out, I suppose...

"Are you all right, Neville?" his mother asked.

Neville looked into the envelope again, but there was nothing more there. He looked at the address again. It had gone to *La Désirée* and then Haslar Hospital and from there was re-addressed to Bury.

"You've gone white as a sheet," said Elizabeth.

He read the short note again. He slammed his fist down on the table and yelled, "NO-oo!" His tea cup jumped and rolled to the floor with a crash, sending the tea and its leaves flying across the floor with shards of china.

"Neville...?" queried his mother.

"I... I'm sorry. I'm sorry. I'll clean it up." He stood to get a cloth.

"Is it from your ship? May I see?" She asked.

"No, you may not." He snapped... "Yes, yes. Sorry. But it won't mean a thing to you. I can scarce believe it myself."

His mother read it and passed it to Elizabeth. "What does it mean?" she asked

"Who are these people?" asked Elizabeth.

Neville knew his face was turning bright red. He knew he could never tell his sister about his history with Marion – or his mother, either. A lie was required. "They... I can't. It's part of that... that thing when I was gone for three years. I'm sorry. I must go think what to do..." He climbed the stair carefully, forcing himself to go slowly and not re-open his wound. *What on earth can I do? I can't leave here yet. I am not healed, and my ship is still away.*

He found his bed and laid down to calm himself and ponder the situation. *How could she do this to me? What more does Georges know of her? His answer was very quick, wasn't it?*

Neville pulled the letter out of his pocket where he had stashed it after his mother read it. A quick calculation led him to understand that there could have been little time between his inquiry through Sir Mulholland and Georges' answer. He and Marion had both left London about the first of September. His letter would have gone to Whitehall in a few short days. Even if Sir Mulholland had sat on it for a week, his note to Georges could have reached the man in France in another week. That would be mid-October. Marion should have concluded her business and sailed home by then, one would think, whether via smuggler back to England and thence to the United States or directly on an American ship out of one of the northern ports. Therefore, he estimated, Georges must have traveled from wherever he'd been, investigated Marion's visit, and penned an answer in only two more weeks. Even the travel would take two weeks. Georges must already have been in Paris. Not unlikely, but was there a connection?

His decision was to write Sir Mulholland asking for two things: more information and a chance to follow his investigation of Stillwater. *If Marion is involved,* he thought, *for what she has put me through I will be happy to let her join in her father's guilt. I will chase them both down, and finalize Sir William's investigation in the process.*

He felt himself growing red at the collar and his blood pressure rinsing again. *I must calm myself, or this thing will never heal. I suppose writing is all I can do for now.*

Mary appeared at her usual hour of ten in the morning. Neville looked at her differently. *She is beautiful, this girl, and she is steady and honest, not at all devious and cunning like Marion. After all this time I can see it again. She is a woman I would be proud to marry.*

"Thank you, Mary, for all your help," he said. "Mother could have done it, I am sure, but I think it pains her to be reminded of the danger I often see."

"It does, Neville, and I don't mind. I have come a long way since you saw me last. Helping you is more than something to do. It make me feel useful again. Do you suppose…"

"Yes, go on."

"After you're better, do you suppose we might… I don't know, go out to dinner or something?"

He reached over and took her hand. "I have thought it myself, but I wasn't sure how you might take it. It seems forward for me, not a year since John's been gone. There have been others, Mary, but I seem to find them less… honest."

"I have suspected. But I am alone again. and my feelings for you are still there."

"I…"

"Nope. No more today. That's it. You're done. I see no bleeding today, finally. You'll be up again soon enough." She leaned over him and kissed him – on the lips – and left him to nap.

Neville's recovery began to gain momentum.

"Only another week to the New Year, Neville. Do you think you would be up to attending church for the Christmas services?" asked Mary.

"I should think so. I have been out for walks with you , although they have been short. I'm sure I will be able to sit on a hard bench for an hour or so."

"That's a good thing. We'll have something to do together. Our mothers are starting to mumble about my visiting."

"Mumble what, Mary?"

Mary blushed. "You know. That you should come to court me now, now this way 'round."

Neville blushed. "Oh. I hadn't seen it like that. But now you mention it, I haven't needed much nursing for a few weeks now, have I...?

"My humble apologies, Mary; I shall indeed turn it 'round."

"So, Neville, you haven't said... it would be nice if... so you would come to court me?"

"Well, I need the air, don't I, to continue..."

"Oh, you impossible prat. Your sister is right. I'll only be back one more time to check that scar, and then it will be all up to you."

Mary stood and stalked to the door. There she hesitated, and then walked back to Neville, grabbed his head with both hands, and gave him a big kiss full on the lips. "You understand, I take it?" she said, and left the house.

Neville was not entirely surprised by the incident. He had been thinking about what he should do. The idea that she was courting him had not occurred to him, and that was embarrassing, but it was also very encouraging.

I think I have reached a decision. I will indeed court Mary with my fullest intention to win her heart – if I haven't already, as it appears. I can give her assurances, but a wedding before I am called back would be almost impossible…

Elizabeth knocked at the door on December twenty-eighth. Her mother opened it, and Neville's sister stepped in to the house brushing her coat.

"Snow again today, Mum, you see?" she said. "Not much, though. I should think it will all melt by noon, and we'll have a nice day."

Neville was sitting in the kitchen warming his feet by the fire. He stood when Elizabeth entered to greet her, and gave her a cheery, "Good Morning, Sis, How are you today? Cuppa tea?"

"No, Neville. I'm afraid I've come with news."

"Good or bad?"

"Depends, for you."

"Depends, why?"

"It's about Mary."

"Mary? She was supposed to be back one last time to check my scar, but I've not seen her these three days past. Is she all right?"

"Yes, Neville, she is. And so is her husband. They've found John alive. He'll be home in a month."

19 - "Passage Home"

"Ellen, can you believe that fool Mr. Stearns showed up here? It was... It was..." Marion spluttered.

"Outrageous, Marion, and very dangerous for us," Ellen suggested, "I just had a word with Mr. Cadoudal about him. How did he know we were here?"

"It is my fault, and I should have told you. I wrote..."

"You wrote and told him? I cannot believe what I'm hearing!"

"No, not exactly. No, really not, at all. He wrote me months ago that he had gone to Washington. Father apparently sent him to New York, but the idiot followed me. He must still think I would have an interest in him."

"Do you?"

"No, not at all. Stop it. I wrote him back a simple letter about our travel and wished him luck in sales. I think I might have mentioned a trip to Paris on holiday in September, but no more. Absolutely no more!"

"Then how do you think a rum salesman finds us at a meeting with Georges in Paris in the middle of a war between England and France? Did you know that he was here before? Is there something more about his appearance here today that we don't know?"

"What do you mean by 'He has been here before'?"

"Here. Here in France, apparently trying to be some sort of spy."

"Spy? Mr. Stearns? That's ridiculous. Spy for whom? Is Mr. Cadoudal not mistaken? Mr. Stearns couldn't scheme his way out of a school yard."

"I've seen worse. You haven't paid him any attention at all, have you?"

"I try very hard not to. He gets the wrong idea very quickly. Not at all like my Neville. Him I have to lead along. Mr. Stearns' main purpose in my life is to steam a little jealously into Neville."

"Forget Neville for a minute, and I don't mean Mr. Stearns' attempts on your affections. His business. What does he do? Have you studied his activities?"

"He's our chief salesman, after Father. He stays in touch with the ships that come and go in order to have an idea what they might buy, and he meets with them to sell rum. Father describes him as his "right-hand man" but I see little of the business that he actually manages. I control the warehouse. Father controls the finances. We all sell."

"Nothing else? What about the guns? Is that only your father?"

"Guns? What guns?"

"The rifles from Harper's Ferry; those your father sells. Surely you have seen some evidence of it. Your father makes no attempt to hide it at home."

"I… I'm sorry. I'm afraid I haven't seen it."

"My goodness. What have I gotten myself into?" queried Ellen to herself, more than to Marion. "No matter," she continued, "perhaps it is for the better. If anything goes wrong you can deny it all and be sent home. You are my travelling companion here, and that does not suppose you have anything to do with whatever business I may conduct."

"What else have you found?" asked Marion.

"Nothing more yet, but my purpose in coming is almost complete. I will ask Georges for more tomorrow, and shortly after that we could leave. Le Havre is the closest port for smuggling ourselves to England, and after your visit to London we could take any American or British ship, I am sure."

"I pray you are as pleased to be off French soil as I am, Miss Stillwater," began Miss Aughton.

"Such formality, Ellen. Have you not enjoyed our comradery?"

"I have indeed. Just practice, I suppose, although I may not be going back to Jamaica with you, you know. I plan to stop awhile in

Boston." She turned to look Marion in the face, and saw that Marion was looking quite dour.

"The Master's most esteemed complements, ladies," said one of the ship's company. "I am sent to ask you to go below while we shoves off. We gets rather busy and we wouldn't want to bowl you over with our ropes or embarrass you with our bad language."

"Yes, of course. We'll go."

"I know," Marion said on the way down the companion to their little cabins. "Another assignment somewhere I suppose. I will miss you greatly."

"And I will miss you." The ship bumped heavily against some immovable object – the pier, probably – and Ellen was thrown into Marion's arms. The two hugged. "Something will turn up." Said Ellen cheerily. "It always does. Did you stop at Whitehall to see that Mulholland fellow?"

"Yes." Marion paused and sighed. "I'm sure something will turn up, yes. I just wish I could tell Neville. It would make all the difference."

The ship was free of the wharf now, and the easy motion of a ship in a protected harbor began.

"It would, I know, but that's what we're into. I would love to tell Joseph, too. I'm hoping he's my next assignment, anyway," Ellen said with a wink.

"What would you do with him?" Marion asked. She felt a glimmer of hope stir within.

"Marry him, naturally."

"Oh, yes, of course. That seems such a distant thing for me."

"Let's take your mind off it, then, shall we?" asked Ellen. "We have the whole passage home to sort out what we know about Mr. Stearns and what he was doing in France – and what we're going to do about it. Here's your cabin. I think it's bigger than mine. Shall we begin?"

"First I must ask, Ellen - is there no chance Mr. Cadoudal made a mistake; that it was not our Mr. Stearns he remembers?"

"Oh, no, Marion. Think about it. I have never known him to forget a face. How do you think he stays alive? Furthermore, was it not Mr. Stearns who recognized Georges first and ran off?"

"It was."

"I suppose it was no mistake, then. You haven't said these last few days in the coach from Paris whether you got anything else from Mr. Cadoudal."

"Well, I couldn't, could I? Not with that smelly, leering French lieutenant in the seat opposite."

"No. No, of course. So get on with it, then, please."

"Georges says that when he was here before - that would be about eight years ago – Mr. Stearns was presented as a tobacco salesman and introduced as being an agent of the United States. But he acted so badly during his visit that Georges and his 'friends' feared they would be outed if Stearns stayed on. He didn't stop talking, and that's always bad. They sent him home with a request that he not be returned."

"Talking's not bad for a salesman, though, is it?" said Marion, "Eight years ago would fit with his arrival in Jamaica."

"Why the United States, I wonder?" queried Ellen. "Georges didn't say, but why would they be spying on an ally?"

"We may never know the answer to that," said Marion, "but the better question is whether they did send him back. This whole thing might be about his chasing me. I told you he wrote me that letter, and it certainly read as if he imagined he was arranging a romantic rendezvous...

"Where do you suppose he went after he ran off?"

"Georges said they followed him to Le Havre. He boarded a ship for Norfolk. That's all they could find out. What do you think, Marion? You know him better than I do. Will he stay in the US or go back to Jamaica?"

"Personally I pray that he stays in the United States. Could he really go back to Jamaica after this?"

"Yes, why not? What does he know?" Ellen asked rhetorically. "First," she said, "he has no idea that you are in the spy game – only that you met Georges and some other men. He may suspect that Georges, whom you did not know, was there to learn what business you had with the others."

"If Georges is a spy for Britain, Ellen, why was he there? Do you know?"

Ellen paused. She looked at the deck beams above her. She looked at the floor. Finally, she looked into Marion's eyes, and she said, "He was there to meet me."

"You, Ellen?"

"You knew who I was – or more correctly, who I represented - before you agreed to participate in this mission. You should have known, or at least assumed, that I am not what I appear to be – ever. I am your handmaiden – your servant. I am your traveling companion – your equal. I am nobody, and I am anyone."

"And what about Joseph?"

"Ahhh. And to him, I am lost. Someday he may know, but not now. Will you agree to that?"

"I will. What was your business with Georges?"

"That you should not ask, so I will not say. But if you allow me, I will continue where I left off...

"Second, he must assume that you and Georges were strangers – that you just met there at dinner – that you were in Paris exactly as put forward... to sell rum to the French navy; that the others at dinner were your customers.

"Thirdly, he must assume that your father expects naught else. You put it forward to him yourself."

"Yes, but it was your creation, Ellen. You cannot deny that."

"I do not, and it has worked marvelously well. I cannot but thank you for your help. I could never have gone there without the cover of a sales visit of some sort and a travelling companion. And I must admit that Joseph was a bonus that I could never have imagined."

Marion sat silently for a minute or two, wondering where to take the conversation next. She took the logical path. "Ellen, what do we do now?"

"Let us go above again. They are done with their dockside nonsense, and it is a nice day. Let us watch Europe disappear behind us and think on it. We have the whole passage, as I said."

One fine day in early October, as the Canary Islands were sinking behind the ship, Marion and Ellen stood on the poop deck under the eye of a very protective captain, enjoying a mid-morning cup of tea.

"King Neptune himself is watching over us today, I think," said Ellen. "I think they call this a 'fair wind' and the waves are quite pleasant. It is a very comfortable motion, indeed."

"When it is like this it is hard to imagine a nicer place to be. This is the sort of thing Neville always talks about."

"And Joseph. I have a suggestion, Marion."

"A suggestion? About my problem at home, I assume..."

"Yes. I am afraid you won't like it, but it is the logical thing. Shall I explain?"

"I think I know what you'll say, so go on."

"I shall say it straight out. Please don't condemn me for it. You should 'cozy up' to Mr. Stearns, if you find him at home acting as if nothing happened. Find out what he thinks he was doing. You must decide for yourself what 'cozy up' means, though, I'm afraid."

"I came to the same conclusion. I certainly don't want the man as a serious suitor." Marion shuddered. "I really can't tell why father likes him, or why he would want to pass his company to him when I could run it just fine, but I do understand that it's in Mr. Stearns' best interest to keep on to see if he can have me as well as the company. I can ask father if he sent Mr. Stearns, but he probably won't say much. If Mr. Stearns is there, he will have told some story of his own already. I'll need a better story about you, too, because he saw you there as my equal...

"And then there's the guns you mentioned...

"You say Father does not hide it at home?"

"He has a little glass award on a shelf in his office."

"Oh, yes. I've seen it; just never bothered to read it."

"You could have. He doesn't know otherwise. Stearns could have seen it as well, and done something with it... his own 'Paris Plan', if you will. Harper's Ferry is very near Washington, and you know he was there."

"I see," said Marion, "Maybe the Americans didn't send him at all. Just another of his brilliant ideas."

"Could you use that to get rid of him? Tell your father that you want in on it. Tell him he doesn't need Stearns for that, either. Maybe that's the last piece of why your father wants him around... he thinks a woman can't handle the arms business?"

"Hmmm. Possibly. I need something."

20 - "Sir William"

"**H**appy New Year, Neville," parroted his mother and stepfather when he came down the stair for breakfast.

"Yes, I suppose," he answered. "I'm sorry, yes, a good morning and Happy New Year to you as well," he responded. "What do you think? 1805 will be a better one?"

"We pray it is one where you don't have a sword stuck through you, Neville," said his mother.

"Ellen…" chided Mr. Blake.

"I'm sorry. I always worry. And a lady to call your own, too, I pray."

"It's all right, mother. I agree with your sentiment."

"There's a note for you just there, dear. A boy brought it this morning. It doesn't look the least official, so it shouldn't be orders to go back to war."

Neville opened the plain envelope. "It's from Sir William. He's here in town and asks that I come 'round to see him this afternoon. I'd best clean up a suit of clothes."

"What, he can't have the rest of us?"

"There's a 'p.s.' here, Mum. It says he'll have the family around later, but this is something navy – and urgent I would guess. Do you have a bit of paper I could reply I'm going?"

Neville scratched a quick acceptance to the invitation and stuck his head out the door to look for some boy who would carry it. *Here's one advantage of living in the city*, he thought. *There's always a boy about who'll hold his hand out for a scrap.*

Neville knocked at the familiar door of Sir William Mulholland at two in the afternoon, as he had suggested in his reply. He was greeted by Spencer, the butler, and ushered him into the parlor where two men were warming their feet by the fire. They sat with their backs to the door. When they heard the rustle behind them and felt the draft from the door, they both stood and turned to face the new guest.

Neville was almost speechless. There was Sir William, as expected. There also was Georges Cadoudal, whom Neville hadn't seen in several years.

"Happy New Year," he said to them, and advanced for a less formal greeting. He and Sir William gave each other a short embrace and a clap on the back, and Georges, as a Frenchman is wont to do, kissed Neville on each cheek.

"You look well, Neville," said Georges. "Sir William advised me you might not."

"He's right, though, Neville. You do look well," said Sir William. "All the better for you to take in what we have to say. It is easier here in Bury. I don't have to smuggle Georges in the back door and all that rot...

"Spencer, bring another cognac, if you would, please."

"That fellow Stearns, Neville," Georges began after they sat themselves, "You have met him, no?"

"The last I saw of him I had run a sword through his shoulder... a duel of his making."

"I assume you have an opinion of him, then. May I ask you for it?"

"Verily. He is a rather sad sack, in my opinion. Rather getting on for the ladies, but quite keen on one who will not have him. He acts the part of a wealthy businessman in Jamaica, but I can't see that he has much of anything to call his. Sort of... well... just another rum salesman to me. Why all this interest in Stearns?"

"You asked for my help in France through our friend here, you remember. I sent you that note."

"A note? About Stearns? It must have gone missing."

"You're sure? It was very brief: 'MS has run, double agent, that sort of thing'."

Neville could physically feel the blood drain from his face and his stomach knot. His chin began to move up and down, but no words were coming out.

"Neville, what is it?" asked Sir William. "You've gone white as a sheet. You'll not have a seizure will you? I heard the wound was severe."

Neville held up a finger for the others to wait while he began gulping and breathing in short gasps. It began to pass. "MS ran?" he finally squeaked. "Michael Stearns? Why would I know he was in Paris? I assumed you meant Marion Stillwater- 'MS'?"

"Marion? Why would I refer to Marion. You asked me to check on her, but in truth, by the time I received Sir Williams' note she had already sailed," said Georges.

"Where is she now, then? I'm sorry. It's a silly question. Why would you know that?"

Neville saw Georges and Sir William look at each other and was sure he saw a tiny nod by Georges.

"She has gone back to Jamaica – to her usual position with the Stillwater Rum Trading Company."

"You know this? Why do you know this?"

"She is one of us, Neville. I am sorry now that I did not tell you earlier – when I learned you had feelings for her, but I was worried that your feelings would have you prevent her from going to France on something more than a rum sales ruse. She is our 'comrade in arms', as they say. She is new and inexperienced, of course, but she works for me, as you do."

Neville's brain was tumbling over itself in an attempt to understand what all this information meant to him. *Marion never deceived me for Stearns – only for her mission. She couldn't tell me... or she didn't know that she could tell me. I must assume she still loves me.*

"She doesn't know about me working for you either, then, does she?"

"She came by Whitehall after her visit to France. I thought about telling her, but I decided that should be left to you. It may be quite tricky, though. I still suspect her father, and I cannot ask her to investigate him. You may need to confront him with our evidence to learn his reaction."

Neville slumped back in his chair and took a long pull on his cognac.

"When might that ever be?" he asked. He did not expect an answer.

"When you get to Jamaica," answered Sir William. He walked across the room to a small writing desk on the far wall and extracted a canvas envelope with the seal and flimsy string of the Admiralty. He carried it over to Neville and handed it to him. "I'd say you are strong enough to sail," he said. "Report to your ship in Portsmouth. She'll be out of ordinary in two weeks.

"If you can keep your attention focused on Georges for a few minutes, though, he will give you all the details he has on Mr. Stearns… it might signify, but it may be that he is no more than an interfering bungler. After that I will review what we have on Mr. Stillwater."

HMS *La Désirée* was swinging easily at single anchor in Spithead when Neville saw her again. Her mizzen course yard was back up where it belonged, as was the fore t'gallant yard. His little shore boat had a small sail up to assist, but was rowing hard to beat the current that was trying to send it west down the Solent.

"Who goes there?" cried a voice from the frigate.

Stroke Oar of the shore boat shouted back, *"La Désirée!"*

A quiet minute passed. *Have they forgotten me or are they dumbstruck with disbelief?* Neville wondered. *Yes, I think I see a glass pointed at us.*

A din began to arise aboard ship; whistles first, then shouting and disorganized drums. It all carried quite clearly across the water. Neville could hear voices he recognized: Foyle, Worth and Towers – even Carlyle the Marine.

How long has it been? he asked himself. *Only two and a half months. It feels like years.*

"Row me 'round to get a look at her, cox'n; and we'll give them up there another minute to compose themselves."

He was proud of his ship. She showed almost nothing of the beating she got at Trafalgar, and all looked ready and willing to go again. The little boat rowed hard forward to clear the anchor cable, slid swiftly down the starboard side under sail, and then rowed hard again up to the larboard main chains.

Mr. Foyle himself took the painter when Stroke Oar threw it, and Neville was aboard a moment later. He tossed Stroke Oar a full pound. Foyle released the painter, and the little boat drifted rapidly astern with the current.

Neville saluted the colors aft, then First Lieutenant Towers, and he touched his hat to the others. A cheer arose from the ship's company as Neville gave each of his officers an embrace and a clap on the back. "Not too tightly, lads," he begged.

21 - "Michael's Dilemma"

Michael Stearns walked down the gangway from the *Virginia Belle* onto the new wharf at Kingston, Jamaica on a sunny afternoon in mid-November of 1805. The passage had been easy. Straight from Le Havre to Norfolk, and then Norfolk to Jamaica, with only one brief stop in Charlestown. Fair weather all the way; it was a good omen for sure.

Everything he saw was familiar – except this new wharf – yet it all seemed different. He knew the same would be true when he walked in to the Stillwater Rum Trading Company: all the same, but all different.

He called for a carriage first, taking his sea chest home to his rented rooms in a large house that overlooked the harbor. His rooms were comfortable, but he did not enjoy the splendor that was the Stillwaters' at *Independence Hall.* He was suddenly very aware of the latter when his house came into view. *There's that, as well,* he thought. *If I had Marion I would also have Independence Hall. People would look at me differently. That lothario Burton and the loathsome Cadoudal have stolen my right – my future.*

Michael Stearns' plan, after a long bath, some clean clothes, and fresh food, was to settle back in to the old grind as if nothing had happened. He would gather his strength for another go at the world. After a nice big steak, why not?

Marion has no idea I'm a spy. How could she? I didn't say anything to her about such a thing, even in Paris where that straw-headed Georges was trying to cut in. He and Marion certainly couldn't have known each other. Nobody other than my contacts in Washington and that other fool

Giroux in Marseille know anything about me. Mr. Stillwater can't possibly know anything – he's too busy trying to make money, and he certainly pays no attention to people. He never let me in on the rifle business, although he should have. I'll have to talk with him about that. Therefore, it is logical that I can go forward with 'business as usual'. I've had plenty of time to prepare my defense against his rantings, which I'm sure will come.

The following day being Tuesday, Stearns dressed in his best workday suit of clothes and walked to the Stillwater Run Trading Company offices on Water Lane. Again he whistled 'Yankee-Doodle-Dandy as he walked, thinking that any Brits who heard him and took offense could damn well bugger off. He opened the door to the scene he had expected: *all the same; nothing ever the same again.*

Chester's head rose from his work when he detected motion at the front door. Stearns chuckled at the instant double-take as Chester's head snapped full upright and the man stared at him. *See? He's never done that before. I'm no longer 'just old Michael Stearns'.*

Chester left his office and walked to the hallway entrance to the lobby. "Mr. Stearns, you grace us with your presence," he said. "This is a surprise! Come in to my office and tell me all about it – where you've been, what you've done, and where you've left my daughter, if ever you were near her at all."

"I have indeed… Chester… I saw her in Paris. She was looking splendid."

Once the two were inside his office Chester closed the door. "I know why she was in Paris," he said. "Why were you there?"

"Didn't you get my letter from New York?"

"I did, and I thought it rather irresponsible for a man in my employ to suddenly take a vacation. What possessed you to go to Paris. Did you know Marion was there?"

Stearns decided consciously to push his luck: "I did, Sir. She wrote me from London that she would travel there in September. You know she has had a fondness for me for some time, and I think…"

"You may overestimate your position, sir," interrupted Chester. He was gaining a slightly pinkish hue.

"I think," Stearns continued, "that she was implying that I should go to share the 'City of Love' with her. Since, as I wrote in my letter, I had al…"

"So you would sneak behind my back to court my daughter? I may have implied myself that you would be a good match, and you have had every opportunity to ask my permission, but I have heard none of that." Chester's face was passing from pink to red, despite the normal tan of a Jamaican resident's skin. "And now you would follow her to a foreign city? Did her letter tell you where she was to stay?"

"No, Sir, it did not. But I have certain skills and contacts."

"Contacts in France?"

"Good salesmen must have contacts, as you know."

"I haven't asked you to sell in France."

"I… I had other interests as well," he fairly blurted. *This may not go well, but I have opened the bag. I had better carry on.*

Chester looked him in the eye, and enunciated clearly, "Other interests, Mr. Stearns? I thought you were working for me?"

"Rifles, Mr. Stillwater. The Harper's Ferry Model 1803 Flintlock Rifle." He sat back haughtily to watch Chester's complexion turn blotchy. The man didn't speak immediately.

"You have some familiarity with it, I believe?" continued Stearns. "I visited them. Nice folks; and they are quite near Washington, where I went to visit Marion. She was no longer there, so I had to do something with my time."

There was still no response from Chester. *He's considering raising my status in the company, no doubt.*

"Since I had decided to go to France, I thought I might have something valuable to sell."

"So you admit that in addition to taking an unauthorized holiday, you followed my daughter, probably with very unsavory intentions, and went behind my back with Harper's Ferry to secure some sort of sales agreement? I should challenge you to a duel myself for all your backhanded insubordination. The Good Lord knows I would win!"

Stearns' disposition flipped from haughty to angry. He yelled back, "You should have let me in on your rifle trade from the beginning, Chester. Why wouldn't you? Am I not, by your own words, 'your right-hand man'?"

Chester responded in kind. "Why? You should know why by now, Michael. You talk too much! This is not rum sales, where talk, talk, talking is the way to go. Talk, in the arms business, will get you killed. Why should I keep you here now? You are a scoundrel after my daughter and my business, and your talk will be the death of both of us. I think you should get out."

"But I won't, will I? I know something you don't want others to know, don't I? After all this time of groveling to you, I have found a way in, and I'm not leaving. Good day, *partner*!" Stearns concluded. He rose from his chair and left the building. He whistled his way to the *Golden Strand Hotel* on Church Street. Once there he ordered an American whiskey. *Very expensive here in Jamaica, but worth it for the celebration. As I thought, it's a new beginning.*

Stearns poked his head into Chester's office. "Mr. Stillwater," he said, "there's a ship come in with news of the war in Europe." Nothing further had happened after their heated discussion on Stearns' arrival. Business was indeed back to normal, except there was now very little communication between the two men. In some way, both were biding their time.

Chester looked up at him with a sour expression, "Mr. Stearns, there is always a ship coming in with news of the war in Europe. Have you nothing better to do than listen to gossip?"

"This is a bit different, I think. You might want to come hear it, but suit yourself." He left Chester's door open and walked into the lobby where a very animated naval purser was telling the story of a great naval battle off Spain's Cape Trafalgar.

The town was alive with the news. A small parade passed in the street waving British flags and making a general mess of singing 'Rule Britannia.'

Michael's thoughts were muddled. A proper Britisher would have no such emotional confusion, he knew, but Americans in business on a British island must wonder whether it is better to have our former allies or our current hosts win such a battle. In Michael's case there was no confusion. He remembered what he had told the American Lt. Leonard in Norfolk years ago, although surprised that he remembered the man's name: *'It was a damned French ship that sunk Father's and it was the damned British who are responsible for that war. He never should have taken advice from a Brit. I was just twelve then. Why join the navy? To get back at the buggers.'*

Michael Stearns returned to his desk and resumed his task of reconciling the warehouse receipts – Marion's job. The disturbing noise outside did not settle for several hours, and finally Michael smiled. *The French took a beating. Whether that's good or bad, I don't care. As long as a great lot of both were killed, the war goes on. When more of them kill each other, it will be just another good day.*

A black thought settled on him. *How likely is it that the stinking Captain Neville Burton was in the middle of it and didn't come out?*

Stillwater's old receptionist looked up when he heard a strange sort of scratching noise at the front doors on the fifteenth of December. A very small boy was trying in vain to pull one of the great doors open. He was defeated in all attempts by the breeze – the so-called 'Christmas Trades' - beginning their annual blow. He could get it no further than a few inches before the immensity of it was beyond him.

The clerk waved the boy off, but he didn't go, so the clerk walked stiffly to the door. His age was showing more now than it had a couple years before, and he was not pleased at anything that caused him to walk. At the door he waited callously until the boy had gotten it open a few inches and then yelled at him, "Get on with you boy. We'll not have you in here."

The boy stopped trying to open the door and held an envelope up against the window for the clerk to read it. 'C. Stillwater', was all there was written upon it, but it was in a very graceful flowing hand – certainly female – that the clerk had seen many times before.

The old man pushed the door open, almost causing the boy to fall into the street. "Gimme that, you ragged muffin. Where'd you get this?"

"Ship's come in, Mister. Miss Stillwater's on it. Will you send a reply?"

"With a gutter snipe like you what can't even open a door? I dunno. Wait there. Right – there," he said, pointing to a tiny corner by one of the meeting booths.

In a moment he returned with a note to be carried, pressed a sixpence into the urchin's palm, opened the door, and shoved him out. "Back to where you got the note, poste-haste!" he cried after him. The boy scampered away with a huge smile on his face.

A ruckus arose in the office. Chester was yelling into the warehouse for a man to fetch him a carriage and for the company delivery wagon to hitch up the horse and go for Marion's baggage.

Michael decided he would stay out of the way while Chester created a minor panic. He wasn't going to the wharf, either, being quite unsure what his reception by Marion would be.

Chester did not reappear that afternoon.

22 - "A Father-Daughter Conversation"

"**O**h, Father, I am so glad to be home," said Marion. They had entered the grand foyer of *Independence Hall.* "You cannot imagine!" She gave him a long affectionate hug.

"I think I can. You're not the first person ever to travel, you know. But it has been a long year alone here. I wish I had never agreed to your 'Paris Plan'. You take your time to clean up, and I'll join you for supper."

Supper was soon served – a meal that Chester knew Marion particularly enjoyed – and the two sat facing each other in their familiar chairs. Marion fidgeted a bit, knowing the conversation would have its difficult moments.

"You're the traveler. Tell me everything first. Then I can give you the boring details of life at home," said Chester.

Marion then launched into the first and easiest part of the trip. "You have all the Washington reports – and the orders. I think Mr. Stearns double-checked all those for you, yes?"

"Why do you say that? I didn't send Michael to Washington. I sent him to New York, and he sent orders back from New York before he took his ridiculous 'vacation' to France. But we'll get to that, won't we? Why would he be in Washington? He is back, you know."

"No, I didn't know. I would say I don't care, but I do. Not in a positive way. Now I'll have to see him." She pushed her christophine across the plate with her fork. "I am sorry to say it, Father, but it will come out. He followed me there. I know it because I received a letter from him – from the *Capital City Rooming House* - the same place I stayed. I hope you had nothing to do with it, because I have flatly denied him. I will not have the man, as I have told you before," she said sternly and rather over-loud for a dinner conversation with her father. She cooled and added, "Anyway, it makes no difference because by the time he got there I was touring England with Ellen."

"Oh!" said Chester with some surprise. "Miss Aughton - she's not with you then, is she? What happened to her?"

"Soon married, I hope, to a friend of Nev… Captain Burton's – one Captain Dagleishe. They met here. Perhaps you met him as Lieutenant Dagleishe of the *Vanguard*?"

"Don't think so. What will you do for a… an assistant now?"

"I'll find someone. Don't worry about it."

Marion then spent a full half hour describing her tour of England and London – without mention of Neville and Joseph, and then launched into her description of the trip to France.

"I was quite surprised at the place, Father. After all I have heard about the country being so beautiful, the city of Paris is far dirtier and poorer than London; much of it quite disgusting, really."

"But you found your way to the meeting with no trouble?"

"Yes, and then… Father, you would not have believed it if you had been there yourself! We are sitting there, Miss Aughton and I and three men, and Mr. Stearns walks in. It was the most awkward situation I could have imagined! He pretended it was a coincidence that he was at the same hotel."

"Was it? How did he know where to find you?"

"I simply do not know. I had written him back in Washington – just a note saying we were enjoying our touring and that I assumed you had sent him there to follow up. And I mentioned that we planned to continue our tour into France in September. No more, Father, I am sure of it. No more!"

"Hmmm."

"The peculiar thing, though, was that when he saw one of the men at the table, he began shouting that I shouldn't trust him, and he turned 'round, upset the next table, and ran out. I saw no more of him, not that it bothered me."

"Who was the man?"

"His name is Georges Cadoudal. He was not among those I dealt with directly, but he seemed to hold great sway with them. His wonderful English was a marvelous help to us, as well."

"I see."

The two concluded their description of the uneventful remainder of Marion's trip back through Boston and Chester's ongoing business at home over the next hour, until Marion declared that she was too tired for more.

"I am so pleased to see you back that I will wait on my breakfast in the morning, just to see you again," declared Chester. They went off to their beds.

In the morning at breakfast, Marion had one last suggestion before they went to the office. "Father, we are both quite curious as to Mr. Stearns' behavior and the meaning behind his strange travel. Although I remind you again that I will not have the man, I guarantee you he would have me in a moment. The company's New Year's party is quite close. I will volunteer as his consort if he will help me with the arrangements – 'cozy up to him', as it were. I have no doubt whatsoever that if I do this he will confide in me whatever I ask of him. We should know his intentions. Shall I do it?"

Chester did not answer immediately, which surprised Marion, but after a minute or two he said, "Yes, all right, but be very careful. I am beginning to distrust the man."

23 - *"Desperate Measures"*

His work day complete, Stearns closed his inventory book, stood to stretch his back, closed his office door, left the building through the back door of the warehouse, and turned toward Church Street. *Let someone else lock up. That's not going to be my job any longer. Chester can do it if he wishes.* It was later than usual, and growing darker fast. Twilight in the tropics is short. It was unlikely he would be home before it was totally dark, but there was a quarter moon this evening, and it was already up. The evening breeze was light and the heat of the day was dropping with the sun to a very comfortable temperature. He stopped at the corner of the alley and Church St., deciding to turn toward the harbor. That decision to take advantage of the beautifully cool evening undoubtedly saved his life. He would walk along the waterfront to watch the last of the sun's light before hailing a carriage to his rooms.

A scuffle behind him on Tower Street, a long block away, gave him pause, but he was headed for an area where he expected to find a few people around. Not much mischief occurs where there are evening strollers or men at work. He did notice a regular tapping sound behind him, but thought nothing of it.

He glanced to the right down Harbour Street before stepping out. Two men ran across it a block away, also heading for the harbor. *What causes men to run?* He wondered. *It's unusual.*

He crossed the street and continued down the gentle grade. The tapping behind him continued, so he turned to see what it was. When he did so, a very large man with a peg leg a block behind him stopped walking and turned to look at the building beside him. *Was there a shop there? Is he looking in its window? I don't remember a shop there.*

Stearns was now more alert. He had had some training years ago on the topic of being followed. It was mostly forgotten, he was sure, but this smelled of it. *Just being followed, or do they mean to harm me?* He wasn't a frail man, but he wasn't armed. He wondered about his options. The one he liked best was simply hailing a hack and riding away laughing, but the city was growing quieter by the minute. He didn't see more than two or three wagons rolling about the street, and those weren't close. He could try hiding in an alley or knocking on some door, but that seemed cowardly. He could just continue with his original idea of going for a walk. If they were just following, they would learn nothing; he had nothing to hide.

Michael opted for the latter, and kept on walking down the street. Maybe there would be more traffic on Port Royal Street, and he would find a carriage there. Suddenly, he knew that wasn't going to happen. Two men - he suspected it was the two he had seen run across Harbour St. – appeared in front of him. Another was coming across Church Street from an alley, and the big man with the wooden leg was closer behind than he thought. They were not just following. Knives were coming out. Michael was not studying them carefully, but he did notice that all wore white shirts with a single silver button in the center below the neck. They began to crowd in closer. Despite being six feet tall himself, he noted them as being tall; the one with the peg leg more so. They came closer, blocking escape in any direction. They were imposing; threatening He smelled rum and something like lemons. He knew he would be lying in a pool of blood soon if he did nothing, so he took his chance. He dove at the wooden leg, putting his shoulder against the knee. The big man shrieked with pain, and his prosthetic, normally held in place with leather straps, came off. *One down*, he thought. *The big one down.* He had a weapon now – a three inch wooden stick about two feet long. He swung it with all his might at the leg of the next closest man, and he went down hard, his knife clattering into the street.

Michael tried to rise, and took a short knife in the right shoulder for his trouble.

"You stupid bugger," he screamed, "Right where that repulsive Burton stabbed me,"

"Ha, ha, ha!" screeched the man in a maniacal tone, "It sounds like you deserve it, gov." Those were his last words before Michael smashed his face in with the peg leg.

One left. The man punched Michael in the face, and he sprawled into the street – in front of a pair of carriage horses on the way to the harbor. He heard men yelling and saw feet landing on the pavement, as if dropped from heaven.

There was more to it, but he did not remember much more than being unloaded – without his jacket - in front of his house and going inside to clean his face and flop into bed.

"**W**hat's happened to you, Michael?" asked Chester. Michael thought he detected an actual tone of concern.

Michael slumped into his office chair. Chester entered his office, as did two men from the warehouse, and Marion watched through his window.

"Why did he even come in?" someone was asking. "Look at him. Bruises and a bloodied shoulder. He should be in bloody hospital or something, muchwhat comin' 'ere.

Marion pushed her way through and knelt beside him. "What happened, Michael?" she asked.

This is why I came in, he thought - *to see if Marion cares for me even as much as she would for a damaged dog. She does, I see, so there's hope.*

He began to ramble about the affair; how he had left the night before and was followed...

"Get him a rum," she said to one of the men.

He drank it and jabbered on for another fifteen minutes. Chester and the other wandered away after they had gotten the gist of it, and he raised his hand enough to grab her arm. "Marion," he said. "I think your father's put them up to it... tried to have me killed because I know about the guns. I can't report him, because I would lose you, you know, but I'm still quite alive and well, you see?"

She turned colder, he could tell, and she said, "Mr. Stearns, you need to take some rest. I will have a doctor come 'round your house to see about stitches in that arm, but you simply must stay quiet a few days." She left this office, and he could hear her giving orders to accomplish what she had told him.

She does care, he thought.

Three days later, after some good rest and a doctor's care, he thought himself well enough to report to work. He would stick to desk jobs – no customer interaction...

"You're well enough to do some good today, Mr. Stearns?" Marion asked when she saw him sit in his chair. His face still showed the scrapes of the cobble on Church Street, and he wore a sling for his right arm, like that which he had worn for months when she was away.

"Nothing to do at home; I can do something here."

"Well, then, I have something you might like. Will you help me make the preparations for our annual New Years' affair? I am quite keen for it, as I missed last year's."

"You didn't miss much. Without you, it was quite dull, in my opinion, with nothing to light the place up. But why would I help with that? I am usually more of a guest of honor."

"Because I need a consort, and despite your infirmities, you might serve," she said.

What a fox. She favors my attentions, and is finding excuses.

"Let me think on it," he said. "What would you have me do?"

"Decisions, mostly. You can sit there, and I'll bring the ideas and what we know of the attendees. We need to create an appropriate seating chart, decide on the wine..."

"Ah, yes, yes. All right. I had forgotten all that. I quite enjoy it, yes. I'll do it." *And have you on my arm all night. Why would I not?*

Marion departed, leaving Michael to fiddle with some business trivia. She returned to ask him about Mr. & Mrs. Freemantle – whether they could be allowed to sit together or whether it would be too disrupting. They laughed about it. She left and came back with another question about the Groogans, and they laughed some more.

She put the whole list of local guests down in front of him and they lapsed into hilarity about the dynamics of Kingston aristocracy.

Chester came across the hall to ask what the ruckus was, and when he found the snickering answer to be 'the guest list', he left, undoubtedly chalking the whole thing up to 'high holiday spirits'. Marion and Michael laughed until the tears rolled from their eyes about the thoughts of 'Mr. so-and-so' sitting next to 'Mrs. such-and such', etc. There was, after all, a long-standing familiarity between them. A pause came at last, and Marion looked Michael in the eyes and said in a far more sober tone, "Michael, we have to talk about the guns…"

The party was a success, as it was every year. Marion was the center of attraction for a dozen captains and lieutenants. Michael reveled in the honor of escorting her in and out, the first dance and a toast. The evening ended with Marion giving him a kiss on the cheek and a heartfelt 'thank you'.

I am returned to Jamaica I love, thought Michael. *It is the life I have always longed for.*

The new year of 1806 stumbled forward into January.

Two weeks later one of the sales associates assigned to cover harbor observation sauntered into the lobby and handed his list to the old Reception clerk. The clerk in turn took his list to Chester's office and set it in his tray. This daily event always caused Marion and Michael to come across from their offices and review it with him – for planning purposes and their own curiosity.

"This third one, *La Desiree*. It's Captain Burton's ship, Father," said Marion.

Is he aboard? My God, what now? thought Mr. Michael Stearns.

24 - "Unraveled"

Neville heard the sentry stomp his boots and a rap at his cabin door. "Jamaica on the starboard bow, Sir," Towers called in. "Thought you might want to view it."

"I do, indeed," He went topside and joined a gathering of officers on the foredeck.

It is a time to see the splendor of the world, he thought. *I have been through my papers and over them again. Now is a time to look toward my home, as she may yet be.* Jamaica lay as a thin brown line atop the water. A thin white line perched upon that, except to the West, where a great pillar of cloud rose up and away into the blue of sky, lit to dazzling white by the morning sun and formed into the shape of an anvil by the winds on high. She would grow as the hours passed, he knew, and the brown line would rise from the ocean and show verdant green as they neared the island's eastern end; *the home of Marion.*

The smoke of the cannons, fired in salute to Fort Charles, hung around the ship as it drifted slowly before the gentle zephyr wafting into Port Royal Harbor.

"Drop anchor in that open area between those brigs, if you please, Lt. Towers," he said, "Have my gig ready to take me in once the anchor's been dropped, if you please. I'm going to stretch my legs ashore and take a look at this new wharf. You may begin to arrange limited shore leave, also."

"Aye, Sir, and thank you. That will be well received."

"**W**hat's Cap'n doing, Mr. Foyle?" asked Lt. Miller. Out of a combined curiosity and ennui, Foyle was watching Neville through a long glass.

"Just pacing the wharf, much as he does the quarterdeck here aboard," said Foyle. "Here. See for yourself." He handed the glass to Miller and walked off.

Neville's purpose in pacing the wharf was far less the exercise than it was waiting for a message boy to return from the *Pig's Tale*. Neville had sent his note there, writing simply that he had missed Marion terribly and was looking forward to seeing her at the earliest possible time. He continued pacing until the urchin returned - much sooner than Neville had expected, and far sooner than he had instructed his gig crew to return. He had been right that Marion would know his ship was in and write him. He had it in hand now, and looked for a place in the shade to read it.

Stillwater Rum Trading Co.
The Happy 12ᵗʰ of January, 1806

I'll fetch you from the New Wharf at half eight on the morrow.
That is when I am normally in my carriage and on my way to
work.
Oh, how I long to see the blue of your eyes.
With all my love,
Marion

The carriage-driver reined his horse in at the juncture of street and wharf. Marion hopped to the street while Neville crossed the last few steps to her. She opened her arms wide as he approached. *She is very much home, he thought. The plumeria is in her hair; I can smell her from here.*

When they embraced, Neville cried out in pain, "Ow, you'll have to watch that spot, Marion!"

He bent over, nonetheless, and they kissed, refraining in the public setting from any more than a polite welcome-home buss. "What's happened to your side?"

"Trafalgar. There was a great battle off Spain. I'm sure you've heard."

"Yes, of course I've heard. This is Jamaica, not a cave. Were you there? Were you injured?"

"Yes to both. The mizzen course yard-arm fell across my chest and a great brute of a Frenchman stuck me with a sword through here," he pointed to his abdomen, "right where you squeezed me. I'll tell you the whole thing, but not now. You are just so beautiful, Marion. It seems over a year since I've seen you. The whole thing is quite a story. I recuperated from the Trafalgar bashing at my Mum's house in Bury St Edmunds and I've had another month and more aboard ship on the way here."

They clambered into the carriage and sat beside each other, holding hands. Marion said, "Driver; to the Rum Company, please."

"Marion, could we talk some before we go there? Drive around a bit, perhaps, or maybe take a walk on the common?"

"To the park, please, driver."

"Yes, ma'am."

"There's something I want to discuss with you privately, but I'll start with just asking about your trip to France and the passage home. There is so much I must catch up on."

"It went surprisingly well, she said. There were a few little problems, but all together..." She summarized her travels in the five minutes it took riding to the park, but left out the part when Stearns appeared in Paris and anything about her actual business there. Neville helped her down from the carriage when they reached their destination, and after commanding the driver to wait, they began a stroll.

"I was touched by your note, Marion," Neville began. "I've never before received a letter from you that ended with 'All my love'. Do you really mean it?" He turned and looked into her eyes.

"I do, Neville, but I haven't told Father a thing about it."

"Speaking of your father, then," he said, "If he agrees, will you marry me?"

She said not a word, but her smile and the twinkle in her eye gave him his answer.

After a moment of just gazing into his bright blue eyes, she said, "He's not been pleased about me even seeing you."

"That's not what I asked, you know."

"I can't just say 'yes'. It's not lady-like."

"All right then, let me tell you about my godfather."

"Does this have anything to do with your question?"

"Not at all, but it seems you aren't going to answer that now, so I'll change the subject. He's not really my godfather; that's sort of a put-on, really. He's a fellow I've known all my life, though. He lives in the same town as me Mum now; helped my family when Dad died and set me up a false muster before I went in the Navy as a midshipman."

"He sounds like a very benevolent friend, Neville, You should be glad of him."

"I am, but you can tell me what you think. I understand you went to see him last September."

"How could I know your godfather? Besides, I was in France in September."

"Yes you were, but then England, and you visited Whitehall, where he has an office."

"How could you know all this? Are you having me followed?" Marion's adoring tone grew swiftly chilly.

"I don't have to have you followed when you visit my godfather."

"Sir Mulholland at the British Admiralty?"

"Yes, Miss Stillwater," Neville said, and then he whispered, "And that will be 'Sir William' to you, if you marry me."

"Oh, we're back to that?"

"No, no; we can go on. When I was recovering at home, Sir William..."

"Mulholland," she muttered again, as if still in disbelief.

"Yes, him. He asked me over to his house to say 'Happy New Year', and there…"

"Just has you over for a cup of tea, does he? To his own home…"

"Yes, Marion, Can we get on? There was your friend Georges. Georges thinks…"

"Georges Cadoudal? That man from France? And I suppose you've known him for years."

"Well, yes I have. We go way back, but that's another very long story, and it has nothing to do with this latest affair."

"Now I'm beginning to wonder if being recruited by the British attaché in Washington was a mere accident. Did you put 'Sir William' up to finding you a bride?"

"Oh, no, Marion. I would never… meeting you is the luckiest thing that has ever happened to me." He continued, although she was now looking quite dubious, "Georges believes your Mr. Stearns is acting as a double agent of some sort… There's something about rifles, Marion. Do you know anything?"

"First, Sir," she said quickly, her voice now truly cold, "He is not *my* Mr. Stearns!"

She hesitated before answering the question, and had obviously warmed quickly with her next thought. "Ellen suspects something, and that there might be some connection to Father. She saw something in his office…"

"Ellen Aughton? Joseph's Ellen? It seems an age since I saw her. What has she to do with this? Sir William didn't tell me about Ellen. Georges knows Ellen? And where is she?"

"She stopped in Boston on the way home. Maybe I shouldn't have spoken, but she was there to see Georges."

"Oh, ho!" laughed Neville, "What a bunch we are. Marion, my real job here is not Ellen's business, I'm sure, but I am to make an arrest – or cause one to be made - if I'm convinced we have a guilty party. I'm to put together a case against Michael." *Or Chester! That might finish me with Marion.* "Is he a real private arms dealer, just trying to become one, or is he a simple bungler?"

"He's a simple bungler, say I," said Marion, "I took the attempt on Michael's life…"

"Attempt on his life?"

"Yes, only a few weeks ago four big men attacked him just after work. One had a peg leg. Michael broke it off and used it against the others, but he was stabbed in the shoulder again, just where... where you... Hmmpf ... men..."

"Did your father know that Mr. Stearns knew about the guns?"

"I'm fairly sure I asked about it."

"Hmm."

"I think the attempt on his life is evidence that he is mixed up in something suspicious," Marion continued, "but there's nothing I could do except write a letter to Sir Mulholland to advise him that I think Stearns is spying on, or at least working against, the British. I asked Michael about the guns, too, but his answers were lame indeed.

"You mentioned that Ellen saw something in your father's office... the little glass award? I've seen it."

Marion put her head down and appeared to gulp. "I went and looked, too, and it's still there."

"Marion, we both know Mr. Stearns was in Paris, but I don't know why. Was he there to sell rifles, or was he really just chasing after you?"

"Ellen only guesses about the rifles, which might mean Father sent him, but I don't believe that. Michael is truly deluded. I know he was following me. He followed me to Washington when Father sent him to New York, and then he followed me to Paris. I've talked to Father about it, and I've told him that I will not have Michael, no matter what he says. And I've told Michael, too, by the way. Even with that I think the fool still believes he has a chance with me. You saw his letter in London. He was thinking it would be a romantic getaway, the silly sod. When he saw Georges, though, he panicked and ran off."

"Yes, I saw Mr. Stearns' letter. It bothered me for months. I thought you were running out on me."

"Oh, Neville, I will never."

"And then I got a tiny note from George in France that said 'M.S. has run', and I thought it meant you, because I didn't know for sure that Stearns was even there – didn't think of him at all. I was crushed; ready to lead a different life. And then I met Georges at Sir William's and the sun began to rise again."

Their carriage clattered to a halt in front of the Stillwater Rum Trading Company. Neville handed the driver a half crown, and the carriage rattled away, leaving the young couple standing nervously in the street by the big wooden doors.

"Shall we, Miss Stillwater?"

"Yes, let's," she said. Neville pulled one of the doors open and Marion entered. When Neville stepped inside, she clamped herself to his left arm like a limpet. They saw Chester's head rise to see who disturbed their door. It was a busy day. Stearns was in one of the sales booths with three men, and six more were in the waiting area. All of those heads turned their way as well. If nothing else, they were a far more handsome couple than was normally seen in those offices. Marion was dressed to greet Neville rather than for work, and Neville, of course, wore his captain's uniform. He would certainly outrank any man from the navy.

Chester, behind his glass windows, stood, but did not come out. Michael continued to sit, and the expression on his face was stoic. Neville chuckled to himself, thinking the man's expression showed more of doom or disaster.

They walked past the receptionist – Neville for the first time receiving no challenge – into the office hallway and thence into Chester's office. Marion was not letting go.

"Mr. Stillwater," said Neville in the cheeriest tone he could muster, "It is good to see you again." He extended his right hand. To his surprise, Chester shook it.

"We have some things we need to speak with you privately about, Father," said Marion. "It might be better at home."

Chester looked around the room, and particularly at Stearns, and finally said, "Give me ten minutes to clear up here. You might wait in your office?" he said to Marion.

Before her door closed, they heard Chester tell the receptionist to call for his carriage. He then walked across to where Stearns was meeting and rapped politely on the door. Michael could see them from where he stood in Marion's office. They passed only a few words, in deference to their customers, and Chester began to give each of the men sitting in the waiting room a short greeting.

"I have brought some papers with me, Marion. It is important to me that you know that they are not of my doing. They are from Sir Mulholland, whom I – we – cannot name as anything but 'Whitehall'. I will show them to you both at *Independence Hall*." He could tell that didn't make her any less nervous. "I'm sure he thinks our conversation is to be about the two of us," he added.

"I expect so. That's one reason I wasn't letting go of you," she said. "And I certainly wanted Mr. Stearns to see it. Ha!"

The carriage ride home was awkward, with Chester sitting beside his daughter facing forward, and Neville sitting opposite, facing to the rear. They passed a little small talk about the year's rainfall and Neville's participation at the Battle of Trafalgar. They all expressed their dismay over the death of Admiral Nelson, although the Americans obviously did not share quite the same concern as the British.

When they arrived at Independence Hall they filed into Chester's office. He waved his butler away and poured them each a glass of rum himself.

"What have you two done, then?" Chester asked.

"It's not about us, Sir," said Neville. "It's about this." He placed his valise on the table, removed a sheaf of papers and spread them on the table like a deck of cards. "I have these letters from Whitehall," he said. They are all from you, it appears… except maybe this one."

He showed it to Marion. Now that he knew her, her flowing hand was obvious. The signature was 'M. Stillwater'. "This first one I picked up in Toulon. It is obviously not the same hand…" He looked at Marion.

"That's mine," she said. "It was about rum sales. Father didn't even want me to take on the rum sales trip. And you got it where? What were you doing in Toulon, Neville?"

"I'm in the navy - I get around. But not now, please; that's another long story."

While Chester was picking up the letters one at a time and looking at them, Neville sauntered across the room to Chester's trophy shelf and came back with a small glass object. He set it down by the letters.

"Mr. and Miss Stillwater, I am dismayed to have to remind you that this is a British Island. Britain considers any trading with the enemy to be unlawful… but this is far worse. Do you have a hand in trying to get something going with the French, or is your guilt only in local dealings? I know you have local dealings, so don't deny that."

"These do look like your writing Father, and all signed by you."

"But they aren't. I didn't write them. This is nothing short of incredible." He was still looking at each letter. "Who could be doing this? And what are all these?" He asked after paging through the letters. At the bottom of the stack he found a large number of pages of tabulated material. "They look like the reports we get from Michael's subordinates about ships that come and go, but they are not identical. They have been re-tabulated."

Marion's mood changed from trembling concern to trembling with anger in moments, "Neville, how could you insult my father this way and still ask for my hand?"

Chester stopped looking at the letters and glared at Neville. "You did what?" he demanded.

"It has nothing to do with this," replied Neville, and fired back, "And you did try to shoot me, didn't you, Mr. Stillwater? Remember that night in the alley – with the same four big men that attacked Michael the other day? That was you, wasn't it – with one of the dueling pistols you sent north with Stearns two years ago. Am I wrong?"

"Father, what have you done?"

"I can't answer that, or he would see me hanged," he said to Marion…

"And I didn't have to put Michael up to anything, Captain Burton. That was all his own doing…

"Did you answer Captain Burton, Marion?"

"No, Father. It isn't lady-like just to blurt out 'yes'. And now I wonder if I should." Neville thought she looked as if she might actually pout. Both father and daughter glared at Neville.

I must keep this calm, Neville thought. "Could it not be Mr. Stearns?"

"That chuckle-head isn't smart enough," declared Marion.

"He just works for me," said Chester. "He does a fair job. He could do well enough to provide for my daughter," he said, sending another mean-spirited glance at Marion.

"Let me see those letters," Marion said. "It may be that..." she said ... "Yes. These are all written with that silly little travel quill and purple-ish ink he has in that little kit of his... and this date..." She picked up another letter, "And this one. And this, and this. These more recent dates are all when he was traveling. Father, Michael was trading on the company name and incriminating you so that he might escape if things went badly..."

"And these tables of ships... they show arrival and departure times, and the navy ships are in different tables. They go back quite a way. Here's your ship *Superieure* in and out, Neville."

"Yes, I saw that... So?"

"There is no doubt of the hand here. It's all Michael's. See here? He makes that thing with all the number twos... and this with the eights."

"So much for Whitehall's theory," mumbled Neville.

"Sir Mmm... Whitehall suspected my father and involved me to... to..."

"That's the sort of job it is, Marion," said Neville.

"What job?" demanded Chester.

Neville took a deep breath. "Mr. Stillwater," asked Neville, "May I have your daughter's hand in marriage?"

"My God, but you're... you're... insolent," stammered Chester, staring Neville in the eyes. You said this wasn't about you."

"Well, it's not; not all of it."

"I don't like everything I see, but I do like the cut of your jib and that Stearns fellow has definitely landed himself in the toilet ... and I've never seen my daughter act this way about anybody, so ... I'll think about it. Now shall we go back and deal with Marcus Brutus? That's a job I will enjoy finishing."

25 - "Unfinished Business"

Conversation in the carriage on the way back to the office was more lively than it had been on the way out, but Chester still sat with his daughter protectively on his side of the carriage.

"Trading with the enemy is against the law," argued Neville, "but if we find Michael to be guilty of the bigger crime of attempting to sell weapons to France, I might just forget your local arms activity if you promise me you'll give it up."

"I have never…" Chester began.

"Poppycock!" interrupted Neville. "I myself have seen boxes being carried from your ship to launches at Bahia de Neiba on the south coast of Hispaniola. I wasn't rum. Rum is in barrels, not boxes. What's wrong with you, anyway? Isn't there enough money in rum?"

"And, you must both quit the idea of rum sales to France, if Marion is to marry me, even if you attempt to legitimize it by selling through the United States. I can't be tied up in any of it, or I will be tied up with all of it and hanged.

"Father hasn't given his approval yet," Marion said. Father and daughter looked at each other. In a moment they smiled, and both looked back at him. He wasn't sure he liked their expressions, which strangely seemed more quizzical than antagonistic. They hadn't said anything, either, so he couldn't tell what they were thinking.

The carriage halted in front of The Stillwater Rum Trading Company, where all three disembarked.

"Allow me," said Neville. He barged through the door with his hand upon the hilt of his sword, and was followed by Chester and then Marion. He saw nobody in the office windows, so he turned to the sales cubicles. Nobody was there, either.

"Oh, hello, Mr. Sykes," said Chester to the one man remaining in the lobby.

"Just leaving, myself," said Sykes. "I don't know what kind of place you're running here. That salesman you've got finished up with the pusser from the *Franchise,* and that was it for him. He said he'd be right back, but all he did was go in that office over there and write something; then he went out the back. I'm the only one waited this long for him, but I can't stay longer today. Good Day, Sirs."

"That's his office. Let's go look."

In the center of a clean desk there was a single note:

> *Marion, I love you.*
> *I never thought you would join up with the damned Brits.*
> *Take care, Michael*

"Whether he's a double agent or a bumbler," said Neville, "he's smarter than we thought, and he certainly tries hard."

The End

Appendix

The Square Sails of a Man-o-War

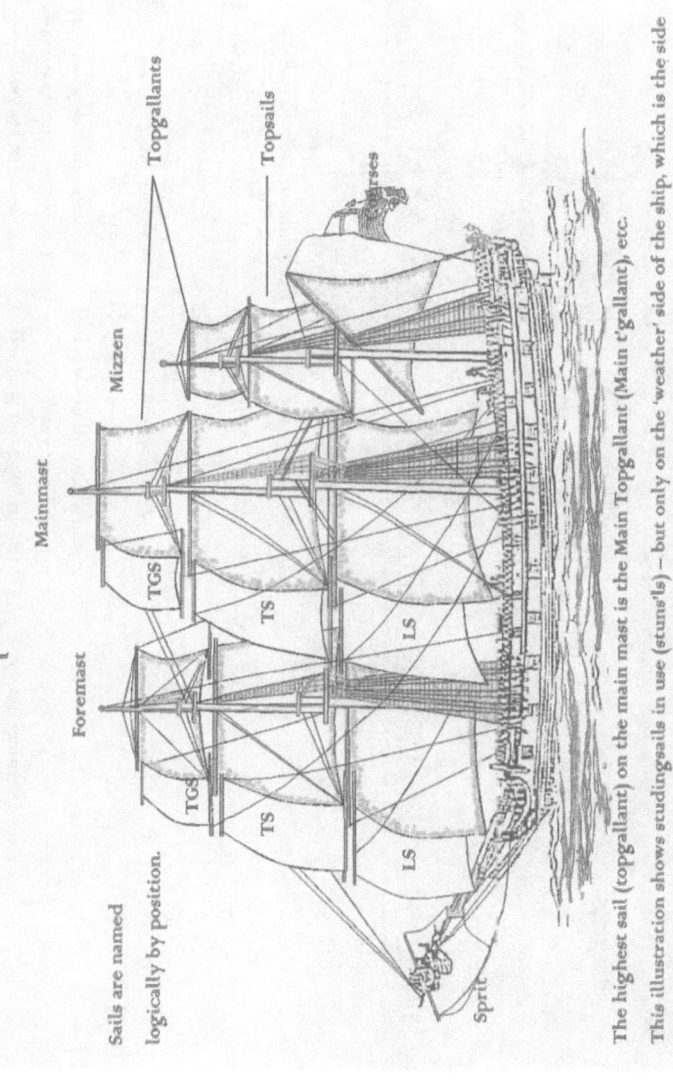

The square sails of a Man-o-War

Sails are named logically by position.

Foremast Mainmast Mizzen Topgallants Topsails ...rses

TGS TS LS TGS TS LS Sprit

The highest sail (topgallant) on the main mast is the Main Topgallant (Main t'gallant), etc.

This illustration shows studdingsails in use (stuns'ls) – but only on the 'weather' side of the ship, which is the side from which the wind is blowing – in this case into the page. The downwind side of the ship is the 'lee' side. There are no leeward (loo'rd) stuns'ls set in this illustration.

Here the studdingsails are labeled LS = lower stuns'l, TS = topsail stuns'l, and TGS = t'g'llant stuns'l. They would be further described by the mast they are on... e.g. TGS on the mainmast = Main t'galant stuns'l

The Fore-and-Aft Sails of a Man-o-War

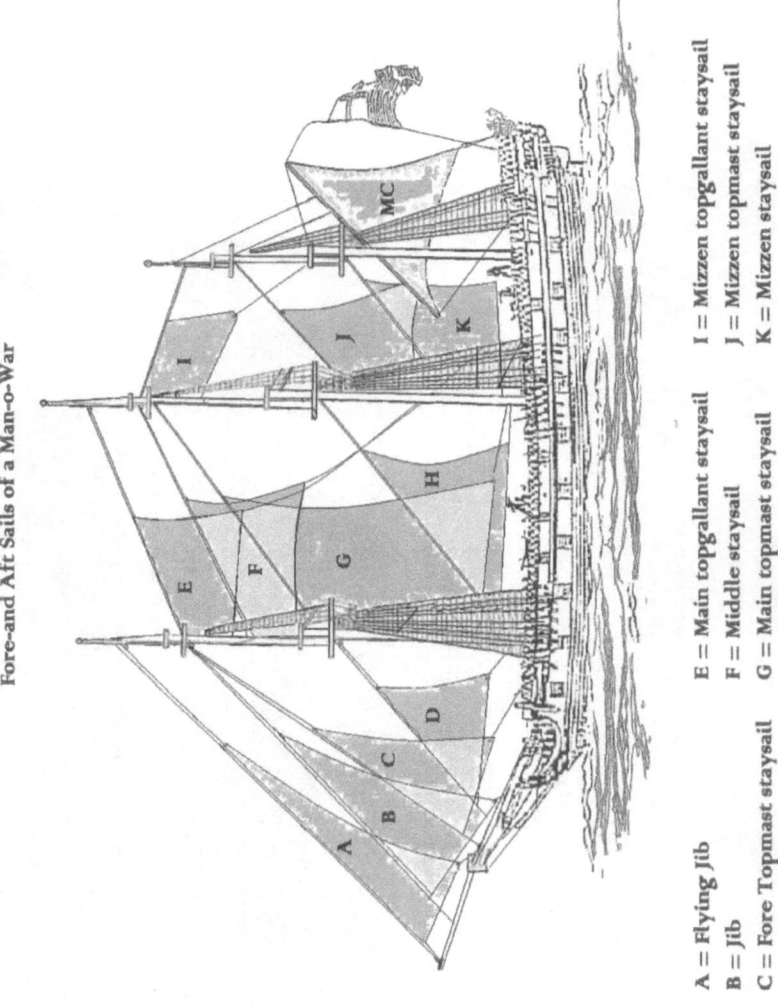

Fore-and Aft Sails of a Man-o-War

A = Flying Jib

B = Jib

C = Fore Topmast staysail

D = Fore staysail

E = Main topgallant staysail

F = Middle staysail

G = Main topmast staysail

H = Main staysail

I = Mizzen topgallant staysail

J = Mizzen topmast staysail

K = Mizzen staysail

MC = Mizzen Course

British Money – pre-decimal (pre-1971)

Britain used a system of **pounds**, **shillings** and **pence**, with coins representing various quantities of each, as follows:

Pound: not a coin before 1817 (then as the gold 'sovereign') – paper <u>notes</u> in values of 1, 5, 10, etc. were used and represented 240 silver pennies (pence): <u>1 pound</u> (£1)= 20 shillings = 240 pence

1 guinea (coin, originally made from gold of the Guinea coast of Africa) = 21 shillings (1 pound + 1 shilling)

1 crown (coin) = 5 shillings = 1/4 pound

1 half-crown (coin) = 2 shillings and 6 pence (stopped in 1970)

1 florin (a beautiful medieval English silver coin) = 2 shillings

1 shilling (coin) = 12 pence (1s)

1 sixpence (silver coin; later called a **'tanner'**) = 6 pence

1 threepence = 3 pence (in sometimes called a 'threp'ny bit' or "thrupence")

1 penny (a copper coin) = one of the basic units (1d)

1 ha'penny (copper coin) = 1/2 penny (pronounced "hay-p-ny"; stopped in 1969)

1 farthing (lowest value coin, a 'fourth-thing') = 1/4 penny (stopped in 1956)

The Prize Sharing system

Shares are to be shared
1/8 to the flag officer
3/8 to the captain (for a private vessel)
1/8 each to commissioned, warrant and petty officers
¼ to the crew

British Navy Watch System (The bells)

(most commonly used in the Age of Sail)

The Navy day began at noon: Sights of the sun were taken by the Sailing Master and/ or officers and any navigation students (e.g. Midshipmen) using an astrolabe, the Davis quadrant (or the English quadrant), octant or sextant as such were invented in order to ascertain the sun's zenith (locally) and determine latitude. When this was done (cloud cover permitting), the one responsible so informed the Officer of the Watch, who then informed the captain. The captain gave the order to "Make it noon and turn the glass", and the order was transmitted to those who performed various parts of the daily ceremony: the hour-glass was turned, the ship's bell was rung 8 times to indicated the end of the forenoon watch, and the boatswain blew his whistle (pipe) to summon the ship's company to dinner.

One bell was rung for each half hour according to the time-keeping device, which was the hour-glass. Two bells were rung on the hour. At one-thirty p.pm. for example, it is 3 bells for the afternoon watch. A watch is 8 bells long (the two dog-watches in the afternoon, which allowed all the men to be fed more easily and rotated the watches for the next day, shared the full 8 bells until after the Spithead-Nore mutinies, when they each have only 4 each).

(See Table next page)

The basic schedule, which did change a bit for make-and-mend day (usually Thursday), Sunday for church, and for any other reason the captain might revise it (such as punishment day – often Saturday).

Bells	Time	
8	noon	**Afternoon watch** begins; hands piped to dinner End of Forenoon watch
2	1 p.m.	Dinner is over
4-8	hourly	Log heaved hourly
8	4 p.m.	**First Dog Watch** (2 hours long); off watch piped to supper
2, 4	5, 6 p.m.	**Last Dog Watch** begins at 4 bells; lights out & off watch to sleep
6, 8	7, 8 p.m.	**Evening Watch** begins
2-8	8 - midnight	**First Watch** begins at midnight; Sentinel's cry "all's well" at each bell
2-8	Midnight - 4	**Middle Watch** begins at 4:00 a.m.
2-7	4-7 a.m.	Hammocks piped up at 7:00 a.m.
8	8 a.m.	**Morning Watch**; hands piped to breakfast
2-8	8 a.m. – noon	**Forenoon Watch**

(Note: one more bell than indicated is rung for the half hour following)

The Caribbean Islands

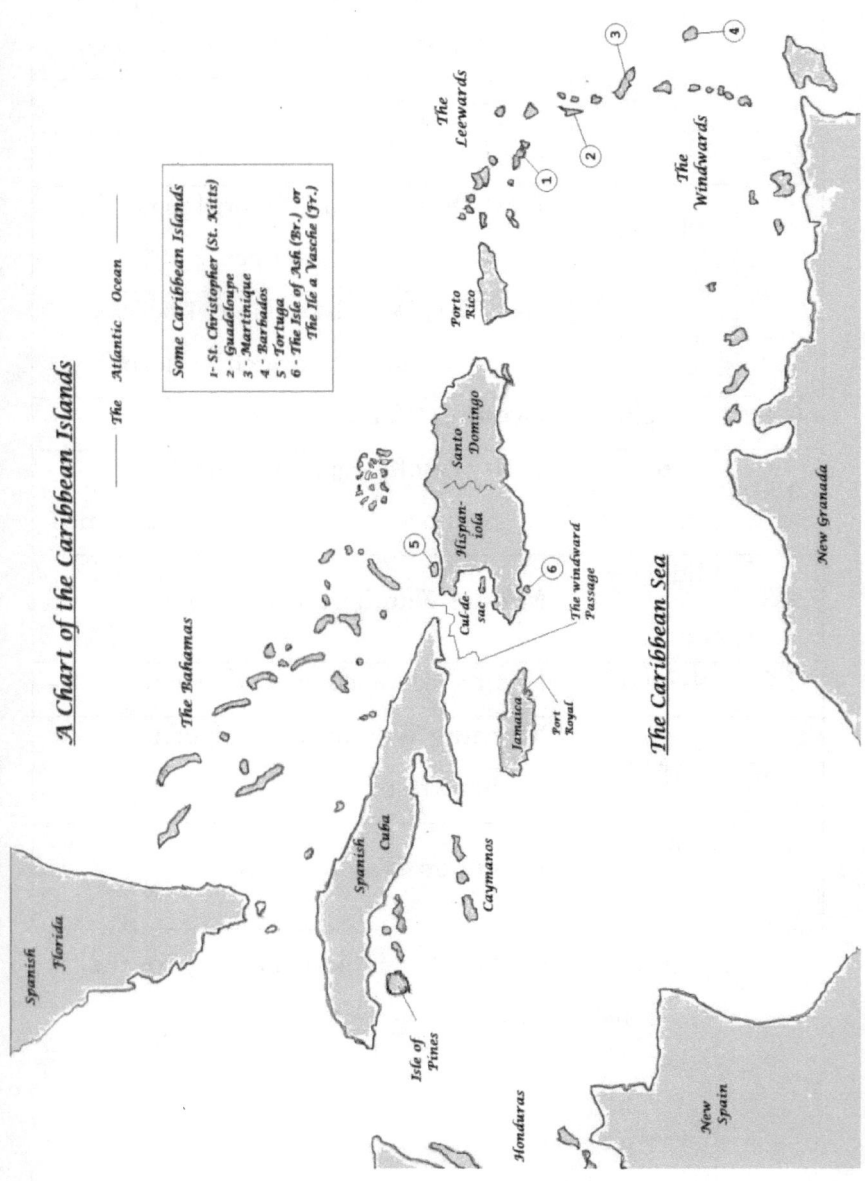

A Chart of the Caribbean Islands

—— The Atlantic Ocean ——

Some Caribbean Islands

1 - St. Christopher (St. Kitts)
2 - Guadeloupe
3 - Martinique
4 - Barbados
5 - Tortuga
6 - The Isle of Ash (Br.) or
     The Ile a Vasche (Fr.)

The Leewards
The Windwards

Porto Rico

Santo Domingo

Hispan-iola

Cul de sac

The windward Passage

Jamaica
Port Royal

The Bahamas

Spanish Cuba

Caymanos

Isle of Pines

Honduras

Spanish Florida

New Spain

New Granada

The Caribbean Sea

Glossary 1.4

aft – The rear or stern of a ship. (the square end, as opposed to the pointy end, called the bow)

abaft – Behind or to the back of, as 'abaft the mainmast'.

ague – A disease involving a series of severe fevers and chills (often or quite likely malaria, which was not understood before the building of the Panama Canal in the early 1900's).

beakhead - The small deck in the bow in front of the forecastle where the boom is mounted and where the crew's lavatories were (from whence followed the term 'head' to mean toilet).

bend – A sailing term meaning to attach the sails. When in place and ready to use they are 'bent'.

blocks - Pulleys.

boatswain – 'bo'sun': A highly skilled warrant officer in charge of deck and rigging operations (not sailing) and the supplies for all repairs. He assigns and oversees all deck work. The bo'sun likely had a private cabin and might eat in the gunroom with the commissioned officers. He would only stand watches on a small ship.

bow – The front of a boat or ship. (The 'pointy end', to which the bowsprit is attached.) The center wooden beam up the very front of it, to which hull planks are attached, is the 'stem'.

bower - A ships' two biggest anchors ('best-' and 'small-'), and their cables; carried at the bow.

bloody flux – A disease: dysentery. It is an intestinal disorder that might be caused by numerous infections, resulting in severe diarrhea with blood and mucus in the feces. The disease is accompanied by with fever and abdominal pain.

Blue Peter – A nickname for a signal flag, letter P (Square of blue with a white square inside it). It was flown in harbor to summon all ship's crew aboard for departure.

braces - Those ropes of the 'running rigging' that were used to turn the yards from perpendicular to a ship's keel to slanted – as needed for sailing closer to the wind. Square sails hang on the yards.

brail up – To raise the aft corners of a sail to cause it to stop drawing.

broach - This disastrous event for a ship occurs when it turns sidewise to the waves in a storm, whether by human error or magnitude of weather. The next wave that strikes the ship on the side may capsize or flood it causing extreme damage and/or injury, and likely sinking.

burgoo – food; not a seaman's favorite. Cheap and easy, so served often. Porridge or gruel of oatmeal.

cable – The anchor line. – OR - A measure of length = 200 yards.

capstan – A rotating machine with a vertical axle mounted through the deck. Above deck, men insert poles horizontally and walk in a circle to rotate it. Ropes (e.g. anchor cables) attached to it below decks are wound up on it to pull - to raise the anchor or sails to raise spars aloft.

careen – To set a boat on the beach at high tide. When the tide is out its bottom can be worked on.

catted / cathead – When something is tied to the cathead (e.g. – an anchor) it is 'catted'. The catheads are beams that protrude sideways from the sides of the ship at the bow and used for jobs like raising the anchors without them hitting the hull.

Cat-o-nine-tails – **'cat':** A whip with many knotted ends used to serve out punishment (ordered by number of lashes). In the navy, it was kept in a red baize bag.

collops – Bacon fried with eggs.

complete (verb) - "To complete" a ship is to finish everything necessary before going to sea; provisions, arms, men, etc., as: '*HMS Swan* was completing at Plymouth'.

commodore – The man in charge of a small group of ships (an admiral would command an entire fleet). He would almost always be a captain, and might be referred to by either word.

confused seas – A sea state in which wind-driven waves, often from distant storms, approach the ship from different directions simultaneously, usually making the motion very uncomfortable

cor – An English expression of annoyance or exasperation.

coxswain – **'cox'n':** The man in charge of a small boat: its captain. He orders the men who row or sail it; a petty officer who commands the captain's gig or barge.

crinkum-crankum - Fancy-work.

cracking on - An expression meaning to raise all possible sail and make haste.

demi-culverin – An old term for a size of cannon: 9- pounder.

farthing – ¼ penny (essentially a 'fourth-thing') – see table on English money.

fathom – A measure normally used for depth, equal to six feet.

fiddle – A raised strip of wood around a surface (e.g. table or desk) that keeps objects from falling off when the ship heels (tilts). A fancy desk might have custom fiddles for items like inkwells.

filibusters – A 17th century term for French-biased pirates in the Caribbean.

forecastle - Usually pronounced 'foc's'l'. It is the foreward section of a ship where the crews quarters were. In most larger ships it was a raised area forward, the top of which is the **foredeck**.

fother – To cover a hole in the hull below the waterline by tying a sail or other canvas over it.

'full and by' – A sailing condition when the ship ss as close to the wind as she can get and the sails are drawing to the fullest. On a square-rigger this would require "bowlines", which are sheets (ropes) from the forward bottom corner of the sail to a point forward (i.e. toward the bow).

glass – A word used consistently for three very different things: a telescope, the ship's timing device, which was an hour-glass, and the barometer. As to timing, the [hour-] glass was reset to local time, if needed, at noon every day when sunsights were taken and the new navy day began. It was then turned every hour, at which time the log was heaved and, if in soundings – the lead line was employed. A 'half glass' is half an hour.

gratings – Rectangular wooden frames with criss-crossed wood strips that are used as hatch covers. (They must be covered with tarps if weather-proofing is needed.) Tipped up on end they were used as a place to tie a man for punishment: being lashed with a 'cat-o-nine-tails'.

gunwale – the top edge of a boat's side. In ships the hull might extend up above the top deck in the waist and effectively act as a solid railing.

HMS - "His Majesty's Ship". Note that *Swan* (Volume 2) is not referred to thus, because the acronym was not officially used in the British Navy before 1789.

head - (see "beakhead") The toilet on a ship.

heave / hove – To pull or push, as on a line. – OR - a ship can 'heave to', meaning adjust sails and rudder in a manner that causes to ship to stop forward motion and lie quietly in rough water. Hove is past tense, as 'the ship is hove to.' Also, come into view, as 'the man hove into view'.

holystone – A lump of soft sandstone used to scrub decks to ensure the hard oak is smooth with no splinters. The deck is then sluiced with seawater, resulting in an almost whitewashed appearance.

idler – A sailor who always works the "day watch". He would normally not stand night watch –e.g. Cook, carpenter, the boatswain and purser, sail maker and cooper and their mates.

Jonas – A person who brings bad luck aboard a superstitious ship.

hounds – Protrusions high on a mast onto which blocks are hung for the halyards used to raise the yards.

langridge – cannon ammunition consisting of a tin can filled with angular pieces of iron to cut down men and damage rigging

larboard – The left side of a ship, opposite of 'starboard'; (now replaced by the term 'port').

lay aft – A command meaning: "Go to the back of the ship," or "Go find the captain on the quarterdeck or in his cabin" or "Go find the officer of the watch," or similar.

league – 3 statute miles (as opposed to the much shorter distance of a cable, about 200 yards).

lead – (or lead-line): A short lead cylinder into the bottom of which a lump of tallow was set. It is affixed to the end of a line knotted at fathoms and tossed over the side (heaved) to measure depth. The tallow picks up evidence of the bottom – shell, sand, pebbles, etc. as an aid to knowing where the ship is. Two different lengths of line were used: one of about 25 fathoms for shallow areas (in soundings) and one of about 100 fathoms for deeper.

lignum vitae – A type of wood grown in Central America that is used for high-wear components like blocks (pulleys). Very salt-resistant; not prone to cracking under load.

lugger – A smaller ship equipped with lug sails. Lug sails are set on booms that are not symmetrical to the mast and may be turned and tightened in a manner that allows these built-for-speed boats to outrun and out-point any square-rigger. Not surprisingly, they were popular with pirates.

martingale – A permanent rope or cable attached near the waterline at the bow and at the tip of the bowsprit to prevent the bowsprit from breaking by opposing the upward forces of the forestays.

minion – An old term for a size of cannon that throws a 4-pound ball somewhat over 200 yards.

mizzen – The aftmost (rearmost) mast in a sailing ship, and its sails (e.g. Mizzen course)

money system, English – see appendix

neaped – An embarrassing situation for the captain (and dangerous if the enemy arrived) when his ship is stuck on land on a high tide that is unexpectedly lower than normal –The ship must wait for the next high tide to be freed.

ordinary – In addition to its normal meaning, a ship 'in ordinary' is out of service; "mothballed". Also, a rating (rank) of seaman which is below 'able seaman' but above 'landsman' or 'waister'

ostler – one who takes / cares for horses for those staying at an inn (or rich person's house)

pease porridge – Food; a dish of boiled, mashed peas.

pinnace – 8-oared ship's boat, often able to fit a mast and sail

pipe – wine cask, also called a butt, equal to ½ tun (which was 240 gal, though it might vary)

poop – The upper aft deck of a ship under / beneath the mizzen sails.

poldavy – A coarse cloth material used by the British for sails or sacks (or for other uses aboard).

priddy – To organize and clean or shine up, as in "priddy the decks".

pusser – The spoken version of the warrant officer's title "Purser". This man is the ships' accountant and normally responsible for purchasing supplies. (See also – "slops").

quoin – a wedge used to manually (and quickly) adjust the elevation of a cannon

reave – To lace a rope though pulleys for whatever its function.

rundlet –small wine cask of about 18 gal = 1/14 tun (which was 240 gal., though it might vary)

saker – An old term for a size of cannon: that throws a 6-pound ball about two hundred yards.

Sham Abraham – An expression meaning those who are happy just to look busy.

sheet / sheet home – Lines (ropes) to the bottom corners of a sail to control it / Sail pulled fully tight & cleated (or belayed).

shilling – A coin of old English money = 12 pennies, or pence. (See English money table)

shot garland – a tube of canvass hung by each cannon to hold its ammunition (cannon balls)

simoom – A dust storm of huge proportion that blows far out into the Atlantic from the Sahara Desert of Africa. Also known in Israel and Saudi Arabia.

skylarking – The game of "follow me if you can" as played by the young boys aboard tall-rigged ships. They would fearlessly climb and swing from rope to rope & mast to mast.

slops – (i.e. "The pusser's slops"): Normally the term referred to ready-made clothes that were sold by the pusser to the ship's sailors, but could include other supplies such as soap or tobacco, but not alcohol. From the older English term sloppes, meaning trousers.

smoke it – An expression meaning to discover a ruse or to understand.

soundings – Depth measurements. A ship is "in soundings" if it is shallow enough that the depth can be measured (usually with the short lead line).

spar – Any of the wooden components of the rigging: masts & booms.

speak – To enable the captains of ships at sea to converse via speaking trumpets, each ship would let its sails loose to stop and "speak" the other. They did not say 'speak to', just 'speak'.

splice – A place where rope is joined to itself to repair it, extend it, or make a loop.

splice the main brace – Although this expression literally means to repair the rope used to rotate the main yard, its true meaning is to reward the entire crew by serving out an extra tot of rum.

starter / to start – A short piece of rope with a knotted end (makeshift whip) or a riding crop used to jolt a man into action. On many ships, used very frequently by the petty officers. Also, the English equivalent of 'apetizer'.

stem – See 'bow'. Front vertical beam of the hull (Leading to the modern expression 'stem to stern').

stern – The aft (back) end of a boat.

starboard – The right side of a ship (facing forward). The opposite of 'larboard' (now 'port').

stone – An old English measurement of human body weight equal to 14 pounds

stroke oar – A person, not a thing: the oarsman in a small boat who controls the pace of rowing; the little boat's 'captain'.

stuns'l – Spoken form of **studdingsails**. (See sail illustration.)

supernumerary – An unofficial extra; a passenger, like a lieutenant being carried to his ship.

sweeps – Long oars used for propelling ships when there is no wind.

taffrail – The stern rail of the stern-most deck (the poop deck or quarterdeck, depending on the ship's construction).

tompion – (pronounced 'tompkin'): a wooden plug for the muzzle of a housed cannon that kept out rain, seawater, etc.

top hamper – The standing rigging & spars above the primary masts: topmasts and above.

truck – The very top of a mast, often being a decoration such as a painted ball above a block (pulley) that could be used to raise signal flags.

van – The front group of a line of ships or convoy, followed by the 'center' and the 'rear'.

waist – The center (top deck) of a ship; the area of deck between the quarterdeck and forecastle.

waisters – Men who normally work in the waist at unskilled jobs; mostly hauling on the lines – sheets, halyards, braces, etc. Usually landsmen; untrained workers.

weather gage – In fighting sailing ships, the advantageous position of being upwind, from which the one with the weather gage can fall down on his enemy in any direction he chooses.

yards (yardarms) – Horizontal spars of a square-rigger's rigging. They are attached to the masts with hoops that permit them to be rotated and raised or lowered for positioning the sails. The sails hang on the yards and are reefed or furled onto them.